ROAD ANGEL

ROAD ANGEL

~

Jilaine Tarisa

INSPIRED CREATIONS LLC

Original songs by Jilaine Tarisa that are referenced or quoted include:

> "From the Heart"
> "Wonderin' Fool"
> "Millennium Blues"
> "Bridging the Gap"
> "Pause"
> "My Love or My Life"
> "Shining Star"
> "Phoenix Heart"
> "Gone for Good"
> "My Choice"
> "Rainbow Bridge"
> "Road Angel"
> "Veil of Illusion"

Author's Note

Road Angel is the second book in the series *The Red Rose Way*, which follows the journey of Caitlin Rose, formerly an attorney for the U.S. Department of Justice.

The time frame for the first book (*A Moment of Time*) is 1996–1998. *Road Angel* picks up where *A Moment of Time* left off, in March of 1998, and ends in July 2000, when a congressional hearing was held by the Committee on Government Reform in Washington, D.C. to investigate the use of mercury in medicine.

Although references are made to public figures, actual locations, and historical events, all characters are fictional and all information is used in the context of a fictional story.

Readers are advised to explore the many resources available concerning the different topics addressed and to reach their own conclusions about matters that are unsettled or that are open to interpretation.

PART ONE

~

SANTA FE

∾ 1 ∾

*C*aitlin adjusted the time on the clock after she crossed the New Mexico state line. She and Lucky had spent the night at a pet-friendly motel in western Oklahoma and were headed for their next destination, Santa Fe.

She stopped at a gas station in Santa Rosa and then continued driving west on Interstate 40. Since leaving the Ozarks, she had—mostly—been following the route mapped out by the motor club, but as she approached the exit for New Mexico's Highway 3, she decided to take a shortcut. A quick glance at the map showed her that Highway 3 would lead her to Interstate 25.

Curious to find out what lay down the dusty road, she followed her instincts—but soon questioned the wisdom of her choice. For miles, the terrain was barren and desolate. No other cars were in sight. The narrow road climbed and fell with the contours of the land, leveling out after a dramatic descent into a valley.

Caitlin parked her car in the lot by the visitor center at a national park and got out to stretch her legs. Seeing a trail nearby, she grabbed a bottle of water and followed the path.

Wildflowers were beginning to sprout, the first signs of spring. In unfamiliar territory now, with no other visitors in sight, she paused to admire the view. Slow-moving clouds cast ever-changing shadows across the mountains in the distance.

She had come a long way, and not just on this journey. The landscape of her life had changed dramatically in the last twenty months. Sudden crises couldn't be foreseen, much less prepared for.

We all hope we will never encounter war, famine, natural disasters. And car accidents.

The transformation she had undergone since her car was struck on a bridge near Alexandria, Virginia had fundamentally altered her life and her identity—maybe even her destiny. She'd left behind her job as an attorney for the U.S. Department of Justice in Washington, D.C. and spent the winter at her family's lake house in the Missouri Ozarks. There, she grieved all the losses she had suffered—her father's death, her broken engagement, the end of her career. Her time at the lake was quiet and uneventful, and she learned to embrace silence.

Once she got over the initial shock of abandoning modern devices for communication and amusement—the telephone, CD player, and television—she came to appreciate the natural world in a way she never had before. She had once been entranced by the gleam of Manhattan's skyscrapers and the hypnotic pulse of electronic music. Now, listening to the sound of the rain and watching the ducks flapping about on the lake—or Lucky hunting down a squirrel—were more interesting pastimes, for Nature was a part of her and she was a part of Nature. That, of course, had always been so, but she had been too preoccupied to notice.

She took a drink of water and slowly walked a bit farther. Free from the throngs that flocked to more popular destinations, the site invited reflection.

She paused again and closed her eyes. The cool breeze felt refreshing after hours of driving. She focused on her breathing, a simple technique that helped clear her mind. Worries about the trip were swept away by a wave of serenity.

Accessing that peaceful easy feeling was easier in a beautiful and remote setting, Caitlin knew. Maintaining a sense of inner calm in the face of adversity was more challenging. Being in the world was the real test of one's ability to remain calm—and to be kind.

The world sorely needs participation by those noble individuals who bring their awareness into the workplace, schools, government, and politics, she thought.

Her job as a civil servant was over, but she hoped her music would inspire and unite people. During the long winter, she had completed eighteen songs. Now, she was hungry for new experiences, new opportunities to engage with the world.

Having lost all sense of time during her reverie, she realized she'd better get going if she hoped to arrive in Santa Fe before dark. The park would close at 4 p.m., a sign had informed her. The gate would close and prohibit entry. She didn't care to wait around to find out if it would also prohibit exiting!

Before turning back, she noticed, in the distance, a small group of people gathered on the top of a mound. The tiny figures looked like colorful dots.

Costumes? Caitlin wondered. Perhaps her imagination was working overtime, but she thought she heard the faint sound of drums and chanting. *Maybe it's just the wind,* she thought as she walked toward the visitor center. She turned to take one last look at the mound. No one was there.

She shook her head and continued walking to her car. Had she crossed into another dimension when she entered the Land of Enchantment?

Ever since the Crash that had plunged her into a coma on July 2, 1996, life had felt a bit surreal. Stripped of her former identity, she was forced to find a new one. The past was dead and gone, but she'd hoped that a change of scenery would help resurrect her belief that dreams really can come true.

When she opened the car door, Lucky opened his eyes and then yawned and stretched.

"Did you have a good nap, cat?" Caitlin asked him.

She started the engine and drove north. Highway 3 soon joined Interstate 25. Patches of snow lay on the ground at the top of Glorieta Pass, but the road was dry and the sky was clear.

Caitlin was eager to see a familiar face, though she'd never felt completely at ease around Melody. She admired Melody's confidence and enthusiasm—and her dedication to her chosen path—but she also felt judged at times. Melody seemed to consider Caitlin's goals and priorities less worthy than her own. She also seemed a little too sure of herself, a little too . . . bossy.

As an attorney, Caitlin had dealt with worldly matters—civil rights, unfair business practices, corporate fraud. Melody taught yoga and meditation and believed that spreading a positive message would have a more profound effect on people's lives than anything a lawyer might contribute. A whole new system was needed, in her view. The old one was beyond repair.

Haughty, Caitlin thought. *That's the word I wanted.*

Her brain didn't function quite as efficiently—or as reliably—as it once had. She had learned to accept her limitations, and she was grateful she had regained her independence. Traveling solo, she was free to come and go as she pleased without having to consider anyone else's needs and wishes.

"Except for you, sleepycat," she said as she reached over and patted Lucky's head.

She parked beside a restaurant on the outskirts of Santa Fe, gave Lucky a treat, and locked the car.

After enjoying a hearty meal of lamb stew with green chile and a salad topped with local goat cheese and candied pecans, Caitlin paid the bill at the register and then called Melody from the pay phone outside.

"Oh good, you're nearly here," Melody said when Caitlin told her where she was. "Take the second Santa Fe exit off the interstate. That's Saint Francis. It's one of the main roads through town."

Saint Francis was Santa Fe's patron saint, Caitlin learned when she stopped at a visitor center to pick up a map and information about local attractions. "La Villa Real de la Santa Fé de San Francisco de Asís" was the full name of the city. "Santa Fe" meant "Holy Faith."

People of many faiths had been drawn to the area, and they had established spiritual centers of various kinds, a woman who worked at the visitor center told Caitlin. A stupa—a consecrated structure adorned with painted murals and a statue of the Buddha—had been built in the 1980s, the woman said as she assembled a packet with maps and brochures.

"A number of Tibetan refugees recently settled here," she said.

At an altitude of 7,000 feet, Santa Fe must have seemed like an ideal spot for people from "the rooftop of the world" to relocate, Caitlin thought.

"Of course, the art scene is what draws a lot of people. Photographers, painters, sculptors—as well as patrons and collectors," the woman added. "The population more than doubles during Indian Market."

"When is that?" Caitlin asked.

"Late summer."

Caitlin picked up the packet. She smiled politely and said, "I expect I'll be gone by then," before turning to leave.

Her own paints were packed away, but she might enjoy a visit to an art gallery or a museum during her stay, she thought. She sometimes missed the diverse cultural events that were plentiful in a city like Washington.

The sun was setting as she headed for the south side of town. Streaks of orange and red streamed across a fiery sky.

"Wow," Caitlin said aloud as she admired the brilliant display.

She parked her car in the driveway beside a small adobe house and coaxed Lucky into his carrier.

Melody opened the door and greeted her with a warm hug. "Welcome to the City Different," she said. "Come on in!"

"Thanks. I'm really excited to be here. And this," Caitlin said as she unlatched the carrier, "is my lucky charm!"

"Oh, right! From Kimo," Melody gushed. "He's precious. Look at the white marks on his crown and heart chakras."

Yep, I'm in Santa Fe, Caitlin thought. *Land of New Age gurus and spiritual seekers.*

"Nice place," she said, looking around.

"I'm staying here while the owner is away," Melody said. "I was renting out the guest room to a friend who came to town after she broke up with her boyfriend and—well, long story short: they got back together and she left. And then you called!"

"Was it someone from Virginia?" Caitlin asked, wondering if she might have met the woman.

"Oh, no. Darcey and I have known each other since we were kids. Let me show you around."

Melody led Caitlin to the room where she would be staying before taking her outside. From the back patio, mountains were visible in the distance.

"I wouldn't leave the cat out here alone for too long," Melody said before going back inside. "Coyotes."

"Thanks for the warning."

"Are you hungry?"

"I'm not, but I'm sure Lucky is. I've got his food and a litter box in the car. I'll bring a few things in."

"I can help."

"That's okay. I need the exercise."

After setting out bowls of food and water for Lucky, Caitlin retrieved her overnight bag and her pillow from the car.

"Tea?" Melody asked her when she closed the front door.

"Sure."

"It's my special blend," Melody said before pouring hot tea from a ceramic pot. She filled two mugs and handed one to Caitlin. "I've been studying herbalism in my spare time. I hope to have an herb garden soon, and harvesting wild sage and nettles is easy, if you know where to look."

"You'll be quite the healer when you're done."

"I'll never be done. There's always more to learn. But I'd like to think I'm already a healer. Honey?"

Caitlin shook her head and sat in a chair by the kiva fireplace.

Melody wrapped a shawl around her shoulders and sat cross-legged on the couch. "We could start a fire if you'd like. Or call Kimo!"

"Not tonight," Caitlin said. "I'm pretty tired. I just want to take a shower and go to bed. It's been a long day. Or three!"

"Did you come over Glorieta Pass?"

Caitlin nodded and said, "I took a back road from I-40 to I-25." She sipped the tea while deciding whether to tell Melody about her stop at the national park.

"I haven't explored that area much," Melody said. "I usually head south to Albuquerque or north to Taos. Was it scenic?"

"I took a short walk and I thought I saw a group of people in the distance," Caitlin said. "They seemed to be gathered around a particular spot. I turned away and when I looked back, they had disappeared! It was . . . strange."

"Hikers maybe?" Melody said. "I don't think there are any pueblos out that way, at least not anymore. The Pecos Pueblo was one of the most powerful in the Southwest at one time. It was abandoned in the nineteenth century. The few families that were left moved in with the Jemez."

The people Caitlin had seen on the mound didn't look like hikers. Intrigued, she wondered who had been out there, on a Thursday afternoon in March, and what they were doing.

"I know of some natural hot springs at Jemez," Melody said. "We should go while you're here, if the weather's good."

"That sounds great!" Caitlin said.

A hot soak would be a glorious way to unwind, she thought.

"There's also a spa here, just outside of town. It costs money, whereas the springs are free, but it's another option. The setting is really quite wonderful."

"I'd love to visit a pueblo. Are any of them open to the public?"

"Sometimes. On feast days, mostly, though some of the ceremonies and dances are private. We can check the calendar. The equinox is this weekend, so there's a lot happening. I'm going to a gathering on Saturday. You're welcome to come. How long are you planning to stay?"

"Oh, I don't know. A week maybe? It's not like I need to be anywhere right away."

Caitlin yawned and stretched before taking her mug to the sink. Los Angeles was her ultimate destination; she hoped to plug into the music community there. She wasn't looking to become a pop star, but she wanted to record some of her material and see if she could carve out a niche for herself on the indie scene. Her songs weren't really right for a club, and she didn't consider herself a folk singer. She wasn't quite sure *what* to call herself or who might be interested in her music; that was why she needed to be around other musicians— to learn and grow and get feedback and advice.

"You said in your message that you've been writing songs," Melody said.

"Uh-huh," Caitlin said as she opened the back door to let Lucky outside. "Stay where I can see you," she told him. She closed the door and said, "I'll play something for you while I'm here. I brought my brother's old guitar with me."

Melody poured herself another cup of tea and said, "I have to stop by the school in the morning, but I thought we could meet for lunch, and I can show you around town a bit afterward."

"Okay," Caitlin said. She knew that Melody had recently enrolled in massage school and her classes were about to begin. "You probably know of some good restaurants. I'm ready for a change of taste. My cooking skills are rather limited."

"I remember!" Melody said with a laugh.

She didn't need to agree so wholeheartedly, Caitlin thought.

"I was thinking of the deli at the health food store. It's quick, and they've got a great salad bar."

Caitlin shrugged. "Okay. Whatever you want."

"I'll leave a note with directions if I don't see you before I leave."

"Sounds good," Caitlin said. "I may want to sleep in."

She opened the door and scooped Lucky up in her arms. "C'mon, Luck. I'll tell you a bedtime story," she told him. "Say goodnight to Melody."

She carried Lucky to the guest bedroom and closed the door. After unpacking a few things, she took a shower and then sat on the bed while she looked through the brochures from the visitor center. When Lucky jumped up on the bed, Caitlin eyed him warily.

"Okay," she said, "but don't think we're going to make a habit of this."

She put the brochures aside and stroked the cat's fur. Lucky's eyes were half closed, and his tail swished gently.

Caitlin began the promised story. "A long time ago, there was a cat named Starcatcher. Now this cat wasn't like his brothers and sisters, who all found mates and started their own families. Starcatcher was adventurous. And he preferred delicacies, like fish, to the mice he could catch around the barn. So he started hanging around the pier, where he was befriended by the captain of a big cargo ship—Captain Juárez. (This was in Spain, you see. Or maybe Portugal. I can't say for certain; it's been a while since Starcatcher told me his story.) The captain fed the cat from his own plate—something that never happened at home, where cats were mostly left to fend for themselves.

"He wasn't called Starcatcher then. He wasn't really called anything, that he could remember. Juárez named him Starcatcher because of the white starburst on his forehead. He had caught a shooting star at the moment of his birth, Juárez said, and that meant he was destined to live an unusually blessed life, even though he'd gotten off to a somewhat rocky start.

"Before long, cat and captain were inseparable companions, and together they traveled the world—South America, Africa, the Orient. Their tale includes shipwrecks and pirates, wine and women. But all that will have to wait for another time," Caitlin said as she turned off the lamp by the bed. "We've had enough excitement for today."

She closed her eyes and smiled, grateful for her friends. Human and feline.

∾ 2 ∾

S am waited until the last monk had left the dining hall. Then, he started mopping the floor of the refectory.

Breakfast, like other meals at the monastery, was simple fare: boiled eggs, oatmeal, brown bread, nut butters and jams. Pancakes were served on special occasions.

Much of the Abbey's produce was grown on site. At harvest time, fruits from the orchard were preserved, and many of the vegetables were frozen. The monks strove to be self-sufficient as ardently as they strove to be self-aware. They learned whatever skills were necessary to feed and clothe themselves. They sewed garments, built furniture, and fished in the Pecos River.

Not a bad life, Sam thought. *For a bunch of recluses.*

Following in the tradition of Saint Antony, the Father of Christian monasticism who had ventured into the Egyptian desert to seek peace through renunciation and asceticism, the brothers and sisters who called themselves Antonites followed strict rules concerning dress, conduct, diet, and, of course, spiritual practice.

Daily activities were organized around work and prayer. The community gathered at 4:00 a.m. for the office of Vigils, which lasted one hour. Lauds, at 5:45, was followed by Mass, and then breakfast was served.

Meals were taken in silence. No jokes, no idle chatter, no probing questions. That suited Sam. He had nothing to say.

Sunday was the only day when socializing was permitted. On Sundays, the Abbey opened its doors to visitors and guests. The light banter that filled the dining hall lifted everyone's spirits. Even Sam's. He never had visitors, but through the conversations he overheard, he learned about the members of this monastic community—and how he came to be there.

Like Antony, Sam had fled to the desert after renouncing his past. He was no saint, however, and he hadn't been seeking God, but perhaps only God could save him. Perhaps God *had* saved him, though he knew not why.

He'd had to put aside his antipathy toward religion early in his stay, but he quickly recognized the difference between this band of peaceful contemplatives and the proselytizing missionaries who sought to convert the world, by force if necessary, to their view of morality and reality. He was so young when he abruptly left the Jesuit high school. Walking away had been necessary for him to be able to move forward with his life once he was able to see Father Brandon for who he really was. Back then, Sam hadn't been able to distinguish between the actions of one individual and the religion he represented. Maybe now he could take an objective look at what he actually believed, if he could free himself from the disgust he felt toward Brandon. He had already abandoned the shared consensus that the set of doctrinal constructs he'd been taught was The Truth, but he sensed that hidden remnants from those early convictions continued to influence his attitudes.

He sharpened a knife in preparation for chopping walnuts. After regaining his strength, he had chosen to stay on a while at the Abbey as a way of saying "thank you" to the community that had nurtured him in his darkest hour.

If inertia can be considered a choice, he often thought when he considered his options.

The peaceful atmosphere, the calm acceptance and demonstrated kindness of the monks, and the freedom from the demands and responsibilities of being a father, a doctor, and an administrator had facilitated his recovery. During his convalescence, he pondered how he could best contribute to the community during the remainder of his stay. He enjoyed tending living things and was thinking he might like to work in the orchard now that spring had arrived. Beyond that, he had no plans.

He put away the mop, emptied the bucket, and glanced up at the clock on the wall. Bells were rung throughout the day to signal meal times and prayer times. The mid-morning prayer office would begin at 9:00. The monks would work until Sext and then eat lunch. The afternoon prayer office, None, was observed at 3:00, after which the hours were unscheduled until Vespers, which preceded a light supper. The day ended with Compline.

Had he forgotten any? Sam wondered as he tied the strings of an apron. The canonical hours had a long history, with fixed times for prayer predating Christianity. Monastic communities had long ago adopted the basic structure of the divine office as the foundation for daily work schedules and prayer rituals. Each office throughout the day was different, just as day differs from night, and the choice of hymns, psalms, and readings reflected the character of each part of the daily cycle.

Sam began chopping walnuts. Brother Henry planned to bake zucchini bread today and he needed chopped walnuts, so Sam chopped walnuts. He did whatever was asked of him. He had learned to follow orders long before arriving at the monastery.

He was grateful that Brother Theodore had been the one to find him, drunk and dehydrated, slumped over the steering wheel of his pickup truck. He had run out of gas somewhere in the vicinity of Clines Corners. The senior monk was returning from one of his quarterly trips to Albuquerque to stock up on supplies and conduct other business on behalf of the Abbey of San Miguel, named for the county in New Mexico where the monastery was located as well as for the Archangel Michael, the patron saint of the Order of the Sacred Flame.

The archangel was a fitting symbol for the Order, Sam thought as he put away the last of the breakfast dishes. Michael was recognized by Jewish, Christian, and Islamic faiths.

Though Christian, the Order was not affiliated with any particular religious tradition. Robert Martin, the founder, had envisioned an environment that was welcoming to modern men and women who were ready to cultivate a connection with Divine Presence through pious living. After a wealthy benefactor donated the land in Pecos, Father Martin and his followers started building. Soon after, the priest died and was buried on the property.

Leaderless, the fledgling group organized their sacred texts and hymns. Under the direction of the new abbot, they taught their version of scriptural interpretation to interested seekers. They drew from the Bible and the Psalms, but far less emphasis was placed on doctrine and recitation of a creed than on maintaining shared agreements and upholding the personal vows that members professed upon acceptance into the Order.

As monastics, the brothers and sisters of San Miguel made a lifetime commitment to stay at the Abbey and serve God. In so doing, they relinquished personal property and attachment to human desires. They supported each other in the individual pursuit of spiritual experience, but each member's faith was his or her private concern. Counsel was available to those who sought guidance on a particular matter, and postulants and novices were instructed in the central teachings of the Order, but individuals were expected to develop their powers of discernment and follow inner authority and guidance, even as they were required to obey the abbot's directives.

As far as Sam could tell, the rules were typical of what one would expect at a monastery, pertaining to chastity, charity, honesty and the like. The schedule was rigid, but he felt at ease. What he lost in freedom he gained in peace of mind. He wasn't pressured to conform. He wasn't criticized for his failings. And he wasn't wasting his energy chasing after unattainable dreams.

The regular periods of prayer proved a soothing balm for his troubled soul. He was inspired to put forth his best effort—not the acts that would win him some coveted position or favor, the ones that flowed naturally from the expression of his innate gifts and talents. The ones that were enlivening rather than deadening. And he had been nearly dead when Brother Theodore and Brother Vincent, a junior monk, happened by.

Brother Vincent was driving the Abbey's van when Brother

Theodore told him to pull behind the truck with the California license plates.

"I sense trouble," Brother Theodore reportedly said. (Brother Vincent remembered Brother Theodore's words as "I smell trouble," but Brother Theodore insisted he never used that phrase. The discrepancy in their stories was the closest thing to a disagreement Sam had witnessed in his time at the Abbey, but, then, opportunities for airing grievances were limited.)

Whether the monks had found out his identity by looking in his wallet or in the truck's glove compartment, Sam couldn't say. No one asked how he had come to be unconscious on the side of the road in New Mexico. No one asked where he had been or where he was going. No mention was made of the pistol he had stashed under the driver's seat. Sam figured the monks had put it somewhere safe and would return it to him when he left. So far, no one had asked him to leave. Was that about to change?

He'd been summoned by the abbot and would meet with him after lunch. Sam had been residing at the Abbey for nearly six months now. The abbot would probably ask about his intentions.

Sam knew he would be expected to become a postulant at some point, if he stayed. In a simple ceremony, he would declare his intention to explore a lifetime commitment to the monastic way of life. He would then wear a short brown tunic over his street clothes to symbolize his identification with the community. But he would not yet take any vows. That step would come later, if he entered the novitiate.

He had been bitter for a long time, and that bitterness had poisoned his ability to enjoy life. He needed to learn about forgiveness. If he couldn't do that here, if he couldn't do that now . . . Well, he was ready to make the attempt.

He removed the apron and hung it on a hook by the door just as the bell rang. He glanced again at the clock on the wall.

Fifteen minutes before nine—that would be . . . Terce?

He would probably be quizzed on all of this someday, he thought as he walked to the chapel.

If he stayed.

∾ 3 ∾

Caitlin walked toward the entrance of the health food store. A vintage car, covered inside and out with hundreds of miniature plastic ornaments, stopped to let her pass.

"Definitely not in Kansas," she murmured.

Once inside the store, she ordered a veggie wrap at the deli counter and then waved to Melody, who was filling a bowl at the salad bar, before choosing a table.

"Tell me about your life here," Caitlin said when Melody joined her. "Who's the current beau?"

Melody stuck a fork into a mound of greens topped with seeds and sprouts, shredded cheese and carrots, and slices of green pepper, cucumber, and radish before answering. "No men. I'm too busy. But I know some great women." She looked up from her salad and said, "I'll introduce you to Shanti and Sable."

"Shanti . . . Is she the astrologer?" Caitlin asked. She remembered Melody talking about some of her friends when they were both staying at Kimo's house in Arlington.

Melody nodded. "Yes. She's very good. She can do both Western and Vedic charts. Lately, she's been studying an ancient card system."

"Playing cards, you mean? Like aces and jacks?"

"Right," Melody said. "You know about the history of the four suits?"

"Hearts and spades?"

"And clubs and diamonds."

"No, not really," Caitlin said before walking to the deli counter to pick up her order.

"Card games were played in ancient China and other lands," Melody said when Caitlin returned to the table. "They became popular in Europe in the Middle Ages, though decks were sometimes banned for fear of encouraging gambling—and divination, which is how the Tarot cards came to be used, with its major and minor arcana."

"Do you use Tarot cards?" Caitlin asked.

"I prefer angel cards. I draw one at every new moon and full moon."

"I remember your new moon ceremony," Caitlin said. "The power went out during a storm recently, and I lit the candle I'd saved from that night."

Melody smiled appreciatively and continued eating her salad.

"What do you hear from Kimo?" Caitlin asked.

"He's graduating soon. Finally!"

"That's exciting. Has he made any plans?"

"He's talking about traveling for a while before he settles into a full-time practice."

"You think he might come out here?"

Melody shook her head. "I doubt it. He mentioned Australia and New Zealand."

"Wow."

"Yeah, right? Can't you just see Kimo trekking around the outback? He'll probably come back with a nose ring or a Māori tattoo!"

Caitlin laughed. "One last adventure before he becomes a licensed professional and has to figure out how to attract a clientele."

Melody finished eating and pushed aside her empty bowl. "I'm not worried about Kimo. He'll find his way." She took a drink of water and then asked Caitlin where she'd like to go. "Canyon Road? The Plaza?"

"Either. Both!"

"All right. I'll drive around a bit so you get a feel for what's here. Then we can walk around the Plaza and maybe end the day with dinner on Canyon Road."

"Sounds perfect," Caitlin said. "Dinner's on me."

"That's nice of you," Melody said before getting up from the table. "I'm gonna stop in the rest room. I'll meet you by the exit."

"Okay."

"Have you got plenty of water?"

Caitlin held up the liter of water she had purchased.

"It's important to stay hydrated. And don't overexert yourself. We're high and dry here."

Caitlin grinned and said, "Yes, ma'am!" She appreciated Melody's concern—and welcomed her advice about the climate—but she sometimes felt that Melody underestimated her intelligence.

She disposed of her trash and then walked toward the exit. A poster for "a new musical," *Millennium Blues*, caught her eye. She walked closer to the community bulletin board and saw that the notice was a casting call. The Playhouse Theater was looking for a mezzo-soprano for the role of Victoria, an "empty-nester in her early forties."

At thirty-four, Caitlin figured she could easily play a forty-year-old. She guessed she was probably a mezzo singer, but she wasn't sure.

"Minimum dance skills required," the poster said.

That's good, because I haven't danced in years, Caitlin thought.

Since regaining the ability to walk, she had avoided high-impact sports that could aggravate her injuries and instead stuck to gentler activities like walking, hiking, yoga, and taiji. She still lacked stamina—and confidence—but she had to start somewhere if she hoped to get stronger. As long as the steps were simple, she thought she could handle a short dance routine.

She was standing by the bulletin board when Melody appeared. Pointing to the address for the theater, Caitlin asked, "Do you know where this is?"

Melody leaned forward for a closer look. "I'm sure I could find it. Nothing in Santa Fe is very far. Are you thinking of trying out?"

"Maybe. I starred in a few musicals in high school. It might be good practice—to audition, I mean. If I'm going to be a performer, I need to get some experience."

Caitlin wrote the address of the Playhouse Theater on the back of a menu she had picked up at the juice bar.

"I could sing one of my songs!" she told Melody as they left the store.

"That's brave."

Caitlin ignored the remark and followed Melody to her car. Could she prepare for an audition on such short notice?

"God, what can I wear? I'll probably have to unload more boxes and suitcases to find anything," she said.

After Melody unlocked the car doors, they both got in the car.

"When is the audition?" Melody asked as she fastened her seat belt.

"Tomorrow. It starts at one."

"You'll miss the equinox gathering."

"Oh, sorry."

Melody started the engine and said, "Don't do anything on my account."

"It's not that I don't want to come—"

"It's fine, really. Let's go find the place now. One less thing for you to have to think about tomorrow. What street is it on?"

Caitlin showed Melody the address she had written down.

"I think I know where that is," Melody said before exiting the parking lot. "But what will you do if you get the part?"

"That's pretty unlikely, so I won't worry about it until it happens."

Melody drove past the Playhouse Theater as well as the State Capitol, the Museum of Indian Arts and Culture, and the Cathedral Basilica of Saint Francis of Assisi. She even drove north of town to the site of the Santa Fe Opera. Then, she found parking near the Georgia O'Keeffe Museum.

"Georgia O'Keeffe's home and studio were in Abiquiú, about an hour north of here," Melody said as she and Caitlin walked past the entrance to the museum. "It's an interesting area, if you ever have a chance to go."

"Good to know. Maybe I'll come back to the museum another time," Caitlin said. She looked around for landmarks she might recognize if she returned.

"Lots of events are held at the Plaza—Indian Market in August, Fiesta in September," Melody said as they neared the city square that was often considered the heart of Santa Fe. "I don't come down here that often." She pointed to a long adobe structure with protruding beams and a flat roof and said, "Let's walk over by the Palace of the Governors. Native American vendors sell their wares under the portal."

"I'd like to buy some jewelry," Caitlin said.

"Jewelry, blankets, pottery—this is the place."

Caitlin had read about the Palace of the Governors in her guide book. Built in 1610, it was the oldest public building in the United States and housed a museum.

"Those wood beams are called *vigas*," Melody said. "The Santa Fe style that you see everywhere draws on Pueblo adobe and Spanish architecture."

Though the more modern structures utilized other materials besides the wood, stone, and sun-dried adobe used by the pueblo peoples, the earth tones and architectural features had been retained, and, in some parts of the city, were required, giving the town a uniform—and distinct—appearance, Melody explained.

"You'll see a lot of covered porches; they're called *portales*. There are some lovely homes here, but most of them are hidden behind adobe walls and coyote fences."

Melody chatted with a street musician while Caitlin purchased a pair of silver-and-lapis earrings made by an artisan from the Santo Domingo Pueblo. Next, she bought a few postcards and stamps at a gift shop. When she was finished with shopping, Melody suggested they walk to a natural foods restaurant near Canyon Road.

"Wherever you want to go is fine by me," Caitlin said. The brisk wind had given her a headache, and she was not yet acclimated to the altitude.

"It's not the fanciest place, but it's got a good mix of Northern New Mexican cuisine and vegetarian dishes," Melody said as they entered the restaurant. "I think we're early enough that there won't be a wait."

They were seated at a table by the window. Across the street, a gallery employee was locking up for the night.

"You should explore some of the art galleries while you're here," Melody said.

The last time Caitlin had wandered into an art gallery she'd met a handsome Scottish artist named Dru and . . . well, all that was in the past. Her experience with Sam had taught her the importance of taking time to get to know a man, of letting him earn her trust.

She opened her menu and said, "You've been a great tour guide, Melody."

"My pleasure. Now, let's eat. I might even have some wine!"

"Knock yourself out!"

"Interesting expression."

Caitlin looked up from her menu. Melody wasn't shy about speaking her mind. Her forthright manner gave Caitlin a better understanding of how other people might feel when she shared *her* less-than-flattering observations about *them.*

I need to work on my people skills, she thought before turning her attention to the dinner specials.

Melody took Caitlin back to the health food store to pick up her car, and then they returned to the house. Caitlin fed Lucky while Melody listened to the new messages on the answering machine. Melody put a kettle on the stove and then helped Caitlin carry a few boxes from her car. After putting Lucky outside, Caitlin joined Melody in the living room for a cup of hot tea. Then, Melody took the cordless phone to her bedroom and Caitlin took Lucky to the guest room across the hall.

Still not sure what to wear for the audition, Caitlin opened a box and looked inside. She recalled the title of the show, *Millennium Blues,* and thought, *Maybe it's about blues music.*

The poster she had seen said she should be prepared to sing something that reflected her vocal range and personality. The first song she had written, "Wonderin' Fool," had a bluesy, torch song kind of feel to it; maybe she should sing that. She could wear the black dress trimmed with lace that she'd worn to a cocktail party at one of the embassies in D.C.—and she knew just where to find it. She had laid her garment bag on top of her bedding and suitcases when she packed up the car.

Finding her black pumps would be more difficult. She rummaged through the boxes, vowing to label everything if she ever went on tour.

Remembering that her sheet music was in her briefcase, she put on her coat and went out to her car to retrieve the briefcase and the garment bag. Finding her shoes would have to wait until morning.

After hurrying back to the bedroom, she unzipped the garment bag and looked around for a place to hang the dress. Noticing a decorative banner made of embroidered silk hanging on the closet door, Caitlin placed the dress and its padded hanger on the same hook. Then, she crawled into bed with a stack of papers.

Looking through the pages of songs she had written at the lake house, she felt a sense of accomplishment. Four months of solitude had unleashed a surge of creativity.

Though she had left the Ozarks only days before, that chapter of her life was behind her now. She was ready to take a step forward. She was ready to take Santa Fe by storm!

∾ 4 ∾

*C*aitlin awoke to the sound of the blender, a sound she had often heard at Kimo's house when she and Melody were both staying there. She put on her robe and slippers and went to the kitchen.

"Good morning," Melody said. "I'm making scrambled eggs. Would you like some?"

Caitlin hesitated, remembering that the scrambled eggs Melody had made for her in Arlington had burned her tongue.

"Sure," she said. "But not so hot this time, please."

She filled Lucky's food and water bowls and then opened the patio door. Lucky was more interested in his food dish and declined the invitation to go outside.

"There's smoothie in the blender," Melody said. "Apple juice, strawberries, banana, and a scoop of protein powder."

"Okay, thanks."

Caitlin poured the last of the thick, pink liquid into a glass and took a drink. "Mmm—Yum!" she said. After rinsing the pitcher in the sink, she took the glass to her room.

She showered and then returned to the kitchen with her wet hair wrapped in a towel. Melody was nearly finished eating, and Lucky was patiently waiting to go outside. Caitlin opened the door for him before tasting the scrambled eggs Melody had put on a plate for her.

"There might be some bread in the freezer if you want a piece of toast," Melody said without looking up from the textbook she was studying. "I'm sure Carolina wouldn't mind."

Caitlin found the bread and dropped two slices into the slots of the toaster. "Carolina's the homeowner?"

Melody nodded. "She's one of my yoga students."

"Where is she now?"

"India. There's an ashram here, just outside of town, and she started going to kirtan there. When the residents planned a trip to visit their guru, she decided to join them."

After buttering the toast, Caitlin spooned the eggs onto one piece and spread strawberry preserves on the other. She brought her plate to the table and sat across from Melody.

"What's kirtan?" she asked.

"A devotional practice with chanting and live music," Melody said, closing her book. "They usually serve food after. You should go sometime. The ashram isn't far, and visiting is a real cultural experience."

"I enjoyed the services I attended at the Ananda Center last year," Caitlin said.

"That's right, you went to Ananda! How long were you there?"

"Just a few days. That's how I got away from Sam, that man I met in Hawai'i. His mother lives at Ananda, so he took me there for dinner one evening, and . . . I stayed. It was my chance to escape without causing a scene. I appreciated the serene environment and the attitude of service. The meditation retreat was a great way to collect my thoughts before returning to D.C."

"Except that meditation is supposed to be about no-thought."

"I wasn't meditating twenty-four hours a day!" Caitlin said. She walked to the sink and filled her glass with filtered water.

"Don't worry about the dishes," Melody said. "I'll get them." With a shooing motion, she added, "Go get ready!"

Caitlin gulped the water and said, "Thanks! I still have to find my black pumps and do something with my hair. I haven't sung publicly since—oh, I don't know. A skit in law school? I'm a little nervous. Can you tell?"

She tended to get chatty when she was nervous, and Melody's blank stare did nothing to put her at ease. She opened the door and said, "C'mon, Luck."

The cat looked around for a moment and then followed Caitlin down the hall.

"I'm going!" Melody shouted through the bedroom door.

"Okay," Caitlin shouted back. She opened the door for Melody and then walked back to the mirror on the wall, where she had been applying mascara to her eyelashes.

Melody entered the room and said, "Wha— Oh!" when she saw the number of open boxes on the floor. "You sure brought a lot of stuff."

Caitlin put the wand back in the tube of mascara and turned away from the mirror.

"Not really," she said, looking at her belongings. "A bit of kitchen stuff. Bathroom stuff. Sheets and towels. Clothes, shoes, coats—it all adds up. I don't know where I'll be or what I might need, and it's easier to bring it than to buy it all again. Besides, I like my stuff!"

Turning back to the mirror, she smoothed her hair, which she had styled into an updo.

"Well, you look terrific," Melody said. She held up a key before placing it on top of the dresser. "Here's a key to the house. I don't know what time I'll get back. Make yourself at home, and good luck. I won't tell you to break a leg. Words are powerful, you know."

Caitlin reached for her purse and pulled out her key ring to add the key. "Thanks for the reminder," she said. She could always count on Melody to point out any word choices that were not, as Melody would say, made "consciously."

"Maybe tomorrow we can have brunch with Shanti and Sable," Melody said before she left.

"All right," Caitlin said. She opened the drawer where she had put the earrings she'd bought the day before.

"I'll be seeing them today," Melody added. "I'll mention it."

"Okay. Have fun."

Caitlin checked her watch: 1:00. She still had time to warm up her voice before driving to the theater.

She remembered the vocal exercises she had learned in a college voice class. Though she had starred in several high school musicals, she'd never had the confidence to audition for any shows at KU. She would have been out of her league, competing with theater majors who planned to pursue professional careers. So what was she doing now, auditioning for a musical after all these years?

It's community theater, she reminded herself.

Or was it? Didn't the poster say something about Equity? If the Playhouse was an Equity theater, then it was run as a professional theater.

"Well, whatever," Caitlin said aloud. "I can do this. I've been practicing for months. I've gotten pretty good, haven't I?" she asked Lucky. He had been watching her movements from his spot on the bed.

Caitlin attributed the resolution of the speech impediment she was left with after the Crash to all the singing she had done while she was composing songs at the lake house. Though she didn't understand the mechanism through which healing had occurred (time, she thought, was probably part of the equation), she imagined that music and singing had reawakened some dormant parts of her brain.

Not all of them, though, she thought as she stroked Lucky's chin. She still didn't remember much about the time she had spent in Ireland with Kimo just weeks before the Crash.

"Just so I remember the words today!" she said, gazing into Lucky's green-gold eyes.

He opened his mouth as if to speak, but no sound came forth.

Maybe he's lost his confidence, too, Caitlin thought.

She put on her coat and, lastly, her shoes. She so rarely wore heels anymore, she felt a bit unsteady on her feet. She picked up her purse, her sheet music, and a bottle of water and walked carefully to her car.

As she drove toward Cerrillos Road, she realized she had forgotten to bring the map Melody had drawn for her.

"Damn!"

Should she go back? She glanced at the digital display on the dashboard. The time was now 2:00. Auditions were well underway. Maybe she could find the theater on her own. Surely there would be signs to the Plaza. She could retrace the route Melody had taken the day before.

But we didn't go from the Plaza, Caitlin realized. *We went from the health food store.*

She did still have the directions for getting *there.* She could stop and check the address on the poster. Maybe someone at the store could tell her the best way to go.

After parking her car, she wrapped a scarf around her head to keep her hair from getting blown around in the wind. She found the bulletin board by the store's exit—but the poster was gone.

She hurried back to her car but felt completely turned around. Unsure which way to go, she drove down narrow, unfamiliar streets. After passing the public library, she found a place to park and went inside. A librarian wrote the address of the theater on a slip of paper and told Caitlin how to get there.

When she walked through the doors of the Playhouse at 4:05 p.m., Caitlin found herself in an empty lobby. She picked up a script that was lying on a long table near the entrance and looked for a sign indicating where auditions were being held. Hearing music and voices coming from the theater, she opened the door. Several actors were onstage, rehearsing. A bespectacled man played the piano. A teenage girl with long, straight hair stepped forward and started singing:

I'm waking up to a new day, rising like the sun

She was joined by a twenty-something man with a thin mustache who sang:

I'm searching for a better way, and I'm not the only one

A petite, dark-haired woman joined in:

An open door to unity is beckoning to me

A heavyset, dark-skinned woman sang:

There's no need to wait to find heaven's gate

Lastly, a blue-eyed man wearing black jeans and a red flannel shirt joined the others:

It's right here, there's no need for fear

Together, they all sang the next line:

When you're living from the heart!

Caitlin was startled when a short man carrying a clipboard appeared beside her.

"Can I help you?" he asked.

Caitlin turned to face him. "Oh—yes. Hi. I'm here for the audition."

"Name?"

"Caitlin Rose."

"I don't see you listed."

As the man looked over his list, Caitlin noticed the name MARK written in bold letters at the top of the page.

"Was I supposed to have an appointment?" she asked.

"That's usually how it's done," the man said, escorting Caitlin into the lobby. "As you can see, the cast is rehearsing. Auditions have ended."

Caitlin took off her coat and said, "Mark. Is that your name? I know I'm a little late, but it's not because I don't respect your time. I'm from out of town, you see, and I got lost. I would very much like to be considered for your show. Is there someone who can make that happen?"

Mark sighed and said, "I'll have a word with the director. Wait here."

Caitlin set her things on a bench and walked over to the framed black-and-white headshots and photos from previous shows that were hanging on the walls. She was imagining how she would feel seeing her photo among them when Mark returned.

"Like I said, auditions have ended," Mark said. "The director is in rehearsal now. But if you care to wait, he'll see you at the next break. Did you bring a résumé and headshot?"

"Oh."

Caitlin gave Mark an apologetic look. Maybe this whole idea was a mistake.

No matter, she thought. *I'm doing it for the experience—and I'm learning what's involved.*

Next time, she would know better what to expect. If there was a next time.

Mark turned and walked down the hall.

Caitlin sat on the bench and leaned back against the wall, using her coat as a cushion. She started reading the script but soon began to feel drowsy. She put the script down, thinking, *I'll just close my eyes for a few minutes . . .*

∾ 5 ∾

"*I*s Caitlin the woman your friend in D.C. was so smitten with? I can never remember his name," Sable said with a sigh. "After all this time. Isn't that strange?"

Sable's big brown eyes and genteel Georgia accent made her seem sweet and innocent, but Melody knew better. Sable was savvy. She knew how to get what she wanted. Melody couldn't keep track of all of Sable's admirers. She had been prom queen in high school and had even entered a beauty pageant while she was in college. With her hourglass figure and flamboyant style, she always drew stares. She didn't seem bothered by the attention. If anything, she encouraged it, chatting with people everywhere she went.

"It's good for business," she would tell Melody as she handed out business cards and showed off her custom jewelry. She was a better model for it than anyone she could hire. Men and women alike asked about her wearable art. Her unique designs were conversation starters. She had been written up a number of times in local magazines, and her work commanded a high price.

Her success was well deserved, Melody thought. Sable was not only talented, she was kind. Melody was pleased to call her a friend.

"Melody's ex-lover, you mean," Shanti said. "Kimo, isn't it?"

Melody smiled and nodded. She had known these women since her earliest days in Santa Fe. She could predict the way either of them would respond in a variety of circumstances, right down to the way Sable bit her lower lip when faced with a hard choice and Shanti raised her left eyebrow when she disapproved of something.

Melody took comfort in that predictability. Familiarity was a sign of intimacy, a bond that was reinforced by their shared history. The three women were very different, yet their friendship had endured in spite of Melody's frequent absences.

Shanti was the oldest of the trio. She had headed a nonprofit organization in Minneapolis before relocating to Santa Fe, where she now offered her services as an astrologer. Sharp and sensible, she was as insightful as she was reliable, and Melody valued her advice.

"Emphasis on the *ex*," Melody said. "Kimo and I are just friends now."

"Honey, men and women are never just friends," Sable said with a laugh.

"Maybe that's why there aren't any men in my life at the moment," Melody said. "All that relationship drama takes too much energy."

Sable grinned. "It's the spice that makes life interesting! Oh, speaking of energy—you know that vortex up on the mesa? I think we should create a labyrinth there. I'm planning some new pieces with a labyrinth design. We could energize them on the land. What do you think?"

"Who owns the property?" Shanti asked, looking around, as if the owner might be present at the gathering. The three women knew almost everyone who had come out, despite the unfavorable weather, to celebrate the start of spring.

"We'd have to find that out," Sable said, moving closer to the bonfire they were standing near. "But would you be interested in helping me run a business? We could sell the pieces in shops and over the Internet. I'd need help with the website and order fulfillment—stuff like that. It could be a way for you two to pick up some extra cash—and for all three of us to work together on something."

"I'd be interested," Melody said. "But I don't know anything about website design. Do you, Shanti?"

"No, but if someone else designs the site, I could learn how to update it—like if you have a special promotion or want to add photos of celebrities wearing your pieces," Shanti said.

"Could happen!" Melody said.

"There might even be a class at the community college that I could take," Shanti added.

"Y'all are the best!" Sable said. "Let's look into the possibilities. I'm going to design the jewelry either way."

"Did we decide anything about brunch?" Melody asked.

"It's fine with me," Shanti said.

"I can't commit to anything before one o'clock," Sable said. "I've got a date tonight, and with any luck, I'll be up late." She grinned mischievously.

"Poor fella," Shanti said to Melody.

"Doesn't stand a chance," Melody agreed.

The women laughed.

"What can I say?" Sable said with a shrug. "I'm a lusty wench!"

"I'm going to get something to drink," Melody said. "Anybody need anything?"

Shanti and Sable shook their heads. Melody walked into the yurt, where tables had been set up with food and drinks. She poured a cup of chai and looked around. Her face lit up when she saw Lu talking to one of the musicians. When they had finished, Melody greeted Lu with a big hug.

"Are you in town for a while?" Melody asked.

"Unfortunately, no. The schedule this year is very full—which is good! The band started touring recently, so we've entered a new phase."

"They sound great."

"A work in progress," Lu said. "And a labor of love! Oh, I just spotted Seva. I need to thank him for arranging all this."

Lu started to walk away but turned back long enough to blow a kiss to Melody. "It's great to see you!"

Melody crossed her hands over her heart. She held Lu in the highest esteem. Their time together was always far too brief. Though she kept a house in Tesuque, Lu was hardly ever there. Still, knowing that bright lights like Lu were present on the planet gave Melody hope. They each needed to do their part to help raise awareness before it was too late, before the damage to Earth and all Her inhabitants was unremediable.

Unremediable—is that a word? Melody wondered.

She was no scholar, but she was careful about her use of language. Lu was the one who had taught her about the power of thoughts and words. Lu was a master of manifestation.

Mistress?

Melody walked back to the bonfire as the musicians regrouped. She was so ready for winter to end. She didn't mind the cold, but the nights were long without someone to snuggle with.

She was taking a break from relationships to focus on massage school, which was starting in two days. Not that there was anyone she especially wanted to date at the moment, but Santa Fe was an easy place to meet people, with a little effort. There was always so much going on. Still, she had been feeling a little lonely lately.

Maybe she should get a pet. *Nah, too much trouble.* She was gone a lot. She wasn't even sure where she would be living next.

For now, the income from renting out Carolina's guest bedroom helped pay the bills. Santa Fe was a hard place to make ends meet without working several jobs. Rents were high, and property taxes burdened the families that had lived there for generations. The influx of celebrities from L.A. who purchased homes to use for an occasional retreat had been a boon to the economy, but it had had an adverse impact on the low-income segments of the population.

Melody was confident that she could figure out the money issue if she put more energy into manifesting abundance. She often set up a table at the farmers' market and other local events to advertise her yoga classes, and once she got her massage therapy license, she would have flyers and business cards for massage, too. Someday, she might even open her own yoga studio. But first she had to get through massage school.

She inhaled deeply and reminded herself to stay focused on the present moment. *The future will take care of itself.*

∾ 6 ∾

*C*aitlin's head drooped as she fought off sleep. When she opened her eyes, she saw a middle-aged man filling a cup at a water fountain by the restrooms. He turned and walked toward her. She sat up straight.

He cleared his throat and asked, "You're here to audition?" in a gravelly voice.

Caitlin pushed aside the strands of hair that had fallen around her face and stood up. "Yeah," she said. "I mean, yes."

"Miz?"

"Rose." Caitlin extended her hand. "Caitlin."

The man weakly returned the handshake. "Which is it?" he asked.

"Both," Caitlin said, flustered. "Caitlin Rose."

"Paul Schaeffer. Follow me."

Caitlin picked up her things and followed Schaeffer into the theater. A stream of actors filed past them, chatting amongst themselves.

A man wearing a black beret was standing by the piano talking to the accompanist. The pair started to leave as Caitlin and the director approached the stage.

"Oh, Ben, would you mind stickin' around a little longer?" Schaeffer asked. "This pretty lady would like to sing for us."

Ben didn't answer but dutifully sat back down. Beret-man picked up a mug and said "I need a refill" before walking up the aisle.

Schaeffer nodded and then called out, "Oh, hey—Gordo." When the man turned around, Paul held out a mug for him to take with him.

Caitlin set her coat and her purse on a chair and walked toward the stage with her water bottle and her sheet music. *Don't trip on the stairs,* she coached herself. *And smile! This is supposed to be fun.*

She set the bottle on a park bench that was part of the set and then handed the sheets of music to Ben, explaining the progression of loose pages.

Ben took one look at the handwritten notes and whined, "Pa-aul!"

"Just follow it the best you can," Schaeffer said. Pencil in hand, he sat at a table near the stage and opened a notebook.

Ben rolled his eyes. Caitlin walked to the center of the stage and waited to hear the brief introduction.

A young woman wearing a bright, colorful, low-cut top approached Schaeffer and handed him a note just as Caitlin started to sing.

Won-der what he's—

Realizing she was off-key, Caitlin said, "Sorry. I'm not used to the desert. Mind if I take a drink and start over?"

The room was silent except for the clicking sound her heels made as she walked across the stage. She took a swig of water, watching as the director whispered something to the woman, who was leaning forward and smiling and nodding. The man with the beret returned and handed Schaeffer his coffee mug before sitting at a separate table.

Caitlin walked downstage as gracefully as she could. She took a deep breath before signaling to Ben that she was ready to begin again.

> Won-der what he's doin' now
> Since we said our last goodbyes

When she focused on her song—rather than her audience—her nervousness vanished.

Schaeffer put down his pencil and leaned back in his chair as she sang the last line:

> Can't help wonderin' what he's doin' now

Ending on a softer note, Caitlin whispered, "I wonder," and bowed her head.

Schaeffer nodded and said, "Very nice. What's it from?"

"Pardon?"

"Is it from a show?"

"Oh, no. It's just something I wrote," Caitlin said shyly. She had no idea if the song was any good. She liked it, but that didn't mean anyone else would.

Schaeffer joked, in high-pitched mockery, "Oh, it's just a little something I whipped up along with the French toast."

Everyone laughed at his jest. The young woman gave him an admiring glance before departing. Beret-man opened a laptop and started typing. Caitlin started to walk away.

"Hang on. I have a few questions," Schaeffer said. "You can go now, Ben," he told the accompanist. "Thanks for staying late."

"No problem," Ben said, friendlier now.

"Do you know what you're auditioning for?" the director asked Caitlin.

"The notice said an original musical."

"Is this your first audition?"

"Yes," Caitlin said. "Well—since, like, high school."

"Uh-huh," Schaeffer said, tapping the eraser of his pencil on his notebook. "A little piece of advice. Find out something about the show you're auditioning for—get a copy of the script if you can. Normally, you'd need an appointment. But I guess you've figured that much out by now." He looked directly at her and smiled, as if to soften the criticism.

"Actually, I just got—"

"Well, never mind. As it happens, I may be able to use you. This is a musical that's currently in rehearsal." He glanced at his associate and said, "We need to replace a cast member on short notice, and we need a strong singer. Do you read music?"

"I play piano, and I write music," Caitlin said.

"Can you come back tomorrow at two?"

"Sure," Caitlin said. "Oh—"

She had promised to go to brunch with Melody and her friends, but she didn't know what time they planned to meet.

"You have other plans?"

"No. Well, yes, but—it's not a problem. Two is fine."

"You've met Mark," Schaeffer said, looking around to see if Mark was in the theater. "He's our stage manager. He'll give you a CD with all the songs from the show. I'd like to hear you sing 'Bridging the Gap' tomorrow."

"All right," Caitlin said. "And thank you, Mister—?"

"Schaeffer."

"Right. You told me that."

"Call me Paul." Checking his schedule, he said, "Better make it one thirty."

"I'll be here. Thanks, Paul."

Caitlin smiled nervously and picked up the sheet music Ben had left on the piano. Her hands were shaking, but she had been called back. She still had a shot.

She took another drink of water before descending the stairs. She liked the brief bit of the show she had seen but realized now that it probably had nothing to do with blues music. Tired and hungry, she left the building after getting a CD from Mark.

Outside, snow was covering the streets and sidewalks. Caitlin stepped carefully to avoid slipping. She put her things in her car and found a pair of boots that she could wear. Then, she started the car and turned on the heater.

Good night for relaxing by a fire, she thought as she brushed snow from the windshield.

After fastening her seatbelt, she inserted the CD into the car's compact disc player and then headed for the health food store.

Melody will understand about brunch. I hope!

"You're home!" Caitlin said when she saw Melody in the living room.

Melody looked up from her anatomy textbook and said, "Yeah, the event pretty much ended when the snow started. So I lit a fire here."

"Good thinking!" Caitlin said. She put down her purse and carried the food she'd bought to the kitchen. Then, she stood by the crackling fire and warmed her hands.

"You don't mind if I eat chicken here, do you?" she asked Melody.

"No, not really."

"I also got quinoa and roasted veggies and greens. You're welcome to have some."

"Maybe later. How was the audition?"

Caitlin removed her coat and took the pins out of her hair. "Okay, I guess. I got a callback, for tomorrow."

"That's good, right?"

"Yeah, nothing's definite yet, but if I get the part I may need to be there all afternoon. What time were you thinking for brunch?"

"Sable can't make it until one, but don't worry about it. You can join us another time."

Caitlin sat in a chair and removed her boots. She rubbed her feet and said, "I don't know if I'm cut out for performing. I felt so . . . *naked* up there. Singing my own material—" She shook her head. "In some ways, it's harder than arguing a case in court. There's a certain protection in all that armor. Losing a trial is one thing, but this—this is like letting people see a piece of my soul. What if they reject that?"

She walked to the kitchen in stockinged feet and took a plate from the cupboard. "Maybe I was fooling myself to think I could just start a new career at my age."

Melody closed her textbook and said, "Oh, Kimo called. I said you'd call him." She held out a shaky hand, her voice mimicking a feeble old woman, and said, "If you can see well enough to dial the number."

"Okay, okay," Caitlin said, laughing. She filled her plate with food and sat at the table. "Did Kimo ever bring strange women home when you lived with him?" she asked Melody.

"Only you, ha ha ha!" Melody laughed. "Why?"

"Just curious."

"Mmm," Melody murmured before picking up the cordless phone and taking it to her room.

∾ 7 ∾

*W*hen Caitlin arrived at the theater, Paul was talking to a man he introduced as Steve, the sound designer. When they were finished, Paul asked Caitlin if she had eaten.

"Yes," she said.

"Well, I haven't," Paul said. "Come with me to the green room. I've got a few minutes before rehearsal starts."

Caitlin followed Paul to a room that was equipped with a kitchenette in one area and furnished with a couch and chairs in a separate area. Three of the walls really were green. The fourth was covered with colorful scribbles that reminded Caitlin of graffiti.

"That's our art wall," Paul said as he filled his mug with coffee from a pot on the counter. "We let each cast have a go at it. Coffee?"

"No thanks. Caffeine makes me nervous."

"I think there's some herb tea in the cupboard."

"Is there filtered water?"

"No," Paul said. He took a paper bag out of the refrigerator and then sat at a small table.

"I'll bring my own," Caitlin said, setting down her water bottle.

She continued to study the words and images that had been drawn, painted, and written on the wall. Some were humorous; others were on the crude side.

Paul removed the wrapper from a roast beef sandwich. "It's always fun to see what's new on there," he said. "People are free to paint over something if they need space. Or if they find something offensive."

"Like these caricatures of you and Mark?"

"Nah, I don't mind stuff like that. I've got a thick skull—er, skin," Paul said with an impish grin. "The down side is, this room always seems to smell like paint."

Caitlin sat opposite him and said, "Not very appetizing, eh?"

"No-o-o," Paul said before taking a bite of his sandwich. "Now then. Do you have any acting experience?"

"Not professionally," Caitlin said. "Some high school musicals. But that was a while ago."

She wondered if Paul had been an actor before he became a director. *If he lost a few pounds and started working out, he'd be quite attractive,* she thought. His blue-gray sweater complemented his pale blue eyes and graying beard.

"How about vocal training?"

Caitlin shook her head. "Nothing formal. But I spent the winter writing songs. And singing them!"

She grinned and then drank some water. She was proud of her compositions, but her audition was the first time she had sung one of her songs for someone else. She realized now that actors were probably judged on what they chose to sing as well as how they sang it. At least her song was original. Directors probably got tired of hearing the same songs over and over when they were holding auditions.

"We've got four performances a week, so the schedule is not too demanding," Paul said. "But you need to know how to care for your voice properly. A good coach will give you pointers on technique, help you develop your own style. Some things will only come with experience." He looked Caitlin in the eye and said, "This ain't no business for the faint of heart. If you plan to go on a lot of auditions, be prepared for a lot of rejection."

"You don't need to worry about me," Caitlin said. "I was once a federal prosecutor, if you can believe that."

"I'll bet you caused your opponents a few sleepless nights," Paul said, his gaze still fastened on her. "There's fire in your eyes. Passion. Determination."

Caitlin fidgeted and looked away. "I admit to feeling a bit out of my element here. But I've always dreamed of being a performer."

"Well, you're in the right place. The Playhouse places a high priority on cultivating new talent. Playwrights as well as actors."

"Is this your theater?"

"I cofounded it, along with Gordon. And someone who's not very involved anymore. We're nonprofit, so we have a board and a managing director."

"Gordon is . . ."

"The music director. My official title is artistic director. Gordon and I usually choose the musicals together, since his role is instrumental. No pun intended." With a faraway look, Paul said, "We've known each other a long time, Gordon and I." He shook his head, as if dismayed by the number of years that had passed. "We got tired of the L.A. scene and wanted to create a venue for experimentation."

"You were a director in L.A.?"

"Shakespearean actor!" Paul said dramatically. "Among other things."

He wiped his face with a napkin, threw his trash in the wastebasket, and refilled his mug before leaving the room.

Caitlin picked up her water bottle and followed him into the corridor, awaiting his decision. Did she have the part?

"Like I said, I need a strong voice in a couple of numbers," Paul told her. He glanced over his shoulder and, lowering his voice, confided, "Christine really wants this role." He gestured down the hall and said, "She works in the office." He paused, as if making a decision on the spot, and then said, "But she's a little young for the part. And I've finally got her up to speed as a swing."

"A swing?"

"It's like an understudy, but for the ensemble roles. We've got two for this show."

"So would I be in the ensemble?"

"Victoria is a supporting role." Quickening his pace, Paul said, "It's a good role for a rookie. You'll get your feet wet. And then you'll know."

"Know what?"

"If you've got what it takes for a career in show biz."

Caitlin hurried to keep up with him. "You think I'm ready?" she asked.

"No," Paul said. "But you will be, opening night."

"When is that?"

"Two weeks."

Paul opened the door to the theater. Caitlin followed him inside, wondering how she could possibly learn everything she would need to know in two weeks.

"Where do I start?" she asked.

Paul scarcely looked at her as he replied, "Get a contract from Christine and see Mark about the rehearsal schedule. I'll speak to Gordon and the choreographer to see if they can meet with you tomorrow. It's an off day—no rehearsal. For now, just take a seat and get a feel for the show. We won't get to your song today, so I'll have you and Beverly and Tina arrive a half hour early on Tuesday. The rest of the cast is off book, so you'll need to learn your lines quickly to catch up."

Paul turned his attention to a woman who had been waiting to talk to him. "Cassandra, what can I do for you?"

Caitlin went to find Christine. As she walked through the lobby, she imagined it filled with people milling about at intermission.

This is really happening! she thought as she wandered down the corridor, past the green room, to the office.

The young woman who had interrupted Caitlin's audition was on the phone, rattling off a speech she had probably recited many times before: "Though you weren't selected this time, we'd like to thank you for auditioning. You're welcome to try again in the future. Look for announcements in *Pasatiempo*. We look forward to seeing you in the audience for *Millennium Blues* and appreciate your interest in the Playhouse."

The name plate on the woman's desk said "Christine Miller." When she put down the phone, Caitlin said, "Hi, I'm Caitlin."

"Yeah, I know. I heard you sing yesterday."

"What's pasa tiempo?"

"You must be new in town. It's the arts insert from the local newspaper," Christine said, searching her desk. "It comes out every Friday." She handed Caitlin a copy of the latest issue.

"Thanks." Caitlin glanced at the cover and then folded the newspaper. "And yes, I am. New in town," she said. "I hadn't really planned on staying. I was visiting a friend and . . . well, this opportunity seems too good to pass up."

"It is, actually. Our regulars fill most of the roles, especially for nonmusicals. It's nearly impossible for an outsider to land a role in a play."

"Paul said I should see you about a contract," Caitlin said.

Christine opened a drawer of the file cabinet and said, "Are you EMC?"

"I don't know, so probably not."

"Equity candidate—you'd get points."

"Oh—how does that work?"

Caitlin knew that Actors' Equity was the professional association that some actors belonged to, but she didn't know anything about how they joined. Membership was considered, by some, to be a hallmark of professionalism.

Christine handed Caitlin a registration form for the Equity Membership Candidate Program as well as a contract for her to sign. Caitlin asked if she could look everything over and return the forms the following day.

"Sure," Christine said before picking up the phone to make another call.

Caitlin returned to the theater and sat behind the tables that were being used by the various directors and their assistants.

Except for Christine, the entire cast was present. Caitlin stood up and waved to everyone when Mark announced that she would be replacing Dara.

She sat back down, wondering who had replaced *her* at the Office of Special Projects. Thoughts of OSP always led to thoughts of Neil, and Neil was not someone she wanted to think about. She returned her attention to the stage. Mark was reminding everyone of the importance of arriving on time for rehearsals. When he'd finished with announcements, he handed Caitlin a rehearsal schedule and then sat at a table in the back of the theater.

"What about costumes?" Caitlin wanted to ask. Did she need to bring anything? Would she get paid?

Everything was happening so fast. She needed to unpack and call her mother and buy more cat food.

Relax, she told herself. *Everything will work out fine.*

Before signing any papers, she would have to talk to Melody about staying on awhile—and find out when Carolina was coming back.

Surely, by then, she thought, *I'll know.*

∾ 8 ∾

*C*aitlin left the theater singing the last lines of the show's eponymous song:

> Life's a good thing, spread the news
> You know the cure's in what you choose
> For these millennium blues
> Millennium blues
> Millennium blues

She returned to the house and fixed herself a sandwich. "Let's go outside," she told Lucky. He peered through the open door for a moment before deciding to go along.

Caitlin closed the sliding glass door and then sat at a table on the patio. Songs from the show played in her head. She'd picked up the names of a few of the cast members and committed them to memory. *It's a start,* she thought, and took a drink of iced tea.

When she had finished eating, she looked over the contract Christine had given her. She would be paid a small salary, she learned, if she successfully performed her role. She would have accepted the offer just to gain experience, so any remuneration was a bonus.

She wasn't sure that she would continue working in the theater after the show was over, but she figured she might as well start earning credits toward eventual membership in Actors' Equity. Signing up for the EMC program would show Paul that she was taking the job seriously—and she was.

Looking over the rehearsal schedule, she saw that the cast had been meeting for over two weeks. Most of the blocking and choreography had already been worked out; she would just have to learn where to walk and stand and when to speak and sing.

Yeah, she thought. *That's all!*

She went inside and listened to the CD several times; next, she read through the script. The play was set in a fictional Big City and centered on a thirty-year-old man named Brad. He has just quit his corporate job, and for the first time in three years he has no important meetings to attend or deadlines to meet. He interacts with people he meets in the park near his office building—and gets to know them quickly when a sudden emergency situation arises.

One of those characters is Victoria, a well-heeled divorcée from an upscale suburb. Victoria has taken the train into Big City for the day. Her kids are grown and out of the house and, like Brad, she wonders what's next.

She's probably restless, Caitlin thought as she tried to get a feel for the role. *And lonely.*

She would join Beverly and Tina in singing "Bridging the Gap." Beverly was playing Estelle, a blind woman with a begging bowl. Tina's character, a teenage runaway, has changed her name from "Alice" to "Elyse." The three women all yearn to break free from limiting circumstances. One by one, they each sing the last line of the song: "Free to be me."

Caitlin had learned the song quickly, but she was glad she would be getting guidance and feedback from Gordon before rehearsing with Beverly and Tina. She didn't want to take up rehearsal time—or draw attention to her lack of experience. As a newcomer, she already stood out.

Gordon had agreed to meet with her on Monday, but Kenny, the choreographer, wanted to wait and work with all three women at the same time. He agreed to come early on Tuesday and go through the number then, before the rest of the cast arrived.

On Tuesday, Kenny took the cast through all of the show's production numbers. Caitlin stumbled along as best she could. She knew her movements were clumsy, but she picked up what she could, and by the end of the day she was no longer bumping into Tina when the three women changed positions during their song. Beverly and Tina were also new in town, but they had been part of the cast from the beginning.

Beverly and her husband, Leon, had moved to Santa Fe from Chicago and were looking for a way to get involved in the community when they learned about the show. They had been singing in a church choir for years—it was how they met, Caitlin learned. Leon had a booming voice that commanded attention. He was playing a preacher in the show.

Tina had acted in a few high schools plays in Albuquerque, but *Millennium Blues* was her first musical. Her father worked for the state, and he'd grown tired of commuting. He'd moved his family to New Mexico's capital city the previous summer.

Caitlin left the Playhouse feeling a little more confident that she knew where to stand and when to enter and exit for the scenes she was in. But she was still relying on the script.

At Wednesday's rehearsal, the cast worked through each scene, time and again, with Paul making suggestions—sometimes politely, sometimes insistently. As the hours passed, his patience seemed to wear thin.

"It's getting there," he told the group when Mark announced a dinner break. Paul reminded everyone that lights and sound effects and costumes would be introduced the following week. The actors were expected to thoroughly know their parts well before technical rehearsals started, and most of them already did.

The role of Victoria was, indeed, "a good role for a rookie," Caitlin thought. She was never onstage alone, so she could take her cues from the others.

Some of the actors knew each other from previous productions at the Playhouse. Rob, the actor playing Brad, was the only member of the cast who belonged to Equity (though Mark, the stage manager, was also a member, Caitlin learned). Rob lived in Los Angeles and was primarily known for his work in films and television, but he had also appeared in a Broadway show. Everyone, it seemed to Caitlin, wanted to be his best friend.

She was focused on getting acclimated and learning her part. After so many quiet evenings alone at the lake house, she was still adjusting to the change of pace. Much of the time, she was in observer mode—watching, listening, and learning. She laughed when someone told a joke in the break room, applauded when someone played a spontaneous tune at the piano, and memorized everyone's names. Other than that, she pretty much kept to herself. She wasn't familiar with the restaurants in the area, and no one had invited her to join them for dinner, so she walked to a sandwich shop in a nearby shopping center and ate alone.

She was nervous about the evening rehearsal, when the cast would run through the songs from Act One. *It's all good,* she thought as she returned to the theater. *Stressful, but good.*

Her song with Beverly and Tina came later in the first act. Caitlin joined the two women onstage. Paul asked them to sing "Bridging the Gap" several times.

He and Gordon had suggestions for all three of them, so Caitlin didn't feel like she had been singled out. At the end of the evening, Paul thanked everyone for their dedication and said that the following day they would focus on the songs in Act Two.

After Mark announced the dinner break on Thursday, Paul approached Caitlin and said, "Let's grab a bite."

Declining the invitation wasn't an option, Caitlin knew, but she wondered if the request was unusual. Did the director spend time, one-on-one, with each member of the cast—or was there a problem he wanted to address privately? She buttoned her coat and followed him into the lobby, hoping he wasn't disappointed with her progress.

Paul didn't hesitate to give the cast suggestions—about where and when and how to move onstage, about the need to project. ("Think about that person sitting in the back row," he'd say. "Can she hear you?") But Caitlin wished he would give more indication of what he was happy with. Was she doing anything right? She had learned all the musical numbers from the show, even the ones she wasn't part of, and she was doing her best to keep up.

Christine was standing alone in the lobby when Caitlin and Paul emerged from the theater. She smiled broadly when she saw Paul approaching. He said hello to her and then held the door open for Caitlin, oblivious to the disappointed look that flashed across Christine's face. Caitlin noticed it, but said nothing.

"There's a diner about a block from here," Paul told her. "The food's pretty good. I eat there more often than I probably should."

"Okay," Caitlin said.

They walked to the diner in silence and then placed their orders at the counter. Caitlin ordered a club sandwich and a glass of iced tea.

"No, better make that hot tea," she told the cashier.

She wasn't accustomed to so much speaking and singing, and her voice was feeling the strain. She selected a lemon-ginger teabag from a box on the counter.

Paul offered to pay and suggested she find a table. Caitlin filled a mug with steaming water at the self-serve station and set it down on a table by the door. She removed her coat and waited for Paul.

He arrived soon after, carrying a tray of food. He handed Caitlin a plate with a tall sandwich surrounded by blue corn chips. Caitlin dipped a chip into the container of salsa that came with her order.

Paul spread ketchup on his hamburger and fries. "You look like you're enjoying yourself up there," he said. "Or is that an act?"

"Oh, no. I am!" Caitlin said before taking a bite of the sandwich. "Everyone has been so helpful," she continued, "and it's fun being part of a group. It feels a lot . . . *safer* than starting out solo. But it's all happening so fast. My head is spinning! I'm still amazed at how perfectly everything has worked out. I had only just gotten to town when I learned about the audition. My friend Melody had a spare room to rent. I'm wondering when the bubble is going to burst!"

Paul seemed amused by her enthusiasm, and Caitlin realized she hadn't had anyone to talk to about the show except Melody, and Melody wasn't interested in hearing about blocking and projecting and costume fittings.

"What made you want to be a lawyer?" Paul asked.

Caitlin's tone changed as she reflected upon her former career. "I wanted to change the world," she said quietly.

"And now?" Paul asked. He washed down the last of his burger with a soft drink and ate a few french fries.

Caitlin was amazed at how quickly he had gobbled up his meal. She had barely touched hers. "Now what?" she asked before taking another bite of her sandwich.

"What's your goal now?"

Caitlin squirmed. "To give up having goals and just ... *live.*" Realizing that she sounded both defensive and aimless, she added, "I'm tired of seeking everyone's approval."

Paul chuckled. "And you want to be a performer?"

"I want to do what I love."

"Approval is the name of the game, honey. If nobody likes you, you don't get to perform. You've got to consider your audience. You've got to know who your audience is."

"I suppose you're right," Caitlin said. She disliked being called "honey" but she knew it was just Paul's way. He was a touchy-feely kind of guy. Whether he was talking to a man or a woman, he didn't hesitate to give a hug, squeeze a shoulder, or put his arm around someone while they were walking. He called men "bro" as often as he called women "honey" or "darling."

"I spent a lot of time alone recently," Caitlin explained. "I'm a little out of practice where cooperation is concerned."

"Theater will cure that," Paul said. "It's true teamwork. It takes everyone from the costume designer to the lighting crew to pull off a quality production."

"I still have a lot to learn."

"You're doing fine."

Paul drank the last of his soda and then tossed two one-dollar bills on the table, signaling that it was time to leave.

Caitlin had only eaten half of her sandwich and requested a takeout box. Back at the Playhouse, she put the box in the fridge in the green room before stopping by the office to ask about cast photos, but no one was there.

She didn't have time to ponder what might have passed between Christine and Paul. This was her first attempt to go off book, and the cast was assembling in the theater.

Later that evening, though, she thought back to her audition and concluded that Christine had, indeed, been flirting with Paul.

"I'll bet there's a story there," she told Lucky before turning off the light.

∾ 9 ∾

Caitlin glanced out the window before deciding what to wear for the final rehearsal before the dress rehearsal, which would be open to invited guests. The directors and designers would all be at the dress rehearsal with their various assistants to check the sound, lighting, music, and choreography. Once the show opened, their jobs would be done. They would only be called in if something went seriously wrong. The stage manager, Mark, would be responsible for ensuring that everything ran smoothly.

Glitches were supposed to be resolved before opening night, during the tech rehearsals and the dress rehearsal. But that didn't mean mishaps couldn't happen during a performance. Caitlin had heard stories about understudies going on without knowing their lines, actors being handed the wrong props, wigs coming unglued and other costume mishaps. The ability to improvise was an asset when things didn't go as planned.

After all, Caitlin thought, *the show must go on!*

The Playhouse had only ever canceled two performances: once because of hazardous road conditions, and once because half the cast was stricken by the flu.

Caitlin finished dressing and walked toward the kitchen. *If they could see me now,* she mused.

What would her father think, if he had lived to see her onstage? Martha, she knew, would be pleased that someone had taken notice of her daughter's talents and believed in her enough to give her an opportunity to shine. *I haven't even told her about the show!* Caitlin realized.

She had called to let her mother know she had arrived safely and was staying with Melody, but that was before the audition. Since then, she'd been so busy she could hardly keep the days straight. And when Melody was at home, she seemed to always be on the phone—as she was now, with her legs draped over the side of a chair in the living room.

"Cait, I'm talking to Shanti," Melody said when Caitlin entered the room. "Can you join us for brunch on Sunday?"

"Um . . . yeah, I think that will work," Caitlin said as she opened the patio door for Lucky.

She had put off meeting Melody's friends long enough, she thought as she filled the tea kettle with water and turned on the burner on the stove.

"Yeah, she'll come," Melody told Shanti. "Where should we go?"

"I'll have to be at the theater by one," Caitlin yelled from the kitchen. "I have a show at two."

She would be tired after Saturday night's performance, so a celebratory breakfast might be a good prelude to Sunday's matinée.

Let's hope I have something to celebrate, she thought.

She filled a mug with hot water, added a teabag, and sat at the kitchen table to go through the script one last time. Melody finished with her phone call and focused on balancing her checkbook.

Caitlin finished her task first. "I guess I'm ready," she said before drinking the last of her tea. "Paul doesn't let me get away with much. I'm enjoying working with him, though. He's been very encouraging. And I'm learning a lot. Some of the actors are really good."

"Just a sec," Melody said as she entered numbers into a calculator. "Let me finish crunching a few more numbers, and then I can give you my undivided attention."

Caitlin peeled a ripe banana and took a bite. Her muscles ached. She rubbed her neck and rolled her shoulders.

Melody put her pen down and said, "Okay, done!"

"When are you going to start offering massages?" Caitlin asked.

"At the school's clinic, you mean? Not for a while. I could practice on people here, I guess, but first I'd need to get a good table. Which will probably have to wait until I see how much the rent will be at the next place."

"You think it will be hard to find something?"

"Dunno. In the past I was always looking for something temporary, because I was going back and forth to D.C. And that's easy enough, if you travel light, because a lot of people only live here part of the time. I've done house sitting as well as house sharing. At one point I had keys to three different houses," Melody said. "Of course, one of those was my boyfriend's place. He'd go on tour with his band, and I'd water his plants while he was away. But now I'm here to stay. Well, at least I think I am. I never know what the Universe has in store until it happens."

"So you're no different from the rest of us?" Caitlin teased.

"Mmm, well, I'm different from most people in that I ask for guidance."

"Like channeling, you mean?" Caitlin had overheard conversations about locals who claimed to be channeling wisdom from ascended masters and discarnate beings.

"We're all channeling stuff all the time," Melody said. "Maybe not from the angelic realms, but from our higher selves, for sure." After a pause, she said, "You write songs—haven't you ever felt like you were a channel and the music was just pouring through you?"

Caitlin nodded. "Yeah," she said. "There's nothing like it."

"You had to cultivate that talent. And you had to be receptive and willing to express it."

"True. But I'm creating something. You're basing decisions on your . . . guidance."

"That's the use I've cultivated," Melody said.

Caitlin thought about Melody's response and asked, "So what kinds of things do you ask about?"

"Anything that's important. And sometimes things that aren't so important. Everything just flows better when I pay attention to what's trying to unfold rather than insisting that things happen a certain way."

"Is it like praying, then?" Caitlin asked before eating the rest of her banana.

"Mmm, I think of prayer as talking to and meditation as listening to. This is more like connecting with. Aligning my personality and will with the divine, all-knowing part of my being."

Melody opened the drawer of a desk in the living room to put away her checkbook, calculator, and receipts. "I don't like to get too philosophical about it," she said, closing the drawer. "It's an inner knowing, not a mental process. I tune in and follow my impulses. I don't know how else to describe it."

"Okay," Caitlin said. She sensed Melody's growing impatience with her questions, but she wanted to understand. "But aren't there different kinds of impulses? Different voices in our heads? Couldn't someone use the same thinking to justify selfish choices?"

"They could if they wanted to. It's all about intention, and when you're on a spiritual path, your intention is to follow the Light, wherever it leads."

"It sounds like it would be awfully easy to fool yourself," Caitlin said. She tossed the banana peel into the compost bin before putting her mug in the dishwasher.

Melody stood by the desk with her arms crossed. "Life gives you feedback, if you're listening," she said. "When you're sincerely seeking to live in accordance with Divine Will, it's amazing how life opens up to support your intention. But first you have to get your ego out of the way. That's where most people get stuck. They can't distinguish guidance from fears and wishful thinking."

The telephone rang; Melody picked it up. After a pause, she said, "Sable, hi!" and walked down the hall. "Can you make brunch on Sunday?" Caitlin heard her say before she closed her bedroom door.

∾ 10 ∾

*C*aitlin headed for the green room, her marked-up script in hand. She'd brought a sandwich to eat later in the day and put it in the fridge.

Paul was rinsing his mug at the sink. "Ready?" he asked.

"No," Caitlin said casually. She watched for the look of concern that she knew would cross his face. "But I will be opening night!"

Paul jabbed her arm with his elbow and said, "Minx!"

Caitlin laughed. "Remind me, how many performances are there?"

"Counting the dress rehearsal, thirteen."

"Isn't that unlucky?"

"I'm not superstitious."

"So you never tell actors to break a leg?"

"I don't," Paul said, "but not for that reason. It's a cliché, and I abhor clichés."

He started the coffee maker and then walked down the corridor at a leisurely pace. Caitlin walked alongside him.

"I'm not directing the next show," he told her, "and this summer is our biennial Shakespeare Festival, which currently consists of one play. Eventually we'll do three, when I can find someone else to direct."

"So you can act instead?"

Paul nodded. "Right now I'm doing both, and it's a bit much. Which is why I need some help," he said, leaning his body into hers. "How would you like to be my personal assistant? It's a highly coveted position."

"There'll be a line outside your door, I'm sure."

Paul was easy to joke with when no one else was around, Caitlin thought, but such occasions were rare. His assistant, personal or otherwise, would be expected to keep up with his demanding schedule—and to put up with his demanding personality.

"What, exactly, would this job entail?"

"Long hours and low pay," Paul said with a wink.

Caitlin laughed and said, "Undoubtedly!"

"Someday, I hope to start an internship program so college students can earn credit. But that's farther down the road."

"Hmm," Caitlin said.

Vague thoughts of ambitious young women being seduced by the allure of power and entranced by their dreams of stardom drifted through her mind.

"I'll think about it," she said.

"What's to think about?" Paul asked, holding open the door to the theater. "It'll be fun."

For you, maybe, Caitlin thought as she walked inside.

What were Paul's intentions? she wondered. She knew little about his personal life, except that he was divorced. She didn't think he had any kids. Was his proposal strictly professional, or was he looking for something more intimate? He was older than the men she had dated in the past, but he wasn't unattractive. And he had a lot of connections—in Santa Fe and L.A. Connections that might help her get where she wanted to go.

Well—why not? she thought.

She wasn't twenty. She wasn't naïve. She wasn't worried about being taken advantage of. She wouldn't do anything she didn't *want* to do. She knew how to say no. She knew how to walk away. She had a place to stay. And she didn't have any other plans.

I will *think about it.*

∾ 11 ∾

S am piled more rocks into the wheelbarrow. He had no idea why the abbot wanted this field by the entrance cleared, but he didn't mind the physical labor. His body was more toned—and tanned— than it had been in years. He felt full of vigor and grateful to be alive.

Who would have thought I'd get buff at a monastery!

He had been given access to the Closet, a small room filled with various donated items and lightly worn clothing the brothers no longer needed. (The women called their counterpart the Boutique.) Community members were permitted to take whatever they wanted from these storerooms without seeking permission. Money for purchases, however, had to be allocated. Monks were not permitted to maintain personal funds. To demonstrate their commitment to the Order, they donated their worldly possessions when they took final vows.

Sam had agreed to take the first step toward joining the Order. As a postulant, he was now known as Brother Samuel. Most of the time, he wore a loose tunic over his clothes, but he could remove it when he was working outside. He was still getting used to the idea of trading one uniform for another, but for now at least, he had no wish to leave the community. If becoming a postulant was what he needed to do if he wanted to stay, then that's what he would do. He was already fulfilling most of the requirements anyway.

He paused to wipe the sweat from his face. He had been working on this piece of land for several days now, removing rocks and vegetation. Easter Sunday was coming up, and he wanted to have the job done before then.

I hope this isn't some meaningless exercise they give to new postulants, he thought. *Chop wood, carry water and all that.*

More likely, something special was planned for Easter. For Christians, Easter was a Super Sunday event. Resurrection was the point of the Christ story. If Jesus hadn't been resurrected, then he was fully human like the rest of us.

Okay, a better human than most of us. But human nonetheless. Not God incarnate.

The Order's teachings focused on living life—and discerning truth—in the present. Their God was a living God, an animating force. Each person was free to decide for him or herself what beliefs to accept about Biblical accounts and historical figures. The monks envisioned a joyful union with the Divine Christ within—a personal resurrection that would enrich the community as well as the individual.

The idea that one needed only to profess a belief in Jesus to be guaranteed a spot in heaven was an oversimplification of how spiritual attainment worked, Sam thought; even he could see that.

He had heard many sermons and recited many prayers as an altar boy, but concerns about the state of his own soul were recent.

Why now and not earlier? he wondered. Had he reached a stage in life when the search for understanding had become important, or a stage in consciousness when the search for meaning had become essential?

Paradoxically, the more he kept his attention focused on the present moment, even in—no, *especially in* moments of stillness—the less he felt a need for answers. Life was simply a mystery, and he was simply a part of it.

That stillness had eluded him for a long time, and he'd sought escape through alcohol and other excesses. He'd expected to find love in marriage, belonging in family life, and fulfillment in work. Maybe what he had really been seeking was *to just feel okay*—and maybe if he *had* felt okay, he wouldn't have made such a mess of his life.

Perhaps the divine part of our nature propels us toward creativity and evolution, but our primitive instincts run our lives if we don't make an effort to tame them.

What, then, was the point of life? With plenty of time now for reflection, he had come to several conclusions—if not about the ultimate reasons for existence, then, at least, observations about human nature.

The first concerned the human capacity for denial. It was, in short, amazing, and it took many forms. Fantasies, addictions of various kinds, even self-sabotage were all forms of denial.

We turn a blind eye and ignore what's going on around us—what's going on in our relationships. We blame others rather than accept responsibility for our own unhappiness.

Fear, he had concluded, was at the root of the unwillingness to change, the inability to see things as they are. Fear of life, and fear of death.

We're afraid we're not good enough. That we're unlovable. That we're not strong enough to meet life's challenges. That we don't know enough or have enough to live fully.

People had to be ready before they could see things differently; there was no quick and easy answer for how to do it. Growth, a natural process, followed natural laws, whether it was physical growth or psychological and spiritual growth.

He hadn't been ready before now. Undoubtedly, there were things he still wasn't seeing clearly, but he was learning to accept where he was in his life without berating himself for not being farther along. He was learning to accept that others were right where they needed to be, too.

And in the end, he thought, *everything in physical form will pass away.*

Lately, he had come to see that the pleasures of the flesh don't need to be renounced because they are somehow dirty or bad; they are simply distractions. People got so attached to their possessions and ideas and beliefs—and identities—that they couldn't let go.

Attachment. The root of suffering, according to the sages. We can't lay down our burdens if we don't let go!

The monks learned to walk with Death, preparing for the moment when they would be called to another plane of existence. As that moment could arrive at any time, they must be ready for it always, for the quality of consciousness at death would determine the nature of experience in the next world.

Sam had no evidence—or experience—to suggest that consciousness survives death, but he was open to the possibility that it might. His ability to see denial at work in his life, however, was growing stronger.

He wasn't quite ready to ask for forgiveness—or to make amends to those he had wronged, though that would be expected of him if he chose to become a member of the Order. If he decided to take vows, he would be required to discuss his failings and his character flaws with a senior advisor. The residents of the Abbey were closely involved in each other's lives. They were invested in the community and responsible for its future. They had a stake in who joined their group. They noticed things. They would know if he wasn't sincere.

He was well aware of his failings. What were his flaws? Anger. Resentment. Bitterness. Were those flaws or just normal emotions that he had allowed to poison his relationships? He was willing to work on his relationship skills, though how he would do that at the Abbey wasn't readily apparent. Did community members *have* relationships?

I guess if you added up enough Sundays, you'd learn about people over the years, he thought.

Of course, words weren't necessary to glimpse a person's character; a lot could be learned through observation. A discerning eye could read volumes about people by the way they carried themselves and fulfilled their duties. Who was naturally jovial and good-natured, who was aloof and serious? Who was overly cautious, and who tended to be a bit careless?

Like the individuals who made up any group, some of the brothers and sisters were leaders, some followers. Some were generous, some were thrifty. Some worked harder than others. As a class, though, they tended to be more perceptive, compassionate, honest, kind, and humble than average. They had undertaken a supremely difficult task: removing all hindrances to union with God.

Never mind confessing his shortcomings to another; Sam had a hard time even admitting his flaws to himself. But he was learning that self-evaluation was not the same as self-condemnation.

He had been taught to avoid showing weakness or fear. Admit to making mistakes? Why? Would you give a wife reason to leave you or a boss reason to fire you by revealing your worst attributes? That wouldn't be logical. But without the threat of punishment—or, in the case of religion, eternal damnation—the exercise could be viewed from another perspective. If one undertakes a course of self-improvement, then *inde sine dicens* one must find the things that need improving. If something could be done—if tools were available to help people change bad habits, if the whole environment offered guidance and support—and incentive—so that becoming a good person was more important than becoming a rich and powerful person—well . . . change *might* be possible.

But even in an environment conducive to cooperation, where role models were plentiful and distractions were few, success was not assured. Some of the people who arrived at the gate, however sincere their intentions, were simply not ready for the rigorous discipline and scrutiny required for monastic life. (One poor sap had recently been asked to leave after the abbot discovered the fellow had been hoarding items from the Closet. He couldn't be accused of stealing, as access to the Closet had been granted, but his behavior was evidence of a psychological issue that was beyond the capability and willingness of the community to manage.)

Sam wasn't sure where he fell on the continuum of readiness. He *wanted* to forgive Yvonne and his mother and Father Brandon, to let go of all the misery he had been creating—for himself and for those close to him—but he wasn't quite there yet.

Maybe Yvonne was right. Maybe vaccines had contributed to their daughter's cognitive deficiencies. Was he to blame for that? No. But he could have grieved with his wife instead of reacting defensively, as he so often did. He could have evaluated the pros and cons with her rather than insisting he knew best. He could have acknowledged that aspects of his medical training had been incomplete. New information sometimes disproved earlier theories and suppositions. He couldn't be expected to know everything there was to know about the human body and how to treat it; no doctor could.

He saw now that his refusal to consider his own role in creating the problems in his life had been due, in large part, to fear. Fear that he would be accused of malpractice. Fear that he would be a poor father. Fear that he was a bad husband. Fear that he was so flawed, no one could ever really love him. Fear that his own mother might not love him.

He'd known no way through the fear. He hadn't yet discovered that it's all an illusion. Still, untangling all that old programming was going to take time. Time and diligence.

He could see now that atonement required efforts to resolve and remedy harms, whether caused intentionally or unintentionally. Atonement was part of the journey to wholeness; becoming "at-one" was the equivalent of becoming "whole." How could someone hope to find God if he was carrying around guilt, shame, anger, resentment, bitterness, and regret? How could he unite with God if he was hostile and defensive? One had to be an open receptacle that Divine Presence and Purpose could work through.

A monk must have a clear conscience before taking final vows.

The monastic path had never interested Sam; even when he was under Father Brandon's spell, he had remained focused on his own ambitions. But now, nearing forty, he was done with ambition, and the Order's teachings were more palatable to him than the dogma he had been fed in his youth.

Strange, he thought as he pushed the wheelbarrow toward the pile of rocks at the edge of the field. *It was only through hitting bottom, being desperate enough to give up everything, that I found something real—maybe the only Reality there is.*

He sensed that his concepts about "God" colored many of his attitudes and beliefs in ways that he wasn't consciously aware of. Slowly—almost imperceptibly—a shift was occurring at some deep, subconscious level. As entrenched patterns were breached, shafts of light shone through the darkness and gave him hope.

The bells rang, signaling the end of the work shift. Sam assessed his progress. Another day or two and he could pull a blade over the ground. Then it would be closer to being ready for building or planting or whatever the abbot had in mind.

Sam walked toward the residence hall, hoping he would have time for a quick shower before chapel. The Sext gathering was blessedly brief. He had usually worked up a good appetite by then and was eager to eat lunch, the main meal of the day.

Following a schedule didn't bother him. He had adapted to military life; he could adapt to this, too.

If he stayed.

∾ 12 ∾

*C*aitlin parked her car near the Playhouse and rode with Melody to the restaurant where Sable and Shanti were waiting.

"Parking can be tricky here, so I always ask the Parking Angel for help with manifesting the perfect spot," Melody said.

She was driving slowly toward the entrance to Pasqual's Café when a car pulled out in front of them, leaving a space available.

"And there it is!" Caitlin said.

"You sound surprised."

Does she really believe in parking angels, Caitlin wondered, *or is she just being playful?* Either way, her prayer was answered.

Inside the café, Caitlin and Melody walked past the crowd of people waiting for a table to the corner booth where Shanti and Sable were sitting.

"Thanks for getting here early," Melody told the two women before introducing them to Caitlin.

"No probs," Sable said. "I love people-watching, don't you?" she asked Caitlin, who sat directly across from her.

Caitlin smiled and opened her menu. Melody and her friends already knew what they wanted, so she ordered last when their waitress arrived.

"Is your feta cheese from sheep's milk or cow's milk?" she asked.

The waitress said she'd check with the kitchen.

"I seem to do okay with sheep cheese," Caitlin explained.

"This is Santa Fe," Shanti said. "I've heard stranger requests."

"I went out with a man once who refused to eat food if anyone else had touched it after it was prepared," Sable said.

"You mean, if you cut up a pie and put a piece on a plate, he wouldn't eat it?" Melody asked.

"Not without blessing and purifying it," Sable said.

"That would be a sight, in the middle of a busy restaurant," Shanti said.

"He didn't get out much, as you can imagine," Sable said.

"Did he want to bless and purify you, too, before he'd touch you?" Melody asked.

"Can't say," Sable said. "We didn't get that far."

The waitress returned and said the feta cheese was from cow's milk.

"Then I'll have the frittata with olives, artichokes, and sundried tomatoes," Caitlin said. "But no cheese."

"They might have goat cheese," Melody said.

Caitlin crinkled her nose and said, "Nah, this is fine."

"Melody tells us you're in a show at the Playhouse Theater," Shanti said.

"Yeah, it just opened."

The show's preview performance on Thursday had been chaotic and stressful; the next two nights hadn't gone much better. Delayed sound cues resulted in some awkward pauses and general confusion and frustration; the actress playing the role of Eve, a hooker, twisted her ankle in her three-inch heels; someone forgot a line and had to improvise. The audience was forgiving, and Caitlin expected that Sunday's matinée would be a more relaxed experience.

"How long does it run?" Sable asked.

"Until the end of the month. I'm not sure opening on Easter weekend was the best idea," Caitlin said, picking up a colorful plastic egg from the centerpiece on their table, "but the show does have kind of a resurrection theme, so maybe it's perfect timing."

"Resurrection?" Shanti asked. "How so? It's a musical, right?"

"I think it's meant to be inspirational," Caitlin said. "You know, enduring a dark night of peril and crisis before breaking through into the light, and being changed by the experience."

"That sounds interesting," Sable said to Caitlin. "I've never gone to a show there," she told Melody and Shanti.

"I don't even know where the Playhouse is," Shanti said.

"It's over by the Railyard," Melody said. "Off Guadalupe."

"Have you been there?" Sable asked Melody.

"Not for a show. But I know where it is."

"Say, do you know where the holistic fair is going to be held this year?" Shanti asked her two friends. "My guidance tells me we should all go in on a booth together. What do you think? I could do readings, Melody could give chair massages, and Sable can sell her jewelry."

Yet another person going on about "guidance," Caitlin thought. Surely all of these people weren't so enlightened that they were receiving messages from beyond.

She glanced at her watch. "My guidance tells me I'm hungry," she said. "The service here seems pretty slow."

"New Mexico is in its own time zone," Sable said with a laugh.

Melody and Shanti laughed, too, but Caitlin wasn't amused. "Where's the restroom?" she asked.

Melody pointed and Caitlin departed. When she returned, the women were talking about the upcoming fair in greater detail. Shanti had her calendar out, but she put it away when their waitress arrived with plates of food.

"Let's talk about it again next week," Shanti said. "I'll pencil it in for now."

"I'll find out how much the booths are," Melody said. "I was planning to get one anyway, so it would be great if we could all share the cost. I know someone I can borrow a massage chair from."

"How do you like Santa Fe so far?" Sable asked Caitlin.

"It feels very . . . remote," Caitlin said. She sampled the fried potatoes and peppers that came with the frittata before adding, "I like that. For now. And I love the skies—I can see why so many painters are drawn here. The light is incredible!"

Shanti had been watching her closely as she talked, Caitlin noticed. "You know who she should meet?" Shanti said to Melody and Sable.

Sable shrugged.

"Who?" Melody asked.

"Lu!"

Melody nodded, and Sable murmured, "Mm-hmm" before taking a bite of her eggs Benedict.

"Who's Lou?" Caitlin asked.

"She ran a women's spirituality group some years back. That's where we all met," Sable said with a smile.

"She moved back to L.A. but she still shows up from time to time," Melody told Caitlin. "Did I tell you I saw her at the equinox gathering?" she asked Sable and Shanti. "She seemed pretty busy, so she may not be around for a while."

"She's always busy," Sable said. "Lu is very charismatic," she told Caitlin. "And very wise."

"She trained as a psychotherapist," Shanti said.

"You just have to meet her," Sable said. She touched Caitlin's hand as if they were old friends.

"When is your birthday, Caitlin?" Shanti asked.

"Shanti's an astrologer," Sable said.

"Oh, right. I don't know much about astrology," Caitlin confessed. "I know I'm a Leo."

"That means the sun was passing through the constellation Leo—in Western astrology anyway—at the time of your birth. Mars and Venus and the other planets were also passing through various constellations, and the subtle qualities of those different energies left an impression on your consciousness. Those patterns continue to influence your life, and understanding them can help you see that whatever you are going through is part of a bigger picture. Events are not random; life is not meaningless. There's a design underlying it all."

"Shanti's readings are great," Sable said. "Even if you don't understand astrologese."

Shanti reached into her purse for a business card, which she handed to Caitlin. "I still do in-depth chart readings," she said, "but I'm also using another method now. I can tell you quite a lot just based on your birth day, even without the time and place, or even the birth year."

Caitlin glanced at the card and then turned to Melody, who was sitting next to her. "Is that the system you were telling me about?"

Melody nodded. "Uh-huh."

"It uses playing cards?" Caitlin said.

"It uses the *symbolism* of the cards," Shanti explained. "It's an ancient system that has—supposedly—been passed along from teacher to student and is now available for anyone to learn."

"Tell her about the birth cards," Sable told Shanti. To Caitlin, she said, "One of the fifty-two playing cards is assigned to each day of the year."

"Except Leap Day and New Year's Eve," Shanti said. "Each card has a defining characteristic, and the way your birth card relates to each of the other cards can help you understand the patterns you're likely to encounter in your relationships, depending upon whether the connections are favorable or challenging."

"What's Melody's card?" Caitlin asked.

"I'm a Six of Diamonds," Melody said before eating the last of her breakfast burrito.

"So what does that tell you?" Caitlin asked, looking from Melody to Shanti.

"On a personality level, the Six of Diamonds is learning about financial responsibility. Most of these influences operate on both a personality level and a soul level. Diamonds represent values, and the Six can be an effective leader once she has mastered her competitive nature."

Caitlin didn't know whether Melody had been a spendthrift in the past but she wasn't a big spender now, and she seemed to track her expenses carefully. As for being competitive, that would explain the not-so-subtle put-downs that Melody fired off when her dominance was threatened.

Shanti continued. "Aries is the first sign of the zodiac. Aries people are good at taking the initiative—that's what makes them self-starters and pioneers. They can channel that fire energy into starting something new."

Caitlin turned to Melody and said, "Oh my gosh, I nearly forgot! You've got a birthday coming up!"

Melody nodded and said, "Wednesday."

Caitlin put her hand on Melody's shoulder and said, "Well, then, your meal is on us." She looked to Shanti and Sable for their assent. The two women nodded in agreement.

"Tell her about the karma cards," Sable said to Shanti. "This is so interesting!" she told Caitlin.

"You know about karma, right?" Shanti asked Caitlin.

"I think so," Caitlin said. "The idea of cause and effect—that actions from the past can have repercussions in the future—both positive and negative. Wrongs need to be redressed. Scales balanced."

"And souls incarnate together over and over again," Sable added. "You may have been the parent before and this time you're the child."

"And if you were enemies before, you might take an instant dislike to someone you meet in this lifetime, for no apparent reason," Melody said.

"Or if you had an unrequited love, there may be an instant recognition—and attraction," Sable said.

"Like a soul recognition," Caitlin said.

"Saturn is the Lord of Karma and the ruler of fate and destiny," Shanti said. "We can't avoid the lessons we need to learn in this lifetime. Other people are often part of those lessons. The soul cards system identifies which birth cards are karmically connected. And when you see the way events play out in people's lives sometimes, it makes sense that Saturn—or karma—is involved. It's the force that draws us together until the soul's purposes are completed."

"You remember the Nancy Kerrigan–Tonya Harding incident?" Sable asked Caitlin.

"The ice skaters?"

"Uh-huh," Sable said, nodding. "Karma," she said decisively.

"Bill and Hillary Clinton," Melody said.

"Could be why she stays with him in spite of his escapades!" Sable said.

"Karmic connections can often explain why people are willing to put up with situations that are challenging and unpleasant," Shanti said. "Not every relationship is meant to be fun and carefree—though positive connections can be present, too, even if there's a karmic tie. It all depends on what your karma is. Some people have a lot of relationship karma to work out, whereas others are blessed with harmonious unions that last a lifetime. Their challenges may lie elsewhere."

"Shanti's readings are always so insightful," Sable told Caitlin.

"You can gain insight into all kinds of relationships," Shanti said. "Family, friends, bosses. Your dentist, even!"

"And all you need is a birthday?" Caitlin asked.

Shanti nodded. "Sometimes you need to dig a little deeper than just comparing the birth cards. When there's something going on that doesn't seem to be explained by the birth card connections, I look at some of the other indicators as well. It gives a more complete picture. It's a complex system, and I'm still learning."

"Sounds interesting," Caitlin said, glancing at her watch. She'd gotten so absorbed in the conversation, she'd lost track of the time. "Oh, heavens! I need to go."

"I'll be offering readings at a fair next month," Shanti said. "You should come by."

"We were just talking about it," Sable said. "The three of us are going to share a booth."

"When is it?" Caitlin asked as she gathered her belongings.

"Same weekend as Mother's Day," Melody said.

"The show will be over by then," Caitlin said. "Right now, that's pretty much all I can think about. It was great meeting you both!"

She left enough money to cover her share of the tab and then followed Melody outside. It was time to transform herself into Victoria for a few hours of make-believe.

∾ 13 ∾

*C*aitlin found a vase on a high shelf in the kitchen and filled it with water. Then, she arranged the flowers she'd bought at the farmers' market.

She had also gone to the Georgia O'Keeffe Museum, where she spent an hour viewing the works that were currently on display. After buying a box of note cards in the gift shop, she decided to pick up lunch at a nearby restaurant and take it back to the house.

After she finished eating, she looked through the different designs on the cards and selected a bright red poppy for Melody. The blue morning glories she would send to Kimo, she decided, along with a graduation gift.

Maybe a Native American drum or rattle. Or a dream catcher! He'd like that.

But what to write in Melody's card? *The less said, the better,* Caitlin decided. The standard "Happy Birthday" would probably evoke scorn, or some glib response like, "Every day is my birthday." She settled on:

> *May your Life be joyful*
> *Your Path be illumined*
> *And your Spirit be free*

She added a postscript: *If you'd like to come to the show sometime, just call the box office and tell them you're using one of my comp tickets.*

She put the card by the flowers and then sat outside. Melody was out with Shanti and Sable. They had invited her to come along, but Caitlin wanted to read through the script again. Performances would resume the following night, and she wanted to be sure everything was fresh in her mind. Having a few days off had given her a chance to catch up on laundry and errands—and sleep.

Was she cut out for the life of an actor? she wondered as she watched Lucky playing with a lizard. Long days, late nights, intense rehearsal schedules, and then—nothing, until the next show. *If there is a next show.*

She loved the theater, and she loved being onstage, singing and dancing, even if her role was a small one. But she worried she might not have the stamina to continue indefinitely. Had her brain recovered enough that she would be able to remember a long monologue? Starring in a musical had been her dream since childhood, but she'd found a new dream when she started writing her own songs. Still, being part of a cast made more sense than trying to launch a solo career as a musician.

The choice wasn't either–or, she concluded; maybe she would do both. For now, she was here, and the only decision she needed to make was whether to accept Paul's offer. Did she want to stay in Santa Fe and continue to be involved with the Playhouse?

As a developing theater, the Playhouse was expected to gradually incorporate the requirements set forth by Actors' Equity. Limitations were placed on the number of hours that actors could be asked to rehearse in a day as well as the number of performances allowed in a week. Breaks had to be taken at regular intervals and rest periods given between rehearsals and performances.

Being an Equity theater helped the Playhouse attract talented actors from New York, Chicago, and L.A. to fill leading roles. With its growing reputation for quality productions, the theater was able to consistently fill seats and generate support from donors. But Paul and the board were concerned with more than revenues; they wanted to treat cast and crew fairly and to create a positive experience for all. Ensuring safe working conditions was a given. Equity's requirements didn't impose great hardships, in their view.

Caitlin sighed. Paul would be expecting an answer soon. He had personally invited her to attend a party at a local entrepreneur's home the weekend after the show closed.

"We hold fundraising events several times a year," he'd said. "Our patrons love having a chance to mingle with our performers. And if it gets them to write us a check, why not? Everyone has a good time."

"A win–win," Caitlin had said.

The plays for the 1998–99 season would be announced at the party, and Caitlin was eager to find out what, if any, musicals were on the list. During the summer, she knew, the spotlight would be on the Shakespeare Festival, which alternated with the New Play Festival.

At the New Play Festival, several unproduced plays were read aloud (by student actors, mostly) and one of the plays was selected for development and a workshop production. Students gained experience with all aspects of the workshop production, which included simple costumes, props, and choreography. The theater department of a local college gave the students credit, and playwrights had a chance to see their plays performed and to hear audience feedback.

That was how *Millennium Blues* came to have its premiere at the Playhouse; it had been selected for development in the summer of 1997. Paul and Gordon had liked the show enough to include it when planning the following year's season. The playwright listened to their input and made significant revisions after the workshop production. He wrote new scenes—and songs—and added another character: Victoria.

I'm the first Victoria, Caitlin realized. *That's pretty cool!*

She yawned and stretched and then went inside to take a nap. She would wait until the party to give Paul an answer, she decided.

〰️

When she took her bows following the show's final performance, Caitlin saw Melody, Sable, and Shanti standing in the front row, applauding enthusiastically. She was touched that they had all come. They were the only people she knew in Santa Fe, other than the gang at the Playhouse.

The audience seemed to enjoy the show, and many of the actors received standing ovations. Caitlin wasn't surprised that Rob got the most applause. His professionalism showed.

She was pleased with her performance, for the most part, she thought as she walked off the stage. She hadn't missed any cues or forgotten her lines or fallen off the stage. But she had continued to feel a step behind the others right up to the final curtain call. She looked forward to being part of a show from the beginning and seeing it all come together—the costumes, the sets, the blocking.

Does that mean I want to stay?

Rehearsals would be starting soon, she knew. But if Paul wasn't directing the next play, when did he want her to start work? She hoped she would have a chance to talk to him at the party on Friday.

And to celebrate!

〰️ 14 〰️

*C*aitlin looked through the pile of clothes she had laid across the bed. The classic style she had favored in D.C. seemed out of place here in the Southwest, but she hadn't had a chance to go shopping for a new outfit to wear to the party. She selected a red silk skirt and a gold top that she'd never worn.

How to stand out from the crowd? Wear bright clothing!

She slid a few bangles over her wrist and put a couple of beaded combs in her hair. Looking in the mirror, she admired her diamond stud earrings and then wrapped a delicate scarf around her neck before spreading bright red lipstick over her lips.

"There," she said aloud. "Positively sparkling."

∽

Expensive cars lined the circular driveway in front of a contemporary home that was clearly designed with entertaining in mind. Caitlin drove to a patch of gravel by the guest house and parked her car.

When was the last time she had gone to a party? she wondered as she walked carefully across the driveway.

Ah, yes—Hallowe'en at Kimo's house, she thought with a smile.

She had answered the phone when Kimo called to wish Melody happy birthday. She asked him about his plans and he confirmed that he was, indeed, going Down Under after graduation. He would be gone most of the summer.

"When I get back I'll figure out how to go about setting up a practice," he said. "I've got some ideas, but travel has a way of changing a person, so I'm holding off on making any firm plans."

"Well, we've known each other a while now, and I can say with certainty that the changes I've seen have all been good ones," Caitlin said.

When she first met him, Kimo seemed directionless and he was stoned much of the time. Since then, he had stopped using drugs and alcohol, had taken up biking and taiji, and had earned a degree in naturopathy.

Caitlin's life had changed a lot during that time as well. She was a long way from Washington and the life she had expected to be living. She could only hope that the changes were for the better and she wasn't just drifting, without a home or a career or even a plan.

She'd always had a plan before—whether she was planning which high school shows she wanted to audition for or which colleges she wanted to apply to or which of her classmates she wanted to date. And she'd usually gotten what she wanted—the roles she had wanted, the schools she had wanted, the dates she had wanted. So how did it all fall apart? How did she end up losing, in quick succession, her fiancé, her career, and very nearly her life?

Rite of passage indeed, she thought as she walked up the steps to the front door of the Chapmans' spacious home. Well, she was here now and she would make the most of this new life, even if it wasn't the one she had chosen—or imagined—for herself.

Whenever she felt the dagger of grief stabbing at her heart, she reminded herself that things could always be worse. Things *had* been worse—much worse. She knew what "pain and suffering" were, and she prayed she would never again have to endure anything as horrific as what she had experienced after the Crash. She remembered feeling as weak and fragile as a newly hatched chick when she was released from the hospital.

Yes, she had come a long way in her recovery, but she knew she might never again have the boundless energy she had once taken for granted. She took more care now with all things—her words, her choices, her body. She was more cautious, more aware of life's uncertainties.

Seeing that the front door was open, she stepped inside.

This must be the place, she thought when she saw the stacks of postcards, brochures, and programs from the Playhouse on a small table. She picked up a leaflet that listed the shows that were planned for the 1998–99 season and saw that *I Do! I Do!* was scheduled for February. *Just in time for Valentine's Day.*

Only two actors would be needed for *I Do! I Do!,* Caitlin knew. A man and a woman.

Now that *would be a great opportunity!* she thought. She put the leaflet back on the table and walked through the living room. Most of the guests were outside on the patio, where live music helped create a festive atmosphere.

Rob had returned to L.A., but many of the local actors who had been part of the cast of *Millennium Blues* were present. They were, by and large, an entertaining lot, Caitlin thought as she headed to the bar for a glass of wine.

"Chardonnay, please," she told the bartender, who filled a glass and handed it to her.

She took a sip and looked around. Paul was making the rounds, shaking hands and patting people on the back.

Caitlin selected a few appetizers from the buffet and then joined Beverly and Leon. The photographer who had taken photos of the cast was standing nearby, chatting with a pretty young brunette who was refilling the dessert tray.

Caitlin turned to him and said, "Are you here to take pictures or to flirt with the catering staff?"

"A little of both," the man said with a laugh. He put down his wine glass and picked up his camera when Paul requested a photo with Caitlin. She could only imagine the dismayed look the camera might have captured when Paul put his hand on her waist and pulled her close to him.

Paul thanked the photographer and then kissed Caitlin's forehead. "You, my dear, have real potential."

"Are you this friendly to all your actors?"

"Only the special ones," Paul said, brushing Caitlin's nose affectionately. "Come with me," he said, taking her hand. "I'll introduce you to some of Santa Fe's finest."

He introduced various people they encountered along their path until they reached the couple hosting the party.

"The Chapmans have been helping keep the doors of the Playhouse open from the start," Paul told Caitlin. "And we greatly appreciate their support." He raised his glass before taking a drink.

"We're glad we can play a part," said Gerald Chapman. "As it were!"

"We love the theater," said Barbara Chapman, "so we want to make sure the Playhouse thrives."

"As long as I'm in Santa Fe, the Playhouse will be in Santa Fe," Paul said.

Gerald Chapman's manner of speech reminded Caitlin of the New England natives she had known in Washington. She could almost picture him at the helm of a yacht. Before she could inquire about his past, Paul whispered in her ear, "I better let Christine know I have a new assistant. You are interested in the job, aren't you?"

"Not if it means you're dismissing her," Caitlin said, her eyes scanning the crowd until she spotted Christine. She was talking to a band member who was on break.

"No, no—she's part-time in the office," Paul said. "That's between her and Sy. Did you meet Sy?"

Caitlin shook her head.

"I'll point him out if I see him," Paul said, glancing around. "He's the managing director. He handles the business side of things—marketing, ticket sales, volunteers." He looked into her eyes and said, "Who I choose to take under my wing is up to me."

Caitlin looked away and thought, *Interesting choice of words.* She had just been comparing herself to a baby chick. She was paying closer attention to language these days—her own and other people's. *Melody would be pleased.*

But what did it mean, exactly, that Paul wanted to take her under his wing? She felt a bit ambivalent about the arrangement he was proposing. It was all so vague, and she liked clear agreements that established boundaries and laid out what was expected of her. Yes, she was new in town and she would surely benefit from being part of Paul's extensive network. She would undoubtedly learn a lot— about the theater and about Paul. She had already witnessed his domineering side. He didn't spare people's feelings.

She watched as Christine laughed and tossed her hair around. *She's attractive, but she tries too hard*, Caitlin thought, remembering the days when she had worn too much makeup and flirted shame-lessly. Young women tended to make foolish choices when they were desperate for attention.

Cinderella is a character in a fairy tale, she wanted to tell Christine. *No matter,* she thought. *She'll learn her own lessons, in her own time. She doesn't need advice from me.*

Aware that Paul was waiting for an answer, Caitlin turned to him and said, "Sure, why not. I don't have any other plans."

He smiled, squeezed her arm, and walked over to Christine, who threw a drink in his face and then stormed off.

"Oh my," Caitlin murmured. Whatever had transpired between those two was probably either common knowledge at the Playhouse or the subject of speculation and gossip.

Caitlin followed Paul to the bar, where he asked the bartender for another gin-and-tonic—and a clean, wet cloth to wipe his face.

"I don't know what she's so upset about," Paul said. "I never promised her anything—or lied to her."

"She's young."

"And I'm getting too old for this."

"Come on—I'll drive you home," Caitlin said. She took the drink from the bartender and set it on the bar. "I think the party's over."

People were starting to leave. Caitlin knew that Paul's departure would hasten the exodus, but she was ready to go, and he was drunk enough that he shouldn't drive—or have another drink.

Guess this is my first assignment! she thought, curious to find out where Paul lived.

He directed her to an exclusive subdivision on the north side of town. The community wasn't gated, but the land was hilly, and no streetlamps lit the way.

"I hope I can find my way back," Caitlin said as she parked her car in Paul's driveway.

Paul nuzzled her neck and said, "You could always spend the night here."

"I'm sure I'll be fine."

"Well how 'bout a little good night kiss, then?"

Caitlin leaned over and lightly kissed Paul's cheek. "Good night, Paul," she said.

"G'night Caitlin my love. I'll call you when I get back from L.A."

"You're going to L.A.?"

"Oh, didn't I tell you? I go a couple of times a year to scout talent and keep up ties."

Paul got out of the car and steadied himself before closing the door. Caitlin opened the passenger-side window. "You need help getting inside?"

"I need help getting into bed," he said, a hopeful lilt in his voice.

"Nice try," Caitlin said.

Paul shrugged. "Can't blame a guy for trying." He fumbled with his keys and said, "I'll be fine. You go on."

Caitlin waited until he had opened the front door; then, she followed the road down the hill until she reached the highway.

Melody was already asleep when Caitlin returned to the house. Caitlin needed to talk to her about staying there a while longer. She didn't think it would be a problem, but she didn't dare assume anything.

Tomorrow, for sure.

She put Lucky outside while she got ready for bed and realized that, for the first time in a long while, she felt happy.

∾ 15 ∾

*C*aitlin helped with the setup for the holistic fair and was first in line for a chair massage from Melody, who was offering fifteen-minute sessions on a donation basis. She wasn't licensed yet, so Caitlin had helped her prepare a release form for people to sign.

Feeling a little looser after some of the tension in her shoulders had been released, Caitlin signed up for a mini-reading with Shanti and then looked over Sable's jewelry. She was happy to see that Sable had taken her advice and brought pieces that would make good Mother's Day gifts. She also brought a copy of an ad she had placed in a few local magazines:

Mother's Day is Sunday, May 10ᵗʰ
Show her how much she means to you
With a gift she'll treasure

Sable set the ad beside the heart-shaped pins, gold earrings, and pendants accentuated with amethysts and other gemstones she had spread across the table.

Caitlin's eye was drawn to the gleaming silver pieces that were resting on a black velvet cloth.

"That's my latest design," Sable said, holding up a silver pendant. "It's a labyrinth. We're trying to find a place where we can create one that people can walk through. I've been talking to the abbot at the monastery in Pecos about setting aside some land there. That way, I can sell my jewelry in the monastery's gift shop. It's not open very often, but the sales would benefit the monks as well as me." She put the pendant back on the cloth.

Caitlin preferred the pin version to the pendant. She picked one up and studied the design. "You could make t-shirts, too," she told Sable.

"That's a great idea, Caitlin! Here—take it!" Sable folded Caitlin's fingers over the pin in her hand and said, "Thank you for that. If this arrangement works out, I'm going to do it. Then I'll give you a t-shirt, too!"

Caitlin appreciated the gesture and fastened the pin to her jacket before checking to see if Shanti was nearly ready for her. The names before hers on the signup sheet all had a line through them. Her soul card reading would be next.

The description said she could choose three people and find out how she was connected to each of them on a soul level, as long as she knew their birthdays.

While she waited for Shanti to signal that she was ready for her, Caitlin thought about which three people to inquire about. She was curious about her relationship with Melody, since they were living together. There had always been some underlying tension in their friendship. It wasn't quite a rivalry, but it felt . . . *competitive* somehow. But delving into her relationship with Melody was not a priority.

She would start with the people she knew best, she decided: her parents and her brother. If none of the information Shanti gave her about her family made sense, then the system probably wasn't very useful.

She sat in a folding chair across from Shanti, who typed her name into her laptop computer and said, "Let's start with your birthday."

"July twenty-sixth."

Shanti entered the date and turned the laptop so Caitlin could view her profile.

"You're a Two of Clubs," Shanti said. "The Clubs are concerned with communication and mental pursuits."

"Well that much fits," Caitlin said. "You probably know I used to be a trial lawyer. And now I'm hoping to communicate something through my music."

"The Two of Clubs doesn't like to be alone. None of the twos do, really, but the Two of Clubs is almost *afraid* of being alone. Though you can find the opposite as well—a recluse. But that doesn't seem like you."

"Actually, I can be a recluse—for periods of time. And I've had a lot of fears to contend with in the last few years. Or, at least, that's when I've become more aware of them. And willing to confront them."

"Well, that's good, because otherwise you risk making poor relationship choices just so you won't be alone."

"There might be some truth to that," Caitlin said, remembering how desperate she thought Christine had seemed for attention—and how she had felt that way in the past.

"You can be quite charming. Except when your fears are controlling you. Then you probably get argumentative."

"You don't want to argue with me," Caitlin said with a grin. "I win arguments."

"You have a sharp mind, but that doesn't always help you in relationships. Here, too, there's a dual quality: you can be very critical of your partner, but you can also overlook problems that you really should be paying attention to."

Caitlin thought about Sam and Neil and Dru and some of the other men she had been involved with. "I haven't always made the wisest choices when it comes to men," she said. "Except maybe my fiancé. We had issues, but I don't regret our time together."

"Do you want to look up his card?" Shanti asked.

Caitlin hesitated. Should she ask about Jayson instead of Bobby?

"No, maybe another time."

"What did he do for work?"

"Jayson's a lawyer too."

"Uh-huh," Shanti said. "You're probably drawn to men who are . . . very macho in some way. Aggressive, domineering, charismatic, or argumentative—even dangerous."

Caitlin sighed. "So what's the solution?"

"You're destined for some fated relationships. They're part of your learning. Some of them might be karmic. You can't avoid those, but otherwise my best advice is to balance your idealism about love with acceptance of your partner's faults. Take time to really get to know someone. How does he treat you? How do you feel when you're with him? And when you do give your heart, try not to be overly critical."

"Good advice."

"Shall we move on to the soul connections?" Shanti asked.

"Sure. I thought I'd ask about my parents and my brother."

"Okay. Who's first?"

"My father. Charles Rose. November twenty-third."

"He would be a Ten of Hearts. What I do here is I look at the top three connections between you. They indicate the main purposes of *why* certain people are in your life as well as the potential and quality of the relationship. Knowing that a relationship is karmic, for example, can help you accept its limitations and focus on learning the lesson or appreciating the gift. With your father, your role is that of a teacher, and this would be a teacher of spiritual lessons." Shanti looked up from her computer and said, "You're not teaching him how to play golf."

"He's . . . no longer living," Caitlin said, her eyes tearing up.

"I'm sorry," Shanti said. "As women, so many of our patterns with men start with our fathers and that first important relationship." She continued to study the information on her computer screen. After a pause, she said, "As a teacher, you were probably somewhat critical of him."

"At the time . . . no, not openly critical. He knew I didn't like his drinking; none of us did. My mother was plenty critical. I didn't need to say anything. I think he was ashamed, maybe, but he also couldn't stop. Or didn't try to. I don't know. I'd probably see him differently now, if he were still alive."

"The challenge for the Ten of Hearts is honesty, and of course, that always starts with being honest with ourselves and then allowing others to see who we really are, rather than covering the truth up with lies. Not always outright lies, mind you, but spinning tales that deflect the true state of affairs."

"Boy, you hit that nail dead on. My father was a journalist—and an Irishman. Stories were his lifeblood. It wasn't till after he was gone that I learned—well . . . Let's just say that after he died I learned some things I hadn't known."

"The parent is supposed to guide and direct the child; it can be difficult when the roles are reversed. But, in some way, you played a role in his spiritual life. That may not have been easy for him, especially if he felt he wasn't living up to his destiny."

"Yeah, well, considering that he took his own life, I'd say he failed to learn a few lessons," Caitlin said.

She still felt a mixture of anger, bitterness, regret, and grief about her father's death. Maybe this role Shanti was describing explained why she felt some responsibility—as if *she'd* failed somehow or could have helped him if only she had known the depth of his despair.

"Beyond that, you two shared a deep love and appreciation for each other. You probably had a lot in common and genuinely enjoyed being together."

Caitlin's tears flowed freely now. Shanti searched her bag and removed a small packet of tissues. She offered it to Caitlin, who took a single tissue and wiped her eyes.

"We understood each other," she said.

"That loving bond would have softened some of the harshness of the lessons," Shanti said.

"Okay," Caitlin said, blowing her nose, "let's move along."

Shanti looked up Martha's birthday and told Caitlin she was a Ten of Clubs. "Interesting that they're both tens. The tens are very driven. A bit restless."

"She always wanted to travel," Caitlin said. "And she doesn't sit still for very long! But her ambitions were never for herself. Not like having a career or anything."

"She might have wanted one but circumstances didn't allow it. Your parents were actually quite compatible."

"They did okay for a while, I guess," Caitlin said.

"As for you two, though . . . there are some challenges. She's one of your teachers. You may not always appreciate her nagging, but she's actually helping point you in the direction of your life's work."

"That's interesting. I hated practicing piano when I was young. I guess I wanted to be able to just sit down and play without having to put in the hours. I resisted and whined and complained, but she didn't let up. And now I really appreciate it. Music gives me so much. I got away from it when I was focused on law—which was something my father encouraged. He didn't want me to waste my life as a struggling artist or musician. And yet, that's where I'm headed now. Well, not struggling, hopefully, but performing. My mother recognized that I had talent, even when I was quite young."

"Sounds like you've managed to access the gifts of the connection, even if it's been challenging at times."

"Really challenging. We didn't speak for several years."

"Interesting. She probably also seems a bit controlling to you."

"Hah! That's an understatement!"

"In her way, she's trying to stimulate you to grow into the fullness of your being. She might encourage you to leave the past behind and risk new adventures. That's a good role for a mom."

"Actually, she was the one who woke me up to the truth about my father. I didn't want to hear it or see it or accept it. She told me to just let it go and live my life. 'Don't stay stuck in the past'—I remember her saying that. She forced me to face facts. I hated her at the time. But now I'm so grateful." Caitlin thought about how easily her mother pushed her buttons. "But that doesn't mean I want to live with her!" she added.

She and Shanti both laughed.

"Okay, let's do a quick check of my brother, Bobby," Caitlin said. "We're probably about out of time, and I know you've got other people waiting."

She and Bobby had never had much in common, but Caitlin had spent the first thirteen years of her life living in the same house with him; she figured she knew him pretty well. When he turned eighteen, he left to join the Coast Guard. Caitlin had no way of knowing what kind of man he had grown into, but she well remembered how he had taunted her, teased her, and put her down. His bullying had left its mark on her psyche. Of course, having to defend herself against an older brother had probably toughened her up, and that toughness proved to be an asset when she entered law. Her artistic side would have been trampled by the demands of law school and litigation. Maybe that was why she had hidden it away all those years: to protect and preserve it.

"Oh this is interesting," Shanti said when she saw Bobby's birth card. "You were surrounded by tens!"

"Seriously? Another ten?"

"Ten of Spades—they're workaholics."

"Does that include workouts? Bobby was really into competitive sports."

"They can go to extremes. And they have to be careful how they use their power. They can be pretty intense."

"Unfortunately, I was often the recipient of that intensity."

"You probably weren't the only one," Shanti said. "But you two do have a lot of Mars energy."

Caitlin looked at her with a puzzled expression.

"Sorry—that's the astrologer talking. Mars can stir up anger, aggression, or competition—hostility, even, if it's not channeled into positive outlets. If the two of you didn't have opportunities to do physical things together—like sports—you could have ended up resenting each other."

"Yeah, that's about the long and the short of it," Caitlin said. "My family spent summers at our lake house in the Ozarks. There weren't many other kids around, except when our cousins came to visit. Bobby and I would ride our bikes or swim in the lake or run around catching fireflies. But back at home, the rest of the year, we were always at each other. And he always won, because he was a lot older and bigger. And meaner."

"Well, I hope I've given you some insights into your makeup and the themes of these relationships."

"*Very* interesting. If I ever think about getting married, I'll check with you first!"

"I hope you'll check with me well before then!" Shanti said. "Save yourself some heartache."

Caitlin paid Shanti in cash for the reading, and then they both stood up and embraced.

Melody was giving a massage and Sable was busy with customers, so Caitlin didn't interrupt them to say goodbye. She went for a long walk to contemplate all that Shanti had told her, and then she went back to the house to write down what she remembered about the session.

"I don't know your birthday," she told Lucky as she stroked his fur. "But I think we're pretty compatible."

Lucky yawned and stretched and then went to the door and waited for Caitlin to open it.

"Okay, but don't wander off," she said. "Stay where I can see you."

Geez, I sound like my mother.

∾ 16 ∾

"*H*appy Mother's Day!" Caitlin said when Martha answered the phone. "I've called a few times, but you were always out and I didn't want to leave a message. I've got some news."

"Good news, I hope."

"For a change! I got a part in a musical here in Santa Fe. Rehearsals had already started and someone dropped out, so they were just replacing the one cast member. I auditioned right after I got here, and the director liked me. So I've been really busy with that."

"That's exciting," Martha said. "I'm so happy for you, honey. Just don't overdo."

"I know. I'm fine," Caitlin said. "The schedule was pretty intense, getting caught up to the others and all. I figure, if I could handle that, then I can probably handle a bigger role in the future."

"You like Santa Fe, then? Are you going to stay there awhile?"

"I don't know, I'm taking it one step at a time. I haven't had a chance to see much of the city yet. I've been focused on the show and getting to know my way around. You remember Melody, Kimo's friend?"

"Oh, yes, the redhead. She's the one you're staying with, right?"

"Yeah, she's subletting a house while a friend of hers is away, so I'm staying with her for now."

"Well tell me about the show. Is it one I'd know?"

"No, it's new. This is the first time it's been produced anywhere. The reviews have been pretty good, and it's got a positive message so I'm happy to be a part of it. To have been a part of it, rather. It just closed."

"I wish I could have been there to see it. Did the reviews single you out?"

"No, I just had a small role, and one of the actors is sort of well known, so a lot of the attention has been focused on him."

"Anyone I'd know?"

"Probably not."

"Well, I'm glad you're enjoying yourself, and of course I'm happy to hear that you're all right."

"Yeah, I'm okay. The director—Paul—asked me to be his personal assistant, so I'll do that for a while. It doesn't pay anything, but it will give me a chance to get to know him better and stay in the loop for upcoming shows. The next one is a comedy, but they usually do at least one musical a year."

"How long can you stay at the house?"

"Another couple of months, I think."

"Will you and Melody find another place together?"

"I don't know. She's mentioned that, but it would have to be furnished since neither one of us has any furniture. We'll see what develops between now and then."

"All right, then. Thanks for the call. And the flowers. They're beautiful."

"I'm glad you like them. I'll talk to you soon," Caitlin said. Before hanging up the phone, she added, "Oh, and Mom . . . thanks for making me practice the piano."

∾ 17 ∾

*C*aitlin missed the flowering trees and bushes that blossomed in the D.C. area each spring. She loved the wide open spaces of the West, and the desert had its own kind of beauty, but the arid climate was too dry for her delicate skin and she often felt parched. She wondered how she would survive the intense heat and sun of the summer months. Maybe she could take a short trip to L.A. Start learning her way around, spend some time at the beach.

Lately, she'd stayed busy by exploring Santa Fe's museums, galleries, and attractions. She had driven to the ruins at Puye—cliff and cave dwellings at the Santa Clara reservation—but she still had not attended a feast day at a pueblo. Melody had suggested a trip to Taos "sometime," but she was always too busy to get away whenever

Caitlin brought it up. Caitlin settled for a solo trip to the Museum of Indian Arts and Culture.

One afternoon in the middle of May, she stopped at a gallery on Canyon Road that featured Native American art. Intrigued by a carving of a bobcat, she was reading about the artist when she heard a familiar voice. She looked up and saw Paul, who was engaged in a conversation with a woman of about forty. Caitlin watched as Paul put his hand on the woman's back. Then, two exuberant children ran over to the pair. The boy, who Caitlin guessed was about five years old, excitedly told the woman, "They've got a real bow and arrow!" Tugging on her arm, he pleaded, "Can I get it?"

Caitlin turned away, but Paul had already seen her.

"Caitlin!" he shouted from across the room. He walked toward her and asked, "How've you been?"

Before Caitlin could respond, Paul introduced the woman and her children. "This is my sister, Sheila. And these two fireballs are my niece, Stephanie," Paul said, tousling the boy's hair, "and my nephew, John." He gestured to the girl, who protested, "*I'm* Stephanie!"

The adults all laughed. Caitlin shook hands with Sheila and said hello to the kids, relieved that she had been spared an awkward moment.

Not all men are devious, manipulative liars, she reminded herself.

She'd had enough of dark secrets. Paul seemed genuine, a what-you-see-is-what-you-get kind of guy. Not terribly deep, perhaps, but a decent man.

Who drinks too much, she reminded herself.

You don't know that, another voice countered. *He might just like to have a good time on special occasions.*

"I've heard so much about you," Sheila said.

Caitlin raised an eyebrow. She'd heard nothing about Paul's family.

Paul looked around and said, "Nice place, huh?"

"Yes, very," Caitlin agreed.

"The owner is a friend of ours, so we thought we'd say hello, but I guess he's not here."

"Can we get ice cream now?" Stephanie asked her mother.

"We were just on our way to get ice cream," Paul told Caitlin. "Care to join us?"

Sheila smiled and nodded, so Caitlin agreed to go along. Having company would be a nice change.

She ordered a cup of raspberry sherbet and then waited outside the shop with Sheila and the kids while Paul paid the cashier. Then, they all strolled down the street together, stopping so Sheila could wipe John's face and hands with a wet napkin after he finished eating his ice cream bar. Stephanie was a head taller than John; Caitlin guessed she was about seven.

"Who moved to Santa Fe first?" Caitlin asked.

Paul pointed at Sheila. "She did. I visited a lot. From L.A. Got to know some folks and decided I'd rather reverse the commute and spend most of my time here."

"Uncle Paul, will you take us to the movies?" Stephanie asked.

"I want to go to the park," John announced.

Stephanie held Paul's hand and said, "Ple-e-e-z," looking up at him with big brown eyes.

"Well, how 'bout we do both?" Paul said. "And pizza after!"

The kids jumped up and down screaming "Yay!" Every time John chanted, "We're going to the park!" Stephanie followed with, "We're going to the movies!"

"If that's all right with you," Paul said to Sheila.

"Take 'em. I'll take a mental health day!"

Paul nudged Caitlin. "Wanna keep me company?"

Caitlin chose an aisle seat for the animated film Stephanie wanted to see. Paul sat next to her. After the lights were dimmed, he took her hand in his. She didn't object.

The kids were nice enough, but she wasn't used to being around children. She decided to skip the outing to the park.

"What, no pizza?" Paul said playfully.

"Maybe another time."

Paul walked her to her car. After a moment of silence, she asked, "How was L.A.?"

"Good," was all Paul said about his trip. "Sorry I haven't called. You know how busy it gets."

"Wasn't that why you wanted help?"

"Yes, but it will take time to show you what's what, and I don't want to ask Christine. Things will settle down soon. I was going to call you later in the week."

"So when should I plan on starting?"

"Monday?"

"I'll clear my schedule," Caitlin said.

Paul smiled and kissed her cheek. "I'll call you."

Caitlin opened her car door and said, "Famous last words."

She had no reason to doubt Paul's sincerity, she thought as she fastened her seat belt. Was she that cynical now, about men and relationships?

Just being realistic. Or trying to be.

～ 18 ～

*C*aitlin was reading a book in the living room when Melody walked in carrying a bag of groceries.

"What's the book?" Melody asked on her way to the kitchen. She set the bag on the counter and then filled a glass with filtered water.

"It's about embracing your inner Venus."

Melody returned to the living room. "Seriously?" she said with a grin.

Caitlin put the book down. "Seriously," she said, chuckling. "I know I'm good at making things happen and getting things done. I'm learning to *allow* things to come to me. Or people, as the case may be."

"The law of attraction," Melody said knowingly.

"That's right. Venus attracts and draws things to herself."

Caitlin rose from the couch and joined Melody in the kitchen.

"It's a simple concept, but one that needs recognition in this action-oriented culture. We are *so* out of balance with nature. We feed growth hormones to livestock to speed up production. Don't even get me started on what happens to chickens at factory farms. Even aside from the harms being done to living creatures, who wants to eat meat that's loaded with hormones and antibiotics?"

Melody peeled an orange. "You don't need to convince me. I'm a vegetarian, remember?"

Lucky wandered into the kitchen to see what all the fuss was about. He jumped onto the counter.

Melody picked him up and put him outside. "No counters!" she said before closing the door.

"I ran into Paul yesterday," Caitlin said.

"Oh yeah?"

"Yeah," Caitlin said, opening the refrigerator door to find something to eat for dinner. "I'll start work on Monday."

"This is the job that doesn't pay anything?"

"I expect there will be other benefits, and I don't have anything else going on."

Melody put away the last of her groceries. "Have you been working on your music? You said you'd play something for me. How about now?"

Caitlin closed the refrigerator door and smiled. "Okay. I'll get my guitar."

She had put her music aside since landing in Santa Fe, and lately she hadn't even been keeping up with vocal exercises. She wanted a rest. Or maybe she needed an incentive, something the show had given her. Maybe she was waiting for a more permanent place to live, a place where she could feel settled. She didn't know the reason. She just hadn't felt motivated.

She thought about which song to play for Melody as she carried her guitar case to the living room. "Oh, I know," she said. "I think you'll like this one. It doesn't need a guitar. But it does need a cat!"

She set down the case and opened the patio door. Lucky walked inside, arched his back, and stretched. Caitlin picked him up and, holding his front paws, danced to the rhythm of "Pause," an upbeat song about taking time out to get centered when life gets you down.

When Caitlin had finished, Melody clapped enthusiastically and said, "I love that!"

Lucky ran for the bedroom. *He probably wants to escape before I decide to write a song about whiskers or some other part of his anatomy,* Caitlin thought.

"You know, there's usually entertainment at events like the

holistic fair," Melody said, "and New Thought churches often have live music at their services. You could put together a set and travel around, performing."

"There's an idea," Caitlin said.

She had wondered how to find an audience for songs like "Pause," and Melody was right—the kind of people who attended programs and workshops about conscious living would probably like her music. She still wanted to put together a CD—or a demo, at least—but she didn't know where to start.

"Maybe after I've done another show I'll have more confidence—especially if I get the lead."

"Yeah, but you don't know when that will be. In the meantime, check out some of the local venues."

"I'll think about it."

"Well, it's a great song. Thanks for sharing."

"Thank you for sharing your space," Caitlin said.

"Do you know yet how long you'll be staying in Santa Fe? I just wondered if you want to find another place together for after Carolina gets back."

Caitlin knew that question would come sooner or later. In truth, she didn't know if she wanted to continue living with Melody. Their friendship might fare better if they lived apart.

"Let me see how this arrangement with Paul goes. I don't want you to be stuck if I decide to move on."

"We've still got some time. But I'm going to start asking around to find out what's coming available," Melody said.

"And I'm going to play the guitar more," Caitlin said, picking up the case. "Starting now."

∾ 19 ∾

*M*elody rose with the sun and took her yoga mat outside. Mornings were so pleasant this time of year.

When she had finished her yoga routine, she went inside to make a smoothie. She added a banana, apple juice, strawberries, and spirulina powder to the glass pitcher and switched the blender on. When the ingredients were blended into a smooth consistency, she poured some of the mixture into a tall glass.

She was disappointed that the business venture with Sable and Shanti hadn't worked out but pleased that Sable's vision would become a reality, if not in the way they had imagined.

The vortex, they'd learned, was located on national forest land. Sable had come up with an alternative site: the Abbey of San Miguel. It was a bit out of the way, but the monastery opened its gates to the public each Sunday. Most of the visitors were there to see residents— or to attend Mass—but the abbot wanted to develop stronger ties with Santa Fe's interfaith community. Until recently, the Order had not sought to attract attention, and few people even knew of its existence. Sable believed the Abbey was an appropriate setting for a labyrinth, and she knew that the site would be well tended by the monks once it was created—according to her design.

That was all good news for Sable, but neither Melody nor Shanti had a role in the new plan, other than as supporters. Melody had agreed to distribute flyers around town and to help spread the word about the labyrinth. A ribbon-cutting ceremony would be held on the summer solstice, but today was the day the path would be laid out.

"We're constructing the labyrinth today, out in Pecos," Melody told Caitlin when she emerged from her room. "Want to come?"

"Oh, no," Caitlin said. "Auditions."

She opened the patio door for Lucky and then poured herself a bowl of cereal.

"Are you trying out for another show?"

"No, but Paul is getting ready for the Shakespeare Festival, and if Paul's working, I'm working. Paul works a lot, I'm finding."

"Can't he make an exception?"

"I'm sure he would if I asked. But I'm still learning my way around the theater, and I'd need to give him more than an hour's notice if I wasn't going to show up."

"Whatever," Melody said.

She didn't know why Caitlin was wasting her time—and her talents—hanging around the Playhouse when she could be pursuing her dreams, but that was her choice.

"Say hi to Shanti and Sable," Caitlin said. "I'll try to make it to the grand opening, but I can't promise anything. It's a Sunday, right? The play opens that weekend."

"Mm-hmm." Melody nodded as she drank the last of her smoothie. "Noon."

Changing the subject, Caitlin asked, "Do you teach a beginning yoga class? I want to get back to a regular yoga practice. What's your schedule?"

Melody washed the blender pitcher in the sink. "My yoga classes are on hold until I finish massage school," she said. "But I can suggest some good teachers." She turned the pitcher upside down and set it on a slatted bamboo drying rack.

"That's all right," Caitlin said. "I can wait."

Melody watched as Caitlin sliced a banana and added almond milk to her cereal.

"You want a few strawberries to go with that?"

"Sure."

"Help yourself."

Melody held out a bowl of strawberries. "You could always join me for yoga here," she said.

"You start a little too early for me," Caitlin said. "It's usually so late by the time I get back. I can't get to bed as early as you do."

Melody didn't contradict her, but Caitlin's choice to stay out late now, when she wasn't performing, was just that: a choice. Caitlin's casual use of clichés—and her mindless chatter—irritated her. She had been the same way, once, and she tried to exercise patience. Knowing the power of words, she chose hers carefully.

Caitlin brought her cereal bowl to the table. "Paul says there will probably be a part for me in the Christmas show," she said. "It's a very popular event, and it sounds like it will be a lot of fun."

"That's great," Melody said. She was getting a little tired of hearing about Paul, but she was glad that Caitlin had plugged into a community that could help her develop her talent. She put her glass in the dishwasher and said, "Well, I better get going. I have to pick up Shanti."

"See ya," Caitlin said.

"You know, I've never been out here," Melody told Shanti as they drove across Glorieta Pass.

"The national park is worth a visit. Maybe you and Caitlin could go sometime," Shanti said.

"She's pretty wrapped up with the theater crowd these days," Melody said. "We keep different schedules."

"How's the massage program working out for you?"

"Good. I'm hoping that between yoga classes and massage, I'll be able to earn enough to have my own place."

"Are you thinking of buying?"

"Gosh, no. That would be a stretch, unless I want to move to Albuquerque or somewhere more affordable. Which I may need to do at some point, but for now, I'm right where I need to be."

"Amen to that," Shanti said. "I'll certainly recommend you for both yoga and massage—and anything else you decide to offer. I can give you some suggestions for flyers and business cards and maybe even a website, when you're ready. I started looking into web design when Sable brought up her labyrinth project."

"Yeah, it's too bad that didn't work out with the vortex land."

"Speaking of land," Shanti said, "a battle was fought near here during the Civil War."

"We should stop on the way back and do a prayer ceremony," Melody said as they passed a pullout in the road.

Shanti smiled. "That's just what I was thinking."

Melody smiled back. She and Shanti understood each other.

"I knew that," she said.

∞

Melody drove past the open gate and parked her car next to Sable's Lexus. When she got out of the car, she saw Sable standing nearby, talking to a monk. He wore a dark brown tunic tied with a sash, and a large cross hung from a thick chain around his neck. Melody knew that meant he was the abbot. Ordinary monks didn't wear ornamentation.

Sable introduced Father Moore to Shanti and Melody. "I'll be in the chapel if you need me," the abbot said said before walking away.

"Thank you, Father," Sable said.

"Is it just the three of us?" Shanti asked.

"Chip and Randy are on their way," Sable said. "Caitlin couldn't come?"

Melody shook her head. "She's otherwise engaged."

"We'll manage," Sable said, looking at the field near the entrance that had been cleared for the labyrinth.

"But first—I have something for each of you," Sable said.

She handed a pendant to Melody and a pin to Shanti.

"These will be available in the monastery's gift shop."

"Which is only open on Sundays," Shanti said.

"As of now, yes," Sable said. "Hey, it's a start."

Melody fastened the chain around her neck. "This is lovely," she said, putting her hand over the pendant and her heart chakra. "It will always be close to my heart."

"What's the plan?" Shanti asked after pinning her gift onto her sweatshirt.

"I've laid rope along the path where the rocks will go. The rocks are over there."

Melody looked to where Sable was pointing and saw several piles of rocks at the edge of the field.

"The rocks will go along the sides of the labyrinth path. We just need to select some good ones and lay them out, next to the rope. Let's try to keep them roughly the same size. I picked out a few to get us started." Sable pointed to the rocks she had placed in a wheelbarrow.

"There goes my manicure," Shanti said.

"I brought gardening gloves," Sable said.

"That's a big labyrinth!" Melody said. She put on a wide-brimmed hat to protect her face from the bright sun.

"Eventually, we can plant lavender or flowers to spruce it up a bit, but for now the path just needs to be ready for people to walk at the grand opening."

"It will be fabulous," Shanti said.

Sable nodded. "It will be—if everything works out."

Melody grasped the handles of the wheelbarrow. "*We're* sure workin' out!" she said.

Three Goddess worshippers creating a labyrinth next door to a monastery, she thought. *Welcome to the new paradigm!*

∾ 20 ∾

*C*aitlin was preparing to leave for the theater when the phone rang. She picked it up when she heard Kimo's voice on the answering machine.

"Hey, Kimo, it's Cait. Melody's not here."

"You two are pretty much interchangeable, right?" Kimo joked.

"Well, we have you in common," Caitlin said. "I'm not sure what else. So you're an official grad now?"

"Yep. Most states don't license NDs, so I guess this is as official as it gets."

"That will change. Acupuncture needles used to be illegal, remember?"

"I do remember," Kimo said. "Thanks for the card. And the gift! I'll bring you back a souvenir from Australia—but you may have to come to D.C. to pick it up!"

"I imagine I'll get back there someday."

"I can't wait forever, you know."

"I wouldn't want you to. Are you ready for your trip?"

"Pretty much. I'll be in New Zealand for the summer solstice. Which, there, will be the winter solstice. What are your plans?"

"For the solstice? I expect I'll be at the theater."

"Are you in another show already?"

"No, just helping out."

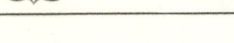

"Waiting in the wings."

"Something like that. I was just on my way over there, actually."

"I won't keep you," Kimo said. After a pause he added, "Though I would if I could."

Caitlin smiled. "Have a great trip, Kimo," she said. "Be sure and send me a postcard. I'll tell Melody you called."

She hung up the phone and put out food for Lucky. He purred as Caitlin scratched behind his ears.

"We'll see him again," she said. "Someday."

When Caitlin returned to the house the following day, Melody was in the kitchen eating lunch and reading the newspaper.

"Hey," Caitlin said on her way to the sink. She filled a glass with filtered water and took a drink.

Melody looked up from the paper and said, "Lucky missed you last night."

"I hope he wasn't any trouble," Caitlin said. "He didn't wander around the house moaning or anything, did he?"

"No. I let him go outside before I went to bed, and I gave him fresh water this morning."

"Thanks. I hadn't planned on staying out all night, but it was getting late and I was tired, so I just stayed at Paul's."

"I figured it was something like that, and you don't need to explain your choices to me, but you could think about calling. So I know not to expect you."

"I thought about it, but it was already late when I decided to stay, and I didn't want to wake you."

Melody set the newspaper on the counter and took her plate to the sink.

"How was your evening?" Caitlin asked.

"Okay. I made some calls about rentals. So what are your plans— should I be looking for a place for myself or for both of us?"

Caitlin sighed and said, "I don't know. I guess we need to decide something soon."

"Uh, yeah," Melody said.

"Paul's got a big house. He said something this morning about letting me move in there, since I don't get paid much."

"That's generous of him."

Caitlin knew that Melody thought she was wasting her time hanging around the theater, but she enjoyed being in the company of actors, and she continued to meet interesting people. After the long, lonely winter she had spent at the lake house, she craved companionship.

She opened the newspaper to see if there was a write-up about the Shakespeare Festival. Paul was not only directing *A Midsummer Night's Dream*, he was playing the role of Oberon, king of the fairies. Caitlin was really looking forward to seeing him onstage.

"So is that what you want to do?" Melody asked.

Caitlin shrugged. "I told him I'd think about it," she said. "And that's what I intend to do." She leafed through the paper until she found the *Lifestyles* section.

"I guess I'll just look for a place for myself," Melody said. "That will probably be easier to find anyway."

"Okay," Caitlin said. "C'mon, Luck. Let's go outside."

She left the rest of the newspaper on the counter and took the *Lifestyles* section out to the patio to read. She needed time alone, to think. She was pretty sure she would say yes to Paul, but she wanted to spend more time at his house before deciding. Carolina had extended her trip to go to Nepal; now she wouldn't be back until the end of July. Caitlin planned to stay with Melody until then. After that, she wasn't sure what she wanted to do, but getting her own place didn't make sense. She wasn't planning to stay in Santa Fe forever.

She and Melody had different rhythms—and interests—but the difference in their schedules was probably more of a problem for her than for Melody, Caitlin realized. She tried to be quiet when she got home late at night, though the effort was probably unnecessary. Melody was a sound sleeper. She made a smoothie every morning and the noise always woke Caitlin—much earlier than she wanted to be awakened. She usually covered her head with a pillow, but sometimes she was unable to get back to sleep until after Melody left the house.

Of course, living with Paul would mean spending even more time with him, and she was already spending a lot of time with him. He had offered her a bedroom of her own, if she wanted it.

So he says . . .

They were starting to get intimate, and Caitlin knew that if they were living together, she would end up sleeping with him most nights; that seemed like the next step in their relationship.

Sleeping with the director . . . what a cliché!

She wasn't in love with Paul, but she liked him. A lot. He made her laugh. She couldn't say that about many people.

Sure, he was a little rough around the edges, but he didn't mean to be unkind. At the theater, he was demanding, and his harsh manner bruised her ego sometimes, especially if he growled at her when actors were present. Caitlin didn't expect special treatment—which was a good thing because she didn't get it. She viewed her time with Paul as an opportunity to develop new skills, and if she wanted to be a performer, she needed to be able to handle criticism and rejection. She also needed to be able to work with different kinds of directors.

Paul was generous with his time. He played games with his niece and nephew and mentored college students interested in a career in theater. Caitlin wasn't the only new actor he had taken a chance on. Whether he would ever give her a leading role, though, remained to be seen.

For the Playhouse to stay afloat, it needed to be profitable, and big names brought big crowds. A few of the Hollywood celebrities who maintained homes in Santa Fe had appeared in productions at the theater. Film actors appreciated an opportunity to perform before a live audience in an intimate space. Many of them knew they weren't ready for Broadway but wanted to try something new. The less experienced actors learned from them and were inspired by their success.

Paul had achieved a good balance, Caitlin thought. With a core group of regular players, the Playhouse could accommodate those with little experience and still remain professional enough to attract Equity actors.

"What do you think?" Caitlin asked Lucky when he rubbed against her legs. "Want to go live in the big house and impress all your friends? Give me one meow for yes and two for no."

Better than flipping a coin, she thought. But Lucky just looked at her quizzically and gave her one of his silent meows.

"Oh, of course you don't know how to answer, furball. You haven't met Paul yet, and you haven't been to his house."

She picked up the cat and carried him inside.

"We'll have to remedy that."

∾ 21 ∾

*C*aitlin brought the two scripts Paul had asked for to his office, where he was discussing the budget for the 1999–2000 season with Sy, the managing director, and Mark. Paul would be directing *Rosencrantz and Guildenstern Are Dead* in the fall. A guest director would direct the two-part *Angels in America* in the spring.

"Thanks, sweetheart," Paul said when Caitlin put the scripts on his desk. "Hey, would you run down to the costume shop and bring me whatever crowns you can find? And grab a couple of swords while you're there."

Caitlin didn't ask why he wanted crowns and swords. She'd learned to follow orders—and Paul gave a lot of orders. He didn't *take* orders well, however; he'd balk if he thought he'd been given an order, so Caitlin was learning to frame her requests and complaints carefully. With Paul, the subtle approach seemed to work best.

Positive reinforcement, she reminded herself. Rather than openly criticizing Paul's wardrobe choices, she steered him toward the clothes she liked with compliments such as, "I love that color on you." Paul seemed more willing to favor a shirt she liked than to avoid wearing one she didn't care for.

The racks and shelves in the costume room were filled with garments, shoes, and assorted accessories. While poking through the headgear, Caitlin noticed a black top hat and tried it on. She wiped the dust off a full-length mirror with a cloth she found lying on a table.

"Hmm," she murmured, imagining herself performing in *A Chorus Line,* one of her favorite shows. She wasn't a good enough dancer to play Cassie, but she would love to see a production at the Playhouse. She would suggest it to Paul. Or, rather, she would find out his thoughts about it. Paul had a way of forgetting where his ideas originated. As long as Caitlin stayed focused on outcomes— and gave up her need for recognition—she often got what she wanted by dropping hints and casual suggestions.

In addition to learning how to handle Paul, she was learning about the various considerations involved in planning a season. A show's popularity, as well as cast size and costume and set requirements, were factors in the decision-making process, but Paul also aimed for balance and variety. A typical season included one musical. A family-friendly offering was a must at the holidays, and the rest depended on timing, budget, and availability—of the rights to the show, and of the right actors.

The importance of casting to the success of a production couldn't be overstated, Paul had told her—even for a small theater like the Playhouse. They had discussed the selection process, for shows and for actors, over dinner the night before.

As an Equity theater, the Playhouse had to cast at least one Equity actor in each show, Paul said. But few Equity actors lived in the area.

"And that's why you hold auditions in L.A.?" Caitlin asked.

"I've got ties to the theater community there, and I usually take in a few shows. It's a good way to stay connected, find new talent, see what's fresh and promising."

"Working with experienced professionals is a lot easier, I imagine," Caitlin said as she cleared plates from the dining room table. "They probably deliver a more consistent performance and have a confidence that amateurs lack."

Paul nodded. "In general, that's true."

Caitlin rinsed the dishes in the kitchen sink before putting them in the dishwasher. She filled a pot with sudsy water and was about to start scrubbing it when Paul came up behind her.

"Occasionally some inexperienced young kid will steal the show," he said before nibbling her ear. "Or a ravishing newcomer."

Caitlin giggled. "Well, I don't know how ravishing I am, but I'm certainly a comer," she said flirtatiously.

"I'd like to ravish you," Paul said, gently biting her neck. "Come on. The dishes can wait."

He took her hand and led her upstairs.

Caitlin smiled at the memory of their bedroom antics and then returned her attention to the costumes. She gathered up the items Paul had requested and also took the top hat and a cane with her; those she hid under a chair in the back of the theater. She had a surprise in mind for Paul, and she was pretty sure he would like it.

On the drive to Paul's house at the end of the day, Caitlin pressed for more information about the play selection process.

"Something old, something new; what works best is tried and true," Paul said.

"I have a feeling you've said that before."

Paul flashed a silly grin. "I can't just think about what plays I'd like to direct," he explained. "I have to consider what people will pay to see, as well as the talent pool. I'm not going to choose something I can't do well. That would be professional suicide."

"Which shows do you direct?" Caitlin asked.

"I usually take the original works that we're premiering. And Shakespeare, of course. Maybe I'll do *Taming of the Shrew* next time. Care to play Kate, Cait?"

Caitlin shook her head. She was quite certain that a Shakespeare play wasn't in her future. But she did want to get a better sense of Paul's tastes and experience.

"Have you ever done a Sondheim show?"

"No, not my favorite. Well—except *West Side Story*, which is exceptional. Sondheim wrote the lyrics, but Leonard Bernstein wrote the score. Jerome Robbins's choreography was brilliant."

Paul pushed the button on the remote control and drove his car into the garage after the door opened.

"Oscar Wilde?"

"No."

"Tennessee Williams?"

"No."

"Arthur Miller."

"Nope."

"Brecht?"

"I'd like to do *Threepenny Opera* sometime."

"*Sweeney Todd*?"

Paul scowled. "Definitely not."

"*Chicago?*"

"Sure, if a generous benefactor wants to fund it."

"*A Chorus Line?*"

"Not enough dancers here who are up to the demands. I like the show, though."

"Mamet?"

Paul nodded. "I've done Mamet," he said, not displeased, implying he might be open to directing another Mamet play sometime.

"*Damn Yankees?*"

"Seeing yourself as Lola?" Paul asked as they entered the house. "We don't normally put on the kinds of shows you'd have seen growing up in— Where was it?"

"Olathe."

"Olathe," Paul repeated. He looked through a stack of mail to see if anything needed his immediate attention. "I look for plays that are edgy or unconventional—and that haven't been done to death."

"And that are practical," Caitlin added.

"Usually. But I'll go out on a limb if I feel strongly about a project. Or a person."

Paul pulled Caitlin close to him, his strong arms locking her into an embrace that was hard for her to resist—or escape.

Good thing I trust him, she thought, allowing her body to relax against his.

Most of the time, she felt safe with Paul, but sometimes she felt suffocated. Was there a middle ground that allowed for more breathing room and yet provided stability? She wasn't sure they would ever find it together. Paul liked a lot of togetherness.

Why wouldn't he?

She was the one who accommodated, who bent to his will. He indulged her—it wasn't as if he was a brute—but she knew that, at some point, she would need to break free and forge her own path.

∿ 22 ∿

"*I* really appreciate you all taking me out for my birthday," Caitlin told Melody, Shanti, and Sable as they lounged in the nude on the wooden deck of a clothing-optional spa in the hills just north of town. "That chocolate mousse cake was divine!"

"Well, we missed seeing you at the solstice," Sable said.

"I wish I could have been there," Caitlin said. "I'll have to wander out to Pecos another time. I'd like to spend some time at the national park."

Her stop at the park upon arrival in New Mexico had been brief—but she remembered her curiosity about the figures she had seen in the distance.

"Go on a Sunday," Shanti said. "That's the only day the gift shop is open."

"At the national park?" Caitlin asked.

"No, at the monastery," Sable said. "That's where the labyrinth is."

A woman with cropped hair and a nipple ring walked past them on her way to the locker room. A large dragon tattoo adorned her breast.

"Ouch!" Sable said. "It hurts me to look at that. I'm sorry, I just don't see the appeal." She jumped into the nearby pool—but was careful not to get her hair wet.

"Where is Paul taking you for your birthday?" Melody asked.

Before Caitlin could answer, Sable swam to the side of the pool and said, "Oo-oh, is there something we don't know? A little romance brewing?"

Melody removed her sunglasses long enough to say, "Caitlin is moving in with her director friend next week."

Shanti and Sable exchanged a worried look when Melody added, "She practically lives there now," before reclining in her lounge chair.

"I think I'll go shower," Caitlin said. "I'm getting a chill."

Melody had been cool toward her since she'd started spending nights at Paul's house. While showering, she decided she'd had enough of Melody's stinging remarks.

She was dressing when Sable and Shanti passed her on their way to the showers. Melody was still at her locker. Caitlin collected her things and walked over to her. She set her bag down and said, "So what it is, Mel? Are you angry that I won't be moving with you?"

"Not at all," Melody said, slamming her locker door shut. "I found a place in Tesuque that's perfect for me. Building up a massage clientele will be easier there, I think. Less competition."

"Are you jealous that things are going well for me?"

Melody scoffed. "Things are going well for me too, Caitlin. I have no reason to be jealous of you. And I know what you've been through. Well, maybe not all of it, but enough. I'm happy to see you succeed—at whatever you choose to do."

"What, then? Why have you been so . . . *distant* lately?"

"It's hard to explain," Melody said, adjusting the towel she'd wrapped around herself.

"Try."

Melody thought for a moment and then said, "It's like there's a missing link with you. The dots don't connect."

"That doesn't make any sense," Caitlin said. She picked up her bag and started to leave. "I have no idea what you're talking about, but I've gotta go. Paul's waiting. Say goodbye to the girls for me. I had a nice time."

"Kimo's waiting for you, too!" Melody blurted out.

Caitlin turned toward her and said, "Kimo! Kimo's in Australia. I doubt he's even thinking about me."

"We each got a postcard from him," Melody said. "Which you'd know if you ever bothered to come home."

"It's not my home. It's not even *your* home! Is this about Paul? You don't like him, do you?"

Melody walked toward the showers. "It doesn't matter what I think."

"I'm not planning to marry him," Caitlin said. "We're just having a good time. Is there something wrong with that?"

Melody stopped and said, "Of course not. But if I knew who my soul mate was—"

"You don't know who your soul mate is, but you think you know who mine is?"

"That's not what I meant. I just know how much Kimo cares for you, and I hate to see you throw away a chance for a real relationship."

"I'm not looking for love right now. I had love—and it let me down."

Caitlin was surprised when her voice faltered. She hadn't realized how wounded she still felt about her broken engagement.

Melody heard the emotion in her voice and took a step toward her. "I know your fiancé cheated on you, but Kimo would never do that."

"How do you know so much about what Kimo would and wouldn't do? And why are you so intent on seeing us together?"

"Because I care about both of you, and I know you belong together. It's . . . it's in the stars!"

Caitlin studied Melody for a moment, uncertain whether to be angry or amused. "The only star in my future is the one they'll hang on my dressing room door!" she said before walking away.

"I guess you haven't learned."

"At least I'm living in the real world," Caitlin said over her shoulder.

Paul was waiting for her to come over for a special birthday dinner, but Caitlin wanted to stop by the house and pick up a few things—including her mail—before Melody got there. She remembered that Kimo had promised to send a postcard from Oz, and she was strangely eager to get it.

She sped up the car, wondering if Melody could be right. Were some people meant to be together? Was fate a genuine piece of the cosmic puzzle or just more New-Age-seeker speak?

∾ 23 ∾

*W*rapped in a plush terry bathrobe, Caitlin waited for Paul's phone call to end. Wherever they were, their date nights were frequently interrupted by calls to Paul's mobile phone.

Caitlin wasn't accustomed to being with someone who was on call all the time. She didn't feel possessive of Paul, but she could imagine eventually getting irritated by the constant intrusions, especially if they needed to have a serious conversation. For now, though, she had nowhere else to be, and their conversations were rarely serious.

As she sat in a chair in Paul's bedroom suite, she tried reading a book by a local author, but she felt woozy from the wine she'd had with dinner. She put the book down and opened the doors to the balcony. The breeze felt refreshing.

She closed her eyes and thought about the evening she'd spent with Paul. He had taken her to La Casa Sena, a restaurant known for its fine food—and for the singing wait staff at La Cantina. Accompanied by a pianist, the entertainers sang show tunes and other popular songs.

"Exploiting the talents of out-of-work actors who are in desperate need of employment," Caitlin had remarked. "Ingenious."

In cities like New York, she knew, actors often worked catering and restaurant jobs so they could be available for auditions—and pay the rent while awaiting a golden opportunity.

Paul knew many of the employees at the restaurant by name, and the manager came to the table to greet him. He introduced Caitlin as his assistant and a "promising new talent" that audiences would "undoubtedly" be seeing more of. Caitlin joked that she might seek a job there if her theater career didn't pan out.

Paul received invitations to a wide variety of events, from intimate dinner parties to black-tie affairs, and Caitlin sometimes went with him. Whether he told people that she was his date or his assistant didn't really matter to her, but she wondered why he had chosen such a popular spot for her birthday. She would have preferred a candle-light dinner in a cozy booth at a quiet restaurant.

"Why *did* you bring me here?" she asked Paul after the manager left.

"It's a fun place," he said. "I know you like show tunes, and I figured you'd enjoy getting a glimpse of the local talent."

"The competition?"

"No, no. Fellow performers! We're all family," he said, holding out a fork so she could sample a bite of his filet. "Lighten up!"

Caitlin nodded and tasted the filet. She'd spent too much time around lawyers. She did need to lighten up.

Paul was not a very romantic man, but he was jovial and good company. An extravert with a lot of energy, he knew how to have a good time. He enjoyed food and festivities and, of course, alcohol. A day hadn't passed that Caitlin hadn't seen him with a drink in his hand.

She looked at the postcard she had stuck inside the book to mark her place. She was grateful her brain had recovered enough to allow her to focus on reading a book. She was still forgetful at times, but she only stammered on rare occasions—usually when she hadn't had enough sleep and was under a lot of stress. But she still had no idea what had happened at the Shannon Pot in Ireland. Kimo had refused to talk about it, but Caitlin could tell by his behavior that something significant had happened.

Less than a year had passed since she'd left Virginia, but she rarely missed her old life. The pace of her new life left little room for regret.

She studied a painting hanging on the wall above the nightstand, an old adobe church at sunset with lavender-tinted clouds hugging the mountains in the distance. She was admiring the painter's bold use of color when Paul appeared.

"You look relaxed," he said before kissing the top of her head. He removed his bolo tie as he walked toward the closet. "That was Sheila," he said. "She invited us over for brunch next weekend."

"Does that mean we're going? I'll add it to the calendar."

Keeping track of Paul's schedule was one of Caitlin's main duties, so she needed to stay informed about his plans. Expecting him to ask her if she wanted to go somewhere, however, was expecting too much, she'd learned.

Paul was hanging up his trousers and didn't reply.

Maybe he didn't hear me, Caitlin thought.

She put the book on the table beside her chair and walked inside Paul's large closet. She was still wearing the high-heeled black pumps she had worn to the restaurant. Stockings were a rare sight in Santa Fe, especially in summer, but she had felt like getting dressed up. She had also thought this might be the night when she would show Paul that she was ready for a starring role. This was, after all, her special day, and she intended to make the most of it.

"I had a lovely birthday," she said, donning the black top hat she had stashed on a high shelf. "And now I have a gift for you."

"Does it involve nudity?"

"Oh yeah. Your place is over there."

Caitlin pointed to the bed with the cane she had borrowed from the Playhouse.

"You're not going to beat me with that, are you?" Paul said meekly before turning down the bedspread. He stuck an unlit cigar in his mouth and settled back to enjoy the show. He no longer smoked, but he still liked the feel and aroma of a good cigar, he had told Caitlin.

She had set up the stereo to play a Joe Cocker song from the mid-eighties, "You Can Leave Your Hat On," with a click of the remote control. She pushed the Play button on the remote and let her robe fall to the floor.

Her hair had grown quite long, and it cascaded down her back. Dressed all in black—bra, panties, stockings and garter belt—she slowly removed each garment in a seductive striptease. Her shoes were the first to go; she strutted and posed before kicking them off.

As Paul hooted and hollered and whistled, Caitlin grabbed hold of one of the bedposts and pulled herself up onto the flat footboard of the king-size oak poster bed. The width of a balance beam, the footboard felt sturdy, if narrow. She hadn't actually rehearsed this routine, but she figured the bed would be a soft place to land if she lost her balance—as long as she fell forward and not backward.

Each time Joe Cocker sang the title refrain, Caitlin lifted the top hat off her head and then replaced it. She moved to the music as she unfastened her garters and rolled off each of her stockings. She tossed each item onto the floor and then wrapped her right leg around a bedpost and leaned back. Next, she slowly removed her panties and twirled them around her index finger.

Paul removed the cigar from his mouth long enough to shout, "Oh, mama!"

Caitlin turned her back to him and unhooked her bra. If Paul's phone was ringing now, she thought, he'd never hear it over the music. She pulled each bra strap down from her shoulders. When the song ended, she threw the lacy brassiere toward Paul. It landed on his cigar. They both laughed.

"Come to papa!" Paul said with open arms.

Giggling, Caitlin crawled toward him and assumed her favorite position: on top.

∾ 24 ∾

*C*aitlin finished packing her suitcase. She was ready to begin a new adventure—or, at least, to take the Paul adventure to the next level. Moving in with him didn't seem like an unreasonable step when she only had a carload of belongings.

It's not as if we're combining households, she thought as she carried her suitcase to the car.

She felt as uninhibited with Paul as she ever had with a lover. When he'd said, "It sure turns me on, watching you perform," she'd asked if he foresaw any starring roles in her future.

"Absolutely," he said.

"When?" Caitlin pressed.

"Well, it won't be *I Do! I Do!* if that's what you're wondering. You need a little more experience before you'll be ready for a principal role."

"But there *are* no other roles in that show, and it's the only musical next season."

"There's the holiday show. I'm sure there will be opportunities then for you to show off your many talents."

Caitlin pouted. "Not the same."

"Maybe better. You know you're a lot stronger as a singer than as an actor."

Caitlin couldn't argue with that.

"Come here," Paul said, pulling her close. "Your time will come," he assured her.

She was thirty-five now; already, she was late to the party if she wanted to be taken seriously as a musician *or* as an actress. She hoped Paul's interest in her was more than sexual, that his promise to help her advance was sincere.

She carried a box down the hall and set it by the front door before taking her cooler to the kitchen. Melody was sitting on the couch in the living room, flipping through the latest issue of *Pasatiempo*.

"Amazing how fast you start accumulating things," Caitlin said as she walked past.

"Yes—you certainly do."

"Oh, right—I'm supposed to speak in 'I' statements," Caitlin said.

She removed her food from the refrigerator and took a drink of apple-cherry juice before putting the bottle in the cooler and closing the lid.

"Own your stuff," Melody said as Caitlin walked through the living room with the cooler.

"I'd rather own than rent!" Caitlin joked as she opened the front door.

Melody responded by going to her room and closing the door.

For someone who preached selflessness and nonattachment, Caitlin thought, Melody could be very judgmental.

Has she even met Paul? Caitlin wondered, and then she remembered introducing them, briefly, after the closing performance of *Millennium Blues*, when she brought Melody, Sable, and Shanti backstage, where Paul was waiting for her. His job as director was over once the show opened, but he made a practice of stopping by the Playhouse at random times during a production to see how things were going, how the audience was responding. That night, he had taken Caitlin out for a late dinner. Melody seemed to have taken an instant dislike to him.

Caitlin remembered Shanti's soul connection system and thought she ought to learn about her tie to Paul sometime. Maybe during his next trip to Los Angeles she would schedule an appointment.

Did Paul and Melody have some unfavorable connection that made *them* "incompatible"?

"Well she's not the one who will be living with him," Caitlin told Lucky as she put him into his carrier for the trip to the north side of town.

North and south—that pretty much sums up Paul and Melody! Caitlin thought. *Same city, different realities.*

She made a conscious decision to put aside concerns about what she was leaving behind and focus on what she was moving toward. She was sorry the situation with Melody had deteriorated to the point where they were hardly speaking, but she was too happy to let Melody's attitude get her down. She could only hope that someday they would be on friendlier terms. She appreciated Melody's friendship.

She returned to her bedroom to get the last box. Paul had offered to come over and help, but Caitlin knew that his presence would only add fuel to the fire.

"I'll leave the key on the table," she yelled.

She closed the front door behind her. Before long, Melody would be offering massages as well as yoga classes, and Kimo would be setting up his new practice. They were each beginning a new chapter of their lives.

Separately.

PART TWO

∾

CENTER STAGE

∾ 25 ∾

The lynx was about to lunge when Lucky jumped onto the bed and licked Caitlin's face, interrupting the vivid dream.

Her heart beating rapidly, she sighed with relief as she oriented to her surroundings. Paul was still asleep. He shifted his position when Caitlin quietly got up from the bed. She put on her robe and followed Lucky down the stairs.

"I know, I know. I overslept."

Lucky meowed and waited by his dish as Caitlin measured a scoop of cat food. These disturbing dreams were becoming more frequent—and more intense. Caitlin sensed they were trying to tell her something, but she didn't know what.

Now is not the time to try to figure it out, she thought as she blended protein powder, almond milk, bananas, and strawberries into a smoothie. She filled two tall glasses, rinsed the pitcher, and then carried the glasses upstairs.

Paul was in the shower, singing. Caitlin smiled and set one of the glasses on his nightstand before taking a drink from the other. Today was the last rehearsal before the preview of the new show, and she needed to get ready to go to the theater.

Nearly two years had passed since she first auditioned at the Playhouse. She had appeared onstage during the holiday shows, and she was selected as an understudy for a couple of plays, but now she was finally getting her big break: a starring role in a musical.

The show, *Park Avenue,* had been workshopped the summer before, and Caitlin's impatience had been palpable. Students from the college took over the production, but, as Paul's assistant, Caitlin was present for many of the rehearsals, and she attended all three of the workshop performances.

She liked the show and thought it would be the perfect vehicle for her to demonstrate her range and talent as a singer. She knew she was a mediocre actress—singing was her strength—but Santa Fe was a good place to take risks. It was a small city yet it drew streams of tourists, some of whom found their way to shows at the Playhouse.

Caitlin wanted to play Emma, the twenty-year-old daughter of Franklin Dawes, a prominent New York City banker. Paul thought she was too old. He liked the college student he'd chosen for the role in the workshop production, and he was thinking of casting her again.

Caitlin hired a voice coach and an acting coach to help her prepare. By the time auditions rolled around, she couldn't have been more ready, and Paul had to agree that she was perfect for the part. The show was scheduled to run for three weeks in February.

Park Avenue wasn't a typical love story, but it offered a glimpse into the courtship rituals of an earlier time, and the production, with its sumptuous clothing and stunning sets, succeeded in creating an aura of glamour and elegance, even as the play underscored the price of keeping up appearances.

The play was set in the spring of 1920. As Emma entered adulthood, women were fighting for the right to vote. (Prior to 1910, only four states—Wyoming, Colorado, Utah, and Idaho—allowed women to vote.) Congress had passed the Nineteenth Amendment to the U.S. Constitution in 1919, and thirty-five states had ratified it— but thirty-six were required for the amendment to be adopted. When that might occur—and whether it would occur at all—was anyone's guess. As the movement gained momentum, reformers stepped up their lobbying efforts. They held marches and rallies, circulated petitions, and, later, picketed the White House.

Opposition was strong. Traditionalists worried that changing roles would have a detrimental effect on domestic tranquility. And Franklin Dawes is a traditional man.

Dawes wants his only daughter—Emma—to marry Jeremy Ford, the son of a wealthy industrialist. Dawes is himself quite wealthy, but he's not in the same league as the most powerful men in New York.

He wants access. Respectability. Influence. Emma's marriage to Jeremy would further his aims. To sweeten the deal, he has promised to build the newlyweds a mansion on Park Avenue as a wedding gift.

Emma was not permitted to join the historic parade on Fifth Avenue in 1915, but her father couldn't stop her from watching it. The parade was hard to miss. Thousands of women, young and old alike, marched for five miles. The event nearly shut down the city!

In those days, women were buttoned up from head to toe. The Roaring Twenties had not yet arrived, and long skirts were the fashion. Well-dressed ladies wore hats and gloves. Young women like Emma were permitted to have acceptable hobbies, such as music or art, as long as their pursuits didn't interfere with their obligations or reflect poorly on their families.

Caitlin's understanding of her character deepened throughout the rehearsal process. She developed a clear image of how Emma would move, speak, think.

Emma is talented, smart—and bold. She likes Jeremy, but she is inexperienced when it comes to matters of the heart. She thinks she is too young to have the responsibilities of marriage thrust upon her. She wants to travel abroad—and not just on honeymoon. She wants to see Paris and Vienna and Italy. Not to shop, but to marvel at art and architecture. She wants to paint wild places and naked people, not bowls of fruit. She fears that being forced to take care of husband and home will crush her spirit. She loves to paint, and she takes her art seriously. She doesn't care a whit about social standing—or social contracts, which is what a marriage to Jeremy Ford would be.

But she has been raised with servants who attend to her every need. She has gone to the best schools and is accustomed to the finest in food and clothing and furnishings. She wants for nothing. Her father has threatened to disown her if she refuses to marry Jeremy. Emma doesn't know if he means it, but is she prepared to take the risk? She knows nothing about managing on her own. How would she survive? Freedom wouldn't mean much if she couldn't even afford art supplies!

Emma has a difficult choice to make: pursue a career in art and risk alienation from her family if her work is too controversial, or marry Jeremy and resign herself to a life of dependency. She could continue to paint—flowers and pets and other tame subjects—but she would probably never achieve anything noteworthy. She would never develop a unique and original style that was all her own.

The playwright had done a good job of establishing what was at stake for Emma, Caitlin thought as she showered and dressed. Emma was a likable and sympathetic character, and the costumes, though uncomfortable, were appropriate for the time and place. New York's exclusive social circles were beginning to open and expand. Emma's father would not have been the only one looking for ways to further his interests.

Growing numbers of women were demanding rights and opportunities—not just to vote, but also to pursue a profession and to choose whether or not to marry and bear children. Caitlin thought the play would speak to women everywhere who were, still, fighting for equal rights and opportunities—and salaries.

She was grateful that she enjoyed more freedom of choice than many of her ancestors—both male and female—but that didn't mean she hadn't suffered the demoralizing effects of sexism. As a lawyer, she had donned a suit of armor as a means of surviving in a male-dominated profession, though she probably wouldn't have seen it that way at the time. She'd been playing the part of Young Urban Professional, and she had acted accordingly. But now she found herself in a more traditional role—and not just onstage.

She couldn't deny that she was drawn to Paul, in part, because of his stature in Santa Fe's theatrical community. And maybe he was attracted to her, in part, because of her involvement with his theater. He had a stake in her success; it would advance his interests, too. But what would happen when she outgrew him, as she had always known she would? She'd been neglecting her own needs, and she was starting to feel restless. Music was her passion. For her, the theater was a stepping stone to a career as a singer-songwriter—a career that would be hers and hers alone.

Unlike Emma, Caitlin was confident about her ability to take care of herself. She was free to leave at any time. She knew that Paul wanted her to stay, and she suspected he might be thinking of proposing; now and then he dropped hints about wanting to "formalize" their arrangement. That was the last thing Caitlin wanted. She wasn't dreaming of marital bliss. If anything, she was wondering how she could gain a little more independence without severing all ties. Paul was an all-or-nothing kind of guy.

At the theater, she accepted his unquestioned sovereignty. She was still learning, still developing, still appreciating the long-awaited opportunity to play a leading role. But she found herself going along with Paul's agenda in personal matters as well. She had grown dependent upon him—she lived in his house, worked in his theater, slept in his bed. She knew he adored her—if anything, he adored her too much. After *Park Avenue* closed, she wanted to focus on her music, but she was afraid of ruining what she had with Paul.

She was fond of him—had grown to love him, even. Couldn't they just enjoy the moment without needing to label it or encase it in cement—and risk killing it? Couldn't love be enough?

No point worrying about it now, Caitlin thought as she finished drinking her smoothie.

She wasn't feeling pressured to make a decision, and no authoritarian father was trying to influence her choices.

Still, she understood Emma's predicament.

∾ 26 ∾

*S*am parked the van near the library and walked toward the entrance. He hadn't left Pecos once in his first eighteen months at the Abbey, but now that he was participating more actively in the Order's affairs, his trips into Santa Fe on monastery business had become more frequent.

He had taken simple vows the previous year, on Easter Sunday. He now shaved his head and wore the full monk's habit. He was undecided about making a full commitment, but he had plenty of time to decide. He wouldn't be eligible to take solemn vows for another couple of years.

Two years and two months, he thought as he caught a glimpse of his reflection in the library's glass windows.

He was still amazed to find himself living in a monastery. Maybe he'd been more disillusioned about religion than antagonistic. Not all religious orders were alike. He had probably needed a long break from theological matters to be able to consider that possibility.

He had started to read in his spare time, and he found that Santa Fe's public library carried a good selection of books on mysticism, Eastern thought, and the power of prayer. He was eager to read the latest book by Larry Dossey, a local physician, but the library's copies were all checked out.

According to a review he'd read, Dossey's book promised an exciting new vision for the future of medicine, a future in which doctors would rely not only on high-tech instrumentation and pharmacological interventions but would also incorporate the healing powers of the mind and the power of intention. The health care system was certainly in need of an overhaul, Sam thought. The practice of medicine had become more of a business than a healing art. Insurance companies dictated coverage, and, too often, coverage dictated care.

He was willing to entertain the idea that thoughts could promote healing. Prayer was an integral part of life at the Abbey, and over time the idea of praying on his own—and not just following along with the prayer books and hymnals—had slowly taken hold in his mind. Daily, he prayed for the other monks, and for Jacqueline. He often prayed for his mother and for his sister, Suzanne. Sometimes he even prayed for Yvonne, his ex-wife. When he was feeling especially magnanimous, he prayed that he would be able to open his heart enough to forgive Father Brandon, for how could he expect to be forgiven by the people he had harmed if he was unwilling to forgive those who had harmed him?

Forgive us our trespasses . . .

He knew he had unfinished business in California. He needed to heal his relationship with his mother—and his relationship with his sister. He needed to establish a new relationship with his daughter. Those relationships all needed tending, whether he took final vows or not. For now, sending occasional notes to his mother was the best he could do. She could share them with Suzanne if and when she chose to. Sam didn't include a return address, so he never heard back.

Forgive me my failings . . .

He found a few books that looked interesting and checked them out with his library card. As he headed for the exit, a poster on a community bulletin board caught his eye. He wasn't looking for secular diversions or entertainment and usually ignored such advertisements, but the name CAITLIN ROSE caused him to look again.

Could it be? he thought as he walked closer.

Other than Jacqueline, Caitlin was probably the person Sam had harmed the most. Yvonne might disagree, but Yvonne's expectations had been unrealistic.

The announcement was for an upcoming show at a local theater— and Caitlin Rose had top billing.

The Caitlin Rose Sam knew was a lawyer, or at least she had been until he ruined her career—and her life. She'd never said anything about acting in their time together, and the image on the poster was an illustration, not a photograph. He had to find out if this Caitlin Rose was *his* Caitlin Rose.

He stopped at the Playhouse and wandered around the lobby until he found headshots of the cast. His heart skipped a beat when he saw her picture.

How in the world did she get here?

He hurried to the box office to buy a ticket. He could use the money he had planned to spend on lunch and a new pair of work gloves.

Opening night was sold out, but tickets were still available for the Sunday matinée.

That would be an easier time to get away, Sam thought.

He could say that an old friend was visiting Santa Fe and was only available to meet for lunch on Sunday. Sure, it was a white lie, but what else was he going to say—that he had a ticket for the theater? No, that wouldn't do.

He returned to the van and stuck the ticket inside one of the books he'd just checked out from the library. Its title was *Radical Honesty*.

Maybe if he took final vows someday he would embrace radical honesty, Sam thought. For now, he would do what was necessary.

∾ 27 ∾

*C*aitlin was putting on a pale shade of lipstick when she heard a faint knock at the door.

"Come in," she yelled.

Stephanie, Paul's niece, entered the room wearing a pink jumper and red shoes.

Caitlin smiled. Stephanie was all girl. She loved dolls and ribbons and bows. She was very particular about what she wanted to wear and would throw a tantrum if Sheila disagreed. She usually got her way.

"Hi Stephanie," Caitlin said. "Does your mother know you're here?"

Technically, no guests were allowed in dressing rooms during the half-hour before a performance. Actors were getting ready to go onstage, and distractions affected their concentration.

"No," Stephanie said. "But she wouldn't mind."

Caitlin turned away from the mirror to give Stephanie her full attention. The girl held out her hand and said, "This is my guardian angel pin. It's for good luck. So I'd like you to have it. For now anyways."

Caitlin was touched. She gave Stephanie a big hug and said, "Thank you! I'll wear it right here." She pinned the small, golden angel to her dress, hiding it under a piece of lace trim.

Stephanie seemed pleased, but she didn't leave. "I'm going to be an actress too," she said. "And a dancer." She demonstrated a movement she had learned in ballet class.

"Very nice," Caitlin said, and then fastened a pearl necklace.

Mark came to the door and announced, "Five minutes to curtain."

"Thanks, five," Caitlin replied, acknowledging she had heard him.

"Are you going to marry my uncle Paul?" Stephanie asked.

Caitlin swept her hair into a bun and said, "I don't know, Stephanie. I can't think about that right now."

"Cuz I'd like it if we were related."

"That's sweet. The show's about to start. You should probably go find your mom."

"Okay," Stephanie said. She turned and ran out of the room.

Caitlin took one last look in the mirror. Touching the pin, she murmured, "Okay, angels. Let's fly!" and headed for the stage.

Caitlin was glad she had a few moments to relax in her dressing room after Emma's argument with her dictatorial father. Because her character was the protagonist, she was onstage for much of the play. She knew that putting on a concert would also be demanding. If she went on tour, she would be the main attraction.

But I wouldn't have to learn so many lines! she thought as she drank a glass of water.

She dabbed her face with a tissue before going back onstage. Her favorite part of the show was coming up, when she sang the heartfelt "My Love or My Life." Then, she would have a break at intermission.

As she took her place next to Timothy, the actor playing Jeremy, Emma's suitor, Caitlin recalled her audition and how nervous she had felt singing her own material. She was still nervous about messing up in one way or another—forgetting her lines, singing off-key, tripping or falling. She didn't want to disappoint Paul after he'd finally agreed to give her the role.

She and Timothy sat on a loveseat as Emma and Jeremy discussed the possibility of spending their lives together. Nearby, a parrot was scratching around in his cage. A vase filled with flowers decorated a table where Jeremy's hat had been laid. On the other side of the stage, an easel displayed an incomplete painting of the same vase and flowers. When Emma brings up her interest in pursuing a career as an artist, Jeremy scoffs at the idea.

Timothy rose from the loveseat and said:

> A career? Why, that's absurd. Out of the question. My resources are more than adequate to maintain a comfortable household.

Caitlin smoothed her dress and said:

> That's all well and good, but there are other reasons to pursue a career besides making money, just as there are other reasons to marry than . . . comfort. What about passion? Romance?

Timothy waved away the suggestion and said:

> I don't have time for romance. I'm interested in what's real and tangible. Family is real. Traditions endure. I want to create something that lasts. I want to build an empire!

Caitlin recited her next line, "You are quite ambitious, aren't you?" to which Timothy replied "Yes" before looking at his watch.

Knowing he can't attain his ambitions without a supportive wife, Jeremy tells Emma that she can paint in her spare time. She's not sure that will be enough for her to fulfill *her* ambitions. Jeremy points out that everyone has to make sacrifices in life.

That was Caitlin's cue to walk downstage and stand beside Timothy as Emma asks Jeremy why he wants to marry *her*.

Timothy turned to Caitlin to explain:

> My father approves. He knows me, and he says he knows the kind of woman that would be good for me. You have grace and poise and a fine physique. You're well-read. You have adequate social connections, and a pleasant disposition.

Caitlin laughed heartily and said:

> Pleasant enough, I suppose. I've been trained well. 'Speak when you're spoken to. Don't talk back. If you haven't got something nice to say, don't say anything at all. Smile, dear, and stand up straight.' But I also have ideas and opinions that I long to share. My pleasant disposition may turn ugly if I am denied opportunities to do so.

Timothy picked up his hat from the table and said:

> That would not bode well for either of us, I'm afraid. It's not just up to me. I have my family to consider, as should you. My father has promised us a home along the Hudson, much as your father has offered to build us a home here, on Park Avenue. All that remains is to set the date.

Caitlin turned to Timothy and feigned alarm.

> Set the date?

The date for the wedding, Jeremy tells Emma. She hasn't agreed to marry him, Emma says. She needs time to think.

Timothy laughed and said:

> To think? What is there to think about?

Caitlin wrung her hands and paused as Emma searched for the right words.

> You must understand: painting is not just an enjoyable pastime for me. It is a means of expression. It is . . . the very soul of me. It's my life.

Timothy bowed slightly and said:

> Very well. I shall await your answer.

Caitlin walked to the table and picked up a silver handbell. She turned to Timothy and said:

> Chester will show you out.

After she rang the bell, an actor dressed as a butler appeared onstage.

> Yes, miss?

Emma tells Chester:

> Mister Ford is leaving.

The butler understands that he is to escort Jeremy to the door.

> Yes, miss.

Timothy put on his hat and said, "Good day." Then, the two men exited the stage. After they had gone, Caitlin stepped in front of the birdcage and said:

> The gall!

The parrot chirped—a prerecorded sound effect—and said, "Hello!"

Ignoring the bird, Caitlin walked toward the easel. Facing the audience, she said:

> Am I to have no say in the matter of how I'll live my life— and whether I want to be married?

The sound effects continued, with an offstage actor speaking the parrot's line:

> Chester will show you out.

Caitlin put her hands on her hips and continued her monologue without acknowledging the bird.

> As if I don't have a mind of my own!

Again, the parrot's voice was heard:

> Set the date. Hello!

Caitlin glanced at the cage.

> Yes, set the date to be . . . put in a cage!

The bird spoke again:

> Set the date!

Caitlin's tone softened.

> Or—be turned loose to fend for myself in the wild.
> And risk . . . freezing to death!

The bird squawked and the audience laughed, right on cue. Caitlin moved closer to the easel and picked up a paintbrush. Too distraught to paint, she put it down again and started to sing:

> And how am I to choose
> When either way I lose?
> My destiny awaits
> But I stand trembling at the gate

The song began quietly but ended with Emma's renewed determination. Caitlin looked from the loveseat to the easel as she sang:

> I cannot know my heart's true call
> Until my mind is clear
> But when the final answer comes
> I will not shed a tear
> For then there'll be no doubt
> I must go on without
> My love
> Or my life!

Applause erupted from the audience. As the lights dimmed, Caitlin took a moment to fully appreciate the enthusiastic response before exiting the stage.

∽

When the show was over, Caitlin admired the bouquet of roses she found in her dressing room. Knowing that Sheila and others would be waiting to see her, she changed out of her costume and hurried to the lobby, where drinks were still being served.

An informal get-together typically followed opening nights at the Playhouse, and Paul was thinking of adding a Q-and-A after certain performances for patrons who wanted to stay and learn about what goes on behind the scenes and how actors prepare for their roles. He and the board were always looking for ways to make live theater accessible and relevant.

Caitlin supported that aim, so when she was approached by Cynthia, the owner of a local bookstore, and asked to speak about women in the theater, she readily agreed. She was eager to meet some new people. Around the Playhouse, "Paul-and-Caitlin" was starting to sound like one name, one entity.

"Have you seen Paul-and-Caitlin?" one cast member might ask another.

"The upcoming fundraiser will be held at Paul-and-Caitlin's house this time," the development manager informed the staff.

"Did you hear the latest? Paul and Caitlin are engaged!"

"What?!"

Caitlin wasn't surprised that their relationship was the subject of gossip, but when she overheard that exchange in the restroom, she wondered if Paul had said something that activated the rumor mill.

She saw him beckoning to her as she stood talking to Cynthia about the local playwright's group that met at Cynthia's store, The Golden Door.

"I'll call you later in the month and we can discuss the details," Caitlin told Cynthia as Paul grasped her arm and guided her toward a stylishly dressed woman with light-brown hair.

"There's someone I want you to meet," Paul told Caitlin.

Who is it now? Caitlin wondered. *Another potential donor?* She was looking forward to some quiet evenings at home when she didn't have to entertain—or impress—anyone.

Go stand on your mark, Caitlin, and recite your lines with feeling, she told herself. *The evening's performance isn't over yet.*

"Luisa, I'd like you to meet Caitlin Rose," Paul said, putting his hand on Caitlin's waist.

The woman shook Caitlin's hand and said, "Caitlin! You have a wonderful stage presence. You were absolutely glowing. Still are— and that's not an act!"

"Thank you for your glowing praise," Caitlin said.

"What'll you have?" Paul asked Luisa.

"White wine."

"Caitlin?"

"Nothing, thanks." She held up a bottle of imported spring water and said, "I'm good."

"Paul and I go way back," Luisa explained after Paul left. "He's very fond of you," she said, watching Caitlin closely to see how she would respond.

Was that a note of concern in Luisa's voice? Perhaps she was reading too much into the exchange, but Caitlin knew when she was being evaluated.

"I'm fond of him, too," she said matter-of-factly before taking a drink of water.

Luisa reached into her purse and retrieved a card from a slim silver case.

"Paul tells me you've written some of your own songs. Send me a demo, if you have one. I'm always looking for good material."

Caitlin read the business card and said, "Oh, you live in L.A."

"I have a house here too, in Tesuque. I travel a lot. I manage a band called the Road Angels. We put on a decent show, but our real purpose for being together is a spiritual one. Performing is our way of sharing on a vibrational level."

Luisa's cell phone rang. She looked at the caller ID and said, "I have to take this, but I'd love to tell you more. Call me when your past catches up to your present and you're ready to embrace your future."

Caitlin's face scrunched into a puzzled expression. "Whatever that means!" she muttered as she watched Luisa walk toward the exit.

Paul returned, carrying two drinks. "Where's Luisa?"

"She left," Caitlin said. "But I'll take that."

She sipped wine while Paul talked to a man from the mayor's

office, and then Sheila and her family came over to say goodnight to Paul-and-Caitlin.

"We've gotta get these two home," Sheila said.

Stephanie and John both looked sleepy, Caitlin noticed.

"Glad you could make it, sis," Paul said, kissing Sheila's cheek. "Good to see you, Ned." He extended a hand to his brother-in-law, and the two chatted briefly about Ned's job.

"I saw you talking to Lu," Sheila said to Caitlin. "I'm glad you two had a chance to meet."

Sheila glanced at Paul before adding, "Let's get together while he's away and go over some details for the p-a-r-t-y." She whispered this last part so Paul wouldn't overhear.

Caitlin figured Sheila was probably used to spelling out words of things she didn't want the children to know, though they weren't paying much attention to what the adults were doing and were waiting as patiently as they could. Even John, now seven, was old enough to spell a simple word like "party."

Caitlin gave Sheila a polite hug and said, "I'll call you."

Did she say "Lu"? Caitlin wondered after Sheila and her family left. Wasn't that the name of the woman Melody and her friends were always talking about?

Caitlin moved closer to Paul and asked, "Will you be seeing her again?"

"Who's that, hon?"

"Luisa."

"I don't know." He kissed Caitlin's cheek and said, "I'll go and get the car. Great job tonight."

Caitlin smiled halfheartedly. She appreciated the compliment, but she had other things on her mind. She drank the rest of her wine and set the glass on a table.

Melody, she thought as she walked toward her dressing room to get her coat and handbag. *I think it's time to visit Melody.*

∾ 28 ∾

*C*aitlin liked to sleep late the morning after a show, if Lucky would let her. When Paul's snoring woke her, she sometimes went to the other bedroom. Paul disliked waking up and finding her gone, but he understood her need for rest.

Today, though, she knew she wouldn't be able to sleep. Paul was snoring and Lucky was hungry and she was eager to read the review of *Park Avenue*. If the review was favorable, she planned to stop at a convenience store to buy a few more copies of the newspaper. Her mother would want to show it to her friends, and a photocopy didn't seem as impressive.

From the feedback she and Paul had received the night before, Caitlin knew that people in the audience had genuinely enjoyed the show, but that didn't mean the critics wouldn't find fault. Still, this wasn't New York, and expectations were lower than they would be for a play opening on Broadway.

Caitlin put on her robe and slippers and went downstairs. She fed Lucky and then opened the heavy wooden door at the front of the house. A layer of fine powder covered the walkway. She quickly retrieved the paper and returned to the warmth of the house.

She brought two cups of coffee upstairs and set one on the nightstand by Paul's side of the bed. The sound woke him.

As soon as his eyes were open, Caitlin asked, "Do you want to read it or shall I?" She stacked several pillows and removed the newspaper from its plastic wrapper.

Paul rubbed his eyes and said, "Is that the Santa Fe paper? Be my guest." Noticing the coffee, he sat up and took a drink. "We'll check the Albuquerque paper later. That subscription goes to the Playhouse."

Caitlin found the review and read the beginning out loud:

> Paul Schaeffer has once again taken a new
> musical from workshop reading to full

> production at Santa Fe's Playhouse Theater.
> *Park Avenue*, a collaboration between
> New York City playwright Tobias Clarke
> and Cleveland-based composer Richard
> Stevenson, is the first original musical—

"I'll let you read that part later," Caitlin said, jumping ahead to the part that interested her.

> The theme of personal sacrifice in the name
> of art will resonate in an arts-oriented
> community like Santa Fe.

"Okay, here we go!" She sat up a little taller as she read the reviewer's critique of her performance.

> Caitlin Rose stars as the (fictional) New York
> socialite Emma Dawes. Coming of age at the
> end of an era, Emma is caught between the
> outmoded mores her father is trying desper-
> ately to adhere to and the emerging freedoms,
> for women in particular, that she is trying just
> as desperately to seize. We watch, entranced,
> as a sheltered young woman grows into a
> confident and capable artist.
> Ms. Rose first appeared onstage at the
> Playhouse in the musical *Millennium Blues*.
> More recently, her spirited renditions of
> such holiday favorites as 'Jingle Bell Rock'
> and 'I Saw Mommy Kissing Santa Claus'
> in the *1999 Holiday Music Revue* delighted
> adults and children alike. With *Park Avenue*,
> Rose takes on her first starring role and she
> handles it beautifully, convincing us that
> Emma's transformation is both natural and
> inevitable.
> Always looking for a fresh voice and
> promising talent, Schaeffer isn't afraid to

gamble on new material and sometimes the gamble pays off. *Millennium Blues* has been produced at several theaters since its premiere in Santa Fe two years ago.

Judging from the audience response on opening night, it's fair to say the future looks bright for both *Park Avenue* and its shining star.

Caitlin handed the paper to Paul so he could read the review for himself.

He took another drink from his mug and said, "See that? They loved ya, kiddo. The show didn't do too bad, either!"

Caitlin snuggled up against him and said, "It was fun."

"Fun?" Paul set down his mug and tickled her. "You want fun? I'll show you fun."

He untied the belt of her robe and spread a trail of kisses along her neck and breasts before gently pushing her legs apart and climbing on top of her.

Caitlin responded to his thrust with a soft gasp. Paul was a large man, and his entry always startled her. Soon, though, she was moaning with pleasure.

After they made love, Paul went to shower.

Content, Caitlin smiled. Her performance had satisfied the critic, and Paul's performance had satisfied her.

∾ 29 ∾

*C*aitlin hadn't spoken to Melody in over a year. They had run into each other once, at the health food store, but neither of them had had much to say. Caitlin wished Melody a happy new year and asked about Kimo. Melody said he had taken a position with a local chiropractic clinic after he returned from his travels. Caitlin guessed that "local" meant the Arlington area.

She sometimes saw Melody's ads in the holistic guide that came out quarterly. Melody taught yoga classes in Santa Fe, but her massage practice was based in Tesuque. The guide listed her new phone number. Caitlin called her on Sunday to ask if they could meet sometime. She was thinking about sending a demo to Luisa, but she wasn't sure which of her songs to record. Knowing more about Luisa might help her decide.

The call went to Melody's answering machine, so Caitlin left a message with the number at Paul's house. She'd met a woman named Luisa recently, she said, and wondered if she was the same "Lu" that Melody and her friends knew.

"I'm free around lunchtime tomorrow," Melody said when she called back—and reached Paul's answering machine.

"I guess we're playing phone tag," Caitlin said when she again got Melody's answering machine. "I don't have a show tomorrow. I can pick something up from the deli and drive out."

Caitlin had only been to Tesuque once, for a dinner party at an expansive ranch that she and Paul had been invited to. On Monday, he was busy getting a haircut and attending to other personal business. Caitlin would meet him later at the house, and then they would go out for a romantic dinner.

Just the two of us, she thought as she stood waiting in the checkout lane of the health food store. *Until his phone rings.*

She had planned ahead for Valentine's Day and made a reservation at a cozy French restaurant, her favorite place for special occasions. The restaurant was usually closed on Mondays, but Caitlin had talked the chef-owner, Claude, into planning a special menu.

"Bouillabaisse, maybe?" Caitlin said with a smile.

"For you, mademoiselle, anything," Claude had said before kissing her hand.

Caitlin didn't really think Claude would comply just because she had asked him to; he was simply being a smart businessman. Valentine's Day was a profitable event in the restaurant business. People were willing to splurge when they were on holiday—and the prices at Claude's bistro were not cheap.

As she drove along U.S. Route 84 toward Tesuque, Caitlin sang a few lines from the new song she had started writing. She'd been wanting to write a song for her mother for some time, and being called a "shining star" by the theater critic had given her an idea.

"Even though I've gone away, I never stray too far. You are the light that guides me home. You are my shining star."

She didn't have much written yet, but the tune was stuck in her head. She hummed the next few bars and glanced up at the gray sky. Flurries were in the forecast, but so far the roads were clear.

Caitlin found the address Melody had given her and parked her car by the guest house. She carried a wicker basket to the entrance. Melody was cool when she opened the door.

"Come on in."

Caitlin took off her jacket and hung it on a coat rack by the door. She set the basket on the table, and then Melody gave her a quick tour.

"Cute place," Caitlin said. "I may need a massage by the time this show is over!"

"I've also been studying energy healing and doing more with sound. Essential oils, too. I incorporate different modalities into my sessions. It's not just massage, it's working with the whole energy body. Much more effective."

Melody put plates and utensils on the small wooden table in the dining area and asked, "How's it going with you and Paul?"

"Oh, you know," Caitlin said, removing a bottle of sparking apple juice from the basket. "He's not, as you would say, my soul mate."

Melody filled two glasses with juice. Raising one, she said, "Cheers," before taking a drink.

"Cheers," Caitlin echoed before tasting the juice. "But he has introduced me to some interesting people, one of whom was a woman named Luisa," Caitlin said as she unpacked the containers of food she'd brought. "She lives in L.A. She invited me to send her a demo of my music. So I guess she's got connections. Or a band, anyway. Maybe she wants material for them to record. Like I said on the phone, I wondered if she could be the same Lu that you and your friends were always talking about."

Caitlin sipped her juice and stood waiting for Melody to tell her where to sit.

Melody set out a plate of sliced pita bread and said, "I would guess so, since Lu and Paul used to be married."

Caitlin nearly choked on the juice. "What?" she said between coughs. "What did you say?"

"I thought you knew, since you and Paul are so close."

"Close in some ways," Caitlin said. "He doesn't say much about his past, especially his past relationships."

"Hmm." Melody sat at the table and spread egg salad onto a slice of pita bread.

Caitlin sat next to her and did the same. "Is that— Is that why you've never liked Paul?" she asked. "Did you hear something about him from Luisa?"

"Nothing in particular," Melody said. She filled her plate with sweet potato and quinoa-and-kale salads. "Just a general impression about his level of awareness."

"Well, granted, he's not one to sit and meditate or read self-help books, but he has other qualities," Caitlin said. "His ex-wife, huh? Well that certainly adds a new dimension to the situation."

"How so?" Melody asked between mouthfuls of food.

"Paul has done a lot for me," Caitlin said as she spooned a small portion of sweet potato salad onto her plate. "I wouldn't want him to feel betrayed if I left here to go work with his ex-wife!"

"As I understand it, they're on pretty good terms."

"Yes," Caitlin said, nodding. "I had that impression, too."

"So maybe there's no conflict. Can't you work on your music with Lu and then come back?"

"That's just it," Caitlin said before starting to eat. "I don't know that I'll want to come back. Not to the Playhouse, anyway. My music is still my priority."

"Glad to hear it," Melody said sincerely. "Then I guess your problem isn't really about Lu. It's about leaving Paul."

Caitlin paused before agreeing. "Yes. Whether I go with Luisa or not, the bigger question is whether I want to be in a relationship with Paul. But I still have to decide what to do about Luisa."

"Have you already sent her a demo?" Melody asked.

Caitlin laughed. "I haven't even *made* a demo yet!"

"Then perhaps your worries are premature." Melody leaned against the back of her chair. "You'll know, when the time comes. Was there something else?"

Caitlin wiped her mouth with a napkin. "Yes. I've been having some pretty intense dreams. *Disturbing* dreams. Did I ever tell you? I sometimes dream about a wild cat attacking me."

Melody shook her head. "I don't remember that. You're wanting to understand what they mean?"

"I guess—if understanding them is part of getting them to stop! I thought you might know someone who works with those kinds of . . . issues."

"What kinds of issues?"

"I don't know, things that have no logical explanation?"

"You mean like trance states and the shamanic realms or dream interpretation? Jungian analysis, maybe?"

Caitlin shrugged and tried a bite of the quinoa-and-kale salad. She didn't know what kind of help she needed. If she knew, then finding it would be easier. Maybe. She hoped Melody could suggest someone for her to consult. Surely these dreams were trying to tell her *something*—whether the message was from her subconscious or from some other dimension of reality.

"I don't think I have the time, or the patience, for something long-term like analysis," Caitlin said.

"The fact that an animal is involved—a *wild* animal—makes

me think of the totems that are part of the native traditions. Some tribes name their clans after different animals—wolf, bear, turtle and such. Native peoples use the things they find in the natural world for their rituals. Some keep eagles for their feathers, which are used in ceremonies."

Melody set out dessert plates and then cut two slices of the carrot cake Caitlin had brought.

"I do know of a Native American healer who journeys into other worlds to help the people that come to her. She's the real thing, from what I've heard. Around here, you have to be careful. Anywhere, I guess. Spiritual wannabes."

"How would I find her?"

"Well, that's the thing. She has to want to be found. You can't just call her up on the phone and make an appointment. You have to develop a relationship with someone who knows her and is willing to make an introduction. Then, she decides whether to offer you the gift of a healing. Apparently, just by being in your presence she knows if she can help you."

"Does she speak English?"

"She might understand some, but she doesn't speak it. One of her relatives translates for her. What I heard was that the old woman feels the tug of Spirit when she's meant to do a reading for someone. Though I'm sure she wouldn't call it a reading."

"Well, I've wanted to visit a pueblo since I got here," Caitlin said. "I guess now I have a reason to. Where is she?"

"She lives at Jemez, but she's a descendant of Pecos, I think. Quite revered by her people, apparently."

"Jemez—where we went to the springs that time?"

Melody nodded.

"And Pecos—is that the pueblo that isn't inhabited anymore?"

"Yeah, it's a national park."

"Right," Caitlin said, remembering her brief stop at Pecos before she arrived in Santa Fe. "So would I go to Jemez or to Pecos?"

As soon as she asked the question, Caitlin knew the answer. When the time was right, she would be guided, somehow, to be at the right place at the right time.

Is this what they all mean when they talk about guidance?

When they had finished eating lunch, Caitlin thanked Melody for her help. She was preparing to leave when Melody said, "There's something else I should probably tell you."

"O-ka-ay," Caitlin said warily.

"Remember that day at the spa—in the locker room—when you asked if I was jealous of you?"

"Ye-es-s," Caitlin said, still on guard. Melody didn't usually fire warning shots; she just launched a full-on assault.

"There was a time when I *was* jealous of you."

"Oh?"

Melody seemed uncharacteristically reluctant to say what was on her mind. *Do I have to draw it out of her?*

"Kimo and I were lovers, back in our party days. After he got arrested and met you, you were all he talked about—how great you were and how knowing you had changed his life. I was still pretty messed up, and I blamed you when we split. Later, when I got straight, I could see that he really did love and respect you in a special way."

Caitlin was shocked, both by Melody's confession and by her acceptance.

"I can see where that would have been hard for you," she said. "So why are you telling me this now?"

Melody shrugged. "I don't know. I guess I just don't want to feel like I'm hiding something. From you or anyone."

But Melody wasn't the only one who hadn't ever mentioned the relationship. Had she and Kimo colluded to keep their history a secret? Caitlin had had enough of secrets.

"Did you and Kimo agree not to tell me?" she asked.

"Oh, no, nothing like that. It just never came up."

"Right," Caitlin said doubtfully. "I gotta go."

She picked up the empty basket and opened the front door. Snow was falling, so she hurried to her car.

Kimo and Melody . . . well that explains a few things.

Now that the affair was out in the open, Caitlin realized she had always suspected that Kimo and Melody had been more than friends. But could she ever look at either of them in the same way again?

If all goes according to plan, I won't be seeing either of them for quite some time, she thought. *I'll be going to L.A. Finally!*

In the interim, she would keep her eyes—and her heart—open for clues about how to find the Pecos healer.

∾ 30 ∾

S am cleaned the kitchen after breakfast was over. The Order's version of Psalm 142 took on new meaning for him as he wrestled with emotions he thought he had vanquished.

Listen to my cry, for I am in desperate need, he prayed, but nothing could banish the thoughts and images that were swirling around in his head.

Caitlin's rejection had been the final insult that caused him to abandon his old life. After seeing her again, his heart swelled with emotion.

Release me from my prison, that I may praise your name.

Days later, he was still affected. Remorse, sadness—and jealousy—overwhelmed his efforts to calmly go about his day. At night, the torment was unbearable. He was too agitated to meditate; he felt the need to *do* something, go somewhere, take some kind of action.

A bottle of vodka would cure what ails me, he'd thought as he paced the floor of his tiny cell the night before. But that fix, he knew, would be short-lived.

He only vaguely remembered the drunken rage that had driven him to smash empty liquor bottles against a wall in his house before he left California. Had he really cut up Caitlin's clothing?

It was all a blur ... but the shame he felt was very real. How could he ever face her again after all he had done to her? She'd never suspected that their encounter on the beach had been part of Neil's agenda. Why would she?

To her, I was just a guy she met on vacation, Sam thought.

And while he might dismiss his behavior in Hawai'i as being part of his mission, his decision to invite Caitlin to his house near Joshua Tree was all on him.

She'd had every right to leave him, the way he'd treated her.

Worse, he couldn't be sure he wouldn't do something rash again. He thought he'd made progress, but Caitlin had always aroused complex longings and desires in him. When they were together, he had felt both at ease and terrified. Why was that?

Transformation, he realized, was the only way. He had to transform himself. He couldn't expect to run away or change his name or read about the journey someone else had taken. He needed to do the work of completely transforming himself. No one could do it for him. He needed to face his past, squarely and honestly.

Maybe he should be in therapy. The monks were not equipped to handle psychological issues, and he might benefit from having someone to talk to about his personal problems. His agitation was probably apparent to discerning eyes.

As Brother Samuel, he was surrounded by people who knew nothing about him or the experiences that had shaped him. Unseen forces dictated his prejudices, his values, his goals—all of which needed to be examined and, when warranted, discarded or transformed.

He finished cleaning the floor and put away the mop and bucket after he poured the dirty water down the drain. Looking at the menu on the wall of the kitchen, he saw that fish would be served for dinner on Friday. It would need to thaw overnight.

Watching Caitlin cozying up to the bearded man after the show had made his blood boil. What did that tell him? he asked himself as he opened the door to the freezer. Was he still attracted to her?

Hell yes!

He emerged from the walk-in with a box of frozen fish fillets. *Not quite enough to feed five thousand,* he thought as he set the box on the counter. How many would be needed to feed the monks? *Always better to have a little extra.*

No doubt about it: Caitlin was attractive. And the way she sang that song about making a choice . . . Well, she was simply *breathtaking.*

Maybe he should stay away from Santa Fe for awhile. The temptations were too great, his will too weak.

～ 31 ～

*W*hile Paul was at the Playhouse for a meeting with the board, Caitlin continued working on the lyrics for her new song, "Shining Star." At noon, she took a break and fixed a sandwich. Leafing through the newspaper while she ate lunch, a headline caught her eye:

Limited Supplies of Preservative-Free Vaccines

Lucky rubbed against her legs as she read part of the short article aloud:

> Pharmaceutical manufacturers voluntarily agreed to remove thimerosal from a number of childhood vaccines after concerns were raised about possible adverse effects from the widely used preservative, which contains trace amounts of mercury.
>
> A spokesman for the FDA said the U.S. Public Health Service supports efforts to reduce exposure to mercury from all sources, but existing data do not support a causal relationship between vaccines and developmental disorders such as autism.
>
> The move to limit the amount of mercury an infant might receive from recommended vaccines was described as 'a precautionary measure.'

The article noted that multi-dose vials could be replaced with more expensive single-dose vials, which did not need a preservative.

Caitlin continued reading aloud:

> Manufacturers declined to recall existing
> lots of vaccines that contain thimerosal,
> citing lack of credible scientific evidence of
> adverse effects in the general population.

"So now we've got manufacturers dictating public health policy," Caitlin said, tossing the paper aside. "And who funds the studies that might *find* credible evidence?" she asked Lucky.

She put her plate in the dishwasher and added detergent. "Of course, if there *were* evidence, we've got people like *Neil* making sure it never sees the light of day!"

She started the dishwasher and then gave the cat a treat. These days, she paid little attention to world news. She didn't have time to dream about travel or curl up with a good book, much less learn about the Internet or follow ever-changing political maneuverings and shifting alliances. Her thoughts revolved around Paul and the Playhouse. She was glad to learn the FDA had asked vaccine manufacturers to provide detailed information about the thimerosal content of their preparations, but she knew that much stronger action was needed.

Perhaps someone in Washington would be interested in knowing about the case she had been working on before the Crash. Because the class-action lawsuit had been dismissed, the matter probably hadn't received much attention.

Not if Neil Morton got his way, Caitlin thought.

Maybe she should tell someone about the way Neil had shut down her investigation and pressured her to seek dismissal of the case. Maybe she owed that much to the children who had suffered adverse reactions and to the parents who were being kept in the dark about potential risks and side effects of vaccines—and preservatives.

She would have to figure out which agencies had jurisdiction over such things or find someone in Congress to complain to, she thought as she dressed.

Soon, she would have time to think about something besides her next performance. Paul no longer relied on her as much at the theater. Christine had recently quit her job, and Sy had hired a new office manager, a middle-aged grandmother named Margaret who was content to work behind the scenes. The Playhouse had received some generous funding, and the board was able to make Margaret's position full-time.

Paul treated Margaret with respect, Caitlin had noticed, and he didn't expect her to work insane hours. Margaret had succeeded in organizing the office—and Paul. Caitlin's days as his assistant ended when she won the role of Emma.

She was eager to sign up for an email account and start learning about the World Wide Web. She'd had an email address when she worked at the Department of Justice, where internal communications were being transmitted via computer more and more. Aside from speed of delivery, email provided a means of tracking who said what.

But she was getting ahead of herself. The show was only a third of the way through its run, and she needed to stay in top form. She couldn't allow anything to distract her from giving the audience her best. Besides, she was having a great time!

Don't miss the moment, she reminded herself. *Right here, right now.*

∾ 32 ∾

Sam hadn't brought his address book with him from California. His plan—to the extent he'd had one—was to disappear. Vanish. Forget everyone he'd ever known. Start over. Reinvent himself.

He no longer had a phone number for Neil Morton, but if Neil was still the head of the Office of Special Projects, finding out his number wouldn't be difficult. Sam decided to go to Pecos after lunch and make a few phone calls.

Trips to Pecos were easier to arrange than trips to Santa Fe. He could always say he wanted to look at mowers or research some other appliance or gadget the Abbey might need in the future. Today, he was picking up seed catalogs in preparation for spring planting. When possible, the monks saved seeds from their harvest, but inevitably some seeds had to be purchased, and Sam was looking to expand the garden and add new vegetables.

He parked his truck near the pay phone outside of the general store. In keeping with the communal sharing practiced at the Abbey, the truck was available for use by any monk who needed it, but that didn't mean the Abbey had taken ownership of it. If Sam left the Order, he would be free to take his truck with him. Until then, the Abbey paid for its upkeep, and Sam's use was governed by the same rules that applied to everyone else. He needed to request permission to leave the property. Once granted, a vehicle was assigned—and then checked back in when it was returned.

Sam dialed the number he was given by directory assistance for the Office of Special Projects at the Department of Justice in Washington, D.C.

I wouldn't be surprised to find out Neil's in jail.

Neil took foolish risks—and Sam had gotten caught in his web.

He couldn't entirely blame Neil. The lure of power was addictive, and Sam was an addict. He knew that now. He was an addict, and he had come to associate Caitlin Rose with danger, an odd sort of arousal that set off an array of reactions as stress hormones flooded his system. He understood the physiological response, but that didn't mean he could stop the rush of intense emotions he was experiencing.

Would Neil take his call? Early on, he had told Sam never to call him or come to his office. Sam was supposed to pretend he didn't know Neil if they ever met in public. But Sam had been unreachable for the last two and a half years. Fortunately for him, Neil's operatives would never think to look for him at a monastery! The idea that he could outsmart a man as cunning as Neil gave him immense pleasure.

His call on hold, he shifted his weight from one foot to the other and furtively looked around. Then he heard the familiar voice.

"Where in the hell have you been?"

"Never mind me. There's something you'll want to see. Or *someone*, rather. You need to get out here."

"Out where?"

"Santa Fe."

"New Mexico? Does it concern national security?"

The Department of Energy maintained a classified laboratory in Los Alamos, thirty-five miles northwest of Santa Fe. The first atomic bombs had been designed and built there, so Sam wasn't surprised that Neil thought he might be calling about something to do with the Lab. Neil might even wonder if Sam's disappearance had been related to work on a classified project.

Let him think that, Sam decided.

"Just get here before the end of the month," he said.

Before Caitlin's show closes, he thought.

He hung up the phone before Neil could respond. Now the tables were turned. Now Sam was calling the shots.

Now you can be my *pawn, Neil Morton. Now* you *can fly across the country on a moment's notice.*

Sam intended to be at the final performance of *Park Avenue,* and if Neil's obsession with Caitlin Rose was anything like his, he would want to be there, too.

Sam called OSP again, this time on a Sunday, when he knew no one would be in the office and he could leave a voicemail message for Neil. He didn't want any questions asked or objections raised. He suggested a hotel where Neil might want to stay when he came to town.

"It's centrally located," Sam said. "Ask the staff for information about a shuttle from the airport in Albuquerque."

Sam had no intention of meeting with Neil, but that didn't mean he wouldn't be seeing him. Knowing where Neil was staying was essential to his plan.

Later in the week, he confirmed that Neil had, in fact, checked into the hotel. Sam had saved the program from the Sunday matinée he'd attended. He left it with the clerk at the front desk and attached a short note:

Closing night is Saturday, Feb. 26

∾ 33 ∾

*K*arl walked to his bedroom to answer the phone. He had finally stopped hoping, every time it rang, that the voice on the other end of the line would be hers. He still thought about her, but less often.

Life goes on.

The house was quiet without Jack and Melody and the others who had lived there from time to time. Karl still had friends over for dinners and gatherings now and then, but his schedule was busier than ever, and, most of the time, a bit of quiet was welcome after working with people all day.

Caller ID might be a useful service to get, he thought as he picked up the receiver. He would make a note to look into that.

He had been researching the health hazards of cellular telephones, and he wasn't convinced that the benefits outweighed the risks. Besides, he didn't really want to be available to everyone all the time.

Caitlin, he remembered, had had a car phone when she was working for the feds. *She's probably got a cell phone by now,* he thought, wishing she would use it—any phone—and call him once in a while.

"Hello."

"Hey you!"

"Melody. Howz it shakin'?"

"Whole lotta shakin' goin' on!"

Karl laughed. He and Melody had been exchanging the same opening lines for years. It was their way of saying: "I know you. We have history."

"Glad to hear it," Karl said. "Whole lotta *building* going on in my world."

"Yeah?"

"Just getting started, really. I found a spot in Pennsylvania and took the plunge."

"You bought some land? That's great! Is anything there? A house or cabin—or trailer maybe?"

"I wanted it done right, so I hired a green architect. He put me in touch with the right people to build it. It should be done by summer."

"I'm pretty busy myself," Melody said. "I'm teaching yoga at a spa and doing massage out of the house. As well as my classes in town, but I usually take a break from those in the summer. And Billy and I got back together."

"The musician?"

"Yeah. We just kinda gravitated back to each other. Things are going well. How about you—anyone special in your life?"

"Everyone in my life is special, but no, not really. Nothing serious. Not yet, anyhow."

"Oh, so there is someone! Details, please."

Karl leaned back against the pillows on his bed. "Not a lot to tell, really. Her name's Angela. We've been spending time together. But if I move my practice . . . Well, I'm not sure she'll want to pick up and move to Pennsylvania. And honestly, I'm not sure I'd want her to."

"Not a keeper, huh? Have you heard anything from Caitlin?"

Karl paused for a moment before answering. Melody probably thought he was a fool, carrying a torch for so long for someone who clearly didn't share his feelings.

"No, not for some time," he said, trying to sound casual.

"She stopped by here a couple of weeks ago, wanting to know about healers. I guess she's been having some intense dreams, so she's looking for answers. I told her about a native woman who's rumored to have shamanic powers."

"So she likes it out there?"

"I think she's getting restless, but her boyfriend gave her a starring role in a musical, so she's happy about that. I told you about him, right?"

"The director guy?"

"Yeah. Well, it was good to see her anyway. Her show is closing tomorrow. I don't know what she'll do next. You remember Lu, my old mentor?"

"Yeah, yeah. I never met her, but I know she was an important figure for you."

"Well, Kimo, let me tell you. Oh, sorry! I keep forgetting to call you Karl. I'll get it. I just need a little more practice. So Caitlin met Lu through Paul, and now she wants to make a demo of her music. Which is great. I think that's what she should be doing, focusing on her music."

"Sounds like we're all where we need to be, for now," Karl said.

"I don't feel any desire to move back East. I guess that could change. I would like to visit sometime, though. Keep me posted on your progress. Send me some pictures! Have you got my address in Tesuque? I'm renting the guest house on Lu's property. She's been offering it to me for years but I never wanted to live this far out before. Now that I'm here I love it! And Lu gave me a great price. She's hardly ever here, so she appreciates having someone looking out for things."

"Melody, I need to get to an appointment. Could you call back and leave the info on my answering machine?"

"No cell phone yet, Kimo? Urrg, *KARL*! Even I've got a cell phone."

"No, not yet. Guess I'm just an old-fashioned kinda guy."

"Yah, right!"

"I'm not sure there'd be any reception out where I'll be. But I might think about getting one for emergencies." Karl glanced at the clock on his desk. "I've really gotta run, but thanks for the call."

"Next time is your call."

"You got it."

Karl hung up the phone and headed back to the chiropractic office for his afternoon appointments. The building wasn't far, so most days he came home for lunch, and in good weather he rode his bike. Taking a break from the office allowed him to return refreshed and ready to give his clients his undivided attention.

Though he disliked the idea of starting over in a new place, his long-range vision required room to grow. He planned to return to Arlington several times a month until he had attracted enough clients in Pennsylvania—and saved enough money—to start a clinic.

Eventually, he planned to hold seminars and invite leading-edge practitioners of integrated medicine to gather and exchange information and ideas. Having the support of peers was important in any field, but developing a strong network was especially important in a country where doctors, insurance companies, and multinational pharmaceutical corporations were aligned against outsiders who took a different approach to health and wellness.

So you see, Caitlin, I'm following my dreams, too. It's up to you to find your way back, Karl thought as he put on his helmet and rode his bike down the street.

Remember. Please. Remember!

∾ 34 ∾

*C*aitlin called Cynthia on Saturday to schedule a time to speak to the playwriting group that met at The Golden Door, Cynthia's "metaphysical and more" bookstore, as her adverts said. Caitlin hadn't been to the store yet, but she knew that Melody often went there—for candles and incense and gifts as well as for books and talks.

"Caitlin, hi!" Cynthia said. "The show's not over yet, is it?"

"Paul doesn't like to close his shows with a Sunday matinée," Caitlin said. "He thinks it's anticlimactic. So tonight's performance will be the last."

She was sorry to see *Park Avenue* end but also ready to get on with some of her other projects and plans.

"Okay, well, March is Women's History Month, you know. We've got some great speakers lined up. Come by and pick up a calendar. You might find something that interests you."

"And the playwriting group?" Caitlin asked. Had Cynthia forgotten about her invitation?

"The playwrights group, yes," Cynthia said slowly, as if to delay the moment when she had to disclose that the group had stopped meeting. "The organizer has decided to move to New York, and we just don't have enough interest to keep it going without her."

"New York is certainly a good place for theater. Who was it?" Caitlin asked. "Anyone I might know?"

"Christine Miller?"

"Ohh. Okay," Caitlin said, putting the pieces together.

She'd wondered if Christine would stick around Santa Fe after leaving her job at the Playhouse. Seeing Paul-and-Caitlin all the time probably got to be too much for her—especially after Caitlin was cast as Emma. *She probably thought it should have been her.*

"Christine was running the playwrights group? I thought she wanted to act."

"I'm not sure she really knows what she wants," Cynthia confided.

"Well she's trying out some new things. Good for her."

"Exactly," Cynthia said. "Thank you so much for understanding. And please do come by. We've got some exciting speakers lined up for— Oh, I already told you that!"

"I will," Caitlin said. "Maybe next month while Paul is in L.A."

"Okay. I hope to see you soon, then," Cynthia said.

"Bye now."

Caitlin hung up the phone and checked "call Cynthia" off her to-do list. She still needed to call Sheila about Paul's fiftieth birthday party. But first she wanted to find a studio where she could record some of her music.

She didn't plan to mention the demo to Paul. Not unless something came of it. He would worry about her leaving him—and the Playhouse—and he might try to talk her out of her plans. Not that he *could* talk her out of anything once she'd made up her mind, but she wanted to enjoy whatever time they had left without him moping and pressuring her, as he was wont to do.

She picked up her handbag and headed to the Playhouse for what might be her final appearance onstage in Santa Fe.

∾ 35 ∾

O n Saturday evening, Sam peered over the railing of the balcony and waited for the show to begin. He hadn't seen any sign of Neil yet, but surely he would come. He had come this far.

Unless . . .

What if Neil had already gotten to Caitlin? Sam couldn't be two places at once, and he couldn't risk a prolonged absence from the Abbey. He'd been off the property a lot lately.

He was looking forward to seeing Caitlin's big number again. There were other songs in the show, of course. The suitor character also had a solo, and Caitlin sang a duet with the art teacher, but her solo was both moving and memorable.

Sam would have preferred a seat closer to the stage, but he didn't want to draw attention to himself. Monks were rarely seen outside the Abbey at all, much less seeking amusement. He planned to stay in the background.

Except at intermission, he thought. By then, he would need to visit the men's room.

The longer he waited, the more agitated he became. He had set events in motion but what, exactly, did he think the outcome was going to be? What did he *want* the outcome to be? And why had he done it—why had he told Neil where to find her? Was he still trying to prove something to Neil? Still trying to hurt Caitlin? Why? Because he couldn't have her?

How selfish, he thought, running his hand across his brow.

He wasn't sure he was even capable of unselfish love for a woman. For the other monks, yes; for his daughter, yes. But for Caitlin? He knew he could be controlling and possessive in relationships.

At least I recognize that much now.

Maybe he was just curious to see what Neil would do. He had never discovered why Neil was so intent on knowing Caitlin's whereabouts that he would send Sam to Hawai'i to keep an eye on her. Oh, sure, Neil said it was all about the vaccine issue. Caitlin supposedly had some knowledge about Neil's covert dealings that he feared she would expose. Or he didn't *know* how much she knew—that was it. He'd wanted Sam to find out what she remembered from before the accident.

The accident you *caused,* Sam thought, berating himself. He *did* feel guilt and remorse; he *did* want to make amends.

Yes, he concluded, that was the main reason he was here tonight— to witness what drama, if any, unfolded between Caitlin and Neil, and to make sure no further harm befell Caitlin. He felt protective of her.

Still trying to play the hero? he asked himself.

He shook his head and thought, *How pathetic.*

∾ 36 ∾

*C*aitlin was dressed and ready and collecting her thoughts when she heard a knock at the dressing room door. She really wished Paul would limit backstage intrusions just before a show. She was in no mood to be disturbed. But it was Paul who stood before her when she opened the door.

"Hey, hon. Just wanted to let you know, there's a man here who wants to bring the show to Washington. The Arena Stage, I think he said. Anyway, we're going to have dinner with him later to find out more."

"I'd rather go to the party," Caitlin said.

It was an informal gathering, but she was looking forward to getting together with Timothy and his wife and a few other actors whose partners were in town for closing night.

"We can go to the party later," Paul said.

Caitlin scowled. "Half-hour," she said, pointing to an imaginary wristwatch. "I need to get ready."

She tried closing the door, but Paul pushed back.

"Hey—this is a great opportunity."

"I'm not interested in going back to D.C.—with the show or otherwise."

She hadn't shown Paul the side of her that was independent and stubborn and argumentative, and he wasn't used to her voicing strong objections to his plans. She had done her best to play the part of the accommodating and agreeable helpmate. She'd wanted to get along—learn from him, advance in his theater—and she'd been willing to put his needs above her own as part of that bargain. She understood that he had to be in charge. He was the director. But now that their run was coming to an end, she was less willing to submit. She wanted her life back—on that much she was clear. She would only tolerate *just so much,* and she was setting a boundary.

"Come on, at least hear him out. I got us a reservation at your favorite restaurant."

"We were just there," Caitlin said, standing her ground.

"So we'll go again!" Paul bellowed.

Caitlin knew that his patience was wearing thin, and she still had to live with him, even if she wasn't working with him.

"All right, all right!" she yelled. "Now go!"

She closed the door. Breathing hard, she tried to calm herself. She and Paul had never had a fight, she realized. *That's because he always gets his way.*

In fairness, he did try to make her happy, she thought as she walked toward the stage.

"Places!" yelled Mark.

Caitlin listened for her cue to walk down the stairs as Emma's parents discussed their plan to introduce her to Jeremy Ford.

It's the last performance, Caitlin thought as she made her entrance. *Don't fuck up now.*

Thoughts about the argument with Paul returned to Caitlin's mind as she left the stage following the heated argument between Emma and her father. She drank a glass of water and then changed her costume. She would drive to the restaurant alone, she decided before going back onstage. That way, she could politely excuse herself if Paul wasn't ready to leave. Maybe that would be enough to placate him. He could come to the party later. Or not.

Act One was going fine until Caitlin walked to the front of the stage during the proposal scene. Timothy had just said, "None of us can, dear Emma. We all have to make sacrifices at times," and Caitlin had replied, "Why me? Surely there are women who are better suited for such a role." Then, she glanced at the audience and saw Paul sitting front and center—and beside him was Neil Morton. Dazed, her thoughts raced.

What's he doing here?

How did he find me?

Is Neil the man from D.C. that Paul was referring to?

An image appeared in her mind that crowded out all thought.

In a desert setting, a man resembling Paul stood guard at the entrance to a temple. He was attacked by an invading army—and Neil was the commander of that army. Caitlin nearly fainted.

When Timothy saw that she had lost her focus, he took her arm and looked into her eyes, as if to ask, "Are you okay?" That simple action was enough to bring her back to the present moment.

"I'm all right, thank you," she said, improvising. "It's such a weighty decision you're asking of me." On this night, her hand-wringing was a sign of genuine distress.

Timothy skipped a line of his dialogue that would have been out of place and said:

> My father has promised us a home along the Hudson,
> much as your father has offered to build us a home here,
> on Park Avenue. All that remains is to set the date.

"Set the date?" Caitlin said, resuming the scene. She stepped forward to sing after Timothy left the stage.

> The times we live in
> Was it all simpler in the past?
> The times we live in
> The world is changing oh so fast
> How can I blame him?
> He wants someone by his side
> How do I tell him?
> I am no ordinary bride
> And if I take a chance on love
> There is no guarantee
> That who I am is everything
> He needs for me to be

The times we live in
What does my future hold?
The times we live in
Will I be left out in the cold
If I choose freedom?
Must my love be sacrificed
If I choose freedom?
Am I prepared to pay the price?
But even if I could agree
To push my dreams aside
A power lives inside of me
That will not be denied

To live without him
Or lose what's mine and mine alone
With or without him
What lies ahead remains unknown
I cannot know my heart's true call
Until my mind is clear
But when the final answer comes
I will not shed a tear
For then there'll be no doubt
I must go on without
My love or my life!

Caitlin quickly walked off the stage when the lights dimmed. Paul would want to know what happened, why she'd nearly fainted. What could she tell him—that her dreams were starting to intrude into reality? That the sight of Neil Morton made her ill? Either way, she would have to explain things she didn't want to explain. Not to Paul.

Geez, Paul! Don't be an idiot, she thought as she headed for her dressing room. *Neil can outmanipulate you. He's a pro. You have no idea. I thought I was free of him.*

She was afraid to close her eyes, afraid she might see more flashbacks. But flashbacks to what?

She paced back and forth and then muttered, "I've got to find some answers!"

It's the last night, she reminded herself. *I just have to get through Act Two and then, God help me, dinner.*

Surely Neil's interest in the show was a ruse. What was he really after?

As she walked back to the stage, Caitlin tried to recall what she used to tell herself when Neil infuriated her. She turned her thoughts to the Office of Special Projects and quickly remembered.

Oh, right. "Hazmat." *Neil Morton is the human equivalent of hazardous material.*

∾ 37 ∾

S am sipped a vodka sour. He hadn't had a drink in two and a half years. It went down easy.

Oh, that's good.

He paid the bartender with a ten dollar bill. He'd been saving the money he was given for meals and incidentals—gasoline, parking, and the like—when he came to Santa Fe on monastery business. Lately, instead of eating out, he often brought bread and cheese from the Abbey and pocketed the cash. But he didn't quite have enough money for a motel, and the outer gate would be locked at ten o'clock. No one ever stayed out this late.

What was the protocol in such a situation? he wondered. Should he call someone? Would he be punished, or asked to leave?

Christ, I feel like a teenager violating curfew.

No matter. It was pretty clear he wasn't cut out to be a monk. Clear to him, anyway. He would think about what to do next after Neil left town. Right now, he was absorbed in the drama that was unfolding before him. He had watched the three of them from the balcony of the theater, just as he was watching them now, from his perch at the bar.

A monk on a barstool—that's gotta be a sight!

Neil and the director looked like they were getting along famously, but Caitlin looked miserable, sandwiched between them. They weren't fighting over her, but Sam knew they both wanted to possess her, like an object. And what did he want?

Forgiveness, maybe. Peace of mind.

He had to make sure that Caitlin came to no harm. The audience had let out a collective gasp when she nearly fell off the stage. Sam had moved toward the exit, standing at the ready. Caitlin continued with her performance, but he'd stayed there, by the door, in case she needed anything. In case anything happened. He didn't trust Neil. He didn't even trust himself.

Okay, maybe he, too, wanted to possess her. Not that he thought he could. And if he was honest, he liked watching her squirm. Just a bit. Maybe he had other motives, too, that he wasn't even aware of.

Engineer a problem and then be the one to fix it. You taught me that, Neil, Sam thought. He raised his glass in Neil's direction before gulping the last of his drink. He was deciding whether to have another when Caitlin rose from her chair.

Ladies' room? Sam wondered. *No, wait—she's heading for the door. And Neil's following her!*

Sam put down his glass and left the bar. Outside, Neil caught up to Caitlin and grabbed her by the arm.

"Hey!" he yelled. "Where do you think you're going?"

Sam ducked into the doorway of an apartment building and listened. He'd gotten good at listening, and the street was quiet, with little traffic. He raised his hood to protect his shaved head from the cold night air.

"Why are you following me?" Caitlin asked, though the question sounded more like an accusation. "And what are you doing here?"

"I could ask you the same thing," Neil said. "You choose this clown over me? An alcoholic who couldn't cut it in L.A.?"

"Leave Paul out of this. He's been good to me. The theater has been good *for* me—and I've gotten good reviews. So why don't you take your fake offer somewhere else!"

"It's a genuine offer. I've got connections, remember? And good reviews where? In the local rag of a town with, what, fifty thousand people? The whole state has a population of less than two million."

"You don't get it," Caitlin said. "You never did."

"Oh, don't give me that crap. You're as ambitious as you ever were, just in a new arena. You must think this guy can help you. Oh, wait—he already has. So it must be about time for you to move on and find some other sucker who can help you get what you want. That's why you fucked me that one time, isn't it? We're not so different, you and I."

So that's it, Sam thought. *They slept together. And then she walked away—just like she walked away from me!*

He could feel anger rising as his fingers formed into a fist. *Stay cool,* he reminded himself. *This isn't your fight. You're just an observer. A witness.* A lot could be learned by watching. Watching and listening.

"Stop saying that!" Caitlin shouted. "And you can tell Paul I'm not for sale!"

She tried to walk away, but Neil grabbed her and threw her against the wall of the building.

"Oh, no. You're not going anywhere! You've got some explaining to do."

Sam decided it was time to emerge from his hiding place. His presence might prevent Neil from doing something stupid.

"What do you want from me?" he heard Caitlin ask.

"I want to know what happened. You treat me like some viper while you play Virgin Mary. I want to hear you say that you wanted it, too—that night that destroyed my marriage. And for what?"

He shook her until she collapsed into tears. Neither of them noticed the robed figure that was approaching.

"Yes! All right? At the time, yes. It's a mistake I've paid dearly for."

Neil let her go as Sam drew near, in time to hear Caitlin's quiet confession.

"I got pregnant."

"You— What'd you say?"

"You heard me. It was only right to tell Jayson I couldn't be sure it was his."

"What happened? Did you—"

"No. I just . . . lost it."

After a long moment of silence, Neil adjusted his tie and said, "Dinner's probably being served by now. I'll see you inside."

Sam glanced back before turning down a side street. Caitlin was slowly walking toward the restaurant.

Drama indeed!

He went back to the van and started it up. He would drive back to the Abbey, he decided. If necessary, he could sleep in the van.

Maybe his return wouldn't set off any alarms.

～ 38 ～

*D*uring dinner, nothing more was said about Neil taking the show to Washington. After he departed, Caitlin walked with Paul to his car.

"Parking will be tight," he'd told her when she suggested they drive separately. Caitlin relented. That was the easier course when Paul had made up his mind about something.

"Let's just skip the party," she told him when he opened the door for her.

He was undoubtedly confused by her behavior, storming out of the restaurant as she had—with Neil close on her heels—but she offered no explanations.

To his credit, Paul didn't inquire, and Caitlin avoided him for a few days. She told him she had a lot to catch up on now that the show was over. But she knew that their relationship would never be the same.

As part of her avoidance strategy, she chose the night before he was leaving for Los Angeles to go over to Ned and Sheila's house. She knew Paul wouldn't complain if she wanted to visit his sister. She also knew he had an early flight and wouldn't insist on coming along.

She *had* promised Sheila they would find a time to begin planning a party for Paul's fiftieth birthday, but, ordinarily, she would have met Sheila for lunch sometime when Paul was busy, or while he was away. She figured that by the time he returned from his trip, the incident with Neil Morton would be far from his mind. She hoped it would all be far from her mind by then, too.

She still felt shaken by the experience, even after Paul left town. But she was also glad that she and Neil had finally cleared the air. Maybe now he would let her be.

She asked around for advice on making a demo of her music. The owner of a guitar store in Santa Fe told her about a recording studio in Albuquerque. Caitlin spoke to Scott Taylor, the owner and recording engineer, before reserving studio time for the following week. A week should be enough time to practice the songs she wanted to record, she thought.

A couple of days before her session, Caitlin checked the weather forecast to make sure no storms were on the way. She had never ventured down the incline to Albuquerque, but she'd heard that Interstate 25 was sometimes closed for hours during snowstorms, especially near La Bajada Hill, which had been named by Spanish colonists at a time when travel down "the descent" was even more treacherous than it sometimes was now.

No inclement weather was expected, so Caitlin made a reservation at a bed-and-breakfast in Albuquerque. She would spend Thursday night there and return to Santa Fe on Friday after a second day in the studio.

She wanted to record three or four of her songs, she'd told Scott. Three would be a stretch, he'd said, but possible if the number of musicians was limited. He warned her not to expect a finished product ready for radio play but said he would do his best to help her accomplish her aims in the time, and budget, she had to work with. He knew the session players in the area and offered to find out who was available.

"Sure, go ahead," Caitlin told him. "But 'Shining Star' only needs a piano, and I play well enough for a demo."

She'd been practicing on the piano at the Playhouse when the theater wasn't in use, and she was eager to send a recording of the song to Luisa.

When Thursday arrived, Caitlin rose early and packed a small suitcase, a few snacks, and her guitar. The session would start at ten o'clock. Not being familiar with Albuquerque, she gave herself plenty of time to find Scott's studio.

She arrived a little early and chatted with Sandra, Scott's production assistant, while he was setting up. Caitlin planned to work as late as necessary—or as late as Scott would allow.

The studio was located on the northeast side of Albuquerque, in the foothills of the Sandia Mountains. *Sandia* meant "watermelon" in

Spanish, Caitlin learned from Sandra, and the range was so named because of the pink blush the setting sun cast upon the hills.

Scott had hired a string quartet to play on "Phoenix Heart" and "Gone for Good," and he was confident those two songs could be recorded that day. He played several instruments himself, he said, and he could add additional tracks later. The following day would be dedicated to "Shining Star." As the song was meant to be a tribute to her mother, Caitlin was excited about playing piano on the demo.

She gave copies of her compositions to Scott and the musicians and explained her general ideas about the arrangements before getting out her guitar. She sang the two songs several times, stopping to indicate, "And this is where I imagine a violin solo," and other details. She would leave the rest to the professionals.

The quartet spent the morning trying out different arrangements. After Caitlin and Scott agreed on the best approach, they all took a break for lunch. They would record the songs in the afternoon.

Scott went home to check on his dogs, and Sandra asked Caitlin if she would like to order takeout from a Mexican restaurant. Caitlin looked over the menu Sandra handed her and then went for a walk while Sandra phoned in their orders. She returned just as their food was being delivered.

Sandra was married to a man from the Santa Ana Pueblo, Caitlin learned. The couple lived in Bernalillo, a town north of Albuquerque, with their two sons.

"I'll bet you've been to lots of dances at the pueblo," Caitlin said. "They look so colorful in the photos I've seen. I haven't had a chance to go to one yet." She finished eating her salad and started on the chicken enchiladas she'd ordered, which were accompanied by pinto beans and seasoned rice.

"Oh yeah! *Lots* of dances!" Sandra said. "My sons have both competed at the Gathering of Nations."

Caitlin scooped up guacamole with a blue corn tortilla chip and said, "Gathering of Nations? What's that?"

"It's the largest pow-wow in the country. It's held at the Pit every April. That's what they call the basketball arena at the university here. You should check it out. Hundreds of tribes come from all over the U.S. and Canada. It's pretty amazing, if you like that sort of thing."

Sandra had dark hair and dark eyes, but she had only mentioned her husband being Native American.

"What's that like, being an outsider," Caitlin asked. "Are you accepted?"

"I'm part Choctaw," Sandra said. "I'm not enrolled, but most people don't know that. They know I'm not from one of the pueblos, but I've never had any problems."

Sandra threw her paper plate and the wrapper from her burrito into the trash and added, "But I don't try to get involved in the politics or anything like that. I mostly just go to the dances and feast days. My older boy won first place last year for Fancy Dance."

"That must be quite an honor," Caitlin said, finishing the last of her meal.

"Yeah, this will be his first time competing as a teen. You should come! If you can."

"When is it?"

"This year I think it's around April 28th and 29th. Whatever that last weekend in April is. The Miss Indian World Pageant usually happens on Thursday night, before the other events. There's vendors and lots of music, not just dancing. Drumming. You know, there's a whole new category of music now at the Grammy Awards for Native Americans. The recording of last year's pow-wow is in the running for Best Album. We're all really excited about it."

"I guess!"

The musicians returned and everyone waited for Scott to get back.

"A friend of mine was telling me about an old woman who lives at Jemez Pueblo but is a descendant of the Pecos people," Caitlin told Sandra, hoping to find out something about the healer she had come to think of as Pecos Woman.

Caitlin threw her trash into the wastebasket and said, "I've been having some strange dreams lately and my friend thought this woman, who's supposed to be a healer of some kind, might be able to help me. Have you ever heard of such a person?"

"Oh, you probably mean Porcingula," Sandra said knowingly.

"What is it?"

"Porcingula—it's a Pecos feast they celebrate at Jemez, but the name is also given to Pecos women. Or at least it used to be. She is very old. I know her granddaughter because she also dances at the pow-wows. She's about the same age as my son Felipe."

"Really?" Caitlin said, intrigued. "Hmm. What do you suggest I do if I want to meet her?"

"Like I said—come to the pow-wow! I can introduce you to Lilly. She sometimes does the translating for Porcingula."

"So they both live at Jemez?"

"Uh-huh," Sandra murmured while nodding and sipping on a soft drink.

Caitlin was elated. She had definitely chosen the right studio.

The following day, the setting sun cast its watermelon glow onto Sandia Peak as Caitlin left Albuquerque. She inserted the compact disc Scott had given her into the CD player to listen again to the three songs Scott had recorded for her. He planned to add some "finishing touches," he'd said, and would send her a stack of CDs by overnight mail when he was done.

Caitlin was pleased with how the songs sounded. Now, she needed to find something to occupy her time while she waited, both for a demo she could send to Luisa and to meet Lilly at the Gathering of Nations. She recalled her promise to stop at Cynthia's store.

This might also be a good time to schedule a session with Shanti, she thought. She wanted to understand more about her connections to some of the people who had passed through her life: Jayson, Melody, Neil—and Paul.

❧ 39 ❧

"*I*'m glad you only need the day and not the year," Caitlin told Shanti. "I know Jayson's birth year, and I could guess at Neil's, but I don't know it for certain."

"Just the day," Shanti said. "For the soul connections, anyway. For a horoscope I'd need the year and the place and, ideally, the time of birth. Where shall we begin?"

"How about with Melody, since we both know her," Caitlin said.

"Okay, the Six of Diamonds."

Shanti looked through her materials and told Caitlin that Melody's role in her life was mostly a positive one, though Melody probably found Caitlin irritating at times.

"Yeah, she gets impatient with me," Caitlin agreed.

"Aries natives are characteristically impatient," Shanti said. "They're ruled by Mars, and this is Mars energy that's being activated between you two. The effect can be irritating at times, but it can also be stimulating. And I think you have stimulated her to get moving in some ways. Not that Aries needs much prodding. They're self-starters, as a rule."

Caitlin agreed that Melody was independent and strong-willed.

"Oh, and there's lots of Pluto energy here, too. That's intense, especially for her. Your presence in her life can be transformational if she accepts the challenge to look at her patterns, which you force her to acknowledge, whether you realize it or not."

"Good to know," Caitlin said. "What about her effect on me?"

"Neptune," Shanti said. "She can teach you about universal love and the spiritual side of life—but Neptunian energy can be deceptive as well as inspirational. It's like trying to drive through fog. You can't see clearly until the fog lifts."

Melody hadn't said how long she and Kimo were together, but Caitlin vaguely recalled that he'd mentioned a girlfriend when he came to her office back in 1994. Later, though, when she and Melody were both staying at his house, Kimo never let on that his relationship with Melody had ever been more than platonic.

Of course, I never asked, either, Caitlin thought. She hadn't wanted to tell them much about her personal life; why would she expect them to talk about theirs? *Best to let that go,* she decided.

"Okay. Let's look at Paul next. His birthday is coming up. May third."

"That would make him a Three of Spades. The threes are artistic. They're very career-oriented, and also a bit restless. They're usually good lovers," Shanti said with a smile.

Caitlin smiled and said, "Well that all fits so far." She didn't want to spend the rest of her life with Paul, but she had no complaints about their compatibility in the bedroom.

"Did you know Luisa when she was with Paul?" Caitlin asked Shanti.

"No. She started the women's group soon after they separated. I think the group was very healing for her. I know it was for the rest of us."

"Did she ever say why they split? What went wrong?"

Shanti shrugged. "I think she just outgrew him. As her spiritual path became more central to her life's work, she was less interested in the same ol' stories that get told over and over, in one form or another. She felt like she needed to get out of the biz. She was Paul's agent, you know. That's how they met."

"In L.A.? And then they moved here?"

Shanti nodded. "She was one of the founders of the Playhouse."

"Oh," Caitlin said. Paul had told her that a "third party" had been involved at one time, but he'd never said who it was. The pieces were falling into place.

"Let's look at the connections between you and Paul. Oh, this is interesting."

"What?"

"Paul and *Melody* have karma."

"I'm not surprised! Melody seems to have an extreme dislike for him."

"Well that's their issue. We don't want to get too far afield. As for you two: Pluto and Venus. It looks like the relationship would be a bit more favorable for you than for him," Shanti said. "You bring up intense feelings for him. Feelings he may not want to have to deal with, but that are important for him to confront. The relationship could be fraught with power struggles as you vie for dominance."

"We've mostly avoided that, because I've pretty much let him call the shots. But I can't keep that up forever."

"No. And why would you want to?"

"Because there are a lot of positives in the relationship, too."

"That's the Venus influence. You two have a lot in common, and there's a strong love bond that probably makes it easier to smooth over any differences. But that Pluto connection can't be ignored. It's the primary reason for the relationship, I think. The Venus connection is what makes it tolerable. And desirable to be in it at all."

"I don't feel I can really be myself with him."

"You probably sense he wouldn't respond well if you said what was really on your mind."

"Exactly."

"But then you're not being honest, are you? You're not showing him the parts you think he won't like or accept."

"True, but there's a lot he hasn't shared with me, either. He's held back a lot, too."

"Is that the kind of relationship you want?"

"Long term? No," Caitlin said. "I knew going into it that it wasn't perfect. But it's been all right during my time here."

"And now?"

"Now I'm getting ready to leave."

"So maybe it's time to be honest. Plutonian energy is ultimately transformational. It's not a bad thing, it just feels . . . *challenging* at times. And intense."

Caitlin squirmed in her chair. "Yeah, I get that. How about we move on to January one."

"And who is this?

"Jayson. My former fiancé."

"King of Spades. Powerful. They can be great leaders, but they have some issues when it comes to intimacy. They fear they'll be betrayed, so they're wary and don't let people close."

"He cheated on me. So he betrayed me before I could betray him? Which I did, of course."

"It happens. The King of Spades likes to keep his options open. He might not want to commit."

"He's the one who proposed," Caitlin said. "It's not like I pressured him."

"Did you ever set a date?"

Caitlin smiled, recalling Emma and her dilemma.

"No. We were busy with our careers and getting established in Washington," Caitlin said defensively. "I didn't see any need to rush it."

"Or maybe you weren't sure about him," Shanti said. "Consciously or unconsciously."

"What about compatibility?" Caitlin asked. "Was he the one and we blew it?"

"I wouldn't say that," Shanti said. "There's a lot of Uranian energy here, so he would probably seem unpredictable to you. From his perspective, you represent Venus. You were definitely the object of his affection—or one of them—but Neptune tells me he may not have been seeing you clearly."

"He told me once that being with me helped him get through law school. What should have been a difficult time was one of the best times of his life. Maybe he thought it would always be that way. I don't know. We just seemed to . . . drift apart."

"So no one was to blame."

Caitlin sighed. "I guess not." After a pause, she said, "Or we all were. We were all consenting adults."

For a long time, she had wanted someone to blame. For a long time, she had blamed herself. But the situation was more complex than that, and she and Jayson and Neil had all made choices.

"Which brings me to the fourth person I wanted to ask about. His birthday is June third."

"Gemini," Shanti said as she looked up Neil's symbol. "Ace of Spades. The card of transformation."

Neil had transformed her life, Caitlin thought. For better or for worse. *Maybe both.*

They had been a good team, for a while. Neil had been her case note editor in law school when they were both members of the law review. He had made a few good suggestions that helped her improve the note, which was later published. At the Office of Special Projects, he had let her choose the cases she wanted to work on—a privilege no one else was afforded, which didn't help Caitlin's popularity amongst her colleagues, but she didn't care. With Neil on her side, she didn't need to worry about her reputation. Her success was practically assured.

"Well now," Shanti said. "Looks like we've hit upon one of your karma cards!"

"You're not going to tell me we're soul mates or anything like that, are you?"

"In a matter of speaking. But the popular notion of soul mates is greatly misunderstood," Shanti said. "There are people—souls, if you will—with whom we've shared experiences over many lifetimes, so you could say there's a soul connection or bond. It doesn't necessarily mean you were meant to marry and live happily ever after. It does mean you were drawn together because there was something you needed to complete or learn together. A karmic connection creates a bond that can be very hard to break until the reasons you came together are successfully handled."

"Geez, you can say that again. Neil showed up here recently, out of the blue. We hadn't had any contact since I left Washington two and a half years ago. And I'd have preferred to have kept it that way!"

"How did the visit go?"

Caitlin shrugged. "I told him what he needed to hear."

"Sounds painful."

"It was. But I'm hoping matters are laid to rest now."

So to speak, Caitlin thought.

The miscarriage had been one more loss to grieve, even if the pregnancy was unplanned. *Ancient history,* Caitlin reminded herself. *What's done is done. Or is it?*

Was Shanti saying that what happened in the past could affect the present, even if we were trying to put painful memories behind us?

"With the karma connection," Shanti said, "the energy is flowing in a particular direction. It's not always fair to say that one person 'owes' the other, though sometimes that's the case. It could also be, though, that two people have a soul contract to fulfill, or maybe one performed some service to the other in a past life and the soul wants a chance to return the kindness. Anyway, in this case, the direction is flowing from you to him."

"Meaning I owe him something?"

"If you prefer to think of it that way. But—" Shanti paused as she looked further into her notes. "Actually, it goes both ways." She looked up at Caitlin. "You may remember I said once that there are layers to this, and if the dynamics of the relationship are not fully explained by the primary connections, I dig a little deeper. While your birth card, the Two of Clubs, is not his karma card, in one of the other connections, it is. The effect is not as strong as when both birth cards are involved, but it's there. So he owes you something as well."

"So will this pattern continue for the rest of our lives? How will we know when we've done enough?"

"You'll know," Shanti said. "When it's done, it's really done."

Caitlin reached for her purse and said, "I think that's enough for today. How much do I owe you?"

She wrote Shanti a check and was given a sheet of paper with a summary of the connections she shared with the people she had asked about.

Knowing she might not see Shanti again, Caitlin gave her a long hug before departing. "Thank you," she said quietly.

"All the best to you. Wherever your journey takes you." Shanti put her palms together and said, "Namaste."

"Namaste," Caitlin said.

With tears in her eyes, she drove back to Paul's house. She felt certain that it was time for their relationship to end, regardless of what she heard from Luisa. She knew in her heart that she needed to leave Santa Fe.

But how to break that to Paul?

∿ 40 ∿

*C*aitlin glanced at the books in the New Arrivals section at The Golden Door before looking over the store's selection of candles, cards, calendars, and gift items. She was pleased to see Sable's labyrinth jewelry on display. After sampling a few essential oils, she picked up a chunk of clear quartz crystal she felt drawn to.

"We've got some great speakers coming up," Cynthia told her when she paid for the crystal. "Have you read any of Athena's books?"

Caitlin shook her head.

"She's a Harvard anthropologist, but she writes popular books under the name Athena," Cynthia explained.

Cynthia gave Caitlin a brochure with information about scheduled events and a flyer about Athena's latest book, *A Time Gone By: Rediscovering the Treasures of the Past*. As part of her book tour, Athena was giving a talk at the store about temple priestesses in early civilizations. The description promised a "lively and enlightening" presentation.

> Imagine a time when women were not only equal
> to men, they were revered for their connection
> to the Divine Mother, Creator of All!

"Sounds interesting," Caitlin said, putting the flyer in her pocket.

"Come by," Cynthia said. "She'll be here on Sunday. Just in time for the equinox!"

Sunday night was when Paul would return from L.A., and Caitlin was planning to cook a nice dinner to welcome him home. She didn't have any plans for earlier in the day, though.

Before leaving the store, she paused to look at the community bulletin board by the door and noticed one of Melody's business cards as well as a poster for *Park Avenue*.

"I guess this can come down now," Caitlin told Cynthia. She removed the thumbtacks that held the poster in place.

"Thanks," Cynthia said when Caitlin handed her the poster. "I know this is silly, but—Would you autograph it for me?" she asked sheepishly.

Caitlin smiled and said, "I'd be glad to." She signed her name below the words:

> For Cynthia,
> Keeper of the Golden Door
> that opens to new horizons!

Not the most brilliant inscription, she thought as she departed the store. *But not bad for the spur of the moment.*

When she returned on Sunday afternoon, Caitlin noticed that the *Park Avenue* poster had been framed and was hanging on the wall behind the cash register. She smiled and followed several people to a small meeting room at the back of the store, where folding chairs had been arranged into rows. About twenty-five people had come to hear Athena's talk. Most were women, but some of them had brought male companions.

Caitlin chose an aisle seat. While she waited, she read the promotional materials that had been laid on the chairs.

A few minutes later, Athena strode to the front of the room and stood next to Cynthia. Tall and lanky, she was dressed in slacks and a navy blazer. Curly brown hair fell about her round face. She took off her horn-rimmed glasses and glanced around the room with bright, eager eyes, quietly listening as Cynthia read a summary of her achievements.

After Cynthia introduced her, Athena asked the audience, "How many of you consider yourselves good, law-abiding citizens?" She held up a hand to see who would follow suit.

Several people chuckled; most raised a hand.

"Well stop that!" Athena scolded.

Laughter rippled through the room.

Athena paced as she spoke. "I'm here to shake up your ways of thinking—about religion, about society, about gender. Because when your thinking changes, so does your behavior. Never underestimate the power of belief."

Cynthia dimmed the lights and turned on a slide projector. Athena put her glasses back on and moved aside to face the screen at the front of the room. The first image was a photograph of Earth, taken from space.

"We'd all like to understand where we came from and why we are here, and our ancestors were no different," Athena began. "People in ancient cultures developed creation myths and cosmologies to explain the origins of the sun and moon and stars, and they told stories—about their heroes and their ancestors and about significant events, like the Great Flood."

Using a remote control, Athena changed the slide. An artist's conception of the Garden of Eden filled the screen. "You've all heard the story of Adam's rib," Athena said. "I'm guessing none of you really believe that a woman could be born of a man. It's the other way around, right? Children are born of the mother."

"What kind of culture would concoct such an absurd story?" Athena asked before sharing her thoughts. "Maybe one that had failed to wipe out the prevailing goddess religion by force. The priests and scribes, who were all men, sought to impose a new belief system, one that cast women as inferior creatures who were unfit to govern— or even to participate in public life in some places. Women began to be seen as objects to be possessed. They were useful for producing offspring, and for taking care of men. In various ways. Yes. Laws were adopted so that offenders could be penalized if they failed to comply, and the penalties were sometimes harsh. Women were often dispro- portionally affected by these laws."

An image of stone tablets with inscriptions appeared on the screen. "Many in today's world still favor rigid gender roles and preach that a woman's place is in the home," Athena continued. "Those who hold such views are often part of a religious tradition which teaches that a Father God created man in *His* own image and gave man dominion over the earth. But it wasn't always this way. In some societies, property and name are passed through the mother. In others, marriage is unknown. Children live with their mothers, and women choose their sexual partners. So it's not hard to imagine an earlier time, when people lacked scientific understanding about everything from conception to the cosmos, when nature-based myths, beliefs, and ceremonies gave a central role to the Goddess, the Mother, the Creator of All."

For the earliest humans, the moon symbolized the cycles of life and death and rebirth, Athena said. She showed a slide with images of the moon in its different phases throughout the month.

"The cycle of the moon repeats thirteen times a year, year after year. Each month, the sky goes dark for three days. The moon always returns, but people came to believe that they needed to make offerings and perform rituals to ensure that She did, for Her cycles were linked to women's cycles, and women bring forth new life. As the moon grows full each month, in the waxing phase, so does a woman's belly grow full and round as she prepares to give birth."

The next slide was a photograph of an ancient stone carving depicting a naked woman holding a bison horn in her raised right hand. As Athena pointed out, the horn was marked with thirteen lines. The moon symbolism was unmistakable.

"In prehistoric times, notations of lunar cycles were common. A woman learned that if she stopped menstruating, she might be pregnant. Knowing that a full-term pregnancy lasts about ten moons, she kept time by the phases of each passing moon. Various systems of lunar notation were devised. The first true calendars were lunar, not solar, and in some traditions a lunar calendar is still used for determining feast days."

The entrance to a cave was shown next. "The cave was the place of transformation," Athena said. "There, people painted animals on the walls and buried their dead. In the great cycle of life and death, new life would emerge again, just as babies emerge from the womb and just as the crescent moon appears after the sky has gone dark."

Athena showed images of round-bellied figurines from the Paleolithic era; these, she said, were most likely created for sacred purposes.

"The naked female image was not painted on cave walls; it was carved in stone and sculpted in bone and ivory. These artifacts were not made to depict individual women, but to honor the feminine principle that gives life and nurtures life. The Goddess was not separate from creation; she was very much a part of it. The Mother loves all her children: humans, rocks, trees, animals, fishes and birds."

Living in harmony with nature was not a utopian ideal, Athena said. It was the only way to live.

"When a mother figure is leader, she emulates the Mother of All. She nurtures her people—she doesn't seek power over them. The differing contributions of men and women are valued. The welfare of the group is paramount, and sharing resources helps the whole tribe or clan to survive and prosper."

Athena described her research into the earliest known civilizations and the information that could be gleaned about these cultures from the artifacts and, later, writings that had been left behind. She believed that a shift occurred when the development of agriculture made the accumulation of wealth possible. The Ice Age was over, and for some tribes, hunting and gathering gave way to planting and harvesting crops and to domesticating animals. People formed settlements and built city-states. They claimed territory as their own. Now there was something to fight about.

Caitlin recognized the ruins of ancient Greece in the next slide. A photo of a painted urn followed.

"Clay pots were used to store food and water—and wine and beer—and trade flourished as new forms of art and decoration were devised. Goddess figurines were fashioned from clay, gold, and other materials to honor the Source of All Life. With the development of writing, oral traditions could be recorded. Rituals and sacred offerings moved from caves to temples. Now, grain sustained life and was considered sacred. And who baked the bread but the women?"

When people lived a more nomadic lifestyle, the notion of asserting dominion over the earth and its creatures would have had little importance. The same was true for fatherhood. "Children belonged to the mothers who bore them," Athena said, "so the first male deities derived their significance from their relationship to the Great Mother: *Her* son and *Her* lover."

A series of slides showed photographs of Sumerian pottery, sculpture, reliefs, architectural ruins, and clay statues and tablets with the cuneiform writing that was used for several thousand years.

"In the Near East, the high priestess was the earthly representative of the Goddess," Athena said. "The holy women of the early temple religions seem to have held positions of great power and influence, as they did in ancient Egypt. Everyone—men and women alike—worshipped the Goddess as the Creator and Holy Spirit, Wisdom."

Caitlin remembered her conversations with Kimo about the theme of the sacrificial king found in the myths of many lands. She wasn't surprised when Athena mentioned these ritual practices.

"In matrilineal societies, the king obtained legitimacy by marrying the queen. A queen needed only one mate to produce an heir. She may have chosen a consort—as Dumuzi was for Inanna—for an annual mating rite. In some cultures, a king reigned for a designated period of time and then was ritually sacrificed. This practice was tied to the dying-and-rising symbolism, of which Dumuzi—later known as Tammuz—was one such representation. The male was probably younger, hence the reference to him being the son/lover. In time, the king assumed a more permanent status, and the practice of human sacrifice gave way to more symbolic offerings."

Like the celebration of the Eucharist, Caitlin thought.

Still focused on the Near East, Athena said that women in Sumer enjoyed many rights and freedoms. "They were not yet viewed as the property of men or as second-class citizens. Ancient religious texts and epic poems mention women as priestesses, poets, astronomers, and rulers. The first Egyptian queen that we know of, Neith-hotep, lived roughly five thousand years ago."

A bronze statuette depicted the goddess Neith with a crown on her head. "Neith is one of the oldest deities in Egypt and was known as the goddess of creation, war, and wisdom," Athena said. "As war became widespread, soldiers and warriors seized control and sought to conquer territory after territory. The first empires were formed, and a supreme male god was given primacy."

Myths reflect cultural norms and expectations, Athena said. As the significance of the goddess religions diminished, the roles of women in society also changed.

She showed a photograph of the bronze head of a bearded king that had been found in Nineveh. "Sargon, often credited as ruler of the world's first empire, used the Akkadian language to unify the diverse peoples he conquered. He appointed his daughter as the high priestess of Nanna, the moon god who was the patron deity of Ur."

The tradition of Mesopotamian princesses serving as high priestess continued for hundreds of years and established a link between the political rulers and the gods. Athena suggested that both Sargon and his daughter may have been born to Sumerian priestesses. Sargon's daughter took the name En-hedu-anna and presided over temples at Ur and Uruk, the leading city-states of the Sumerians.

"As a means of uniting the Akkadians and Sumerians in one common culture, elements of the Sumerian religion were incorporated into a new religion rather than rejected. Thus, the Akkadian goddess Ishtar came to be associated with the Sumerian goddess Inanna. Ishtar/Inanna was considered the daughter of Nanna, the moon god."

Caitlin struggled in vain to recall what Kimo had told her about Inanna visiting the Underworld. Her memories of what was said or done shortly before the Crash—cases she'd worked on, conversations she'd had—were hazy, which was almost worse than not remembering at all. The fragments of memory hinted at information she could no longer recover, information that was as lost as the civilizations Athena was describing. She returned her attention to Athena's presentation.

"Now the moon, for so long the symbol of the Goddess and the cycles of life, was ruled by a male god. The high priestess, originally the earthly representative of the Goddess, came to be seen as the wife of a god. But she still mated with a chosen consort in a sacred rite to ensure continued abundance and the renewal of life."

When a priestess was impregnated as part of a sacred ceremony, the identity of the father was irrelevant, Athena said. "Her children were not labeled illegitimate or scorned and ostracized, as they would be in patriarchal societies."

The new patriarchal systems considered women and children the property of men, and men controlled their fates. "Now we begin to see gender-specific laws, and the denial of rights for women."

Although adultery was sometimes a crime for men as well as for women, men often enjoyed more sexual freedoms. Purity was demanded of women. Prostitutes were scorned.

"And who was the most famous prostitute in history?" Athena asked.

"Mary Magdalen," a few people murmured.

"His-story has reviled her as a whore, though she seems to have played a central role in Jesus's ministry. As a powerful woman, she would have threatened the dominance of apostles such as Peter, who didn't understand her favored position. Perhaps she was trained in the ways of the Goddess, and used herbs and ointments in her work as a healer. Then as now, there were different sects of Jews, and their beliefs and practices differed somewhat."

Athena showed pictures of modern orthodox Jews, who, even today, wore distinctive hairstyles and clothing. "In the Hebrew tradition, the discharge of bodily fluids—as occurs monthly for menstruating women—renders one impure for a period of time," she said.

She noted that early Christian Church Fathers extended the impure idea to all sexuality and encouraged abstinence and celibacy. "The Christian Son of God was immaculately conceived. Even after giving birth to other children, the Mother miraculously remained a Virgin."

Athena suggested that the proponents of the patriarchy may have even downplayed the importance of their own mothers.

"We find many references to the son of man in ancient scriptures and in the synoptic gospels. The term seems to have been used in different ways at different times, but in pre-Christian writings, the expression usually referred to a human being. Could it be that these men, who were so focused on expanding their kingdoms, and on dominion and glory, sought to downplay the fact that they had been born of women? In any case, a mythology had to be invented to justify putting men in charge of earthly affairs."

Athena noted that in the Book of Enoch, a figure known as the Son of Man was expected to reward the kings and the mighty who were righteous but would "break the teeth" of sinners. "In the Psalms," Athena said, "we hear a similar plea: Lord, break the teeth of the wicked. Over in Sumer, a century before Sargon, the king of Lagash instituted a number of legal reforms. While acknowledging that in earlier times women were permitted to have more than one husband or mate, now polyandry was made a capital offense. And while aristocratic women enjoyed many freedoms, the other classes didn't fare so well. The punishment for a woman saying something offensive to a man? Her teeth would be crushed with a brick. A woman who steps out of line is considered wicked."

Athena turned off the slide projector.

"With the rise of empires came the drive to consolidate wealth and power. No longer would men and women be accorded equal status—in the home, in the temples, or in society. Now we had a supreme male deity, and his earthly representative was the king. Now we had hierarchy, with the king and the royal family at the top. Religions and governments enacted laws to force compliance. The old ways were attacked as wicked, demonic, sinful—and made illegal. This went on for hundreds of years, with the Inquisition and other means of suppression, some overt and some subtle. Sex and procreation—and women—had to be controlled once men took over. Men had to be sure their children were really theirs. Why?"

"So they could pass their property on to their sons," someone in the front row said.

"You've been paying attention! Under patrilineal systems, property passes to sons, not daughters. The best way for men to justify their actions? This is the way God wants it. This is the natural order. Well, don't you believe it!"

Athena took off her eyeglasses and said, "You can read all about the shift toward patriarchy in my book, but what I want to leave you with isn't about the past, it's about the present and the future and the kind of world we want to live in, the kind of world we want to pass to the next generation."

She paused to take a drink of water and then continued. "I'm not suggesting we go back to living in caves or that we should revive the worship of pagan goddesses. Humankind has made great strides in scientific understanding and technological achievement. Now we need humanitarian advances. After five thousand years of patriarchy, it's time to take an objective look at the structures of society and develop policies that promote the health and safety of individuals, families, towns, and the planet on which we live. We must evaluate costs and benefits not only in financial terms but in terms that take into account quality of life and the costs to the human spirit when we are forced to live and work in dehumanizing and oppressive conditions. When we fear our neighbors, when the air we breathe and the water we drink are polluted, we all suffer."

Many heads nodded, and someone near Caitlin shouted, "Amen to that!"

Athena chuckled and then continued with her parting remarks. "What can I do, you ask, that will make a difference? I vote. I donate to worthy causes. But I can't change society.

"It's true that change is often slower than we might like. That's why you can't think of making a one-time contribution and then you're done. Change is a process, and we all need to be vigilant and persistent. One by one, we are waking up. And when we are awake, we value the sanctity of life. We confront injustice wherever we find it—at work, in society, in our own homes. We call it what it is. We don't deny or rationalize or make excuses. But this is not about a battle of the sexes. Men, too, suffer when relationships are toxic, when our cultural values emphasize winning and conquest, and when our leaders teach, through their policies and their own behaviors, that violence and force are acceptable means of achieving desired outcomes. Boys, too, suffer from neglect when their parents don't have adequate support to properly care for their families. It's not about fault or blame; it's about change. We must change our ways, make different choices, and learn—from our mistakes and from our successes—both individually and collectively.

"Don't let anyone tell you that male dominance is what nature intended, that inequality has always been necessary for a society to thrive. A society can be structured in a variety of ways. We still don't have an Equal Rights Amendment. We do still have a glass ceiling, and wage inequality. We can create sane policies and institutions that truly offer equal opportunities for all. That's not likely to happen if we keep electing leaders who don't even see a need for change, much less have a long-range vision for introducing reforms.

"This isn't just about having more female bodies in positions of power. That's important, but women who have adopted the conventional value system as their own will only perpetuate it. Women shouldn't have to behave like men in order to succeed. We need to be free to be ourselves—all of us: black, white, indigenous, men and women, heterosexual and homosexual, young and old. We need to change how we think and behave, how we talk to each other and how we talk to ourselves. We each need to examine our fundamental views about life and what it means to be human. When we disown the feminine, we create an imbalance. The individual—or the society—is then incomplete. It's lopsided. What happens when something is lopsided?"

"It falls over," someone shouted.

Athena nodded. "It requires a greater expenditure of energy to sustain it in its unbalanced state. Eventually, it topples. When we value cognitive understanding over intuitive sensibilities and our felt sense of what is needed, we miss out on a lot of important information. When science and rational thought supersede the collective wisdom of the ages, shamans are seen as misguided primitives, energy healers are all considered quacks—and women are dismissed as weak and irrational."

Strong women look great on the big screen, Athena said. "But in real life? Do you find yourself criticizing strong women? Ask yourself why. Do you go to movies that perpetuate the objectification of women and stereotypical views of minorities? We need to stop glorifying violence and teach tolerance, respect, and compassion. Yes, of course we should honor the heroes who defend our freedom, the pioneers who explore new territories—on Earth and in space—and leaders who guide nations through times of great change and upheaval. But alongside of them, let's not forget the contributions of artists and musicians, visionaries and innovators, poets and spiritual teachers."

We must attend to the needs of the spirit, Athena said, and not just the needs of the body. "How can we hope to have healthy relationships with others if we are filled with shame and self-loathing? When religions tell us we are sinful and the media tells us we are ugly, we lack self-worth. When we believe we are fundamentally flawed, we don't see any point in attempting to change. We're disempowered. When we're disempowered, we're unwilling to take risks. The refusal to take risks stifles creativity. Civilization doesn't advance if we simply perpetuate the same old ideas, products, and stories."

Athena suggested that when we disown our feelings we lose our center. "We focus on what we're trying to be rather than developing the courage to be who we are."

In order to be able to acknowledge our strengths and weaknesses, and to express our confidence and our vulnerability, we need to feel our feelings. "Whether you have been sexually abused or traumatized by war, you need to allow yourself to heal. You can't open your heart to others if you are carrying around anger and resentment. You can't respect others if you don't respect yourself."

When emotions are denied healthy outlets, they manifest in destructive tendencies. "We turn to drugs and alcohol or seek thrills and intensity. We fill up our lives with stuff and keep ourselves busy so we don't have to be alone with our thoughts—and our feelings. We're constantly dissatisfied and craving and searching. It doesn't have to be this way."

Athena ended her talk with an upraised fist. "I'm here to start a revolution!" she declared. She lowered her arm and spoke quietly. "A quiet revolution. This isn't just about women's issues; it's about strengthening our communities so that the individuals within them can thrive. Look beyond your own interests. Take what you need—and leave some for others. Support your local businesses, like this wonderful bookstore. Shop at the farmers' market. Start a co-op. Vote for candidates who care about the environment, our planet, our home. It's the only one we've got, and we're all in this together. Increasingly, we act on a global stage. It's time we attempt to live in peace as one human family. We've had Her-story and His-story. Now it's time for Our Story. Thank you."

Cynthia announced that Athena would be signing copies of her book, which was available for purchase, in the back of the room.

Caitlin bought a copy, but she didn't stay to have it signed. She wanted to get back to Paul's house and start preparing dinner. If he wasn't too preoccupied, maybe they could go to bed early and enjoy some intimate time. Reconnect.

As she walked to her car, she wondered if Athena's talk would inspire people to take action. She liked Athena's acknowledgment of the importance of art as well as activism. Caitlin had chosen a career in civil service because she'd wanted to make a difference. As a lawyer, she *had* fought against corruption and injustice—and she *had* experienced sexism and unfair treatment by those who never stopped to question their assumptions about men and women.

Her mother had quit work when she got married. She stayed at home to be a wife and mother until Caitlin started school; then, Martha took a couple of part-time jobs, serving lunch at the senior center and helping out in the office at the church a few mornings a week. Had her father ever changed a diaper in his life? Caitlin wondered.

Well, the part about men not being sure if children are theirs is certainly true, she thought as she drove to the north side of town.

When she discovered she was pregnant, she told Jayson the truth: he could be the father, but unless they got a paternity test, they couldn't know for sure.

"It was just the one time, on Valentine's Day, when you said you had to work. I knew you weren't working—not alone, at least. I was angry and hurt. But I didn't do it to get back at you. Neil had been coming on to me for years. I went to the office, and he was there. It started to snow and he ordered Chinese food and opened a bottle of wine. I appreciated the company and . . . it just happened."

Jayson confessed that he'd been having an affair with his paralegal for several months. "I guess we've grown apart," he said.

If she had married Jayson, Caitlin knew she would have been responsible for child care and cooking and cleaning, even if she also worked full-time. Jayson was more enlightened than many men, but he would have balked if she had suggested keeping her name or sharing household chores. In the one conversation they'd had about "household help," he'd objected to the idea of hiring a nanny or a maid. It didn't fit with his image of home and motherhood. At the time, Caitlin didn't say much about it. She decided she would use her own money to get whatever help she needed.

How many times in her life had she refrained from speaking her mind in order to keep the peace? she wondered. Sure, she'd gone to law school and learned to be assertive. She knew what her rights were. But expectations, assumptions, traditions, and biases— in the workplace, in the media, and at home—meant that women were still expected to be supportive and submissive, agreeable and polite. Maybe they no longer needed to worry about having their teeth smashed with a brick, but women who spoke with authority and objected to unequal treatment were labeled as demanding or controlling or worse.

If Jayson had been willing to accept the child as his own, Caitlin might have married him despite his infidelity if they both agreed to work on improving their relationship. Her miscarriage spared her from having to make any difficult choices. When her pregnancy ended, she moved out. Soon after, the paralegal moved in.

Before long, Neil's marriage ended in divorce. Caitlin kept her distance from him, as much as possible, while she grieved—the end of her engagement, her father's death, the termination of her pregnancy. She was in too much pain to try to explain how she felt, much less tell Neil about the miscarriage. What would be the point? It was over and done. She wanted to focus on her career and get on with her life. She didn't want anyone—any men, especially—to get too close. Not Kimo, and certainly not Neil.

Paul's car was in the garage when Caitlin reached the house. She knew he was unaware of the many ways she felt invisible when she was with him. Athena's talk provided a good reminder: if she wasn't expressing her needs, then she was partly to blame. But the attempts she had made had fallen on deaf ears. She could see that Paul wasn't interested in changing, and she accepted him as he was, knowing that she would leave someday.

If she wanted to be in a different kind of relationship, she needed to be with a different kind of man. She would have to look elsewhere if she wanted to co-create an equal partnership with a man.

∾ 41 ∾

*A*fter his return from L.A., Paul was around the house a lot until rehearsals started for *Angels in America*. It was a big house, and Caitlin was glad she didn't have to clean it. Paul's housekeeper of many years came once a week to clean. She also did his laundry.

Caitlin usually fixed breakfast, but now that she and Paul were following different schedules, they each fended for themselves at lunchtime. Paul sometimes met friends at a café on Canyon Road; other times he picked up a wrap and ate it at the Playhouse. When he was at home, he fixed a sandwich or heated up leftovers.

Sometimes on Sundays they went out for brunch, and afterward they would come back to the house and make love. In the evening, they might watch a movie or go for a walk or sit out on the balcony and gaze at the stars. Caitlin cherished those quiet times as much as she enjoyed the gala black-tie events they occasionally attended together.

Most evenings, Caitlin cooked dinner. When Paul wasn't there, she listened to music while she cooked. When Paul was there, he watched the news on television. He liked the volume turned up loud.

Caitlin disliked hearing about wars and murders and other disturbing events and did her best to tune out the content. Occasionally, however, some piece of news caught her attention—like the announcement that a congressional committee was investigating potential causes of autism and the possibility that vaccines played a role. She missed the first part of the report when she was rinsing vegetables in the sink, but she heard enough to know who she could contact in Washington.

> Congressman Dan Burton, Chairman of the Committee on Government Reform in the House of Representatives, has initiated a series of hearings investigating whether

there is a connection between vaccines and the rising rates of autism. The most recent of these hearings concluded this week in Washington. The committee's next hearing will examine the detrimental effects of mercury in the body, including vaccine preservatives derived from mercury.

Caitlin dried her hands on a dish towel and moved closer to the television. A brief clip was shown from an interview with Congressman Burton before a commercial break interrupted the broadcast.

Dan Burton, Caitlin repeated silently. *Bingo!* She found a pen and paper and wrote herself a note.

She would write to the congressman, she decided, and let him know about the class action lawsuit that had been dismissed before she'd finished investigating the claims against the manufacturers that used thimerosal in their vaccines. She would convey her concern about the way cases were handled at the Department of Justice when injuries allegedly caused by vaccines were involved. The Department's policies seemed to hinder, rather than facilitate, resolution of cases that could not easily be dismissed or settled. She would tell Burton about her conversation with a DOJ attorney who was familiar with the functioning of the Vaccine Injury Compensation Program and suggest that the committee consider investigating whether the VICP was functioning the way Congress had intended when it passed the National Childhood Vaccine Injury Act.

Satisfied with her plan, she finished cooking dinner and called Paul to the table.

The next day, Caitlin went to the public library and signed up to use the computers. When one became available, she created a free email account and then looked up contact information for Dan Burton on the World Wide Web. She found a transcript of the April 6 hearing and read through the testimony of the parents and experts who had appeared before the Committee on Government Reform. These parents were convinced that vaccines had triggered the regression of their young children. Their children were not expected to ever recover or function normally.

Remembering Jasmine Wells and her autistic son, Marvin—and still hoping for a child herself someday—Caitlin felt moved by the suffering these families were experiencing. The parents thought they were protecting their children by having them vaccinated but, in hindsight, many wished they had taken the time to research side effects and learn about the additives and preservatives used in vaccines before blindly agreeing to the immunization schedules their pediatricians recommended and their school districts required.

Caitlin drafted a letter to Congressman Burton. In 1996, she told him, she was working as an attorney for DOJ's Office of Special Projects. She offered to share what she knew about the dismissal of a class-action lawsuit concerning the mercury-based vaccine preservative thimerosal.

She had done a lot of research on vaccines in general and thimerosal in particular. She no longer remembered all the details of what she'd learned, but she clearly remembered Neil badgering her to file for dismissal of the case. She had refused, but that was before the Crash. After the Crash, the case disappeared—from the docket and from Caitlin's radar. All her energy went into her recovery. She stopped keeping up with current events. While she was at the lake house, she rarely heard news of the outside world. Finding a new direction for her life took priority.

Now she had the time, the energy, and the will to follow up on the matter. She believed the role of government, where health matters were concerned, should be one of protecting and promoting the public welfare and not just the financial interests of the pharmaceutical industry and its lobbyists, and she was prepared to put her thoughts on record.

> If that case had not been dismissed—if it had received widespread attention in the media—might it have helped raise awareness so that some of these parents might have been alerted to potential dangers? Informed consent requires factual disclosures that

permit meaningful weighing of the risks
and benefits before allowing children to
be injected with thimerosal-containing
vaccines. I can't help but wonder: *Could
some of these devastating injuries have
been avoided?*

Caitlin printed two copies of the letter and drove to the post office. She signed and mailed one copy. When she returned to Paul's house, she put the other copy in her briefcase.

By then, it was again time to fix dinner.

∾ 42 ∾

*K*nowing that she might soon meet Porcingula's granddaughter, Caitlin went to the Plaza in search of a gift. After browsing through several shops, she settled on a silver bracelet with turquoise stones and had "For Lilly" engraved on the back.

Later, she called Sandra to find out what time her son would be competing.

"I'll be there," Caitlin told her.

"Great! I'll watch for you. It can get pretty crazy in the Pit!"

On Friday afternoon, Caitlin again descended La Bajada Hill on her drive to Albuquerque. After parking in a lot on the University of New Mexico campus, she paid the entrance fee for the Gathering of Nations.

The competition in Felipe's dance category wouldn't start for another hour, so Caitlin listened to live music for a while and then wandered around the grounds. Seeing all the vendors, she realized she could have found a gift for Lilly there. *But it probably wouldn't have been engraved.*

As the time for the Teen Boys Fancy Dance approached, Caitlin entered the Pit and made her way through a sea of colorful regalia.

Costumed performers wearing beaded garments and feathered headdresses swirled around her. The sound of chants and drums and bells filled the arena. Some people greeted acquaintances; others watched the dancers with rapt attention.

Sandra waved when she saw Caitlin and then introduced her husband, Joe, and her sons, Felipe and Joe Junior. Lilly was there to watch Felipe dance, so an introduction happened naturally as they all waited for the first dance to begin.

"Sandra told me you would be competing today, so I brought you something," Caitlin told Lilly. She handed the girl a narrow white box and added, "For good luck."

"Oh, wow!" the girl said when she opened the box and saw the silver-and-turquoise bracelet inside, resting on a pillow of cotton. "Thank you! That's very kind. I'll wear it home later."

"Caitlin would like to meet your grandmother," Sandra told Lilly.

"Oh sure, no problem," Lilly said. "Come to Mass on Sunday. We have lunch after. You'll be my guest." The girl stood up a little taller, as if pleased she had something special to offer.

Caitlin enjoyed watching the competition with Sandra's family. When Felipe's dance was over, Joe told his son he'd done a fine job.

Lilly waved to them all and said, "I have to go get ready now. Bye!" Looking directly at Felipe, she said, "Bye Felipe!"

Felipe was refilling his water bottle and looked up when he heard his name. He smiled at Lilly and, distracted, spilled water on the floor.

Caitlin pretended not to notice. She turned her attention to Sandra.

"Are you hungry? Would you like to get something to eat?"

She had seen a few food stands and hoped to eat a quick snack before driving back to Santa Fe.

"Sure, Joey and I could do that," Sandra said. "Felipe will want to stay with his friends, I think."

"When do you find out the results?" Caitlin asked after they'd left the dance floor.

"Tomorrow evening," Sandra said.

"And what about you, Joe? Do you plan to dance, too?" Caitlin asked the boy. He shook his head and said no, he was going to be a drummer.

Sandra steered Caitlin toward a food vendor she liked.

"My treat," Caitlin said. "I never would have known about this if it weren't for you."

They found a place to sit and eat, and Caitlin told Sandra she also had a gift for her. She gave her a small box containing a pair of silver hoop earrings.

"These are lovely!" Sandra said. "Thank you so much!"

"I hope you like them."

"Real silver? What's not to like!"

When they had finished eating, Sandra and her son returned to the competition and Caitlin left the arena. Much as she enjoyed seeing representatives of so many tribal nations, she needed to get back to Santa Fe.

"Bye Joe," Caitlin told the boy. "Keep drumming!"

"I'm so glad I got to see your son dance," she told Sandra before they parted ways. "And thank you again for introducing me to Lilly. Oh, and tell Scott he did a fabulous job! I'm really happy with how the songs turned out."

Caitlin was thrilled with what Scott was able to do in such a short time, especially for "Shining Star." She'd sent a CD to Luisa and was anxiously waiting for her feedback.

She hadn't told Paul—that she'd sent a demo to Luisa, that she knew he'd been married to her, or even that she was going to Albuquerque for the day. He rarely asked her what she was doing. If he had taken more of an interest—in her thoughts, her feelings, her aspirations, even her past—she might have shared more of herself with him.

The Playhouse kept him occupied—the current show, the next show, the cast, the board, the budget. These days, he was busy with rehearsals for *Angels in America*. He was unfamiliar with the director, and he wanted to keep a close eye on the show's progress until it opened, he'd said.

Caitlin didn't want to ruin his birthday celebrations, so she kept quiet about her upcoming departure. She was planning to take him out for a nice dinner on Saturday. His birthday would fall in the middle of the following week, and his surprise party would be held at Sheila and Ned's house that evening. Caitlin was bringing the cake.

After that, she thought, *we'll talk.*

∾ 43 ∾

Caitlin called Melody on Saturday to tell her she would be attending Mass in Jemez the following day. "I met the healer's granddaughter. Oh, and her name is Porcingula."

"The granddaughter?"

"No, the healer."

"Be sure to bring a tobacco offering."

"Cigarettes or loose tobacco or what?"

"I don't think it matters. You know there's a brand called Native Spirit or something like that. It might have fewer additives."

"Good idea," Caitlin said. "I'd like to bring a gift for Porcingula but I have no idea what she might need or want. I don't want to bring the wrong thing and offend her."

"Yeah, you probably don't want to bring her a blanket with a design from a different tribe or something."

"Maybe I'll just ask Lilly, her granddaughter."

"Can't hurt."

That evening, Caitlin took Paul out for dinner at Claude's bistro. She wanted his fiftieth birthday to be special, and Claude's had become their place for quiet, romantic evenings. When they returned to the house, they made sweet love.

She would miss their lovemaking, Caitlin thought as she lay awake listening to the far-off cry of coyotes. She looked over at Paul, sleeping soundly. She couldn't imagine being in Santa Fe and not being with him. He was so much a part of her life there. But in a new place? She might be too busy to miss anyone.

I won't miss the snoring, she thought as she reached for the earplugs she kept in a drawer in the nightstand. *Or the drinking. Or the constant phone calls.*

Would Paul miss her? she wondered. *Not for long.* The Playhouse kept him occupied. He met a lot of people there. He would find someone to keep him company, no doubt. *Angels in America* would be opening soon, and the Playhouse would be abuzz with activity. Paul would be in his element. He would hardly notice her absence.

In the morning, Caitlin fixed an early breakfast before leaving for Jemez Pueblo. She planned to allow plenty of time to find the church—and then find Lilly.

"You're going to Mass why?" Paul asked her before she left.

"A teenager from the pueblo invited me to meet her family."

"How come?"

Caitlin shrugged. She and Paul had never discussed spiritual matters. She didn't plan to start now. "Because I expressed interest in her culture," she said. "Her family is having lunch after Mass."

"All right. Maybe I'll go over and see Sheila and the kids," Paul said.

"Find out what time she wants us for dinner on Wednesday," Caitlin said.

"Oh, right. Dinner."

Paul knew they had plans for dinner; that part wasn't a surprise. What he didn't know was how many people had been invited.

"Oh, and would you give Stephanie her angel pin?" Caitlin retrieved the pin from a drawer and handed it to Paul. "I keep forgetting."

After Mass, Caitlin pulled Lilly aside and said, "I'd like to get a gift for your grandmother. Do you know what she might want or need?"

The girl thought for a moment and said, "She likes animals. People bring her wounded birds so she can take care of them. But I don't think she wants any pets." She thought a little longer and said, "Oh, I know! Candles. She uses lots of candles."

"Thanks, that's a great idea!" Caitlin said.

Lilly was wearing the bracelet Caitlin had given her. When she saw Caitlin eyeing it, she said, "She liked my bracelet. She likes turquoise, too. C'mon, let's go over to my auntie's house and I'll introduce you to everyone."

"I'm so honored to be here," Caitlin told Lilly's aunt, Estella.

Estella gestured to the kitchen table, where a buffet was spread out along with plates, napkins, and utensils. "Grab a plate," she said.

Caitlin hadn't known what kind of food to expect, but she recognized most of the dishes: a pot of chili, a green bean casserole, a bowl of macaroni and cheese, and a colorful gelatin dessert with marshmallows. Next to a tray of neatly arranged deviled eggs was a platter filled with chunks of cheddar cheese on one side and rolled-up slices of turkey held together by toothpicks on the other side.

Caitlin took a small amount of each food, not wanting to offend anyone by refusing their contribution—or by taking too much. Lilly appeared beside her and said, "My mom made the fry bread. Try it with cinnamon and honey."

Caitlin complied. "Mmm. Heavenly!" she said as she licked honey from her fingers.

She sat in a chair in the corner of the living room and observed the family and friends who had gathered to share a meal. The sense of community, of belonging, was evident.

As she ate the food on her plate, Caitlin thought about the times she'd been part of a community. Being so closely involved with Paul, she had been welcomed into Santa Fe's theater community. Yet, they didn't feel like her people, not in the way Lilly was woven into the fabric of her community, or even the way Melody and Shanti and Sable had bonded in Lu's group and continued to remain close friends. Caitlin had been blessed with good friendships throughout her life, but her friends were a diverse lot. She had loved college life, but most of those friendships had fallen away. Perhaps that sense of belonging was what she was searching for, she thought as she quietly ate the last of her lunch. A place where she could sink deep roots and build a meaningful life with kindred spirits.

One of Lilly's cousins came by with a pitcher of iced tea and asked if anyone wanted a refill. Caitlin smiled and held out her glass. She knew enough about the history of native peoples in the American West to know that their past had not been rosy. She sincerely hoped the future would bring peace and prosperity to the pueblo.

Lilly took Caitlin's plate from her and set it on a table. "Come with me," the girl said. "I'll introduce you to Grandmother."

Caitlin followed Lilly to an adjoining room, where several people were gathered around a wizened old woman who nodded and smiled often, revealing gaps where teeth were missing.

As Lilly and Caitlin stood before Porcingula, the teenager spoke to her grandmother in their Towa language. Caitlin watched intently and smiled when the old woman looked at her and nodded. The man sitting next to Porcingula offered Caitlin his chair, so she sat down. The woman turned toward her and gazed into her eyes. Then, she took Caitlin's hands in hers and closed her eyes, bowing her head slightly. After a few moments, she nodded and then spoke to Lilly.

"She says you can come to her and she will do a ceremony," Lilly told Caitlin.

Porcingula spoke again.

"The night before the new moon," Lilly said.

"When is the new moon?" Caitlin asked Lilly.

"I don't know," she said. She asked her grandmother and then said, "The new moon is Wednesday night," Lilly said.

"So I would come back on Tuesday night?"

"Yes," Lilly said. "You can meet me here and I will take you to Grandmother. We usually finish with dinner by seven o'clock."

"Seven o'clock," Caitlin repeated. "Okay, I'll see you then." She smiled and bowed her head toward Porcingula, and then thanked Estella for her hospitality before walking to her car.

The next day, Caitlin went shopping for tobacco, candles, and turquoise. She hadn't known that turquoise came in so many varieties and colors—or that much of the turquoise sold commercially is treated with additives. She bought the most natural turquoise stones—and tobacco—she could find as well as an assortment of unscented candles.

She arrived at Jemez Pueblo on Tuesday and parked in the lot by the post office. Carrying a box full of gifts, she walked the dusty road to Estella's house. Lilly was waiting for her and led the way to a small one-bedroom adobe house with a flat roof not far from the Jemez River.

Inside Porcingula's simple home, Caitlin was surprised to see Christian art alongside native crafts and furnishings. *Well, she is Catholic after all.*

Several candles had been placed around the room, the hot wax caught by small dishes that looked handmade. A blanket was spread on the floor of the living room, and a white buckskin had been laid on top of it. Assorted objects were arranged on the buckskin, including several bowls, a large feather, a tortoise shell, and a gourd rattle painted with symbols of the sun, moon, and stars. Lying in the center was a prayer stick.

Porcingula wore a woven belt around her waist and strings of shells and beads around her neck. Turquoise-and-silver jewelry adorned her wrists and fingers. She sat on a cushion on the floor and gestured for Caitlin to take a seat opposite her. Lilly sat in a chair in the corner of the room.

The old woman picked up the rattle and shook it as she chanted in her native language. She gazed into a bowl of water for a long while. Then she gazed at Caitlin for a long while.

She took some of the tobacco Caitlin had brought and sprinkled it into the tortoise shell along with crushed herbs she took from another bowl. She handed the shell to Lilly, who lit the mixture before handing the shell back to her. Porcingula then picked up the feather and spread the smoke in Caitlin's direction while she chanted.

Caitlin closed her eyes and tried not to cough. When she opened her eyes, Porcingula was putting the turquoise stones Caitlin had brought into four small piles around the prayer stick. Caitlin guessed that they represented the four directions, but she wasn't sure.

Porcingula motioned for Lilly to come and help her get up off the floor. Holding a bowl full of cornmeal, she stood behind Caitlin and sprinkled some of it over her head.

Aside from feeling uncomfortable when the smoke wafted into her face, Caitlin hadn't felt much of anything up to this point. Now she felt an almost uncontrollable desire to laugh. Not wanting to appear ungrateful or disrespectful, she fought the urge by thinking about how much she missed her father. Thinking of him often still brought tears to her eyes. Still, the desire to laugh was overpowering, and Caitlin couldn't help but smile as she sat being showered with cornmeal. But it wasn't only because she found the situation amusing. She felt something she hadn't felt in a long, long time: unbridled joy. She wanted to jump up and hug the old woman. Knowing that such an emotional outburst would be inappropriate, she waited, as patiently as she could, for the ceremony to end.

Lilly handed the prayer stick to her grandmother, who gestured to Caitlin to stand facing her. Lilly translated when Porcingula spoke. "It is because you are kin to us in spirit that I am able to help you." She held the prayer stick out to Caitlin and spoke again.

"You must go to the sacred land tomorrow, when the moon begins her monthly journey, and plant this prayer stick into the earth. There, you must pray that the pieces of your soul that have flown away will return to you," Lilly said.

Caitlin looked from the old woman to the young girl and said, "But I don't know where the sacred land is."

Porcingula understood and addressed Caitlin's concern. "But you have been there," Lilly said. "You have seen."

Caitlin stood, bewildered, for a moment before she realized what the woman was talking about. "Oh! The land near Pecos?"

Porcingula smiled and nodded and squeezed Caitlin's hand. "You go," she said.

"Okay," said Caitlin, nodding. "I'll go. Tomorrow."

She said goodnight to Porcingula and walked with Lilly to her house. After thanking her again for her help, she continued walking to her car. She felt strangely hopeful about her life and her future.

With no moonlight and few streetlights in the village, she stumbled down the road in a state akin to intoxication. She had no idea what time it was. That she would find herself here, wandering down a dusty road in a remote Indian village late at night, was a bit surreal if she really thought about it.

A long way from Kansas indeed!

The parking lot at the post office was well lit. As she slowly walked toward it, Caitlin gazed up at the canopy of stars overhead, awed by the sheer number of luminaries in the heavens.

Paul was reading a book when Caitlin joined him in bed. She kissed him on the cheek and said "Good night" before putting in her earplugs and drifting into a peaceful slumber.

∾ 44 ∾

*P*aul was still asleep when Caitlin left the house on Wednesday morning. She wanted to arrive at the national park as soon as it opened. She had promised to help Sheila prepare for Paul's party, and she wasn't sure how long this adventure would take.

She parked her car in the same spot as two years before, when she was on her way to Santa Fe. This time, she went inside the visitor center and looked around. She learned that the pueblo, built early in the fourteenth century, had been inhabited until 1838, when the last residents abandoned the village and crossed mesas, mountains, and the Rio Grande River to arrive at Walatowa, home to the Jemez, who spoke a similar dialect. The two tribes were merged by an act of Congress in 1936. The land that had been home to the Pecos people for hundreds of years was now part of the national park.

Situated on an upper branch of the Pecos River, Cicuyé Pueblo was a thriving community of more than 2,000 people when the Spaniards arrived in the sixteenth century—and renamed the pueblo. Franciscan Fray Andrés Juárez had a great church erected there early in the seventeenth century, but it was destroyed during the Pueblo Revolt of 1680. Disease, raids by other tribes, and poor treatment at the hands of the Spanish led to the demise of the Pecos people, who numbered just over one hundred at the beginning of the nineteenth century.

Once a thriving center of trade, Pecos Pueblo had lost its dominance by 1821, when the Santa Fe Trail brought a new wave of traders bound for Santa Fe. Mexico had just won its independence from Spain, and the territory known as New Mexico would be annexed by the United States in 1848, at the end of the Mexican–American War.

The ruins of the pueblo buildings, the mission church built by the Franciscans, and surrounding areas were excavated by an archaeologist early in the twentieth century. Thousands of skeletons and other artifacts were shipped to a museum in Massachusetts. In 1990, Congress passed an act requiring the return of human remains and some funerary artifacts to the living descendants and culturally affiliated tribes. The largest repatriation to date occurred in 1999, when nearly two thousand remains and artifacts dating to the twelfth century were returned to Pecos.

The remains were reburied in a historic ceremony. Retracing the route that their ancestors had walked in 1838, some Pecos descendants, joined by their Jemez neighbors, walked for three days to their ancestral homeland, which they still considered a sacred site. Many more arrived in vehicles. A procession was led by the current Pecos Governor. The Governor of Jemez was also there, along with representatives of the Massachusetts museum and the commissioner of New Mexico's Office of Indian Affairs.

Caitlin asked a volunteer at the visitor center about the site where the ceremony had taken place the year before. "It's closed to the public," she was told.

A couple of middle-aged tourists asked about the trail to the mission church that had been built just south of the pueblo. When they exited the building, Caitlin followed. She walked slowly to put some distance between herself and the couple. When they veered off toward the church, she walked in the other direction, toward the spot she had seen from a distance two years earlier.

The wind blew her hair into her face. She pulled a hat out of her pack as she considered where—and how—to plant the prayer stick she had brought with her. She knew the removal of ancient artifacts was against the law, but what about leaving something there? She wouldn't be littering, but she would, in a sense, be interfering with the site.

As she reached the top of the mesa, she saw two poles protruding from a hole in the ground and surrounded by a stone circle. Walking closer, she realized that the poles were part of a ladder, and the hole was the entrance to a kiva. She looked around and, seeing no one, climbed down the ladder.

"Great, now I'm trespassing on federal property," she muttered.

But I was given permission by Pecos Woman herself! she imagined saying in her defense.

Ah, but law enforcement authorities would arrest Porcingula as readily as any other trespasser, Caitlin knew.

She hadn't seen any signs that said entry was not permitted, but knowing that she had been asked to perform a sacred ceremony here, she felt keenly aware of the need to be discreet and not attract attention.

The roof of the kiva was made of wood beams, which the earth above concealed. The circular enclosure contained a firepit but nothing else. The underground space was illuminated by a shaft of light streaming through the entrance. The walls, made of plastered adobe, seemed stark and bare without any images painted on them.

Turning to look around, Caitlin understood what Porcingula had meant when she told her to stand "in the center" and honor the directions by sprinkling the cornmeal she'd been given. She removed the pouch with the cornmeal from her backpack, and after taking a moment to quietly center herself, she spread the contents in each of the four directions, starting with the east.

Next, she was to lie on the ground with her palms open and ready to receive. She was to stay this way until she received a message, however long that took.

What if a message never came? Caitlin wondered as she lay still. How long would she wait? How long before tourists would start to arrive—or park rangers?

She zipped up her jacket and tried to relax. She was safe here in this womblike chamber, she reminded herself. Safe from storms and coyotes. And snakes! She closed her eyes and was drifting into a twilight state when she heard a familiar voice inside her head.

"The cat is back!" the voice said.

Caitlin jumped to her feet. She was not alone.

As if she'd been transported back in time, she saw images of people dressed in their native attire. They looked worn and solemn. Some danced; others shook rattles and banged on drums.

Caitlin looked down at her own clothes. She wore a blanket that was knotted at one shoulder; a woven belt like the one Porcingula wore circled her waist. Her hands were bony and wrinkled. Her legs were wrapped, and on her feet she wore leather moccasins. She knew that this dance was one last desperate attempt to save the pueblo. She was old; she would not leave. She would die in the place where she had lived her entire life. And her people would not leave until they had performed the traditional rites after her death.

Caitlin wept. She had been there before, she knew, just as surely as she was there now. As a toddler, she had been rescued from the clutches of a bobcat, a type of lynx. Her face was scarred for life, but the mark was no disgrace; it was more like a badge. When the bobcat was killed, its spirit was transferred to her, granting her psychic powers and creating an affinity with the animal kingdom in general—and with cats in particular.

Or so we believed, Caitlin thought.

Bobcat Woman had helped many during her lifetime, but at her death her heart was heavy. Her people had been conquered, decimated, and driven from their village. Caitlin still carried that sadness within her.

But she sensed that healing was possible, and not just for her. She removed the prayer stick from her pack. It was painted with white, black, red, and yellow stripes. A feather had been tied to the stick with string.

Caitlin prayed for all her relations, past and present—for everyone in her vast circle of kinship, throughout time. Then she planted the prayer stick firmly in the ground.

After climbing the ladder and exiting the kiva, she shielded her face from the bright sun while her eyes adjusted. Then, she walked farther down the trail, to an overlook where she could view the landscape. She would not gaze upon this site again, she knew. When she felt ready to leave, she turned and walked slowly back to the parking lot, too overcome with emotion to question the workings of the psyche—or the universe.

～ 45 ～

*S*am washed the pots and pans after the noon meal. He felt strangely agitated, for no apparent reason. Outwardly, not much had changed in the last two months.

He'd been keeping to himself more than usual, going for walks along the river or holing up in his cell in his spare time. He went about his chores and didn't leave the property.

Father Moore had suspended his vehicle privileges after his late-night return from Santa Fe. The abbot hadn't asked a lot of questions, but Sam had felt the need to explain. He told Father Moore about the anguish he'd felt upon discovering that "an old girlfriend" was in town, and his need for resolution.

"Seeing her that night helped me achieve that, I think," Sam said. "I didn't need to talk to her. I just needed to see her."

Maybe his confession helped put the abbot's mind at ease, assuring him that Sam's infraction was no more serious than pining for an old flame. It wasn't like he was out dealing drugs or selling the Abbey's art collection or planning a terrorist act. To Sam's relief, Father Moore hadn't lectured him or punished him or asked him to leave. He merely told him to look deep inside of himself to discern what he needed to do next—and whether the Abbey was the place for him to do it.

He had been doing just that. The heated discussion on the street between Caitlin and Neil had made a strong impression on him. That they had been able to go back to the restaurant after that scene surprised him. Working through problems had never been his strong suit. Shutting down all opposition had been his unstated objective, but that was no way to build healthy relationships.

He was, he realized, finally ready to begin to mend his relationships with his family. His request for permission to make a long-distance phone call to his mother was granted. From the notes and postcards he had been dropping her now and then, she'd have been able to tell that he was in New Mexico, but he'd never said precisely where. He'd never given her a way to contact him. He just wanted everyone to know he was all right, and that he was thinking of them. Beyond that, he hadn't had much to say.

He hadn't called her yet. He was still pondering what he wanted to do. But his agitation was building, as if prodding him to get on with it.

He took a deep breath and walked toward the building where the telephone was located.

Time to bite the bullet.

∾ 46 ∾

*C*aitlin was hardly in the mood for a party when she returned to Santa Fe from Pecos. She showered and then dressed in a colorful flowing skirt paired with a beige top. After choosing a belt and suede boots, she added a bracelet, earrings, and Sable's labyrinth pin. She looked at her reflection in the full-length mirror. Something was missing.

The top was too plain, she decided. She wrapped a silk scarf around her neck. Now she was ready. She went downstairs and picked up her keys.

Paul was in the kitchen, looking through the mail. Caitlin kissed him on the cheek and said, "I'll go on ahead and help Sheila get things ready." She started walking toward the garage but paused when the phone rang.

Paul picked up the receiver. "Thanks, hon," he told the caller.

Caitlin turned toward him, wondering who he would call "hon" besides her. After a few moments, she concluded that the caller was Luisa.

Caitlin still had not mentioned the demo to Paul—and he would not be happy if the first he heard about it was from his ex-wife. He looked up as he said, "Sure, hang on. She's right here." Holding out the phone to Caitlin, he said, "Luisa called to wish me happy birthday, but she wants a quick word with you."

"O-ka-ay," Caitlin said tentatively. "Hi Luisa," she said into the phone.

"Thanks for sending the CD," Lu said. "I liked your songs, and I think you would like our little group here. Why don't you come out and meet everyone? We're in the midst of recording an album. You could sing backup on a few of our songs, and we've got the studio through the end of next week, so if you'd like to record one or two of your songs, the Road Angels can back you up as well. How does that sound?"

"That sounds great. Can we talk about this tomorrow? I'm on my way over to Sheila's. Paul won't be joining me for another hour or so, so you can continue catching up with him." Caitlin looked directly at Paul as she said, "I can fill him in on your news later on, if that's okay."

"I get it," Luisa said. "You want to tell him yourself. I won't say a word."

Caitlin smiled and handed the phone back to Paul. "I'll see you over there," she said before quickly exiting.

She had put together a scrapbook of mementos of her time with Paul—a collection of newspaper clippings, photographs, ticket stubs and the like—and she hoped to give that to him after the party, if he was still sober. If not, she would wait until the following morning.

She drove to the bakery to pick up the cake she had ordered and took it to Ned and Sheila's house. *It's been grand,* she thought as she walked to the front door. *But let's quit while we're ahead.*

Twenty of Paul's friends had been invited to the celebration in honor of his fiftieth birthday, but only a few had arrived early to help with decorations and last-minute preparations.

"Where are the kids?" Caitlin asked when she realized the house was strangely quiet.

"Spending the night with friends," Sheila said. "I promised to save them some cake."

Caitlin took a picture of the cake and then helped Sheila spread a tablecloth. She arranged a centerpiece for the table and greeted guests at the door. She had met most of them before, though several people brought dates that she didn't know. When Paul arrived, she steered him into the kitchen, where Ned and Sheila were busily getting ready to serve dinner, buffet style.

"Where are the kids?" Paul asked.

"You might check the living room," Sheila said casually before glancing at Caitlin and grinning.

Caitlin hurried around to the other entrance to the living room so she could take a few photographs as the guests all shouted, "Surprise!"

Mission accomplished, she thought as she returned to the kitchen. She put on an apron and then carried a stack of plates to the dining room. After everyone else had helped themselves to the buffet, she filled a plate and took a seat in the living room.

"And there's the lovely Caitlin," Paul said when he saw her. "I suspect she had something to do with this event." He winked at her.

Caitlin shrugged and feigned innocence.

"As some of you die-hard theater fans may know, I'll be directing *Taming of the Shrew* this summer, and I'll also be playing Petruchio. Caitlin won't agree to be my Katharina, though," Paul told the group. "She wanted a break to work on her songs, and the Bard doesn't seem to interest her much," he said with a chuckle.

Feeling like the laugh was at her expense, Caitlin didn't respond.

"She's no shrew, though, I can assure you," Paul added. He held up his glass to her from across the room.

Caitlin smiled politely and then joined Sheila in the kitchen. Sheila closed a drawer and said, "Um, did you happen to bring any candles for the cake?"

"Oops."

"Yeah, we overlooked that detail."

"I'll run out," Caitlin said. "I know just where to find some." She must have seen every candle in Santa Fe while shopping for something to bring Porcingula.

The party supply store at a nearby shopping center was still open and had large wax numbers to put on the cake. Caitlin bought a "5" and a "0" and drove back to the party. She sang along when "Refugee" by Tom Petty and the Heartbreakers came on the radio.

She parked next to Paul's Mercedes and removed the key from the ignition. She was about to get out of the car when she suddenly felt disoriented. Closing her eyes, she was shown a ceremony in a cave.

Melody was there. They were both priestesses, but it was she, not Melody, who had been chosen to succeed the oracle, the Pythia.

Though prophecies were no longer delivered in the name of the Goddess since the installation of the priests of Apollo, the temple at Delphi was the stuff of legends, and the Pythia was one of the most powerful women of her time.

As quickly as the image of ancient Greece faded, another temple appeared. These images were similar to those Caitlin had seen during the last performance of *Park Avenue*. Neil's army killed Paul before entering the temple and restraining Kimo; then, they hauled her away. Heartbroken, she was taken to a cold, dank cell.

Next, she was running from flowing lava after a volcanic eruption. She tripped and fell and everything went black. But then . . . there was light.

And then she was back at the Shannon Pot, standing with her back to Kimo, both of them dressed in animal skins. Her eyes widened as she again watched the lynx leap toward her. She heard the voice she'd heard at Pecos; it was telling her not to resist. And then she bounded over the path of hot coals as if possessed by the spirit of the cat.

Bobcat Woman, Caitlin thought.

"It was real," she whispered. "It was all real."

But the torrent of images was not over. The angry face of Sam Burns appeared, moments before the Crash. The traffic light had just turned green. Caitlin had looked into the rear view mirror. Headlights were rapidly approaching. As she drove onto the bridge in Alexandria, nearly home, she glanced over at the black GMC that was now beside her. She looked into the angry face of Sam Burns before he gave the steering wheel a sharp turn and swerved into her car, forcing it into the cement barrier.

"Oh my God!" Caitlin shrieked, over and over. It was Sam Burns who had crashed into her that day. And he had done it intentionally. The Crash wasn't an accident.

Caitlin closed her eyes, but the image of Sam's face would not go away. Hunched over the steering wheel, she sat in the car and sobbed.

When she finally opened her eyes, Caitlin realized that the sky was dark. *How long have I been sitting here?* she wondered.

When she felt ready to face the guests at the party, she entered the house and put the candles on the kitchen counter. Sheila emerged from the living room and asked, impatiently, "Where have you been?" Seeing the state Caitlin was in, her tone changed. "You look terrible! What happened?"

"You wouldn't believe me if I told you," Caitlin said wearily. "Go ahead and serve dessert. I'll go freshen up."

She walked to the powder room and splashed cold water on her face, glad she hadn't had time earlier to put on any makeup. She heard the group singing "Happy Birthday" to Paul and hoped someone had snapped a photo.

Returning to the kitchen, she picked up the plate of cake and ice cream Sheila had set aside for her. She found a clean fork and walked into the living room, choosing a chair at the edge of the room, not far from the front door.

"There she is!" Paul announced as she sat down. "Hey, sweetheart, how about a song to go with dessert?"

"Oh, no, really, I—"

"Aw, come on. This is no time to be shy!" Paul pressed. "It's my birthday. You can't deny me my birthday wish."

Someone brought her a guitar. Reluctantly, Caitlin put down her plate. She searched her mind for a quiet song. Only one came to mind, and it was blessedly short.

"All right, well, this is a work in progress," she said. "I'm calling it 'My Choice.'" She strummed the guitar and sang:

> I've always known it was
> My choice
> Not to go
> I stayed and played the game
> Your way
> The way you
> Said to play
> You don't listen
> Anyway
> Why?
> Tell me why should I
> Stay
> And go along
> Anymore
> The game is over
> It's time
> For me to find
> A piece of mine

It's up
To me to cut
The ties
That keep me
Stranded
By your side
It's up
To me to find
A better way
My way
And so
I choose to go

Caitlin didn't look up once as she sang. When the song ended, she quietly set aside the guitar and picked up her plate. The ice cream had melted.

The room was quiet for a moment until, finally, Paul started clapping slowly and others followed suit. A few people took their dishes to the kitchen, excusing themselves with remarks about how late it was and they really must be going. "Need to relieve the babysitter," one said. Soon, only Paul and Caitlin remained.

Paul poured himself a drink and said, "Got something you want to tell me?" before again sitting on the couch, across the room from Caitlin.

"Yeah, I kinda do actually," Caitlin said after eating the last bite of her cake. "I hadn't really planned on it happening this way, but you pushed. As you so often do."

"Apparently."

"I'm sorry if I embarrassed you."

"Oh, hell, you know I don't embarrass easily. It will all be forgotten soon enough. What's on your mind?"

"I was going to wait until tomorrow, after I've talked to Lu more, but she mentioned something earlier about maybe having me sing backup on a few songs. Her group is making an album, I guess. She offered to help me get a couple of my songs recorded while I'm there."

"You'd sing with the Road Angels?" Paul asked.

"Uh-huh," Caitlin said, too exhausted to be excited about the plan—or anything.

"Interesting group," Paul said, sloshing the liquor in his glass around. "You might like them."

"Let's talk about this tomorrow," Caitlin said. "It's been a really long day." She walked over to Paul and leaned down and kissed his cheek. "I really didn't want to ruin your birthday."

She took her plate to the kitchen and said goodbye to Sheila and Ned.

"Sorry I can't stay to help you clean up," Caitlin said.

"Don't worry about it," Sheila said.

"I might not see you again," Caitlin told her before giving her a long hug.

"I heard," Sheila said. "Congrats. If it's what you want."

Caitlin nodded. "It is." She hugged Ned and then told the pair, "Say goodbye to the kids for me," before leaving with Paul.

Back at Paul's house, Caitlin undressed and got into bed. Paul put his arm around her. She moved away when he started snoring, wondering what kinds of dreams she would have that night.

They couldn't be any stranger than this day has been.

∾ 47 ∾

*I*n the morning, Caitlin cut up fresh strawberries and scrambled some eggs while Paul read the newspaper in the living room. She put two slices of bread in the toaster and then walked over to the stereo.

Something soothing, she thought as she looked through Paul's music collection. She inserted a compact disc of Native American flute music into the CD player and pushed Play.

"Breakfast is ready," she told Paul on her way back to the kitchen.

He set aside the paper and brought his mug to the kitchen table.

"Oh, let's eat in the dining room," Caitlin said as she carried their plates to the adjoining room. "There's more space." She was eager to show Paul the scrapbook she had made for him.

They ate in silence. After they'd finished, they looked through the scrapbook together, reminiscing about good times and laughing over awkward moments.

Caitlin pointed to a photo of the two of them at the fundraising event they had hosted at Paul's house in the fall. Paul was open-mouthed, mid-sentence, and Caitlin was leaning away from him, scowling.

"Remember this?" Caitlin asked. "You'd just suggested that maybe we should host all the fundraisers here."

"We raised more that night than we ever had," Paul said. "And it was fun. This house is great for entertaining. That's part of why I bought it."

"Yeah, well, all *you* had to do was show up! I'm the one who organized it all. Once, I didn't mind. Much. But twice a year? Every year? No thanks!"

The next fundraising event—the following day—was again being held at the Chapmans' house. Caitlin would be on her way to L.A. by then.

Paul closed the scrapbook and said, "That's a thoughtful gift. I'll cherish it always."

Caitlin cleared the dishes from the table and loaded the dishwasher. "Will you be here for dinner?" she asked Paul when he set his mug on the counter.

"If we can eat early. I want to check in on the rehearsal since I missed it last night."

"I'll pick up some steaks," Caitlin said, adding the mug to the dishwasher before starting it. "I'm thinking of driving out to Tesuque to see Melody this afternoon."

"Okay," Paul said. "I'm heading to the gym."

After he left the house, Caitlin retrieved her suitcases from the closet in the spare bedroom.

She remembered Sam's house in California—and how he had shredded her clothes while she was at the Ananda Center. The image of his face, moments before the Crash, still haunted her. *Vile man!*

Knowing she'd had sex with Sam made her want to crawl out of her skin. He had touched her, been inside her. How could she live with this knowledge? How could she cleanse herself of him, forget him?

As she packed her sweaters, she paused, remembering how she had longed to have her memories back—and now she did.

I'd rather know the truth than be kept in the dark. If remembering means I have to remember all of it—the pleasure and the pain, the successes and the failures, I can live with that. That's life; that's relationships. You can't just take the good parts. You have to take the whole package. Or not.

She didn't have to *stay* in a bad relationship, and she could get smarter about her choices, pay attention to the warning signs.

Paul had his faults, but he'd never harmed her. He was hard on her when she was in a show, but that was understandable. The Playhouse was his arena. As a partner, his flaws had more to do with omissions, things he didn't do.

Caitlin realized that, as far as Paul knew, their relationship was humming along just fine. He was happy; he had what he wanted. They didn't ever talk about what was going on between them or share their innermost thoughts. Caitlin hadn't seen any point in complaining. She enjoyed the parts that were good and tolerated the rest, knowing the relationship would end at some point. That time had arrived.

She packed all she could fit into the suitcases and then called Melody to tell her the news: she was leaving for California. "What would you think about taking care of Lucky for a while?" she asked.

"I could do that," Melody said. "I'm home more these days, with my massage practice here. He can join me when I see clients if he wants to. Cats are great healers, you know."

Caitlin looked over at Lucky and smiled. "Yes," she said. "They are."

She decided she would stop by The Golden Door and buy a gift for Melody on her way to Tesuque. But first she wanted to talk to Luisa.

"It's the lawyer in me," she told Lucky as she gathered up his toys. Until she and Lu had discussed their arrangement, she would spend her time getting organized.

She would need to take Lucky's cat carrier and litter box to Melody's. And his food and bowls. She should also write Melody a check to cover expenses.

Anything else? she wondered as she looked around at the pile of boxes and belongings she had brought downstairs.

She hadn't accumulated much during her time in Santa Fe—clothes, mostly, and those she would take with her, along with her guitar and cooler and snacks for the road.

And my pillow. I want my own pillow.

Some things, like kitchen supplies and bedding, she hadn't needed at Paul's house; those boxes were already packed. She would need a few more boxes for the other things she wasn't taking with her. Maybe she should rent a small storage unit. She wanted to travel light, and Melody's place wasn't very big.

Best if I don't leave anything here. Paul might think I'm coming back.

A clean break would be easier. As far as their relationship was concerned, she was already gone.

∞ 48 ∞

Sam checked the glove compartment before driving away from the Abbey of San Miguel for the last time. No pistol.

No matter. He didn't anticipate needing it, and Ananda wouldn't allow weapons on the property anyway.

The monks had been gracious about his departure. They filled the tank of his truck with fuel and offered up a Mass for him as a way of honoring the completion of his time in the community.

When Sam brought his habit to the abbot's office, Father Moore rose from his desk to greet him. He said he appreciated Sam's contributions to the Abbey, his care in tending the gardens. Brother Gregory brought an envelope, which Father Moore handed to Sam. With his right hand, the abbot made the sign of the cross and told Sam to "go in peace" before returning to his desk.

Sam didn't open the envelope until he got to his truck. Inside, he found one hundred dollars. Whether there had been cash in his wallet when Brother Vincent and Brother Theodore found him, he couldn't say, but the money would help him get where he needed to go. His credit cards were all expired. If he ran out of funds, he would have to call his mother.

"Come home, son," she had said when Sam called her the day before.

"What home?"

The women had figured out a way to rent out his house, he learned. They were all angry at him—his ex-wife, his sister, his mother; they didn't care if he would be unhappy about their actions. None of them were the type to stand by and do nothing, and bills needed to be paid.

They all knew about his abrupt departure. His sister had spoken to his supervisor at the base when no one had been able to reach him for weeks. They didn't suspect foul play, so no one filed a missing person's report. Sam couldn't be presumed dead until five years had passed with no sign of him surfacing anywhere. All anyone could do was wait.

Sam understood. He *had* behaved irresponsibly, and he knew, in calling his mother, he would be chided for it. That was part of why he hadn't called sooner. He had to be ready to listen. And he'd had his own rage to deal with.

Yes, it had been selfish of him to take off and not tell anyone. But he'd been in bad shape at the time and didn't care about anything or anyone. He didn't think any of them cared about him. He didn't know where he was going—or if he would ever return.

"You always have a home here, with me," Satchidananda said.

Sam had paused a good long while to let that idea settle.

Maybe he could stomach staying at the Ananda Center now, after his time at the Abbey. At least at Ananda people talked to each other. Some people took vows of silence for periods of time, and silent retreats were offered regularly, but there were also programs that taught communication skills, and time was allotted for residents to share their views—and their feelings—about various matters.

Sam figured he could probably benefit from living in the community for a while. He knew he wasn't ready to return to secular life just yet, not after two-and-a-half years at a monastery. Visitors regularly streamed through Ananda—program participants, devotees, guests of residents. Maybe he would meet some interesting people.

He wouldn't need to live with his mother—whom he would have to refer to as Satchidananda when speaking of her at the Center. She rented a one-bedroom apartment. She said she would find him a room while he waited for the housing committee to assign him a place to stay—when one opened up. There would be a trial period of living in the community, and then, if all went well, he would be approved as a "long-term visitor." If he wanted to stay.

He'd be starting over wherever he went, and he had little desire to return to his house in the desert. Maybe he would sell it. He would deal with all that after he was back in the area.

He understood now the importance of a clear conscience, and of making amends. He would do his part to reestablish a relationship with his mother and his sister. He would apologize to Yvonne for not taking her concerns about vaccine safety more seriously. He would get to know Jacqueline. He was even willing to investigate alternative treatments that might help her. He wouldn't fight Yvonne every time she wanted him to contribute to the cost of some of the wacky therapies that were, in his view, peddled by quacks.

Maybe someday he could bring himself to apologize to Caitlin Rose. He was glad to see that she had recovered and was living a full life. She didn't seem to have a lot of lingering challenges or impaired functioning, as far as he could see. She was in a relationship and pursuing a new career path. She was all right. He could stop worrying about her and focus on finding a new direction for his own life.

He felt fully alive, and, for the first time in years, optimistic about his future. Not a reach-for-the-stars kind of optimism; a calm, serene, and steady assuredness that he *had* a future.

He would try to arrive at the Ananda Center before Mother's Day, he thought as he turned onto Interstate 25. That was over a week away. He could take his time getting there and camp along the way, explore some of the natural beauty of the West. Maybe he would stop at the Grand Canyon.

And the ocean. He really missed the ocean.

∾ 49 ∾

*D*éjà vu, Caitlin thought as she carried Lucky's carrier to Melody's front door.

Melody opened the door and said "Hi there, old friend" to Lucky as she took the carrier from Caitlin.

"Thanks," Caitlin said. "I didn't know where else to take him." She set Lucky's food and water dishes on the floor in the kitchen and then returned to the car for his litter box.

"Where do you want this?"

"Mmm—right there by the door, I guess," Melody said, pointing.

"I'll miss you," Caitlin told Lucky. "But I'm sure Melody will take good care of you until we meet again."

"Oh, yeah. We'll be fine. You go be brilliant!" Melody said.

"I've got something for you, too," Caitlin said. "Be right back!"

She'd found a large gong at The Golden Door and thought Melody might like it for her yoga and sound healing classes.

Melody banged the gong with the mallet that came with it. "I love it!" she said as the tone reverberated. "I'll put it in my treatment room for now."

"And here's a check," Caitlin said. "For food and kitty litter and whatever else. I've written down the vet's number, in case anything comes up."

"When do you leave?"

"In the morning. Assuming I get everything done."

"You will." Melody hugged her and said, "Give my best to Lu. Now scoot!"

"I'm not abandoning you," Caitlin told Lucky before she left.

Still, she felt like she was. She was surprised at how attached she had become to her feline friend.

"Okay, time to switch gears," she murmured as she moved the gear selector from "park" to "drive."

After racing back to Santa Fe, she secured a small storage unit.

She bought packing tape and a few empty boxes while she was there and then headed to the grocery store.

Kebabs might be an easy dinner, she thought, picking up beef, onions and potatoes, red and yellow bell peppers, and mushrooms.

Back at Paul's house, Caitlin cut the beef into cubes and mixed a marinade in a bowl. She added the meat, put the bowl in the refrigerator, and then took the empty boxes upstairs.

Hoping to take a load to storage before Paul got back, she hurriedly packed books, paint supplies, and files into separate boxes and then piled the boxes into her car. She set out the skewers for the kebabs and left a note for Paul. Then she drove back to the storage facility.

Paul had started grilling the kebabs and was opening a bottle of red wine when Caitlin returned. "I'm ready for some of that!" she said when she saw the wine.

She was happy to stop rushing around and eager to enjoy a relaxing dinner before resuming packing. Paul would be out for the evening; she would have time to herself to wash her hair and call her mother and plan her route.

They ate dinner outside on the deck, as they often did when the weather was nice. To Caitlin's relief, they talked and joked as if this wasn't their last night together. But then Paul removed a small box from his pocket and said, "I know why you have to leave. But I'm hoping I can entice you to return." He set the box on the table and slowly pushed it toward Caitlin.

Caitlin stared at the box, wide-eyed. She really didn't want to have to do this.

"Open it," Paul said.

Curious, Caitlin opened the lid. *Maybe it's not what I think it is.*

It was.

She didn't remove the ring from the box. "It's beautiful, Paul," she said. "Really. It is."

He leaned back in his chair and sighed. "But."

Caitlin leaned over and grasped his hand. "But I'm not coming back. I'm sorry."

"You're not happy here?"

"I have been happy—with you, with the Playhouse. But

long-term . . ." She shook her head. "You've built a life here. I need to do the same, somewhere."

"Why can't you do that here? You can make trips to L.A., like I do."

"You know, you never once asked me to come with you on any of those trips," Caitlin said. "Well, it doesn't matter now." She shrugged. "Santa Fe just doesn't feel like home to me." She closed the lid of the ring box. "That's the bottom line."

"I thought we were pretty good together," Paul said, taking back the ring. "Well, you know where to find me, if you change your mind."

"We were good in some ways. But this is your home. The Playhouse is your theater. We spend time with your family, and we go out with your friends. When was the last time we had my friends over?" She knew the answer to that was "Never."

"We could," Paul said.

"But we don't. It's not entirely your fault. I've been content to lose myself in your world. I think I knew it wouldn't work any other way. Or that's what I believed anyway, whether it was true or not."

"Where will you go?" Paul asked.

"I don't know. I'll see what happens when I'm in L.A. That's where I was headed when I first came here. I'm sure it's all leading somewhere. I just can't see where yet."

After a pause, Paul asked, "Did you ever love me? Because I love you. You know that, right?"

"I know," Caitlin said.

Paul had never actually said the words before, never even signed a card "Love Paul." It wouldn't have mattered, but if Caitlin had wanted a long-term relationship, those kinds of gestures would have been important to her.

Her eyes filled with tears. "There's so much that I'm grateful for. You've given me a home for nearly two years. You made it safe for me to try new things, and you've always encouraged me to follow my dreams. This is a big step for me, and there are no guarantees. I'll always remember what we've shared. But there's a different life waiting for me now."

"Well, I had to ask," Paul said, putting the ring box in his pocket. "I wouldn't want to think back and wonder."

Caitlin smiled, remembering their first meeting, at her audition. "Yeah, then *you'd* be a wonderin' fool."

Paul understood the reference. "We'll always have Polaris," he said, looking up at the sky.

No stars were yet visible, but they had spent many evenings gazing at the heavens and pointing to the few constellations they knew.

"Here's lookin' at you," Caitlin said before drinking the last of her wine. "Nice meal."

"You made it easy for me."

Caitlin smiled. "I tried," she said. "No regrets."

"Nah, me neither."

Paul squeezed her shoulder before taking his plate inside.

Caitlin feigned sleep when Paul came to bed later that night. She had nothing more to say to him, nothing more to give.

Some people are only meant to be in our lives for a season or two, she thought. That didn't diminish their importance, but it did limit the possibilities. No matter how much they both might want a particular outcome, the choice was not always theirs to make. Their souls had come together with an agenda that superseded human desires and wishes. Their souls would lead them where they needed to go.

The stirrings of the soul could be silenced for a while, Caitlin had learned, but they couldn't be banished. The more her awareness of the spiritual dimension deepened, the more willing she was to follow where she was led, even when she didn't know the reason.

She knew that kind of faith was foreign to most people. They couldn't understand how she could just pick up and go. Her life in Santa Fe was comfortable. What was the problem? They wouldn't understand the changes she was going through, that her spiritual life was becoming her priority. They would think she was being unrealistic or ungrateful or too picky. They'd say things like "Every place has its problems" or "You may never find what you're looking for" or "The perfect man doesn't exist," as if she hadn't already come to those conclusions and needed to be stopped from making an awful mistake. They would think she was crazy for wanting to join a group of traveling nomads.

Caitlin knew how people thought. But she also knew that something better lay ahead.

She did love Paul, but if she told him that he would think there was a chance she might come back someday—that if things didn't go well, she would return to Santa Fe. That wasn't going to happen. Paul would not be part of her future. It had nothing to do with what she wanted or dreamed of or hoped for. Relationships were either in the cards or they weren't.

Kimo would understand. And being with people who understood was becoming more and more important.

∾ 50 ∾

*M*elody walked around the property, as she did every night before going to bed, making sure nothing looked amiss. The walk helped her shed any worries or cares that had crept into her mind during the day.

Life was quiet, but that was by choice. Caitlin could go chase the spotlight—more power to her for following her dreams and pursuing her passions. Melody's focus had been more internal lately. She'd made peace with the past, and, for the moment, she was content in her life. Sure, she got a bit lonely now and then. Having Lucky around would actually be a welcome change.

Kimo had finally moved on, it seemed; he had a new love interest now, Angela. He didn't call very often anymore. It was probably best that way, Melody thought. Maybe she shouldn't try to stay friends with old lovers. Maybe that prevented them both from moving on and being fully available to their new partners.

She still saw Billy now and then. He was sweet, but he was gone so much of the time, touring. Melody sighed and thought, *Musicians.* She was drawn to talented and creative people, but if she wanted a day-to-do life with a partner she could co-create a future with, she might have to find someone a little more . . . *regular.* Summer was Billy's busiest time.

These days, her only male companion was her gay friend, James. He'd been coming to her yoga class in Santa Fe for a while, but they hadn't really gotten to know each other until she started going to his salon to have her hair trimmed. They met in town for lunch now and then.

Almost all of her massage clients were female, she realized as she returned to the guest house. Living in Tesuque, she wasn't as involved as she'd been in Santa Fe. She might need to make more efforts to socialize. Get to know some new people.

"Until then, I've got you, Little Lucifer!" she told Lucky before giving him a treat.

Kimo had taught her that the true meaning of "Lucifer" was "light bearer."

Karl, she thought. *I have to remember to call him Karl.*

Lucky jumped up on the futon in the living room. Melody turned out the lights and went to bed.

∾ 51 ∾

Caitlin made a smoothie when she got up in the morning. She was eager to get on the road and didn't want to take the time to sit and eat breakfast.

"I'll stop in Albuquerque for lunch," she told Paul when he came downstairs. After a tearful goodbye, she drove away from Santa Fe and didn't look back.

She remembered the Mexican restaurant Sandra had ordered takeout from but forgot that today was Cinco de Mayo. The restaurant was packed. Caitlin waited for a takeout order and then drove to a park with a picnic table to eat. Next, she followed the signs to Interstate 40 and headed west.

She would spend the night in Sedona, Arizona and then drive south to I-10, which would take her all the way to Santa Monica, where Luisa lived. She figured she would arrive at both destinations around dinner time.

After driving in the rain for a while, she crossed into Arizona and soon spotted a rainbow. She exited the highway and pulled over to the side of the road so she could get out of the car and take a few photos.

From her vantage point, the rainbow looked like a bridge connecting distant rock formations.

Hmm. A rainbow bridge.

Maybe she should write a song about it, she thought.

Inspired, she started singing as she drove back to the entrance ramp for I-40.

"Follow me through the night, to the stars burning bright. We will conquer the darkness together."

Finally, she was being given the chance to bring her songs to life.

The muses were pleased.

PART THREE

∾

SHINING STAR

∽ 52 ∽

*C*aitlin exited I-40 in Flagstaff and followed the directions she had printed out before she left Santa Fe. The Internet made travel planning easier.

Living in Santa Fe, she had grown accustomed to the year-round availability of fresh produce grown without pesticides. She shopped for farm fresh eggs laid by hens that had access to outdoor pastures, dairy products from animals that hadn't been fed hormones, and packaged foods that didn't contain artificial colors and flavors. She wasn't as careful as Melody, but she was willing to go a bit out of her way to find healthy food, and she was pleased to see a variety of prepared foods at Flagstaff's "all natural" grocery store.

After a stop in the restroom, she decided on chicken salad and cinnamon-dusted roasted butternut squash for dinner. She filled a small container with hot vegetable soup and then noticed the array of desserts. *Why not?* she thought, and added a brownie to her basket before checking out.

The winding road to Sedona descended through Oak Creek Canyon and required her full attention. Darkness was encroaching by the time she pulled into the parking lot of the hotel where she had made a reservation, and she was eager to get settled in for the night. The concierge told her about an early morning guided hike that still had space available. "I'll see what time I get up," she told the man.

After unpacking a few things, she ate dinner and then took a quick shower. Traveling was easier without a cat to consider, but she and Lucky had never been apart for more than a few nights. He had lived with Melody before, though; she was familiar. Before long, he would feel right at home, Caitlin assured herself, and Melody would let her know if any problems arose. She spent some time working on her new composition and then turned out the light.

The restaurant in the hotel opened for breakfast at 7:00 a.m. Short on time, Caitlin opted for the buffet and filled her plate with scrambled eggs, hash browns, and a pancake. She added melon balls to a small bowl and then headed to a booth to eat what she could before joining the hiking group. When it was time to go, she gulped down a glass of freshly squeezed orange juice and rushed to the lobby.

At eight o'clock, the sun was already shining brightly. Seven women and one man had assembled and were waiting for their guide to arrive. Soon, they were greeted by Ed, a bearded man dressed in blue jeans and a long-sleeved cotton shirt. He directed them all to a waiting van.

As he drove to the parking lot at the top of a mesa, Ed pointed out notable sights and landmarks and shared fun facts about the town's history as a backdrop for Hollywood films.

"John Wayne, Henry Fonda—even Elvis—were on location here," he said. "Everything's got a name. The buttes, the mesas, the canyons. Up ahead is Airport Mesa. I'll leave it to you to figure out why it's called that."

Everyone got out of the van and admired the panoramic view. Caitlin took a deep breath as she gazed at the rock formations in the distance. The scene captivated her in a way that Santa Fe's landscape never had, and she wished she could stay longer to explore the area. She had heard about Sedona's famed vortexes and wondered if these supposed energy centers were real.

Ed waited while people took photographs and then he led the group on an easy hike to a medicine wheel. Rocks had been placed on the ground to form a large circle. A second circle in the center was made up of smaller rocks, as was a cross that divided the wheel into quadrants.

"There's tours that come here to do ceremonies, if any of you are interested in that sort of thing," Ed said, "but I just think it's a peaceful spot for reflection and enjoying the beauty of the day."

Caitlin agreed. The hike wasn't too long or too strenuous. She had a chance to get a bit of exercise and fresh air before spending another day in the car, and she was able to see a place she never would have found on her own in the limited time she had for sightseeing.

"We'll have about thirty minutes here," Ed announced. "The trail continues, if you want to hike more. I'll be right here, playing my flute." He held up his cedar flute and then sat on a slab of rock near the medicine wheel. "So I'll see you all back here in half an hour."

Caitlin put on her hat and walked a short distance. This part of the trail wasn't shaded, but the sun wasn't too hot yet and she knew she wouldn't be outside long. She sat on a flat section of rock and noted the time on her watch. A small plane flew overhead after taking off from the municipal airport nearby. After the noise had stopped, Caitlin closed her eyes and savored the moment. She was thinking about how much she enjoyed travel—in particular, the feeling of liberation she experienced when she was in a new place and every day felt like an adventure—when a sudden awareness came upon her that was as clear as the cloudless sky.

I need to talk to Kimo. It's time.

They hadn't spoken since she moved in with Paul—no doubt Melody had filled him in on that development. Caitlin wanted to tell him about her life as Bobcat Woman and her recollection of the ceremony at the Shannon Pot. They had shared a profound experience in Ireland, one that no one else could ever begin to understand.

The ache in her heart told her she was now open to the possibility of a more intimate relationship with Kimo—or Karl as he now preferred to be called. She was glad this realization had come while she was nowhere near a telephone. The intensity of the impulse would fade by the time she returned to the hotel. She would have to think about how to approach Karl. She couldn't just show up on his doorstep and expect him to welcome her with open arms. First, she would get a sense of what was going on in his life.

If he had a girlfriend, Melody hadn't mentioned it. On the contrary, Melody was always encouraging her to call him—and to give a relationship with him a chance.

She thought about how to proceed as she walked back to the medicine wheel. Should she call Melody and find out Karl's status?

For now, she needed to stay focused on her music. Maybe she would go on tour with the Road Angels, if they invited her. That would keep her busy for a while.

But, oh, how happy they would both be when they could finally be together! Wasn't that what Karl had been wanting all along? Caitlin had grown to appreciate his friendship, but Karl was different from other men she had known—and dated. He was younger than her and into things that she had considered bizarre.

"Oh, you mean things like chakras and past lives and shamanic ceremonies?" she said aloud as she drove south on Interstate 17. Now that her conventional belief system had been shattered, a new understanding was dawning that this lifetime was part of a greater journey.

At Pecos, she had glimpsed other times and places. Was it possible that her soul had incarnated on Earth before? Her personality and her soul were separate, but connected. Her identity as Caitlin Rose would die with her body, but her soul would live on—and perhaps return to Earth again.

Knowing about some of her other lifetimes gave her a deeper understanding of herself and her present life. Some of her fears and proclivities and talents and interests could have carried over from earlier times. Some of the people in her life could be souls she had first encountered in the distant past.

If she accepted the idea of karmic rebalancing, then she had to accept responsibility for all of her choices and actions. Acts that were intended to cause harm to others and their interests *would* have consequences . . . sometime.

This new belief system made sense. She felt at peace with her new outlook—and optimistic about her future.

"I guess we don't know until we're ready to know," she murmured.

Undoubtedly, there were things she still didn't know, things she was still in the dark about. But wasn't that why we were here? To learn, to grow, to experience. To love.

To help each other. And share the journey.

And there was no one she would rather share the journey with than Karl Marx Owen.

∾ 53 ∾

*C*aitlin parked her car behind the other vehicles that were crammed into the driveway. Luisa met her at the door.

"Welcome! We've been expecting you."

Caitlin put her suitcase down and followed Lu to a large open space where fourteen people were sitting in a circle. They all looked up when Caitlin and Lu entered the room.

"Caitlin Rose, meet the Road Angels!"

Lu started the introductions with Pete. Then, the young woman to Pete's left said her name, and on around the circle. Some added "Welcome" or "Namaste" with a smile or bowed head.

"Okay, I think we're done here," Lu said after everyone had been introduced. "I'll show Caitlin around and see you all here for yoga in the morning."

"Don't worry about remembering names," Lu told Caitlin after the group dispersed. "You'll have plenty of time to get to know everyone. Are you hungry?"

Caitlin shook her head.

"How about a cup of tea?"

"Tea would be nice."

"I'll show you to your room, and you can settle in while I put the kettle on."

Luisa gave Caitlin a quick tour of the house. The room they were standing in would typically be considered the living room, though this one was sparsely furnished and seemed to be functioning as more of a multipurpose room that could be used for yoga classes as well as group meetings, Caitlin thought as she looked around. Bookshelves lined one of the walls, and large cushions were stacked in a corner of the room along with rolled-up yoga mats and folded blankets.

Instruments and cases were scattered about the adjoining music room, as well as a few music stands. The glass chandelier suggested that the room had been intended for dining.

The long wooden table in the kitchen reminded Caitlin of the table at Kimo's house in Arlington, though this table was flanked by two benches. Looking through the sliding glass door, Caitlin saw that there was additional seating outside on the patio.

Large calendars hung on the walls of the office, with tour dates and other group commitments written in different colors. (Green for performances, blue for rehearsals, red for deadlines, and purple for everything else, Caitlin later learned.)

"You'll be sharing with Cara," Lu said as she showed Caitlin to her room upstairs. "She's our newest member."

Caitlin carried her suitcase up the stairs and down the hall. She was surprised to see some of the cramped spaces that were being used as sleeping nooks.

"Does everyone in the band live here?" she asked.

"Yes," Lu said. "It's part of the experience!"

Two twin beds were made up in the simply furnished bedroom. "Ask anyone, if you have questions or need something," Lu said before leaving Caitlin alone. "Come on down to the kitchen when you're ready."

Caitlin unzipped her suitcase. Two empty dresser drawers were available for her to use, as well as half of the small closet. Sheets and towels were provided, as Luisa had told her on the phone. "Just bring yourself," she'd said. "We've got costumes and pretty much anything you'd need. Shampoo, even!"

Caitlin was glad she had traveled light—by her standards. Someone like Melody, who practically lived in yoga attire, would undoubtedly think she had overpacked, but Caitlin was particular about the brand of shampoo she used, and she liked having a variety of clothes and shoes to choose from. She would rather keep a few extra things in the trunk of her car, she had decided, than leave them in a storage unit 800 miles away.

When she had finished putting away her things, Caitlin joined Luisa in the kitchen.

"I won't bombard you with too much information tonight," Lu told her. "I'll save that for morning!"

She held out a plate of apple slices before selecting a piece for herself. As she spread nut butter on the slice, Lu said, "We've got a full schedule, so you'll need to hit the ground running."

"That's pretty much how it went when I got to Santa Fe," Caitlin said before taking a sip of chamomile tea.

She planned to watch Luisa closely, and not only because she wanted to learn from her. She also wanted to learn *about* her. Melody, Shanti, and Sable spoke of her in reverential terms. They practically idolized her. Paul, on the other hand, had said little. Caitlin would form her own opinions, but so far she found Luisa intriguing.

She was also curious about the group. Would she fit in or regret jumping on board with few questions asked?

"Being a friend of Melody's, I'm sure you know that spirituality is a large part of why I started the Road Angels," Lu said.

"So you did start it."

Caitlin didn't know anything about the band's history, only that the group traveled around the West, performing in various venues and conveying a positive message through lighthearted entertainment. The intention was that everyone would leave feeling uplifted, Melody had told her—including the members of the group.

Luisa murmured "Mm-hmm" as she sipped her tea.

"When Paul and I moved to Santa Fe, I decided to get a degree in counseling. I found a graduate school with a curriculum that's designed to be transformational—and it was! After I finished school, I was in private practice for a while, but I got restless. I wanted to find a way to draw on my years of experience in the entertainment industry that also aligned with my values and my spiritual path. Santa Fe was a little too remote and isolated for me. I love to go there for a getaway, but I prefer to be where the action is."

Caitlin drank the last of her tea. "Sounds like you found a good blend," she said. "I haven't discovered a way to use my legal training since I left Washington. Other than knowing my rights!"

"That's no small thing these days," Lu said. "Maybe I'll ask you to review our contracts!"

"That was my worst subject in law school, I'm afraid. I passed the course, but I steered clear of the business-oriented electives. I was more interested in due process and family law than in corporate entities or employment law. Though I ended up learning about those things, too, when I worked for the government."

"More tea?"

"No, thanks," Caitlin said, yawning. "I'm feeling a little sleepy."

"I won't keep you up any longer. It's an hour later on your time clock. We start each day with yoga and meditation at five thirty, but you can skip tomorrow's session if you want to sleep in. Breakfast is at seven. After that, we head to the studio."

Caitlin went upstairs and showered and then got ready for bed. She was turning down the bedspread when Cara came into the room. Caitlin acknowledged her, but neither of them attempted to start a conversation.

Caitlin turned out the light by her bed, and, before long, Cara did the same.

∾ 54 ∾

*O*n Sunday morning, Caitlin slept until nearly seven. Cara's bed was made up and her personal items put away.

An ideal roommate, Caitlin thought as she made her way to the bathroom down the hall. *Neat and quiet!* She dressed quickly and hurried down to breakfast, eager to get acquainted with her new bandmates.

You're only a probationary member, she reminded herself.

Undoubtedly, there would be hurdles to clear before she could become a full-fledged member of the band. And only through immersion in the group would she know if she *wanted* to become a member.

A place had been saved for her at the long table in the kitchen. Luisa was sitting at one end and a woman named June sat at the other end. As soon as Caitlin took her seat, she was approached by Cherry, a tall brunette wearing an apron.

"We've got scrambled eggs this morning, and we always have oatmeal, nut butters, toast, juice, and tea and coffee," Cherry said.

"Eggs, please," Caitlin said. "And toast. And coffee."

Meals were not self-serve, she learned. Food was set on the counter, buffet-style, and dished out by someone from the kitchen team.

Everyone in the group was given chores and responsibilities. Laundry, shopping, cooking, cleaning and other chores were handled by teams. The kitchen team, headed by Cherry, took care of preparation, serving, and cleanup for all of the group's meals, though June ordered most of the groceries. Team assignments rotated every three months, so no one was stuck cleaning toilets forever.

Because of the expertise required, tasks related to touring, performing, and management of the band didn't rotate. Assisted by June, Luisa handled public relations, marketing, and bookings. Other members maintained the tour bus, oversaw the purchase and upkeep of costumes, sound and lighting equipment, and musical instruments. Caitlin was assigned laundry duty along with Seth and Crystal, the group's choreographers.

Seth, who wore his long hair pulled back in a ponytail, played the saxophone. Caitlin noticed the tattoos covering his arms and wondered what they depicted. One, she could tell, was a serpent, but from across the table she couldn't see the others clearly.

"I'm in charge of the costumes for our performances," Crystal said. Dressed in workout clothes, she was sitting to Seth's right.

The members of the band all looked young and fit, Caitlin thought as she looked around. Rick, who was seated next to June, was a little pudgy, and June and Luisa looked older than the rest of the group. Of the musicians, Caitlin guessed that she was probably the oldest, though Cara might also be in her thirties.

Probably one of the reasons Lu put us together.

June told Caitlin that Crystal often accompanied the band with rattles, chimes, a tambourine, or hand clapping, as appropriate. "She has an excellent sense of rhythm," June said. "She also helps involve the audience members when the band plays at private events."

Sitting on Seth's left was Jordan, a recent college graduate who had joined the band four months earlier. She played the piano and electronic keyboard, she said, and she was starting to work on some of her own compositions.

No one asked Caitlin any questions, but everyone seemed willing to answer her questions. A few people shared information about how the group functioned.

The tour bus was used for traveling to performances and not much else, Seth told her, so people carpooled for trips to the store and other errands and appointments.

"We usually go out in pairs," Jordan added. "Unless it's a very short trip, like to the neighborhood market if we forgot something."

Even dental appointments were scheduled so that two people could go at the same time, said Marya, who was sitting next to Jordan.

They had learned to maximize their use of time, which they considered a precious resource that wasn't to be wasted, June explained. Idle chatter and purely pleasurable pursuits, such as lying on the beach reading a novel or going out to a bar for happy hour, were discouraged. People could do that on their own time, when the group wasn't in session. (They thought of the group as a school, June said; "session" didn't refer to a recording session.)

"When the group is together, each person is expected to be fully present and to fully participate," June explained. "Personal time is used for creative pursuits and purposeful activities, whether it's composing music or writing in a journal, completing chores, or sharing a meaningful encounter with another member of the group."

"Meaningful" could apparently be anything from discussing spiritual principles to sharing a talent.

"Everyone shares whatever gifts and training they have to offer, whether it's massage therapy or astrology readings or energy healing," June said.

Talking about the latest films showing at the theater in the mall, however, seemed to be frowned upon.

"We do take breaks from time to time," June added, "so people can visit family or go on vacation. But if people start wanting too much time away, it's considered a sign that they're ready to transition."

Noticing that June and Luisa looked at each other when June talked about transitioning, Caitlin wondered if someone was preparing to leave the group.

After breakfast, Lu suggested that Caitlin stay behind and work on one of the songs she wanted to record. She wasn't needed at the studio yet, so her time would be better spent preparing.

She had played Caitlin's demo of "Shining Star" for Rick and David, Lu said. "As long as you have the master, we won't need to rerecord your vocals on that one. Rick and David will add more instruments and create a fuller sound. I guarantee you'll love it. So let's focus on getting something else ready to record while we have the studio reserved."

Had Scott given her a master for "Shining Star"? Caitlin wondered. She wasn't sure, but she could easily find out.

Before leaving for the studio, Lu showed Caitlin the band's rehearsal studio.

"So this is where you hide the piano!" Caitlin joked when they entered the renovated garage. She spotted a keyboard, drum set, amplifiers, and a variety of instruments and audio equipment. Lu gave Caitlin the code for the keypad to unlock the door and told her she could use the space anytime—"day or night."

They returned to the house, where the band was waiting and ready to go. June conferred with Luisa and then scribbled in her notebook. "I'll be in the office if you need anything," she told Caitlin before disappearing down the hall.

Caitlin carried a few more things from her car to her room and spent some time writing in her journal. As she had missed the morning yoga class, she unrolled a mat and did some stretches.

At noon, June took food to the group at the studio. When she returned, she invited Caitlin to join her on the patio for lunch.

"Who are Rick and David?" Caitlin asked.

"Rick is part of the group," June said. "He doesn't play in the band. He mostly works behind the scenes, like me."

"What does he do?" Caitlin asked.

June bit into a bean burrito before continuing. "He handles the sound at concerts and works with local crews when the band is on tour. Stuff like that."

"So he's the sound engineer and the production manager," Caitlin said before dipping a corn chip into a bowl of guacamole.

June nodded. "Most of us fill several roles," she said.

"And David?" Caitlin asked.

"He owns a local recording studio. He's committed to helping the band finish their first album on time. Lu's putting together a tour, and she plans to sell CDs at shows. So we need to have CDs ready to sell."

June finished eating her lunch and added, "Rick seems to be learning a lot from David."

Caitlin asked June how she got involved with the Road Angels. "For that matter, how did Lu get involved with the Road Angels?"

When Lu returned to L.A. after splitting up with Paul, June said, she heard a band playing at a whole life expo and thought they sounded pretty good.

"They were singing about love and kindness and positive experiences, but they weren't sappy or preachy; they were very entertaining."

Lu approached them with the idea of being their manager.

"None of the members of that group chose to be part of the band that Lu eventually put together, but she learned a lot about the music business during those early days," June said. "Her vision requires a willingness to go deeper into spiritual development than most people are prepared to commit to," she added.

Lu prepared a mission statement so prospective members would know in advance what they could expect if they joined the group.

"What did it say?" Caitlin asked.

"The thrust of it was that we should consider ourselves emissaries of light, spreading positive vibes through our interactions and through our music. And though we may pursue whatever we wish to in our individual lives, when we're together—and especially when we're representing the Road Angels—we strive to express our highest potential and reign in our selfish tendencies," June said. "Of course, Lu worded it more elegantly!"

Caitlin could tell that June was an excellent source of information about the group—and about Lu—and she wanted to learn all she could from her.

After lunch, June went back to work in the office and Caitlin sat at the piano practicing "Rainbow Bridge" for a while before warming up her voice with vocal exercises. When she felt satisfied with her readiness to perform the song for the group, she sat on the patio and wrote in her journal.

The afternoon was warm and sunny, and the neighborhood was quiet, except for a barking dog. Caitlin allowed her mind to wander and realized that June had never said how she met Lu or got involved with the band. The conversation had turned to the group's mission, and Caitlin's question never got answered.

No matter, she thought. She would find out another time. Or not. She was curious; that was all. She didn't need to know.

She liked the idea of being an emissary, spreading positive messages of hope and inspiration through her music, whether she was part of a group or performing as a solo artist. Having experienced a spiritual transformation herself, maybe now she had something to say. But what would it be like to be a Road Angel?

"It's been four years now since I packed my bags and sold my Frigidaire," she sang aloud.

How long had it been since she'd sold her townhouse in Alexandria? Not quite three years, she calculated. But four had a better ring to it.

I know—I'll write a song about being a Road Angel. Maybe the group will record it. And if they like it, maybe they'll put it on their album!

A song about being a Road Angel belonged on the band's album, not hers.

She spent the next hour playing around with lyrics until she came up with a verse she liked. She sang the lines several times so she would remember the melody:

> It's been four years now
> Since I packed my bags
> And sold my Frigidaire
> Told the boss goodbye
> Let the caged bird fly
> And I left with just a prayer
> Gonna find what fate
> Lies beyond that gate
> Feel the magic in the air

She had told Neil goodbye, all right—and thought she would never see him again. She was far from Washington now, but also far from Kimo. Her heart ached when she thought of him, an ancient yearning that whispered, *"You belong to me."*

The kitchen team returned from the studio and started preparing dinner. Caitlin took her journal upstairs and lay on her bed, resting, until Cara arrived.

"Is everyone back now?" Caitlin asked her.

"Yeah," Cara said. She set a letter that had arrived in the mail on the table by her bed and then brushed her shoulder-length hair.

"How'd it go?" Caitlin asked. "At the studio."

"Oh, I'm not the best person to ask," Cara said. "There's a lot I'm still figuring out!"

"I understand," Caitlin said.

The two women walked downstairs together shortly before six o'clock. Several different salads had been set on the kitchen counter.

"There's usually a hot entrée, too," Cara said just as Cherry brought out a hot casserole dish.

"Looks like lasagna," Caitlin said, peering at the dish. "Always vegetarian?" she asked Cara.

"Yes, though I've heard that when they—when *we* go on the road—we have more options if we're eating out."

Cara had not yet performed in public with the band. She was learning how to play the flute and taking lessons, she told Caitlin.

André, the group's drummer, set out a bowl of steamed broccoli. He was on the quiet side, and Caitlin hadn't learned much about him yet, but she knew that his family had immigrated to the United States from Portugal when he was a child.

"They're not the only members of the kitchen team, are they?" Caitlin asked Cara.

"No!" Cara said with a laugh. "Nearly everyone is on the kitchen team. There's a different shift for each meal, so it's not so bad. The cooks don't have to clean up after their shift, either."

Luisa arrived with a man Caitlin hadn't seen before. Everyone stood around the table and joined hands. Lu waited until the room was quiet and then she bowed her head and said, "We give thanks for this nutritious food, for family and friends and soul mates. For the many blessings in our lives and for all the beautiful music we have yet to create together. Tonight we welcome David, our brilliant recording engineer, to our table. Namaste."

Some people murmured "amen," others repeated Lu's "namaste," and Caitlin also heard an "aho," which she remembered a few of Melody's friends using to indicate agreement with something that was said.

During dinner, Caitlin listened attentively when anyone spoke about the recording session. She would be going to the studio the next day to add her voice to the mix. (Backing vocals were typically recorded last, June had told her.) She knew that the time allotted for her songs would be limited, as it had been in Albuquerque, and she was eager to get started.

After everyone had finished eating, Rick and David returned to the studio to work their magic on the tracks that had already been recorded. Everyone else was given half an hour of free time before the group would gather in the living room, which people referred to as the "main" room, if they referred to it by name at all. Usually, Caitlin discovered, Lu simply announced, "We'll gather at seven" or something similar. People understood that if a location wasn't specified, they would all meet in the large room on the main level.

"I imagine Caitlin has some experience with mediation as a process for resolving disputes without going to court," Lu said at the start of the evening session.

"Only in a superficial way," Caitlin said. "I have lots of experience, though, with negotiating outcomes. Settlements. Plea bargains, even."

"Ah," Lu said. "We'll call on you if one of us gets hauled into court. In the meantime, you can be our official mediator if any problems get too hot to handle through our usual practices."

"Okay. Sure."

"In a group like this one," Lu continued, "you are each expected to accept responsibility, not only for your actions and your assigned roles, which should go without saying, but also for your personal development. That's not to say you're expected to be perfect or to be in a good mood all the time or that you're always strong and dependable—no. We all have wounds and issues and sensitivities—and feelings and opinions and preferences. We're all unique individuals, and clashes can be expected from time to time. There's no judgment around having problems. It's how you deal with them that matters. We're all going to discover a lot about ourselves—and each other—on this journey together, so there's no point trying to hide. We strive for authenticity, and many of the exercises and practices that I introduce are designed to help you become—and express—your most authentic self. The only way we can all feel comfortable in sharing our vulnerabilities and feelings is if we create a safe container in which we honor and respect each other. Gossip and backstabbing have no place here. Whether we are in session or not, you are expected to maintain confidentiality regarding what you learn about each other as part of this experience."

"And what we learn about you?" Caitlin asked with a sly grin.

"Well, that would be appreciated, though I'm not terribly concerned about myself at this point," Lu said.

"No memoirs, then?" asked Cherry. *"My Life with the Road Angels?"*

Of the current members of the band, Cherry had been around the longest, Caitlin had learned from Cara. Early on, the band got gigs at local events in Southern California that had a spiritual or holistic theme. New Thought churches and outdoor festivals were popular venues, both for playing music and for distributing flyers about upcoming concerts, some of which were held at Luisa's house. Members of the group came and went; Lu adapted by changing the set list to fit the talents of the current members. The band had slowly developed a following and now toured all over the West Coast, having outfitted an old bus so that it met their needs when they were on the road.

Lu had been busy planning the band's first-ever cross-country tour for several months, June had told Caitlin at lunch. Though most venues had to be booked months in advance, sudden opportunities sometimes presented themselves. When possible, openings were worked into the schedule.

Everyone was tired that evening, so Lu kept the session short. "We'll just have our check-in," Lu said, adding, for Caitlin's benefit, "We never skip check-in, except when we're performing."

Starting with the person to Lu's left, everyone was invited to share something. "What's on your mind or in your heart that needs expression?" Lu asked.

"I'm really happy to be here, and I'm enjoying getting to know all of you," Caitlin told the group when her turn came. "I look forward to getting better acquainted with your music, too." Grinning, she added, "And I'm excited about joining you in the studio tomorrow."

Lu closed the evening with a short meditation. Afterward, some people headed to their bedrooms, while others went to the rehearsal studio in the garage or to the music room.

Caitlin went upstairs and got ready for bed. She looked over the notes she had written for her newest song and jotted down a few ideas for additional verses before turning out the light, ready for sleep.

∾ 55 ∾

*C*aitlin was given headphones to listen to the playback of the song that she, Marya, Cherry, and Allison were adding backing vocals to. They had rehearsed in the lounge while André, the drummer, and Sky, the bass player, were in the studio, recording. Their harmonies sounded good, Caitlin thought.

David agreed and recorded several takes before sending the women back to the lounge to rehearse their next song while Pete was in the studio.

Several people had told Caitlin that Pete was the band's most versatile musician. He had composed the music for a lot of their original songs, and he had also written some of the lyrics. (The lyrics of Pete's other songs had been co-written with Matt, who played electric guitar.) Pete sang lead on about half of the band's songs; Cherry sang lead on the rest.

Crystal and Jordan arrived at the studio and set up the buffet table for lunch. Caitlin asked Crystal if she would be joining the women singing backup. She already knew that Jordan didn't sing.

Crystal shook her head and said, "Oh no. You know how women with lovely voices are sometimes called songbirds?"

Caitlin nodded. "Yes."

"Well I sound more like a screech owl!"

Caitlin laughed but thought, *I can see why Lu asked me to come out and sing backup.* Three of the female members of the group—Cara, Crystal, and Jordan—didn't sing at all.

Because of the group's spiritual focus, Lu didn't turn away anyone who was genuinely interested in being part of the band. She considered each person's interests and aptitudes and found a way for everyone to get involved.

Lu and Paul were a lot alike in that way, Caitlin thought. They sought to include others and help them grow as artists. Lu encouraged members of the Road Angels to try new things. She paid for music lessons and bought instruments for people who didn't have their own, though the instruments remained the property of the band, ready for the next person to use if someone left.

Members didn't get paid for performing, June had told Caitlin. Not in cash, anyway. People were free to leave anytime if they didn't feel they were gaining something of value by being part of the group, and they were never asked to pay for anything or to make financial contributions. Food and essential items were covered, but extras were not. Requests could be made—for a favorite meal or a particular kind of guitar string—but if someone had a craving for a burger and fries, he was on his own.

When Pete was finished in the studio, David called the four women in to record their vocals. After listening to their harmonies, he made a few suggestions and they sang the song again. David liked the change and asked them to sing the song several more times. When they were done, he announced from the control booth, "Thank you, ladies. I think we've got what we need."

Back in the lounge, Crystal and Jordan were serving lunch: a huge tossed salad with homemade dressing, broccoli-and-quinoa salad, hummus and pita, and a beet-with-vinaigrette dish. Caitlin gobbled up all the food on her plate.

Lu arrived, and Rick and David accompanied her to the control room so she could listen to the songs they had been working on.

As people finished eating, they left the crowded lounge to get some air. Caitlin was about to do the same when Luisa appeared.

"Everything's coming along nicely," Lu told Caitlin, Cara, and June. "I've worked out the set list for our concert in Santa Barbara. I'll post it on the door to the office, so spread the word. I need to get back to the house. Oh, and Caitlin, I've included 'Shining Star.' As it's Mother's Day weekend, I think that will fit right in."

Caitlin's heart skipped a beat when she realized she would be performing one of her songs before a live audience in five days.

"Oh wow. Great," she said, flustered.

Thoughts and questions flooded her mind. What would she wear? Was she going on early in the show or later? Who could she tell? Her mother, for sure. Caitlin had sent Martha a couple of postcards, but she hadn't had a chance to phone her since arriving in Los Angeles.

"Maybe—" Caitlin blurted out suddenly as an idea occurred to her.

"Yes?" Lu said. She had been talking to June about her schedule for the afternoon.

"Sorry. I didn't mean to interrupt. I was just wondering— Would it be okay if I invited my mother to the concert? I mean, would she be able to get tickets? For her and her husband, probably."

Caitlin was, by now, over her antipathy toward Ray. She wasn't eager to meet him, but she was open to not hating him.

"We can get them tickets if they're able to come," Lu said. "I'd love to meet them."

Caitlin borrowed June's cell phone and stepped outside to call her mother.

"I'll look into flights right away," Martha said when she heard about the concert. "We'll drive out if necessary!"

Caitlin was ecstatic. This was the opportunity she had been waiting for, and she was ready to seize the moment.

She returned the phone to June, who had finished packing up the bowls and utensils to take back to the house. (There never seemed to be any food left over, Caitlin had noticed.)

After June had gone, Lu said, "Let's discuss the other songs you're interested in recording." She gestured to the chairs in the lounge and said, "We'll probably have time for two of yours when ours are finished."

"I've been thinking about it," Caitlin said after she sat down. "I've got one that's ready to go, but what I'm hearing will almost require an orchestra, with strings and horns as well as piano and guitars."

"Seth plays sax," Lu said, "and Pete has a trumpet and a trombone, so I'm guessing he can play them."

Lu's phone started vibrating. She glanced at the screen but put the phone aside.

"A lot can be done electronically, you know, without needing to hire session players. Rick and David can truly work wonders in the studio—you haven't heard any of their finished songs yet. So the question is: Do you want to wait, possibly indefinitely, until you can work with an orchestra to get the sound quality you desire, or do you want to use this opportunity to create a similar effect sooner than later?"

"Well, when you put it like that . . ." Caitlin said. "I guess, with any luck, I might have the opportunity to perform that song live someday, too."

Lu nodded. "You could record a live album."

"I'll need a few more songs for that," Caitlin said. "I just hope these recordings turn out well."

"Are you ready to play something for the group?"

"Yes."

"Okay. We'll listen to one of your songs after dinner," Lu said, rising.

"Am I done here?" Caitlin asked. Everyone else seemed to have something to do. "I've got an idea for a new song that I think would be perfect for the group, and I'd like to keep working on it. At the house."

"Sure," Lu said. "You can ride back with me."

Caitlin collected her belongings and settled into the passenger seat of Lu's Mercedes. She'd hoped the ride might give them a chance for casual conversation, but she was beginning to realize that little about Luisa Martinelli would be considered casual. Lu's choices—and her use of time—were intentionally designed to maximize effectiveness and minimize wastefulness. She was already on the phone, making arrangements for a new stop on the tour, a theater in Boulder.

"I'm not sure we can fill the theater," she told Caitlin after her call ended, "but we might, if I can arrange an interview at one of the radio stations in Boulder. I've got to get busy with promotion. June sixteenth will be here soon enough!"

"So the group will have some time between the concert in Santa Barbara and when you leave on tour, from the sound of it."

"About two and a half weeks," Lu said as she parked the car in the driveway by the house. "Oh, I've been meaning to ask you: How would you like to take Cherry's place on this tour? She's feeling like she needs some time out. She's thinking about going back to school, actually."

Caitlin's eyes widened for the second time that day. "Well, I'd need to know the details, but yeah, I'd love to, if everything lines up. I'll need to think through the logistics. Melody is taking care of my cat. Stuff like that. How long the tour would last. Where I'd leave my car!"

"June can tell you a lot. She's an integral part of the team, both here and on the road."

"She comes on tour?"

Lu gathered her purse and other belongings to take inside. "Oh, yeah," she said. "June is my right hand!"

Caitlin got out of the car and closed the passenger door. "I'm impressed with all you've been able to achieve here," she told Lu as they walked toward the house.

"Thanks," Lu said sincerely. "That means something, coming from you."

Caitlin was surprised by the compliment. Maybe Lu didn't view her as the neophyte she thought she was. Maybe the admiration was mutual.

Caitlin brought her guitar to the garage and found a few chords she liked for the chorus of her newest song, "Road Angel." Only the hook—"I'm a road angel"—repeated, but the tune was catchy, and Caitlin was motivated to finish the song quickly, knowing she might soon be singing it all over the country. It could well become the group's signature song. As it was evolving, it had a country-western feel to it. The lofty imagery she had used in phrases such as "you'll find me up on high" would probably appeal to a wide range of people, she thought.

"I'm a road angel, freedom is my song. So don't take me for granted, 'cause I won't be here long," she sang.

An angel is a messenger, she recalled Kimo telling her.

She smiled, remembering the sometimes-goofy guy she had spent time with in the Washington, D.C. area—and in Ireland. Maybe she would continue to think of that person—the one she had known in the past—as "Kimo" and reserve "Karl" for the man she intended to form a relationship with in the future.

A glance at the clock on the wall told her that dinner would be served soon. She packed up her guitar and notes and walked over to the house. The song still needed work, but a few of the verses were done, and Caitlin liked the melody she had come up with.

Hopefully, Lu and the others will like it, too, she thought.

At the evening check-in, Lu told the group to expect long days and late nights for the foreseeable future.

"We will continue with morning yoga and meditation, but our evenings will be spent rehearsing—and that includes stage choreography," she said, glancing at Seth and Crystal. "This tour will be different because we're only performing our own music."

Looking at Caitlin, Lu explained, "We've played in different kinds of venues, so sometimes we've done covers of pop songs we like. And sometimes we focus on a theme, like Valentine's Day or Christmas."

"Show tunes," Cherry called out.

"Yes, we've incorporated show tunes for some of our private events," Lu said.

"Weddings," Seth added.

Lu nodded. "Yes, we've played at a few weddings. As I was saying, this show will be different but still lively and upbeat, as always. We're all about positive messages and spreading peace and love and good will."

"And harmony," Crystal shouted.

"And harmony," Lu said, chuckling. She gestured toward Caitlin when she said, "Caitlin's songs will fit into our program well, I think. She'll be playing with us in Santa Barbara, and possibly longer."

Caitlin grinned and nodded.

"We need to learn a few of her songs so we can accompany her in the studio this week and on stage after that," Lu continued. "We're going to close the show at the Lobero with 'Shining Star,' so we'll have to work out an arrangement for the live performance. She has already recorded that one, though, so tonight we'll focus on learning one of the songs she plans to record this week. Caitlin, why don't you tell us a little about the song and then we'll head over to the rehearsal studio to hear what you've got. You're on piano again for this one?"

"For this one, yes. I've got another one I'm working on that's built more around the guitar."

"That you're working on?" Pete said. "You mean it's not even finished yet?"

"It was a recent inspiration," Caitlin said. "It's almost done."

"What's the name of the song we're going to hear tonight?" Lu asked.

"'Rainbow Bridge.'"

Lu smiled and said, "Nice! I like it already."

Caitlin described the symphonic sound she was imagining for the song and sang it through once, a cappella.

Lu suggested that she focus on singing and let Jordan play the piano. Caitlin wasn't sure what Lu's reasoning was, but she was willing to give that approach a try.

After a short break, the group gathered in the converted garage to work on Caitlin's song. She played it several times on the piano and indicated to Cherry, Allison, and Marya where background vocals should come in.

Sky picked up his bass and chatted with André while Matt and Troy worked out their guitar parts. Caitlin turned the piano over to Jordan. She told Pete she wanted him to experiment with both the trumpet and the trombone for certain parts of the song.

"I can't play both instruments at the same time," Pete said.

"You can play them separately in the studio, though. Why don't you play the trumpet first and then later we can see about the trombone."

Pete shrugged and went to get his instruments.

"Want to try out your flute?" Caitlin asked Cara. "I can suggest a couple of places in the song where a flute would fit in nicely."

"I can try. But I'm really not very good yet."

"Might as well get some experience playing along, even if you're not ready for the recording studio."

"True," Cara said, nodding.

When everyone was ready, Jordan played the piano as Caitlin sang, "Follow me through the night to the stars burning bright. We will conquer the darkness together."

André joined in on drums, and Cherry picked up a tambourine.

"Look ahead, not behind. It's not easy to find. There's a place where love reigns now and forever."

Caitlin signaled to Cara that she could play a few notes before the next verse, and then she listened closely to Pete's trumpet and decided to use it, sparingly. She told the background singers to hold off on singing until the music started to come together.

By midnight, the group had made a good start on putting together a sound that Caitlin and Lu were both happy with.

"Good job, everyone," Lu said. "We'll head to the recording studio after breakfast."

"Will we have more time to rehearse before we start recording?" Caitlin asked Lu.

"Yes. We'll want David's input as well. He'll know what will sound best in a recording."

"When can I hear 'Shining Star'?"

"You'll have to ask him if it's ready yet. I think he's focused on getting all the tracks recorded at this stage. He'll continue working on the mix while we're getting ready for Santa Barbara, but we have to make sure he has everything he needs from us while we have the studio time."

"Sure, I understand."

Being unfamiliar with David and Rick's work, Caitlin felt a little uneasy about entrusting everything to them. She would have preferred to have more oversight—and input. But Lu was footing the bill for all of this, and Caitlin retained the rights to her work. She really had nothing to lose. If she didn't like the recordings, she didn't need to use them. Either way, she was gaining valuable experience— and having a good time in the process.

∾ 56 ∾

*C*aitlin stayed at the house on Tuesday morning to continue working on "Road Angel" while the band was at the studio. She and June joined the group at lunchtime.

While everyone was eating, Lu made a few announcements. "We're done recording our songs," she said, "so the remaining time in the studio will be devoted to Caitlin's music." They would begin with "Rainbow Bridge."

Caitlin felt panic creeping in as her certainty that a fiasco was looming cast a shadow over her fantasies of having a successful recording career.

This is going to be a disaster.

The band had only just started to learn "Rainbow Bridge," and Caitlin had noticed the previous night that the skill level of the musicians in the group varied widely.

Cara was right. She's definitely not ready.

And as Pete had somewhat rudely pointed out, "Road Angel" wasn't quite ready to go, either. No one had even heard it yet. There was no way this scenario could have a happy ending. She would walk away with nothing.

Well, almost nothing. Maybe Rick and David would be able to turn "Shining Star" into a marketable product, as Lu had promised. She would have to be content with that. The band would need a week to rehearse "Rainbow Bridge," she thought, and they didn't *have* a week. She just couldn't see how this was going to turn out well. Swamped by fears of failure, her enthusiasm was starting to wane.

Lu noticed the shift immediately. "Everything okay?" she asked as people finished eating and left the lounge area.

"One night of rehearsal . . . I just don't think we're ready to start recording."

"That's the beauty of tracks," Lu said. "Rick and David can isolate the parts that aren't working and fix them. David hasn't even heard your new material yet. He'll have ideas about how to make the song great. We're not done rehearsing. We've got all afternoon. That should be plenty of time. Jordan spent the morning practicing the piano part. As long as we get a good recording of your vocals and her piano, the rest can be polished later, as needed."

"You mean we don't have to have a finished product by Friday?" Caitlin asked.

"No," Lu said, laughing. "Not for your songs. Just ours. So let me do the worrying. You focus on the singing. How's that?"

"Okay. But the other song I'm working on *is* for the group. It's called 'Road Angel.'"

Lu's face lit up. "Intriguing," she said, smiling. "I can't wait to hear it."

"As soon as we're done recording this one," Caitlin promised.

"Well, let's get to it!"

Caitlin was tired after dinner, but she was also eager to share "Road Angel" with the group, and after such intense work on "Rainbow Bridge" in the afternoon, she was ready to think about something else.

She was excited about making a contribution to the Road Angels' album. She wasn't only there to get their help on her projects, she was there to be part of the group—for however long her participation lasted.

She nervously opened her guitar case after the evening check-in. Her song would undoubtedly change once the members of the band started improvising their different parts, and that was fine; this was meant to be their song. They should make it their own, using her chords and melody as a starting point.

Just so they don't change the tempo, she thought. *Or the lyrics.* For now, she would be the one singing it—and playing her acoustic guitar.

She'd never been part of a band. She would have to learn how to play along with Sky's bass, Matt's electric guitar, and André's drums. She didn't plan to play any instruments for the band's other songs; she would be filling in for Cherry, who sang lead on about half of the band's songs and backup on most of the others. But she did want to play piano for "Shining Star" and guitar for "Road Angel" when those songs were performed live.

Troy was the band's rhythm guitar player, Matt had told her. "Pete and I trade off playing lead and rhythm guitar," he said. "And sometimes we both play lead. It just depends on the song."

"But Pete always plays guitar? I mean, he can play other instruments, right?"

"He can play the keyboard, but so can Jordan, and she's really good, so he usually plays guitar. I'd never seen him pick up the trumpet—or the trombone—until you asked him to."

Matt seemed to find the idea of Pete playing a trumpet amusing, Caitlin thought as she glanced around the circle before taking her seat. She wanted horns on "Road Angel"—when the band played it live as well as on the recording. She hoped Pete would be willing to honor her request, but she had noticed that he seemed to like being in charge. He deferred to Luisa, as they all did, but when she wasn't around, he often ran the show—or tried to.

Caitlin referred to her notes several times while she sang. She knew she wouldn't remember all the lyrics to the song. She had changed them too many times.

"I'm a road angel, wherever I am is home. With new friends to share and lots of love to spare, you know I'm never alone."

The room was quiet for a moment after she finished singing.

They hated it, she thought, afraid to look up. And then, enthusiastic applause and laughter erupted around the circle.

It was perfect for them, they all agreed. They wanted it on their album.

"That might even be our single," Lu said, beaming.

Caitlin was so relieved she wanted to cry.

Pete, she noticed, said nothing.

∾ 57 ∾

Caitlin approached Luisa before the band started rehearsing in the morning. "Um ... I was hoping Pete might play the trumpet on this one," she said quietly. "And I'm not sure the sax will really work."

Lu stood up and said, "Seth, you can sit this one out. And Pete, we'd like to hear you on the trumpet. Caitlin will be playing guitar. She'll tell you where she wants you to come in. Seth, why don't you go help out the kitchen team, if you don't mind."

Lu sat back down and continued working on her laptop computer.

"Thanks," Caitlin said.

She walked over to where the musicians were set up. "I thought we'd start with the chord progression and go from there," she told Pete, Matt, Sky, André, and Troy.

The lunch team (Jordan, Crystal, Allison and, today, Seth) came by after they had finished preparing lunch. By then, Caitlin's fingers were sore. She was ready for a break. The band played "Road Angel" one more time so the members of the lunch team could hear their progress, and then everyone went back to the house to eat.

"I'm starved!" Caitlin heard Matt tell André.

"Yeah, I hope it's something good today, like veggie burgers. I'm getting tired of salads," André said.

The lunch menu featured Indian food—basmati rice and garlic naan along with dishes of creamed spinach, chickpeas, vegetables, and lentils. For dessert, the team had made a rice pudding.

Caitlin glanced around the table while she ate, curious to know what people thought after spending the morning working on her song. The group seemed uncharacteristically quiet. She had no idea what that meant, if it meant anything. Maybe they were also ready for a break, and enjoying their lunch.

June packed food for Lu to take to Rick and David and stayed behind when everyone else left for another day at the recording studio.

〰

The afternoon session was similar to the day before, but because "Road Angel" was a song the band would record for their album, people voiced their opinions more forcefully than they had for "Rainbow Bridge." Should they use the Fender or the Les Paul? Would including a flute part be a good idea? With so much input, Caitlin was glad that Rick imposed some order on the process. As producer, Lu had final approval on whether a song was finished or not, but she deferred to Caitlin's preferences on her songs. Caitlin, in turn, appreciated guidance from those with more experience.

David listened to several variations of the song and steered the group toward the sound he liked best. The band rehearsed until everyone agreed they were ready to start recording. Rick checked all the microphones and then David recorded tracks of André's drums, the guitar and bass parts, and Caitlin's vocals.

Before the group left for the day, David said he would play a rough cut for them in the morning. Unlike the songs that the band had been playing for a while, the development of Caitlin's song required continued refinement, even after the recording process was underway.

"We're still finding the sound," David told Caitlin when she asked for his thoughts. "We'll get there," he assured her.

After dinner and the evening check-in, Lu announced that evening exercises would resume. She asked everyone to pair up.

Caitlin felt drawn to some people in the group more than others. She respected Pete's talent as a musician, but he had rubbed her the wrong way on more than one occasion. She felt at ease sharing a room with Cara, and she had enjoyed her talks with June. Always aware that she was the newcomer, she knew she had a lot to learn. She waited to see who would approach her—or who would be left as the odd person in need of a partner.

Rick asked her if she would be his partner, and Caitlin was glad that he did. He and David would decide on the mix for her songs, and she appreciated a chance to get to know him better.

They chose a spot by the glass doors that led to the garden and sat facing each other on pillows on the floor. Lu's instructions were to gaze lovingly into each other's eyes, projecting warmth and acceptance.

"It's not a staring contest," Lu said. "Blinking is allowed!"

Caitlin took a deep breath and tried to relax. She felt awkward at first, sharing such an intimate encounter with a stranger. Would Rick notice the scar on her chin, she wondered, or the other imperfections in her appearance that she was so aware of? Rick didn't fidget or look away, and though his face remained expressionless, his eyes seemed friendly.

Can we smile with our eyes? Caitlin wondered. She decided to give it a try, imagining sharing all the love in her heart with Rick.

After a while, her awareness of Rick's features faded and she felt enveloped in the energy field that the two of them were jointly creating. The experience was almost mystical, Caitlin thought, though it couldn't come close to the experience she had shared with Kimo at the Shannon Pot. She couldn't wait to talk to him about it, now that she remembered what had happened there.

Be here now, she reminded herself, breathing deeply. As the exercise continued, she felt as if she caught a glimpse of the truth expressed in the statement "We are all one." Beneath the personality traits and beyond the differences that separate people there exists an essential unity of spirit. Finding it required a clear mind, an open heart, and a willingness to accept *what is* rather than attempting to change or control anything.

Two beings who achieved this state, Caitlin sensed, could dance together and co-create something magical—if they could stay in alignment and get their egos out of the way. She doubted that many people were capable of sustaining that kind of high-level interaction, but perhaps that was where evolution was leading humanity—to a greater ability to subdue selfish agendas and instinctual urges and live together in peace and harmony. Perhaps Lu had envisioned a similar ideal that she was attempting to lead the group toward.

As Caitlin allowed her spirit to harmonize with Rick's, the sounds in the room that, at first, seemed to intrude on her attempts to concentrate no longer bothered her. Crystal clearing her throat. André shifting around to find a comfortable position. The clicking sound made by the cord of the ceiling fan. For a moment, Caitlin was aware only of a shared experience with the man sitting across from her, and he could have been anyone. *She* could have been anyone. Deeply moved, her eyes teared up.

When the exercise was over, Lu turned on the lights.

"Wow," Caitlin said to Rick. "That was powerful. Have you done that before?"

Rick shook his head and calmly said, "No."

"Feel free to share your experience with your partner," Lu told the group.

"I can start," Caitlin offered.

Rick shrugged. "I have no preference."

"At first I was really aware of feeling self-conscious. I guess that's a good thing for a performer to get over!" Caitlin said. "But after a while, I noticed a shift, and I really felt your energy and it was like we were in a field, just the two of us. I'm probably not describing it very well, but it felt . . . peaceful. Not like we were two strangers who'd been thrown together—more like we were . . . *connected* in some way."

Rick nodded and said, "Well—and I'm not a performer, so I totally get what you're saying about feeling self-conscious—but my experience was a little different. I'm not very attuned to subtle energies. I'm more of a techie, so I'm good with computer programs and instruments and those kinds of nuances and details, but when it comes to people—and especially when it comes to women—I'm not always sure I'm reading the cues right. So I was really aware that I sometimes get nervous when I have to talk to women, but we didn't have to talk at all, so that was good for me, to experience just being with a woman and sharing something that's . . . wordless. Well, something other than sex," Rick added with a chuckle. "I was able to relax. For me, that's a start. I have some issues with intimacy."

"Ah," Caitlin said knowingly. She searched for some positive feedback she could give Rick. "'Wordless.' I like that."

"You may wish to complete your sharing with a hug, if both partners feel comfortable with that," Lu told the group.

Caitlin and Rick embraced politely, and then everyone quietly left the room.

Caitlin was glad she'd had a chance to establish a connection with

Rick, but it was Karl who was on her mind as she got ready for bed. After the concert in Santa Barbara on Saturday, she would figure out when might be a good time to call him.

And what she might say.

∞ 58 ∞

*C*aitlin was the first person to come downstairs on Thursday morning, other than the kitchen team. "Just tea and toast," she said when Jordan asked her what she wanted to eat. She was too nervous to eat much.

This was the band's last day at the recording studio. Anything that needed to be recorded—or rerecorded—had to be done by the end of the day. After that, Rick and David would be busy mixing the Road Angels' songs, which would then be sent off for mastering. When that was done, Caitlin's song "Rainbow Bridge" would be finalized. But today she might finally get a chance to hear the final mix for "Shining Star."

She sat at the long table in the kitchen and was soon joined by Cara, Crystal, and Marya. Breakfast was not preceded with a blessing, and people often trickled in at different times when the group wasn't first meeting for yoga or taiji practice. The household was a mix of night owls and early risers. Some people took a plate of food and went off by themselves to eat in peace.

Today, though, everyone seemed energized. They were all eager to hear the songs that would be included on the band's album—thirteen including "Road Angel." After the kitchen team finished cleaning up, Rick drove the entire group to the recording studio. Lively chatter filled the bus.

First, David played the band's album. Luisa invited comments; most were positive. Next, David played "Shining Star." Caitlin was happy with it, though she didn't have a lot to compare it to, other than the demo she'd made in Albuquerque—which had sounded good to her at the time. The effects Rick and David had added were interesting—and might even make the song more appealing to some listeners—but simple arrangements worked best for some songs, she thought. Something magical got conveyed in a live performance, she realized, even if it wasn't as technically perfect as a studio recording.

Maybe because *it's not perfect,* she thought.

In the old days, she could have released two songs on one 45 rpm record, with an A side and a B side. "Does anyone still make 45s?" she asked, remembering the vinyl records she used to buy as a teen—and play over and over again.

"No," said David. "Well—none of the big labels, anyway."

"Then how does a single song get released?"

"MP3," said Rick. "It's the new digital format. But I'll send out promo copies of the band's CD to deejays."

"Oh," said Caitlin.

She must be getting old, she thought. She hadn't kept up with the latest technological advances, and she had no idea who the hot new artists and celebrities were. She didn't even have a mobile phone. She was happy to leave the final decisions to Lu and Rick and David. They knew the music business better than her.

They seemed satisfied with her vocals on "Rainbow Bridge"; it was the added instrumentation that they were still fiddling with. The band would spend the day waiting around in case anything needed to be redone. The time for experimentation was over. Fine tuning was all that remained, and the members of the band had no role in that.

Caitlin asked Cherry to go over her parts with her so she could start learning the band's songs.

"So Santa Barbara will be your last concert," Caitlin said as they walked toward a couch in the lounge.

"Yeah," Cherry said wistfully. "Back home, I sing in the choir at church, but I'm not a songwriter and I don't play any instruments, so unless I join another band later on, I'll probably just sing for my own enjoyment. This has been a great experience, though, with Lu and the group. I had to overcome a lot of my insecurities to be able to put myself out in front as a lead singer. But I'm ready to step back."

"I'm really looking forward to seeing the show," Caitlin said. "As a spectator."

"The Lobero is a wonderful old theater," Cherry said. "We've never played there, but it will be a grand setting for my final performance. The band's first paying gig outside of L.A. was in Santa Barbara, you know."

"Were you with the group then?"

Cherry nodded. "Yeah, though I wasn't singing lead. I'm glad I got to sing on the album. I can play it when I'm missing everyone."

At the evening check-in, Lu thanked everyone for their dedication and hard work during the recording process.

"I think we've put together something really special," she said. "The CDs won't be ready in time for Santa Barbara, but we can take orders and . . . We've got merchandise now!"

She held up a t-shirt with "Road Angel" printed on the front in purple script. "Mugs and t-shirts will be sold at our shows," she said, "and Rick is working on a website. We can sell everything through there, too."

Lu passed around the t-shirt so everyone could see it up close.

"I'm guessing we'll each get one," Matt said when the shirt came to him.

"There's a box in the office. Just let June know what size you need and what color you want."

Continuing with announcements, Lu said, "It's only a two-hour drive to Santa Barbara, so we won't be staying overnight."

"Aww," said Crystal.

"I know, we'd all love to hang out in Santa Barbara for a few days, but we don't have the budget for that. The show is at eight. Caitlin, what have you heard from your guests?"

"My mother and her husband are driving out. They should be in Vegas by now."

"Anyone else need tickets?"

Cherry raised her hand, as did André and Crystal.

"Let June know how many, ASAP," Lu said. "We'll have a quiet evening tomorrow, after check-in, so you can have some time to yourselves. For tonight, I thought we'd learn a bit about energy fields. So find a partner and pair off. For this exercise, you'll want to be with someone you feel comfortable with."

Caitlin and Cara gravitated toward one another. They were

already coexisting in a shared energy field every night. Perhaps, Caitlin thought, she could learn about the nature of that field.

"Last time, we practiced projecting warmth with our eyes," Lu said. "Tonight we want to bring our attention to the energy that radiates from our hands. Begin by holding your palms together, in a prayer position."

Lu demonstrated as she stood in the center of the room.

"Next, slowly separate your hands and then move them toward each other. Can you feel warmth as your palms get closer together?"

Caitlin spent a few minutes focusing on her hands. She didn't notice anything unusual, just body heat.

"As many of you know, we each have an aura," Lu continued. "The aura surrounds our physical body and emits light and color, which some gifted psychics are able to see. We're not going to spend time on trying to see auras, but we do want to become more aware of our individual energy fields and how we are affected by other people, and by electromagnetic fields, and by our thoughts. Our intention in this group is to keep our own vibrational energy field clear and to thereby be able to transmit uplifting energy to others—not just through our music but through our presence. So it's important to purify ourselves so that we're suitable channels for this undertaking. Because?" She paused, waiting for a response.

"Because you can't give what you don't have," Pete said, repeating what was evidently an oft-heard refrain.

"That's right," Lu said. "You can't share positive vibes if you're filled with negativity. With practice, we can develop awareness of the field that is generated during an interaction, whether it's with one other person or an auditorium filled with people."

Lu dimmed the lights and said, "Let's start by closing our eyes and taking a few deep breaths, allowing all our worries and tensions to fall away. Next, I'd like you to imagine being showered with white light. This light penetrates your aura and clears away any impurities, traveling down your spine and legs and continuing on down into the ground through your feet. Allow Mother Earth to receive all the refuse you're letting go of. She knows how to recycle these energies, just as other waste products are broken down through natural processes."

Caitlin followed along as Lu led the group through several exercises, from sensing the energies of other people to sending them healing and restorative energies with the intention of creating balance and harmony. Afterward, Lu invited questions and comments.

"Is it the person's own energy that is being transmitted, like from an energy healer?" Allison asked. "Wouldn't that deplete the healer?"

"Great question," Lu said. "This is why it's so important to keep yourself in balance, so that you are not giving away your energy—or taking on other people's negativity. When done properly, the healer is not in danger of either. But if you are getting depleted, you need to figure out what's going on and address it. We're a long way from becoming trained energy healers—that's a specialized path and a great one, for those who are drawn to it. Here, I'm introducing you to some of these principles so you can begin to put them to use immediately. Does anyone want to share anything about their experience? Did you feel energy moving through you to the other person? We're all different in terms of how sensitive we are, so don't worry if you didn't notice much happening. The intention is what's important."

"I was more aware of the energy that I was sending than what I was receiving," Crystal said. "But that could just be because that's where my attention was focused. It was subtle, but I did feel energy moving through me."

"And what does that tell you about sharing with others?"

Crystal thought for a moment. "That giving and receiving are the same?" she said tentatively.

"Can you say more?" Lu asked.

"Well the energy has to come through me in order for me to pass it on. It's like you said earlier, you can't give away what you don't have. So if I don't have any money, I can't gift it to anyone. It has to come to me first. It's the same with energy. I have to open myself up to it, and receive it, and allow it to move through me to someone else. So in the process of giving I'm also receiving."

"Excellent," Lu said. "We'll end here, and you can continue to ponder the implications of that principle. You've all heard, I'm sure, that you can't love another if you don't love yourself—that's a related concept. Think about what it means when you are filled with negativity. When you harbor bitterness, resentment, hatred, and contempt toward others, those states and feelings become your reality. Why would anyone choose misery over bliss? For it is a choice we make when we stay stuck in negativity, and there are tools and practices that can help us shift our experience. We can help each other stay on track as well. Namaste."

"Namaste," Caitlin repeated along with others in the group.

As she walked upstairs, she remembered the name that Sam's mother had chosen when she joined the community at Ananda. "Satchidananda" translated as "bliss consciousness."

Had Mrs. Burns been successful at finding bliss? Caitlin wondered.

∾ 59 ∾

"*I* hope I don't regret this," Sam thought as he turned onto the road that led to the ashram.

He also hoped he wouldn't have to stay with his mother for long. He knew the community had rules—and committees—for just about everything. Hell, he couldn't spit on the sidewalk without somebody complaining about it.

He would probably have to state his intentions in his application for long-term housing. Why did he want to live there?

He didn't, really, but how bad could it be? He would do what was expected of him, as he always had. He didn't plan to stay forever—just long enough to sort some things out. Get to know his daughter. Apologize to Yvonne—show her he had changed, and prove he didn't need supervision when he spent time with Jacqueline. Chances were good that his mother would want to be involved anyway. Sam wouldn't deny her that. He had caused them all enough pain.

He wasn't interested in rekindling a flame with Yvonne—she didn't need to worry about that. But he did want to be on better terms with her. And with Suzanne, his little sister.

He realized he had a lot of proving to do to regain their trust. He was ready to try. But none of that required living at the Ananda Center.

He would focus on his recent monastic experience in his application, he decided, and say that although the monastery in Pecos hadn't been the right place for him for the long term, he had appreciated the lifestyle. The spiritual path had brought him peace of mind.

He had begun to develop a relationship with—should he say "God" or "Spirit" or what? Maybe he would just say that his spiritual life was his top priority at this stage of his journey.

Yeah, they'll like that. These New Age types are always talking about life as a journey. And even though ashrams had been around for ages in India, the residents of the Ananda Center were pretty much white, middle-class Americans.

Of course, the whole reason he had been visiting Ananda all these years was because of his mother's involvement, Sam thought as he trudged up the stairs to her apartment.

"I'd like to explore Ananda's approach to spirituality and community and see if I would fit in here," he could say. *"And I'd like to be closer to my family."*

He would probably only be approved on a short-term basis anyway, to start. He didn't anticipate any problems getting that far, as long as housing was available.

He knocked on the door.

Maybe they could put him in one of the rooms they used for guest accommodations. He wasn't particular—but it wouldn't take long for sleeping on the couch in his mother's one-bedroom apartment to try his patience. He would do his best to get along, but he knew how easily his mother pushed his buttons.

Why invite trouble?

∾ 60 ∾

*O*n Saturday, the bus departed for Santa Barbara. Luisa and June sat in the back and went over various arrangements and task lists. Caitlin sat by a window and looked at the passing scenery. She had seen little of L.A. during her stay, and if she joined the band's tour she would be leaving California soon.

When the bus exited Highway 101, Lu sat next to her and asked, "Have you been to Santa Barbara before?"

"No," Caitlin said, gazing out at the red tile roofs. "It looks lovely."

Lu nodded. "Very popular destination for weddings and honeymoons." She craned her neck to see where they were. "We performed at a festival here a while back. The organizer liked us and hired us to play at her wedding. So we've got some fans who will come out to hear us."

Caitlin smiled, amused that Lu considered herself a member of the band. She didn't set herself apart. Caitlin liked that, even if, in reality, everyone else considered Lu more of a boss and a leader than a peer.

"This is the downtown area. We're nearly there." Lu stood up and said, "I'll need to tell Rick where to park."

Caitlin watched Lu walk to the front of the bus. She was excited about her first concert—and also a little nervous. A lot of work went into recording an album and planning a tour. She was glad she wasn't trying to do it all on her own.

Tonight would be a good trial run, she thought as she stepped off the bus. She would sing lead for "Road Angel," the first song of the night, and then she could enjoy the band's music until she sang "Shining Star" at the end of the show.

Someone from the Lobero's staff escorted the group into the theater. Caitlin followed along, wondering if Martha and Ray were in town yet. They had expected to arrive in Southern California Friday evening and planned to find an inexpensive motel somewhere. Today, they would be driving to Santa Barbara in time to enjoy a nice dinner before the concert.

After the band's equipment was unloaded and set up, everyone gathered for sound check and then Crystal handed out costumes. Caitlin's costume was pink. She really disliked pink, she realized as she dressed. She would have to talk to Crystal about that.

Perhaps Lu and June hadn't wanted to spend the money for new clothes when they thought she would only be appearing in one show. But surely they would want her to feel comfortable and confident, and pink just didn't suit her.

Red or gold, she thought. *No pink.*

She couldn't blame the costumes, though, for the less-than-stellar performance they all gave for their first song. "Road Angel" was new to all of them, and they hadn't rehearsed it much. There hadn't *been* much time to spend on it. "Shining Star" was practically a solo; for that one, Caitlin wouldn't need to worry about anyone's performance except her own.

"It'll get better," June said when she saw Caitlin's frown.

Caitlin dabbed at her face with a towel and took a drink of water. Watching from backstage, she paid close attention to Cherry's numbers, knowing that she might soon be taking her place.

This is probably a good time to be a newcomer, she thought. The band had been performing together for a while, but on this tour they would only be singing their own material—no covers. They were entering a new phase, with new choreography and new venues lined up. Caitlin wouldn't be the only one figuring things out.

The feel-good nature of the show helped shift her mood, and soon she was smiling and swaying to the music. The time passed quickly, and before long it was her turn to go back onstage. Cherry introduced her.

"And now, here with a special tribute to her mother, who is in the audience tonight, please give a warm welcome to Caitlin Rose."

"You're on," June said with an encouraging smile.

Caitlin lifted her hand in greeting to the audience as she walked across the stage toward the piano. Cherry joined the other backup singers after saying, "And to all the mothers out there, happy Mother's Day." The rest of the band stayed onstage, in the background.

Caitlin played the introductory notes for "Shining Star" before starting to sing.

"Here is your foolish child, running reckless like the wind . . ."

Cherry, Allison, and Marya joined in with their *oohs* and *aahs*, and Cherry repeated the last line of the song, "You are my shining star," timed to fill the space when Caitlin paused.

When the song was over, Cherry thanked the audience for coming, and the members of the band all stood in a line at the front of the stage to take a bow together. Caitlin stood in the center.

Looking out at the sea of faces, she was surprised to see the glowing screens of mobile phones that had been lifted up by many of the people in the audience. Was this a thing now? she wondered, recalling that cigarette lighters had been a common sight at the arena concerts she and her friends attended during college. *Probably safer this way,* she thought, though the effect wasn't quite as enchanting.

Half the group exited the stage to the left, while the other half walked off in the other direction. Caitlin looked to the left and then to the right, unsure which way she was supposed to go. *Probably doesn't matter,* she decided.

She was eager to find her mother, but seating was general admission; Martha and Ray could be anywhere. Finding them would be easier after the crowds thinned. Backstage, she drank a bottle of water and waved her hand to fan her face. She was surprised when her mother and her stepfather suddenly appeared. Lu had spotted them and introduced herself.

Caitlin hugged her mother and shook hands with Ray, sizing him up while Lu spoke.

"You won't have much time for a visit tonight," Lu told Caitlin, "so I invited Martha and Ray to come by the house on their way back to Kansas." Glancing at the couple, she added, "But they're not sure when that might be."

"We'd like to visit some of the wineries in the Santa Ynez Valley," Ray said.

"It's a beautiful area," Lu said. "Caitlin might have told you, we're getting ready for our first national tour, so it's been a hectic time."

"Yes, I think she mentioned something about that," Martha said.

"Did she also tell you we invited her to come along?" Lu asked with a sideways glance at Caitlin. "Because she hasn't given me her answer yet."

Caitlin knew this was Lu's way of asking about her decision.

"I wanted to give you a chance to back out if I completely embarrassed myself tonight," she said.

"Far from it," Lu said. "I think I'll keep the set list exactly the way it is. It worked great."

"It was fun," Caitlin said. "Once I got out there. Of course, in the future I'll be onstage the whole time, so I won't be standing around worrying about the final number!"

"Is that a yes?" Lu asked.

"Yes," Caitlin said with a nod. "I would love to go on tour with the

Road Angels. But I'm not actually a Road Angel, so would I get billed as a special guest?"

"Already making demands!" Lu joked. "We can talk about it. Now if you'll excuse me, I need to check on how everything is going behind the scenes. It was a pleasure to meet you both."

Lu shook hands with Martha and Ray and said, "I hope we'll meet again. Please feel free to stop by if you're in the area."

"I need to go, too," Caitlin told Martha after Lu had left. "I'll have to change for the ride back. But I'm glad you could be here."

Feeling in love with the whole world, Caitlin hugged both her mother and Ray.

"I wouldn't have missed it," Martha said, her eyes brimming with tears. "I'm just so proud!"

"Well, maybe the tour will take us through Kansas City," Caitlin said.

"Yes!" said Martha. "Why don't you get in touch with the country club?" She turned to Ray and said, "Wouldn't the ballroom be perfect for a concert?"

Ray nodded.

"Between the two of us, we know lots of people who would love to come to a show like this!" Martha said.

"I'll mention it," Caitlin said. "Let me know what you decide to do. We'll be in town for another couple of weeks."

"We were thinking we might like to drive north a ways, to see the Hearst Castle," Martha said.

"We've been wanting to see a bit of the country for some time," Ray said. "We enjoyed Las Vegas. We're going to stop at the Grand Canyon on the way back, and maybe the Hoover Dam."

"And Ray's got family in Colorado he'd like to visit, too," Martha said.

"So we're all going on tour!" Caitlin said.

Ray chuckled and said, "Right!"

I guess he's not so bad, Caitlin thought. Her mother seemed happy anyway.

"Okay, honey," Martha said before giving Caitlin a parting hug. "You go join your friends."

Caitlin smiled and nodded and then turned to leave.

"You look great!" Martha added.

Caitlin turned back and smiled and waved. She knew that her mother wasn't referring to her costume.

She felt deeply satisfied with how her life was going, she thought as she walked to the dressing room she shared with the other women in the band. But she did wish she had someone special to share her good fortune with.

Now that the recording was done and the concert was over, she was ready to think about contacting Karl.

∾ 61 ∾

*O*n Sunday morning, the kitchen team served a pancake breakfast for Cherry's last meal with the group. After everyone had been served, Luisa invited people to share something positive about Cherry.

"What have you admired or appreciated about Cherry in the time you've known her?"

"I admire Cherry's composure," Caitlin said when it was her turn. "She handles difficult situations gracefully, while also exuding energy and enthusiasm. I've appreciated her willingness to help me step in as her replacement." After a pause, she added, "Though I'm not sure she can really be replaced," and winked at Cherry.

Pete had the last word, remarking that he would miss the "other" lead singer. Caitlin tried not to take it personally, but she suspected Pete wasn't happy that she would be taking over for Cherry.

Cherry put her hands over her heart and said, "I'm grateful for having known each and every one of you. And I can't thank Lu enough for all she's done in orchestrating this whole experience. I know the tour is going to be phenomenal."

"Who's going to head up the kitchen team now?" Marya asked as the breakfast plates were cleared from the table.

"We'll change team assignments when we regroup after the tour," Lu said. "Now that our work at the recording studio is finished, we can start preparing to go on the road. We've been neglecting the landscaping and the housekeeping lately, so we'll need to do a thorough cleanup this week."

Caitlin had wondered when the laundry team would take care of its chores.

"When is our next concert, exactly?" asked Crystal.

"We leave here the first of June," Lu said. "That's a Thursday. The next show is on Friday, in Sedona."

"Where are we playing?" Sky asked.

"There's a new center there that will be a wonderful setting for us," Lu told the group. "I've also talked to one of the ministers at the Unity Church in Sedona. I was thinking Caitlin's 'Rainbow Bridge' would be a good song for the Sunday service, and we can follow up with an afternoon concert. What does everyone think? This model could work for several of the cities we'll be visiting that have New Thought churches."

"Great idea," said André.

"I used to attend a community church when I lived in Asheville," Marya said. "They have two Sunday services. Lots of upbeat people go there."

"Give June the name and we'll look into it," Lu said.

"Oh, and my mother suggested we play at a country club where she lives, near Kansas City," Caitlin said. "If we're going that way. She and her husband know a lot of people and can help spread the word. If they get back in time, that is! They're enjoying a second honeymoon, it seems."

"Do you know the name of the club?" June asked.

"No, but I can ask her to call you. As soon as I hear from her!"

"I was going to bring this up later, when we discuss last night's concert, but since we seem to be having announcements now, I'll mention that we took fifty orders for the CD," Lu said. "We also sold quite a few t-shirts. I'm not sure how well the mugs are going to sell, and they're breakable and heavy. We'll take some along with us, but we might end up using them for promotion. Give them to deejays at radio stations maybe."

"Are we doing radio interviews?" Matt asked.

"We've got two set up," June said. "Lu has a lot of contacts in New Mexico, so we were able to book a great venue in Albuquerque.

We're giving away a number of tickets, there and in Boulder, Colorado, so we'll want to help the stations create some buzz by going on the air the day before."

"All of us?" asked Troy.

"Probably just the two lead singers and myself," Lu said.

Caitlin glanced over at Cherry, wondering if she had any regrets about skipping the tour.

"Well, if you'll excuse me," Cherry said, "it's time I got on my way."

Everyone stood up and took turns hugging her, with promises to keep in touch.

"Can I help you with anything?" Matt asked her.

"Um, sure," Cherry said.

She handed Matt the framed photo of the band that June had given her. Everyone had signed a card, and Lu promised to send a copy of the band's CD when it was available.

"Don't forget your mug!" André said, holding out the mug Cherry had left on the table.

Matt and Cherry walked to the main room to collect Cherry's suitcase and purse.

"Free day, everyone," Lu announced. "Go enjoy the beach or a movie—this may be your only chance for a while. After cleanup, that is! We'll serve lunch and dinner for whoever is here, and then we'll gather at seven. So be back by then. Enjoy!"

"Hey, Caitlin," Marya said as she walked toward her. "Crystal and I would love to go to the beach, but neither of us has a car. Are you interested?"

"Sure," Caitlin said. She asked Cara, who had been sitting next to her at breakfast, if she wanted to come.

"No thanks. I want to spend a little time with my flute."

"Half hour?" Caitlin asked Marya and Crystal.

"Fine," said Marya.

"Great!" said Crystal.

Caitlin and Cara walked upstairs to their room.

"I'm glad we're going to Sedona," Caitlin said. "I spent a night there on my way here. I was hoping I'd have a chance to go back."

"Magic happens!" Cara said.

It does when Lu is involved, Caitlin thought.

∾ 62 ∾

O n Monday morning, Caitlin showed up for laundry duty with Seth and Crystal.

"Did you have fun at the beach?" Seth asked the two women as they folded sheets and towels. "Where'd you go?"

"The girls wanted to go to Venice Beach," Caitlin said.

"It was fun," Crystal said. "Marya bought a belt from one of the vendors, and I got a pair of sunglasses."

"And what did you get?" Seth asked Caitlin.

"Some cool photos," she said. "There are a lot of interesting characters at Venice Beach!"

"That's for sure," Seth said.

What Caitlin didn't tell Seth was that the women had gone for a hike in the hills north of Santa Monica after they'd had enough of the beach and the sun—and the crowds.

In the late afternoon, before returning to the house for dinner, they'd found a secluded spot to meditate. They spread out their beach towels and sat quietly for twenty minutes before chanting several rounds of *Om mani padme hum.* Then, they headed back to Caitlin's car—but after she unlocked the doors, Caitlin had a sudden inspiration.

"I'll just be a minute," she told Crystal and Marya.

She grabbed her camera and walked to a nearby overlook. As she gazed out at the Pacific Ocean in the distance, she had a strange feeling she'd witnessed the scene before.

Maybe I dreamed it, she thought.

Knowing that Crystal and Marya were waiting for her, she didn't linger. She snapped a couple of photos and returned to the car. But she'd been in a pensive mood ever since. Her attention wandered back to the scene in quiet moments, but she never figured out why she felt such a strong attraction to the place.

Oh well, she thought. *There may not be a* logical *explanation, but I'm sure there's* some *explanation—even if I never know what it is!*

She was putting clean sheets and towels into the linen closet when she heard the lunch bell.

The ritual was the same at lunch and dinner. Everyone stood around the table and held hands while Lu said a blessing, and then the kitchen team served the meal. Seating, however, was more random for meals than it had been for yoga practice, when people seemed to return to the same spots each morning.

Caitlin and Crystal decided to eat outside on the patio.

"There you are," June said as she walked toward them. She handed Caitlin a letter and said, "Looks official."

The letter was sent from the office of the Committee on Government Reform, the committee chaired by Dan Burton—the congressman Caitlin had written to from Santa Fe. It had been sent to her at Paul's address, and Paul had forwarded it.

Probably just some "thank you for contacting us" form letter, Caitlin thought, setting the envelope aside.

Her first rehearsal as a lead singer with the band was starting soon, and she wanted to review a few of their songs before then. The letter could wait.

With an hour of free time before dinner, Caitlin opened the envelope from Washington, D.C. and lay down on her bed. She was surprised to see that the enclosed letter was signed by the chairman. After reading it, she sat up and said, "Holy—"

She was being invited to testify at an upcoming hearing that Congressman Burton was convening on July 18. She wasn't required to attend, the letter said; her participation would be entirely voluntary.

The Committee on Government Reform had broad authority to investigate "any matter" at "any time," the chairman wrote, and it was specifically charged with conducting the oversight of "the operation of Government activities at all levels." Recently, the committee had been investigating various aspects of vaccine safety.

Burton said he appreciated that Caitlin had been concerned enough about her experience with the Department of Justice to contact his office. He was interested in hearing more about the case she had worked on, and he was considering dedicating a future hearing to an inquiry into how well the claims process was working from the perspective of claimants and attorneys alike.

Caitlin recalled that claims filed under the Vaccine Injury Compensation Act were handled by attorneys in DOJ's Civil Division. She hadn't been involved in that process, but she could suggest legal protections that Congress shouldn't overlook—even if some bureaucrats might prefer that they did. Individual rights and liberties had to be balanced with societal interests, she knew.

And with financial interests, she thought.

Money played a key role in politics, as in so many endeavors. Politicians needed campaign funds, and pharmaceutical companies made big donations to candidates who were viewed as potential allies on Capitol Hill. Profits could be affected if legislation imposed too many burdens and restrictions on operations.

Although the committee hearing was scheduled for July, Caitlin was only given a week to respond.

A week from when? she wondered as she checked the postmarks on the envelope. *From when I received it?*

How would testifying fit in with the tour? When was the tour supposed to be over, anyway? Where would she even *be* on July 18?

She looked over the forms that were attached to the letter with a paper clip, a Truth in Testimony Disclosure Form and Witness Instruction Sheet. As she was a non-governmental witness, she would need to submit a draft of her proposed testimony in advance of the hearing as well as a curriculum vitae.

I don't teach or do research so I don't have a vitae. Do they want my résumé? She had a copy of her résumé in her briefcase, along with other important papers she'd made sure to keep with her.

Burton's letter referred to a "short biographical summary." *Yes, my résumé should do,* she thought.

She would need to find time to collect her thoughts. Once the band got on the road, she might not have much access to a computer, and thoughts about the federal oversight of vaccine manufacturers would be far from her mind.

She would type up a draft of her testimony soon, she decided, and then review it closer to the time of the hearing.

∾ 63 ∾

Sam waited until his application for short-term housing was approved before removing the rest of his things from the truck.

Mother's Day had been tolerable. The community celebrated with a special brunch, so his first visit with Suzanne was less awkward than it might have been if they had met in a more private setting. She seemed to be making an effort to be civil, which he appreciated. She was six years younger than him, and they'd never been especially close. After his father's death and his mother's move to the Ananda Center, Sam had taken off in search of adventure and a different kind of belonging.

He was ashamed to realize how little he knew about his sister's life. She had married after high school and moved to San Diego, where her husband had taken a job. At the time, Sam was 2,300 miles away, in medical school. He didn't even attend the wedding. He was wrapped up with the demands of his training—and with trying to win Yvonne.

Yvonne and Suzanne bonded after Jacqueline was born, while Sam was stationed at China Lake. Yvonne didn't know anyone in California, and she never really took to military life. Suzanne was childless and loved being an aunt. She welcomed Yvonne as the sister she'd never had. Sam was glad the two women got along. He longed for a happy home life. For a brief time after his daughter's birth, he was hopeful.

During their brief visit, Suzanne was undoubtedly watching to see how long it would take for him to lash out or get defensive. He'd expected that. He was willing to submit to her scrutiny. In small doses, anyway. Mercifully, his sister and his mother went for a drive after brunch, so his visit with them consisted of polite conversation in the crowded dining hall. He couldn't say he *enjoyed* his sister's company, but his efforts were sincere.

He had sent Yvonne a card for Mother's Day and wrote a note

saying he looked forward to meeting with her soon so they could straighten out any misunderstandings and set up a schedule for him to visit their daughter. Jacqueline would be starting school in the fall, and the current plan, apparently, was to place her in a program for children with special needs.

Sam hadn't heard back from Yvonne yet, but he was praying for all of his family members and learning to focus on their positive attributes rather than expecting the worst. His reactivity and his tendency to jump to negative conclusions were just habit patterns. He was confident he could change them.

While he was unloading the truck, he found the large envelope he had picked up off the ground near Caitlin's BMW at the crash scene in northern Virginia. He had looked through it at the time, but with all the distressing events that transpired that day, he had little memory of the contents.

He moved his things to his new quarters—a single room with shared facilities—and opened the envelope. Inside he found information about the Vaccine Injury Compensation Program and the claims process. A timeline outlining the history of thimerosal's use in vaccines. Photocopies of a few newspaper articles about parents who believed their child had suffered neurological damage after receiving multiple vaccines at the same time—vaccines containing the preservative thimerosal. Some anecdotal accounts of exposures to mercury that had resulted in neurological symptoms—and death. Nothing that could be considered classified, or even confidential.

Sam set aside the pages about the claims process and read through the information on thimerosal. And, for the first time in years, he cried.

He could make excuses for his refusal to listen to Yvonne's concerns, but the fact was: his baby girl had regressed and no one knew why. He still believed vaccines were important weapons in the fight against infectious disease, but he hadn't known much about how they were produced or what they actually contained. Thimerosal had been used in a variety of products for decades, and everyone had just assumed it was safe—the CDC, the FDA, the pediatricians.

He might never know the cause of Jacqueline's disability—the vaccines she'd been given might *not* have had anything to do with her decline. But he'd been arrogant to assert so strenuously that there was *no way* a vaccine had been the problem. He was, after all, the one who had insisted that her immunizations be kept up to date. Adverse reactions were rare, but they did occur—no one could dispute that. There *were* risks. He'd thought Yvonne had been listening to too many baseless conspiracy theories. She didn't know enough about medicine to make an informed decision about whether or not to vaccinate. He had dismissed her objections outright. He hadn't been willing to listen—or to explain his own thought process.

Of course, at that time, little information about thimerosal had been available. Only in recent years were the concerns of parents like Yvonne starting to be taken seriously.

About all he could do now was attempt to make amends. Be involved in his daughter's life—and in her care. Help Yvonne, rather than be a hindrance.

If she'll let me.

Maybe he could demonstrate his remorse by learning about the latest promising treatments for spectrum disorders. Surely the Ananda Center must have computers for residents and guests to use. No doubt Yvonne had explored various approaches to managing Jacqueline's condition. Sam needed to be familiar with the options so he could have an intelligent conversation with her and they could, hopefully, work together going forward.

Regardless of the reason for Jacqueline's decline, there might be developments that would help her maximize her strengths and minimize her challenges. Maybe Sam could put his training to good use in a new way.

He had his work cut out for him. Whether he stayed at the ashram or not, he would almost certainly be staying in California for the foreseeable future.

∾ 64 ∾

*O*n Thursday, Caitlin spent some time typing up her notes about the thimerosal case she had worked on at OSP after notifying the committee of her intention to testify at the July hearing. She asked June for a diskette so she could save the file, but she didn't tell her what she was working on.

After dinner, she hurried to the office to use the computer before the group's evening session started. She typed a draft of her testimony and then left the diskette and her shoes by the door of the main room.

Luisa was standing at the front of the room and facing the rest of the group. When everyone was assembled, she spoke about the ancient Chinese practices of taijiquan and qigong.

"In Chinese philosophy, taiji is the source of all things. The two complementary forces, yin and yang, emanate from this undifferentiated infinite potential. Qi is the vital force that moves in each of us. By developing the ability to direct the flow of energy, we are able to increase our power, both physically and spiritually. Usually, however, when we speak of taiji we are referring to taijiquan, a movement practice that can help us develop balance, strength, and coordination. Though it is also practiced as a martial art, our focus here will be on the health and meditative benefits. I like to think of taiji as meditation in motion."

The group would focus on qigong practices in the upcoming week, Lu said, and the following week they would learn the taiji forms that they would be practicing while on tour. Both practices would help remove energy blockages.

"Tonight I will demonstrate the entire taiji routine you'll be learning."

After taking a moment to center herself, Lu moved gracefully from one form to the next. When she had finished, she said, "Through these different movement exercises, we learn how to flow with the Tao. Eventually, as we incorporate this way of being—being with ourselves, each other, and the world—we find that many times throughout the day we are calling upon this Force, and in doing so, our lives become more harmonious. We flow effortlessly from task to task."

Caitlin thought the routine looked similar to the one Kimo had taught her. She wished she had been more diligent about practicing what she remembered, but after she landed in Santa Fe her life had gotten very busy very fast. Caught up in the excitement of it all, she had allowed some of her healthy habits to slide. Resuming a regular practice would be easier if the whole group was participating.

She went upstairs when the session ended. Soon after, June knocked on her door and said, "Phone call. You can take it in the office if you want."

"We're leaving California tomorrow," Martha told Caitlin when she came to the phone, "but Ray wants to avoid the traffic in L.A."

"Where are you now?"

"What's the name of the town?" Martha asked Ray before returning to the phone.

"Ojai," she said. "I can't look at the spelling, it only confuses me."

Caitlin smiled. "I passed along what you said about the country club, and June wants to follow up on it."

"Yes, I already spoke to her about it."

"Okay, good. So you told her who to contact?"

"Yes."

"Perfect. So maybe I'll see you then."

"When do you all leave?" Martha asked.

"In two weeks."

After Sedona, they would stay at Lu's place in New Mexico for a while. Lu and June were planning a house concert there for local friends and supporters. Caitlin was looking forward to seeing Lucky again before the group traveled to Colorado.

While she was in the office, she printed out the draft of her testimony so she could look over it one more time before setting the matter aside.

She hadn't forgotten about calling Karl, but the group's chores, activities, and rehearsals kept her busy, and in her spare time she had been working on her testimony.

Maybe Sunday, she thought as she turned out the light in the office. Sundays seemed to have less going on.

Relatively speaking.

∾ 65 ∾

On Sunday, Caitlin's time was taken up with costume fittings and a short promotional video that Rick was shooting; it would go on the band's new website, along with brief descriptions of each member. That meant getting dressed up, putting on makeup, and waiting around between takes.

In the evening, Lu made a few suggestions about tour preparations.

"You're welcome to bring a yoga mat if you wish, but remember that space is limited—both on the bus and in some of the places we'll be staying, so choose wisely when you're packing. For our practice, the emphasis will be on taiji and qigong, which don't require mats. So there won't be any more group yoga for a while."

Lu paused as she looked over her list of announcements.

"June will fly back here once or twice to take care of bills and mail and whatever else needs attention, so she'll start up all the cars while she's here. We're hoping they will all fit in the driveway. As most of you know, the gate at the end of the driveway will be locked while we're away, and the alarm system will be on. So everything should be pretty secure."

Lu put down her notes and said, "Touring can be fun and exciting and rewarding—but also challenging, frustrating, and exhausting. Inevitably, there will be delays and frayed nerves and temper flares with long days in close quarters. For those of you who are going on the road with us for the first time, you'll find out whether or not this is a lifestyle that you want to embrace, but I guarantee the experience will change you in some way. You're in for quite a ride, both literally and figuratively."

"When exactly does the tour end?" Caitlin asked. She hadn't yet mentioned the congressional hearing to Luisa or June.

"We've still got some gaps we're hoping to fill," June said. "As of now, the last concert we have scheduled is around the summer solstice, in Asheville."

"That's North Carolina," Caitlin said, thinking aloud.

"Yes, the western part of the state," June said.

"How'd that work out with Kansas City?" Caitlin asked.

"Overland Park is a go," June said. "Your mother invited us to stay at her house, if people don't mind couches and floors. I told her we usually bring along sleeping bags and a few air mattresses for just such occasions."

"And the bus is always an option," said Seth.

"Yeah, but who wants to stay on the bus any longer than they have to?" said Pete.

"Rehearsals have been going well, I think," Lu said. "The music is coming together. Now we need to make sure that *we're* all coming together. I'd like to spend some time on interpersonal dynamics and conflict resolution—maybe tomorrow evening. Be thinking about what your triggers are. What kinds of people and situations push your buttons, and what is your usual reaction? We want to learn to stay calm and to respond rather than react."

She stood up and said, "It's a lovely evening. Let's go for a walk in the neighborhood. We can meditate on surrounding the whole area with a blanket of light."

∽ 66 ∽

Caitlin hurried downstairs on Friday morning, eager to learn about the group's new practice. The room was large enough for people to spread out and still see what Lu was doing.

"Qigong can be used to address specific imbalances and to restore health as we learn to coordinate our breathing and our bodies," Lu began. "We aim to achieve greater awareness of Spirit moving through us. Qi is all around us. Through our breath, we draw in energy from the cosmos."

Lu inhaled deeply and lifted her arms over her head with a scooping motion. As she exhaled, her hands swept the front of her body and cleared her energy field.

"We learn to gather energy and to direct it to the energy centers of the body. And to expel negative energies." She demonstrated this last point with a flicking motion of her hands.

"Traditional Chinese medicine holds that there are twelve primary energy meridians that run through the body," Lu said. "Qigong opens the flow of energy through the meridians."

Caitlin knew that acupuncture was also used to balance the flow of energy through the meridians—but that required going to someone licensed to practice acupuncture. These practices Lu was introducing could be done at home or in a park or airport or just about anywhere.

"There are thousands of forms of qigong," Lu continued. "Taiji is one form."

They would begin with standing postures, she said; eventually, they would learn the taiji routine she had previously demonstrated.

"Later on, we'll practice expanding and contracting qi, and maybe we'll do some partner work. We'll start slowly and continue to build on what we've learned. For now, we simply seek to get in touch with our bodies and the life force that flows through each of us. We don't seek to control it, just to gently awaken it and befriend it. Often, we suppress our innate urges rather than allowing them to guide us to greater well being. As you learn to access, trust, and follow your inner wisdom, your connection to Source will grow stronger and stronger."

She returned to her starting position and said, "Begin with your feet hip-width apart, your knees slightly bent. Allow your arms to hang gently at your sides. Touch the tip of your tongue to the roof of your mouth and inhale deeply, extending your abdomen as your lungs fill with air. As you exhale, contract your abdomen and expel the air, first from the bottom of your lungs and then from your chest. Experiment with different rates of breathing and find what feels comfortable for you."

Caitlin closed her eyes and focused on her breathing. Lu continued talking.

"In our qigong practice, we cultivate deep listening. Relaxation is important, as are intention and focus. Breathe out all stress and worry and let the tension melt from every part of your body as you connect with your infinite nature. Feel your connection to heaven and earth. And to each other."

Lu exhaled and said "Re-laax" in a soothing voice. Next, she led the group through some gentle warm-up exercises: swinging the arms from side to side, swaying the hips, and bending from the waist.

"Allow your body to move in harmony with the flow of your qi— whatever that means to you," Lu said.

Caitlin looked around to see what others were experiencing as they got in touch with their qi.

Allison's torso moved vigorously from side to side as she stood with her feet planted firmly. Watching Cara bobbing up and down, Caitlin was reminded of the pogo stick she had been given when she was a child. She had always had good balance, whether she was learning to ride a bicycle or walking the balance beam in gym class.

She bent her knees slightly and continued to focus on her breathing as she allowed her body to relax. After waiting for what seemed like half an hour (but probably was more like five minutes, she realized), she felt something.

It was subtle at first—an urge to move her arms in a particular way. She followed the urge, moving her legs as well as her arms and then bending with a swooping motion. She remembered Kimo telling her to move from her center, the dantian. When she returned to her starting position, her body seemed to vibrate with a gentle hum. She almost wanted to hum along with it!

Lu's instructions continued. "Now, shift your weight to the balls of your feet. Notice how that feels. Visualize the energy channels that pass through the front part of your body, beginning at your feet and moving along your legs and torso, hands and arms, face."

Caitlin had noticed a large chart on the wall in the back of the room that depicted the different acupuncture points in the body. She made a mental note to spend some time familiarizing herself with the primary meridians.

"Shift your weight to your heels and notice the back part of your body," Lu said. "Imagine the energy flowing down the back of your head, down your arms and spine and the back of your legs and then continuing down into the earth."

After several more exercises, they all went outside for a walking meditation in the backyard.

The rest of the morning was taken up with chores and tour preparations. Lu wanted the group to have a full dress rehearsal before they went on the road. She had approached several local venues about hosting the band as a charity fundraiser, but with such short notice, she wasn't able to arrange anything. "So we'll do it here," she announced at lunch. "Maybe Saturday night. Just us."

"I'm glad to know that not everything works out for Luisa, either," Caitlin told Cara as they walked to the rehearsal studio after lunch. "Shatters the illusion that she's Superwoman!"

"Oh yeah," Cara said casually. "False starts are an accepted part of the process. I've heard her say that we should accept roadblocks as indications we're either heading in the wrong direction or the timing is off. No point forcing something that's not coming together."

"Or taking it personally," Caitlin added.

At dinner, Lu announced that she had some exciting news to share with the group that evening.

"It must be really good if Lu's excited about it," Cara murmured.

Caitlin nodded. From what she had observed, Lu was usually a model of self-containment. She rarely got worked up about anything and seemed to take everything in stride. But now she seemed genuinely excited, which made everyone especially curious.

"I almost wish she hadn't said anything," Caitlin told Cara. "Now I just want to get through dinner to find out what it is!"

"She probably did it as an exercise in self-control," Cara said. She and Caitlin both laughed.

Caitlin had asked Cara about her background one evening as they got ready for bed. Cara said she had been teaching at a high school in the Midwest until budget cuts threatened some of the music programs. Though her job wasn't in immediate danger, she was ready for a change.

Another Midwesterner, Caitlin thought. *Maybe that's why we get along so well.*

Cara had been playing cello in a string quartet, she said, but there wasn't much call for a cello in the Road Angels—so she had taken up the flute.

"Is there much call for flute music?" Caitlin had asked.

"Hee hee," Cara laughed. "Maybe not! More than cello, anyway."

Cara explained that her degree was in music education.

"I've got some proficiency with a variety of instruments," she said, "but the band seemed to have enough guitar and piano/keyboard players. Lu approved it, so . . ." She shrugged as her voice trailed off. "My background is in instrumental music, so pop songs are kind of a new thing for me. If that's what you'd call what the band plays. That's certainly what they *were* playing before they started recording their own songs."

Caitlin asked Cara what had drawn her to the group.

"After my mother died, I felt like I needed to take care of myself for a while."

"Were you her caregiver?"

"Her last summer I was. It was tough going back to teaching in August. I was exhausted."

She had been meditating for many years and had traveled to India on a tour organized by her meditation teacher, Cara said, but she thought Lu's group would help her bring her interest in music together with her interest in spirituality.

"That's probably a good description of why a lot of us are here," Caitlin said.

When the group gathered after dinner, Lu said, "I got a call today from Washington, D.C. We've been invited to sing 'America the Beautiful' on the Fourth of July."

"All of us?" asked Jordan.

"I was thinking Caitlin, Allison, and Marya could carry the song. Everyone else would sing backup."

"And play instruments," Pete said.

"Yes, you'll play your instruments. Along with the National Symphony Orchestra."

"Whoa!" said Matt.

"Wow," said Rick. "Quite an honor."

"Wait a minute," Caitlin said. "Is this the concert that they have every year, on the National Mall? The one that's on television?"

"The very same," Lu said.

"Don't they usually choose big name acts for that?" asked Crystal.

Lu shrugged. "Who knows. It's a new millennium. Maybe they wanted more diversity. Or maybe someone influential saw us perform somewhere. I'm sure there will be plenty of celebrities in the lineup."

"I've never been to Washington," said André.

"I'd like to visit the White House," said Troy.

"Will we be able to do any sightseeing?" asked Allison.

"Perhaps," Lu said. "In terms of scheduling, this means that after Asheville we'll head straight to Washington. And that will be the end of the tour."

"That's quite a finale!" said Sky.

Talk about the show and the tour continued, but Caitlin was too distracted to listen. She was still absorbing the news. She would be singing at the concert that she and the gang from the Office of Special Projects used to attend on Independence Day!

She could hardly believe where her journey had taken her. She had dreamed of acting on the stage and that dream had come true. This opportunity was beyond her wildest dreams. And the person she most wanted to tell was Karl.

But when?

She looked around, as if she would discover the answer in a place she hadn't looked before. The house phone was in the music room, and that room was often in use. During the day, June and Lu were usually in the office, or close by. Calling after the group's evening session wouldn't work; they often didn't finish until nine o'clock, so with the three-hour time difference between the West Coast and the East, it would be after midnight in Virginia.

She would have to stop looking for the perfect time, she decided, and just call.

∞ 67 ∞

*C*aitlin used the phone in the office to call Karl after dinner on Sunday. He didn't answer, and she didn't leave a message.

No message could adequately convey all that she wanted to tell him. She needed to talk to him. She would try again another time. He was probably at work during the day, but what else was he involved with, now that his training was complete? How did he spend his time?

She wanted to know all about his life, all about him. They had so much to catch up on, and her eagerness could no longer be contained.

We need to talk, she thought as she walked down the hall for the group's evening session. *Well, I* need to talk, *anyway! And I'm also ready to listen.*

After the evening check-in, Lu walked to the front of the room. The rest of the group stood and watched her.

"The more you practice these exercises, the easier time you'll have, both in remaining calm through life's challenges and in regaining your composure after an upset," Lu said. "You'll become more resilient and flexible."

She demonstrated the first three taiji forms and then said, "Getting to that calm place inside is half the battle. When you can detach from the need to have situations turn out a certain way—or to have people behave or think the way you'd like them to—remaining calm and centered is much easier. You expand your energy rather than dissipating it through conflict and resistance and negative tendencies. By surrendering to a Higher Power, you align your personal will with that of the Creator."

She invited everyone to follow along as she demonstrated the movements again.

"Of course, life isn't always filled with sunshine and harmony, and you won't always feel like doing the work. But when it's hardest is often when it's needed most."

After the group had practiced the three forms for a while, Lu took a break. "Being part of a group like this—and, sometimes, being part of an intimate relationship—intensifies the transformational process," she said. "We're in a cauldron here. From time to time, the heat gets turned up, and depending on the circumstances, some people are likely to feel it more than others. Stick around long enough and you'll be the one in the hot seat, so don't think you'll be spared. If you get too complacent or feel superior when you see others struggling, know that your turn will come. And then you will be humbled!"

Lu's warning evoked nervous laughter from some of the newer members of the group and a few nods from those who had been around awhile.

"Let's spend our remaining time this evening doing a partner exercise. Find someone you'll feel comfortable sharing something deeply personal with."

With a laugh, Rick said, "And what if we don't feel comfortable sharing deeply personal things with anyone?"

"Then you'll need to move out of your comfort zone," Lu said. "Surely you've all had to do that at some time since arriving here?"

"Only every single day since I got here," Seth said as he and Jordan headed to a corner of the room.

Caitlin had been paired with Cara often enough, she decided; she, too, would step outside her comfort zone and work with someone she didn't know as well.

She asked Crystal to join her. They sat across from each other on pillows that they placed in the center of the room and then waited for Lu's instructions.

"Let's work on forgiveness. First, I want you to close your eyes and take a few cleansing breaths. What are you ready to release? Who do you need to forgive? What's holding you back from being your most radiant self? Is it anger? Jealousy? Resentment? Ask your heart. What do you need in order to be fully healed? It could be to feel heard, or to speak your truth, or to yell or cry or be held."

After a pause, Lu said, "Take a few minutes to listen for the answer. When you're ready, you can begin. Decide who will share first, and support your partner in whatever way seems appropriate."

Caitlin invited Crystal to go first.

"It's my sister," Crystal said, nodding. "She's younger than me and, well, I just don't get her. She distorts the facts and makes me sound like a spiteful, malicious ogre!"

"The way she talks to you, you mean?"

"Well, it's mostly my mother that I hear things from. And, in fairness to Jenny, my mother probably adds her own flavoring to the mix. But even when Jenny complains directly to me about something, she never remembers it quite the way it happened. Or at least not the way I remember it happening. And she never seems to recall all the times I've gone out of my way to help her."

"I can see that this relationship pattern really bothers you," Caitlin said. "But what, exactly, is it that you need to let go of? Or that you need to forgive? Can you put it into words?"

Crystal thought for a while and then said, "Expectations, I guess. We're just never going to have the kind of relationship I'd like to have with a sister. I mean, I know she'll never be interested in the things I'm pursuing—spirituality and all—and she doesn't understand my choices." She glanced around the room as she said, "She doesn't know anything about what goes on here."

Crystal sighed. Caitlin thought she seemed sad or disappointed. She waited for Crystal to say more, when she was ready, and hoped she felt supported as she got in touch with her feelings.

"But even normal stuff," Crystal continued. "Confiding in each other, wanting to spend time together and . . . I don't know, go shopping?"

"So, really, all you can do is love her and bless her and try to be patient with her shortcomings. And, like you said, let go of expectations."

Crystal frowned. "Yeah, but it makes me sad because I've been keeping her at a distance more and more. Fewer opportunities for misunderstandings that way."

"So maybe if you can calmly address the problems that come up, you can show her how people work through things together, using the tools that you've learned from being part of the group. What do you think motivates her behavior when she distorts the facts? Do you think it's intentional, or maybe she isn't even aware of when she's doing it? Does she just remember things differently than you do, or interpret situations differently? Do you think she wants a closer relationship with you?"

"Well if she does she's sure got a strange way of showing it!" Crystal said. "I honestly don't know what her issue is—if she's jealous of me or she just doesn't even like me or what. But *my* issue is that I'm done trying. I've tried everything I know to try, and I'm just letting go. I'm not pushing her away—I'm here if she's ever ready to stop this game she's playing. But I'm not bending over backwards anymore to try to fix things between us."

"Amen!" Caitlin said, affirming Crystal's clarity and determination to not let her sister's behavior get her down.

Crystal was right to focus on her own thoughts and behavior, Caitlin thought.

We're all affected by other people, but we can't control how they think or feel. We can't make them love us or appreciate us or treat us the way we want to be treated. If our best doesn't seem good enough, if our pleas fall on deaf ears, sometimes we have to let go. The situation can change, but we can't assume that it will.

"How about you? What baggage are you ready to unload?" Crystal asked with a laugh.

Caitlin took a deep breath and said, "I don't know how ready I am, but I know I need to take a step in that direction. The whole theme of forgiveness struck a chord when Lu said that was the focus this evening."

"Okay, so who do you need to forgive?"

"My father." Caitlin nodded but didn't say more.

"For?"

"For giving up."

"On you?"

"On everything. On himself. On life."

"Is he still living?"

"No. He died eight years ago. He was having a hard time. Everyone seems to think it was an intentional overdose, and maybe it was. I guess I'll never know," Caitlin said glumly. Her mood lightening, she added, "Unless he comes and tells me!"

"Hey," Crystal said, "could happen."

Caitlin laughed. "It could, actually."

She had heard of people communicating with souls who had departed and believed it was possible. She was convinced now that the soul has an existence that is greater than a single lifetime. The soul might even influence some of the choices we make—and some of the talents we have—in ways our conscious minds don't understand.

"I have been pretty angry at him, though," Caitlin said, her eyes welling up with tears. "I think in some way I took it personally, like he'd betrayed *me*. But he was just trying to deal with his pain." She took a tissue from the box Crystal handed to her. "Or *end* his pain, I guess."

"And forgiving him doesn't mean you think what he did was right," Crystal said.

"No," Caitlin said. "It means I'm willing to remember his life as a whole, and not just how it ended."

"And to get back to the love I'm sure you had for him," Crystal said, squeezing Caitlin's hand.

"I think part of what has taken a while is that I've had to change my whole image of him. Of who I thought he was. And I can see where I'd been in denial about some things, like his alcoholism. He drank. He always had. It's what I grew up with, so I didn't analyze it. It was a problem, sure, but it was a problem we just dealt with. I'd never known him any other way, never wondered if he *could* be any other way. Never wondered if there was help available. Who was I to tell my father he needed help? He was who he was." Looking up at Crystal, Caitlin added, "And I did, I loved him anyway."

She shifted her position on the floor and sat up straighter. "But now, I want to be strong enough—and clear enough—to see things as they really are," she said with growing confidence and enthusiasm. "To the extent that we ever can, anyway. I don't want to be like your sister!"

They both laughed.

"Seriously, though. In all my relationships. I want them to be . . . authentic. I know not everyone is capable of meeting me there, but I'll hold up my end."

"That's all we can do," Crystal said.

Lu struck a tuning fork to signal the end of the exercise, and Caitlin and Crystal hugged before putting their cushions away.

Next, everyone stood in a circle and held hands.

"Let's close our eyes and take a moment to honor ourselves for our willingness to share our deepest truths and heal our deepest wounds. For as we become more whole, we also become more free, and we empower others to transform their lives, too. We're all on this Earth journey together. What we do matters. Namaste."

Walking to her room, Caitlin felt a little lighter. Maybe some of the pain she had been carrying had been lifted from her heart. The waves of grief came less often now than they had in the past.

She was willing to change her mind about her father, see him as he was. As a man, not just as her father.

Perhaps we can't ever really know another person. I'm not sure we can even fully know ourselves!

How many lifetimes had she experienced that she didn't know about?

Only the soul knew its true reasons for taking on a new personality. And when the time had come to depart.

～ 68 ～

The first day of June, Caitlin thought when she opened her eyes. *Today's the day.*

Downstairs, the house was buzzing. After a hurried breakfast, Matt, Seth, Sky, Rick, and Pete loaded the bus with instruments and equipment and suitcases. André and Troy cleaned up in the kitchen while Marya and Allison packed the lunch they had prepared for later. June was overseeing the whole operation, and Lu was on her cell phone, confirming arrangements for the group's stay in Sedona.

Caitlin placed her suitcase by the door and walked to the office. She had called Karl's landline every day since Sunday. Sometimes in the morning, after breakfast; sometimes right before dinner. No answer. She decided to call one last time before the group left for Arizona. If she still didn't reach Karl, she would ask Melody if she knew anything about his whereabouts. The band would arrive in New Mexico the following week. She and Melody could catch up then.

It's nearly noon in Virginia, she thought as she dialed Karl's number.

"Hello."

Caitlin's heart fluttered at the sound of Karl's voice. "Hey, stranger! I've been trying to reach you for days!"

"Caitlin? I've been in Pennsylvania this last week. You know I bought some land there, right?"

"You're building a house?"

"The house is done and I'm slowly moving in. I brought a load of stuff up. I'll be fully moved in by the end of the summer. I've still got a few clients here, so I'll have to figure out how often I need to drive down to see them. Anyway, I got in late last night, so I'm still in bed if you can believe that."

"Sorry if I caught you at a bad time," Caitlin said. "I'm about to get on the road myself, and I was hoping we could talk before I leave."

"Where to this time?"

"Actually, I'm headed your way. I've got so much to tell you. I hardly know where to start. I'm going on tour with a group called the Road Angels. Did Melody ever talk about them?"

"No, I don't think so."

"It's a band that Lu started. I'm sure she's told you about Lu."

"Oh yeah."

"I met her in Santa Fe, and she invited me to come out to L.A. to record a couple of my songs and—well, now I'm joining the band on a national tour. The first show was last weekend, in Santa Barbara. My mother came, actually."

"Glad to hear it."

"Yeah, she and I are on pretty good terms now. She and her husband drove out."

"No shit! You finally met your stepfather?"

"Yeah. It went okay."

"You sound great. I guess you were right—L.A. was the place for you."

"For my music anyway. I'm not so sure it's the place for me, long term. But I haven't even told you the best part."

Before she could tell Karl about the ritual in New Mexico or recovering her memory of the Shannon Pot or the invitation to testify or the Fourth of July concert, June knocked on the door and said, "You've got five minutes. We're about ready to go."

"Okay," Caitlin told her.

"Sorry?" Karl said.

"I'm gonna have to go in a minute. But I wanted to tell you—"

Caitlin heard a female voice asking "How many eggs do you want, hon?" and then she heard Karl's muffled reply. "Uh, two I guess. Thanks."

"Are you eating eggs now?" Caitlin asked. The last she knew, Karl was committed to a vegan diet.

"Occasionally," he said.

"Well, it sounds like you've got company. Here I've been babbling on. I didn't think—"

"That's okay," Karl said. "I'm really glad to hear from you." After a pause he said, "Angela and I have been together about six months now."

"Oh," Caitlin said, taken aback. She wasn't quite sure what to say next or how much to share, but she felt her energy field contracting. Had she waited too long? Should she pour out her heart, let Karl know how much he meant to her?

Even if she wanted to, she didn't have time. The bus was ready to go. And he had someone there waiting for him, too.

"Okay, well, I'll be in town next month," Caitlin said. "Maybe we can get together. You've been on my mind a lot since—well, a lot has happened. I . . . I remember."

"You remember?"

"The Shannon Pot. I remember what happened."

"Oh!"

"And I just want you to know," Caitlin started to say before getting distracted by the sound of a horn honking. "I wanted you to know that I love you."

She knew she was about to start crying. "I've gotta go. But I'll be in D.C. for the Fourth of July. I'm singing 'America the Beautiful'! Can you believe it? Well, along with two other women. So maybe I'll see you then. Take care."

She didn't wait for a reply. She'd heard all she needed to hear. She hung up the phone and hurried to the bus. Once seated, she pulled out her handkerchief and blew her nose.

She could forget any romantic ideas she'd had about Karl welcoming her with a bouquet of roses and declaring his undying love for her.

No one would be waiting for her at the end of the tour, so she'd better stay focused on each step of the journey.

Hopefully, the music, the camaraderie, and the joy of performing would draw her attention away from the ache in her heart.

PART FOUR

FULL CIRCLE

∾ 69 ∾

The bus left Arizona on Monday morning. Caitlin settled into her seat by the window and reflected on her return visit to Sedona. Other than an annoying buzz in the sound system at the venue where the band played Friday night, everything had gone well during the group's stay. Days were warm and sunny; nights were clear and mild.

On Saturday, Lu had given everyone a free day. Crystal, always on the lookout for costume ideas, went in search of thrift stores to hunt for bargains and novel wardrobe items, and Marya went with her. Allison and Jordan went to a movie; Cara relaxed by the pool. Troy accompanied Rick, who was eager to take pictures of the scenic vistas. The rest of the guys went hiking.

The group's accommodations were within walking distance of shops and restaurants, and Caitlin enjoyed having a day to herself. After wandering through an art gallery's outdoor sculpture garden, she bought a t-shirt and a chunk of amethyst at one of the shops and then found a restaurant with a few organic items on the menu. She ordered roast chicken with sides of pasta and asparagus and enjoyed the view of the red rocks before returning to the hotel, refreshed.

She hadn't heard of Unity centers before and was surprised to learn that the movement had originated in the Kansas City area. The Sunday celebration was more uplifting than the church services her family had attended regularly during her childhood in Olathe, and Caitlin enjoyed chatting with people afterward about her song "Rainbow Bridge." A potluck luncheon was provided, and quite a few people stayed for the band's afternoon concert. The tour was off to a good start.

After several hours on the bus, Caitlin began to feel drowsy. She put her head on her pillow and slept until the bus came to a stop at a scenic viewpoint near the Laguna Pueblo. Rick stood up and announced, "We're about forty miles from Albuquerque."

A few people wanted to get out and take pictures. Caitlin could see the whitewashed mission church from her window. She smiled, remembering her time at Jemez with Lilly and Porcingula.

Hard to believe that was only a month ago!

She wasn't surprised to find herself retracing the route she had recently driven, but she hadn't expected to be returning to Santa Fe via tour bus.

The group would be staying at the house Luisa kept in Tesuque. When the band was on hiatus, which happened several times a year, Lu escaped from the City of Angels and spent time at her own personal retreat.

When everyone was back on the bus, Troy got behind the wheel and headed east on I-40.

Caitlin thought about the diverse backgrounds of the people in the band. She and Lu were the only licensed professionals; she and Cara were the only ones in their thirties. Caitlin guessed that Pete, Seth, Crystal, Marya, Sky, and Matt were in their mid-twenties. Troy, André, Allison, and Jordan were the youngest members of the group. Rick was probably in his late twenties. Luisa and June had to be in their forties. June was the only parent. Divorced, she had a daughter in college.

Caitlin was well aware that her biological clock was ticking. She would be turning thirty-seven soon. She was running out of time if she wanted children. Did she?

Having a child on her own wasn't something she was prepared to attempt; she was clear about that much. Even if she never married, she could create a full life for herself, but she had always imagined— almost *assumed*—that she would have a family.

Of course, family can mean many things, she thought, looking around the bus. *I guess it will all come down to finding the right partner.*

She wouldn't have children with just any man. Her partner would have to be patient and kind and supportive, and he would have to allow her the freedom to continue her creative and professional pursuits. He would also have to have a strong identity and value equality. She had been on her own far too long to allow herself to be dominated by an overbearing spouse, and she didn't want to become a nagging wife, either. Her marriage would be a respectful, loving union of two complementary souls—or she wouldn't marry.

I'll just have cats!

Thinking of Lucky brought a smile to her face. *I hope Melody won't mind keeping him a little longer.*

She hadn't called Melody to let her know she was coming to New Mexico; she figured Lu had told her about the house concert she was planning. Undoubtedly, Lu had contacted everyone she knew—including Paul. *Should I call him?* Caitlin wondered.

Without a car, she wouldn't have an easy way to get around. But she would be at Lu's house for over a week. Would Paul be offended if she didn't call him? Did it matter? Maybe she would ask Lu if she thought he would come to the concert.

Caitlin turned and saw that Lu was standing in the aisle talking to Pete and Matt as she made her way to the front of the bus.

"Okay, everyone. Listen up!" Lu said. "We're really weighted down, and we're coming up on La Bajada, which is a very steep incline. So we want to give our bus—and our driver—the confidence to climb to the top! Let's all think light thoughts—"

"Like in *Peter Pan*?" Cara shouted.

Caitlin understood the reference to the scene in the musical when Peter teaches the Darling children to fly, though she wasn't sure the younger members of the group would get it.

"Exactly," Lu said. "Let's fly to the top. What shall we sing to help get us there?"

"'Fly Me to the Moon'?" offered Seth.

"Don't know it," said Sky.

Allison suggested "Up Where We Belong," and then Crystal said, "Oh, I know! 'Chitty Chitty Bang Bang'!" Everyone laughed at that idea.

"Hey, don't knock it," Crystal said. "The car can fly, after all!"

"How about 'Don't Stop Believin''?" said Pete. "We all know it."

When others agreed, Pete sang the first few lines, followed by Matt. Marya sang the next verse. Everyone joined in for the chorus, and as the song neared the end, Caitlin sang a line solo.

The bus crept up the long hill, and the passengers grew restless as they neared Santa Fe. Pete and Matt threw paper airplanes, Seth played "Fly Me to the Moon" on his sax, Crystal and Marya looked through a fashion magazine for ideas about hairstyles, and Lu and June conferred about their to-do lists.

After exiting Interstate 25, Troy made his way to U.S. Route 84. Before long, Caitlin saw the sign for Tesuque. She had driven this way to Melody's guest house.

Wait a minute—that is *Melody's guest house!*

Troy drove down the long gravel driveway and, once again, Caitlin found herself shaking her head in amazement.

Makes sense, I guess.

Melody probably either got cheap rent or didn't pay any rent in exchange for looking after Luisa's place, Caitlin thought as the bus came to a stop in front of the main house.

She stood up when Lu walked by and said, "I hadn't realized this was your house when I came to visit Melody here."

"She's in the casita," Lu said. "She's been helping me spread the word about Friday's concert. Well—Saturday's, too, for that matter!"

Lu continued walking toward the front of the bus. She had told the group the weekend would be busy, with back-to-back concerts in Tesuque and Albuquerque, but they would have plenty of time to relax after that, as they didn't leave for Colorado until the following Wednesday.

Caitlin gathered her things and followed the others into the house. Lu gave them all a quick tour.

The house was spacious, with three bedrooms upstairs and a fourth bedroom downstairs, near the front door. Another small room was set up as an office. The large living room would be the setting for the house concert. The family room would serve as a lounge where people could visit, and the long table in the dining room could be used for serving refreshments as well as displaying the t-shirts and CDs that would be available for purchase.

The master bedroom was upstairs; Lu would share it with June.

Caitlin's room was furnished with twin beds. She chose the bed by the window and was again sharing with Cara. An adjoining bathroom connected their room and the room next door, occupied by Crystal and Marya. Allison and Jordan were assigned the downstairs bedroom. The men would sleep on couches and air mattresses.

After all the groceries had been brought inside, the kitchen team started preparing dinner. Caitlin brought her things to her room and looked out the window. She could see the guest house from there, but she didn't see Melody's car.

She walked over to the casita and checked the door. Locked. She looked through a window, hoping to catch a glimpse of Lucky. Realizing that if he spotted her he wouldn't understand why she didn't come inside to see him, she walked back to the house.

Luisa was in the kitchen, putting rice and pasta and condiments on shelves in the pantry.

"Do you know if Paul will be coming to the concert?" Caitlin asked.

"I don't know. I expect he'll come if he can, but you know how busy he is."

Lu closed the pantry door and put on an apron. "Oh, by the way," she said, picking up a large bag of carrots. "I've arranged a radio interview for you and Pete in Albuquerque on Friday. The morning show. You'll have to leave early to get down there in time. June and I need to stay here to get everything ready for the concert that night, so you two will have to go on your own. Melody said you could take her car. You know the way, and you're a friend of hers, so I suggest you do the driving, if that's all right with you."

"Sure," Caitlin said. She watched as Lu started scrubbing a couple dozen carrots and noticed a juicer on the counter. "Can I help with anything?"

"There are glasses in the cupboard behind you," Lu said. "There should be enough for everyone."

Caitlin put the glasses on the counter and left the kitchen when Lu turned on the juicer.

She didn't mind driving to Albuquerque, but she wasn't thrilled about spending several hours alone with Pete. He'd been the least friendly member of the group.

Probably Lu's way of forcing us to relate to each other.

∾ 70 ∾

*C*rystal was on breakfast duty and had volunteered to get something ready for Caitlin and Pete before they left for Albuquerque. She was already in the kitchen when Caitlin went downstairs.

Caitlin walked past her and sat at the kitchen table, humming the theme song from *Chitty Chitty Bang Bang*.

Crystal laughed. "What song would you have chosen for the drive up the hill?" she asked before setting out the beverage selections.

Caitlin thought for a moment. "Um . . . 'Ain't No Mountain High Enough,' maybe?"

"That's good, too!" Crystal said. "Oatmeal is ready, or I could boil some eggs if you'd like."

"Oatmeal will be fine," Caitlin said. "I think I'll have some tea. I can get it myself. If that's okay."

"Oh, yeah, go ahead. Things seem a little more relaxed here than in Santa Monica."

"Only because no one is up yet!" Caitlin said as she poured steaming water into a mug. "Lots going on today."

Crystal set a bowl of oatmeal on the table for Caitlin and a plate with a slice of toast for herself. She stirred a cup of coffee and sat across from Caitlin. "So you used to be a lawyer," she said before spreading strawberry preserves on her toast.

"Mm-hmm," Caitlin murmured. She mixed raisins and walnuts into her oatmeal and said, "Still am. I'm just not practicing."

"What kinds of cases did you work on?"

"All kinds. I worked for the Department of Justice. In Washington. But it's a little early in the morning for me to think about all that. I'm wondering what this interview at the radio station will be like. I'm surprised Lu would send Pete and me off on our own. I don't really know what to expect."

"I'm sure you'll be able to handle whatever comes up."

"Pete and I seem to lock horns a lot," Caitlin said quietly.

Crystal laughed. "He can be a little hard to take sometimes. I'm hoping Marya will be a good influence on him."

"Oh, are they—"

Crystal nodded and sipped her coffee. "It's recent."

"Hmm," Caitlin said. Changing the subject, she asked Crystal about her background.

"I grew up with MTV and wanted to dance in music videos," Crystal said. "But then I got injured. That pretty much put an end to those dreams."

"I understand how that goes," Caitlin said before drinking her tea.

Crystal stood up and took her plate to the sink. "I met Seth at a choreography workshop," she said. "He had just joined Lu's group and he was encouraging her to add more movement to the show." She glanced at the clock on the wall and said, "I wonder where Pete is. He won't have time to eat if he doesn't get his butt in here soon."

Caitlin smiled. "I think I'll go grab my things and get ready." She rose from the table and pushed in her chair. "Thanks for the breakfast. And the chat!"

"My pleasure!"

Pete opened the door to the kitchen just as Caitlin was reaching for the handle. He walked past her and asked Crystal, "Any bagels left?"

Caitlin closed the door behind her and went upstairs. She put on lipstick and mascara and then looked at her reflection in the bathroom mirror. *It's radio,* she reminded herself. *You don't need to look good!*

She tiptoed into the bedroom so she wouldn't wake Cara.

Maybe not, she thought, *but I need to* feel *good.*

Sometimes the right attitude—and the right outfit—helped set the tone for a meeting. *If nothing else, it boosts my confidence.*

She picked up her purse and the sweater she had laid on a chair and walked downstairs. Lu had said she would leave the keys to Melody's car on the kitchen counter.

Pete was leaning against the counter—right in front of the keys—chatting with Crystal. Caitlin reached around him and grabbed the keys.

"I'll be in the car," she said before leaving.

Pete followed, taking his half-eaten bagel and a cup of coffee with him. When he got into the passenger seat of the car, coffee spilled onto his jeans.

Caitlin rolled her eyes and started the engine, thinking, *This is going to be a long day.*

The deejay's casual manner helped put Caitlin at ease. He had seen her in *Park Avenue* and brought up her time in Santa Fe while they were on the air, asking about her involvement with the Playhouse and the switch from stage actress to recording artist and musician.

"It seemed like the natural progression in my evolution as a singer," Caitlin said.

She realized that the conversation was focused more on her than on the Road Angels, but that wasn't her doing. She didn't want to be rude. She answered the questions that were put to her.

"And what about 'Shining Star'"? Did you write this about you and your mother?"

"Strictly speaking, no, it's not autobiographical. The lyrics toward the end of the song are about being a mother, which I'm not. I hope to be someday, but I think there are things you don't really understand about being a parent until you are one yourself—or are old enough to be able to put yourself in your parents' shoes and realize the struggles they had and the sacrifices they made. So I'd say it was inspired by my relationship with my mother and my appreciation for her after we worked out some of our issues. Which, probably, all mothers and daughters have, I'm guessing!"

"Issues."

"Yes."

"Well, let's have a listen," the deejay said.

When the song finished playing, he announced, "And that was 'Shining Star' by our guest here in the studio, Caitlin Rose, backed up by her band, the Road Angels. Caitlin, Pete, thanks for joining us today. And all you listeners out there in Radioland, stay tuned for your chance to win tickets to Saturday's concert."

Caitlin didn't have a chance to correct him until after they were off the air for a commercial break.

"It's not my band," she said. "If anything, I'm their guest!"

She glanced at Pete, who was glaring at her.

"Oh, gee—sorry," said the deejay. "But honestly, no one's going to know the difference."

Caitlin and Pete both thanked the man for his time.

"Thanks for stopping in," the deejay said, shaking their outstretched hands. "I'm looking forward to the show."

"Me too!" Caitlin said, flashing a big smile.

The promotional part of the tour seemed to be going well, she thought. Pete apparently disagreed.

"That's just great," he muttered as they left the station. "We all work and slave for months and then you come along and take all the credit!"

"I didn't steer the conversation that way. I just answered his questions. I can't help it if he's a fan. I lived in Santa Fe for two years."

Caitlin opened the doors to Melody's car and got inside. Pete stood outside for a moment, as if he wished he could find another way back to Tesuque. Then he sat in the passenger seat and slammed the door.

"The Playhouse is a popular theater," Caitlin said as Pete sulked. "And you should be glad about that, because some of those same people who saw me in a musical there will probably come to the show on Saturday. And that will benefit the whole band, not just me."

Now she was worked up. She wanted to add, "Save the temper tantrum for your girlfriend!" but kept quiet.

She drove out of the parking lot and headed toward I-25. She was thinking of stopping at the Mexican restaurant where she had eaten on her way to L.A.

"Are you hungry?" she asked, breaking the silence.

"It's ten thirty," Pete stated emphatically, as if Caitlin had asked a ridiculous question.

"By the time we order and get our food it will be after eleven," Caitlin said. "We'll probably miss lunch with the group. And I don't know about you, but I'm not normally a vegetarian, so I look forward to opportunities to eat out."

The food served by the kitchen team was good—and healthy—but Caitlin wasn't a fan of soy products and she didn't normally eat so many grain dishes. Eating out occasionally satisfied her need for variety.

"Fine," Pete said. "Whatever."

He never said whether he was a vegetarian, but he ordered beef tacos so Caitlin guessed he wasn't.

She also guessed he would never admit it if she did something that pleased him. He had made up his mind about her, and he intended to remain disapproving, it seemed.

They didn't speak during lunch. Caitlin decided that was just as well; she would rather save her voice for the concert that evening.

On the drive to Tesuque, she played one of Melody's CDs of Native American flute music. Back at Lu's property, she parked the car by the casita. Pete walked to the main house. Caitlin knocked on Melody's front door. The door was unlocked, so she went inside to visit Lucky.

"Hey little fella!" she said after setting Melody's car keys on the table.

Lucky meowed and rubbed against her legs. Caitlin picked him up and said, "How are you today?" She had been visiting him every day, usually more than once, but she hadn't had a chance to talk to Melody yet.

She found the brush she had left with Lucky's toys and brushed his fur, talking to him all the while. "I'm heading back to Virginia soon, you know. So maybe I'll see our pal Kimo. He's got a girlfriend now, I guess. I'll have to ask Melody what she knows about their relationship and if it's serious."

She was still coming to terms with the idea that Karl was seeing someone.

Heck, maybe Paul is too, she thought. He wasn't one to stay unattached for long.

She put the brush away and said, "Well, I better get back and see what's going on with the group. I can just imagine what Pete's been telling everyone."

Melody couldn't have gone far without a car, Caitlin thought as she walked across the gravel driveway. *Maybe she's over at the house.*

"She went to Santa Fe with Lu for supplies," June said. She and Allison were spreading a cloth over the long table in the dining room.

The radio in the kitchen was tuned to the station in Albuquerque, so Caitlin figured that everyone had probably heard the interview.

No one said anything about it, though, so she went upstairs to her room. Cara was there, playing her flute. She set it down when Caitlin came in.

"Was everybody mad?" Caitlin asked. "Pete threw a fit after we left the station."

"Oh, well, yeah—that's Pete for ya," said Cara. "I don't personally know what Marya sees in him."

"Is that allowed?" Caitlin asked. "I mean, are there any rules about couples in the group?"

Cara shrugged. "Anyway, I don't think anyone was bothered about the interview. We all know you were something of a star when you lived here."

Caitlin felt her eyebrows go up. "Oh, I don't know about *that.*"

Was that why people kept their distance from her a bit? Did they think she thought she was special? She hadn't ever behaved like a prima donna—but, then, she hadn't been assigned to kitchen duty, either. Cara had recently been added to the kitchen team, replacing Cherry. Wouldn't Caitlin have been the logical replacement? She had taken over Cherry's role in the band.

Not that I want to volunteer for kitchen duty! she thought as she headed for the stairs.

She was, after all, a guest of the band, not a permanent member. Maybe different rules *should* apply. When this tour was over, she didn't plan to live in Santa Monica with the group. She wasn't quite sure what she would do, but she still had time to decide. She would have to go back to L.A. to get her car at some point, and she still had stuff in storage in Santa Fe. She and Lucky could always go to the lake house for a while if no other opportunities presented themselves, though she didn't really want to spend another winter there. She didn't know a soul in the area.

As she walked down the stairs, she passed André, Sky, and Troy, who were taking their belongings upstairs to the bedrooms in preparation for the concert that evening. They didn't seem to mind the sleeping arrangements and took it all in stride.

They could expect more of the same if they all stayed at Martha and Ray's house, Caitlin thought. She hadn't ever been there, but how big a place could it be?

Maybe we could swing by the lake house for a night after that.

It wouldn't be too far out of the way, and though the house was small, it was surrounded by a lot of land. Maybe some people would want to camp outside. The setting was peaceful, and they would have the place to themselves. She would ask June for an update on the itinerary, she decided.

I know I'll be ready for some down time after a night with my mother and Ray.

∞ 71 ∞

"You've got to be kidding me," Caitlin murmured when the bus pulled up to the KiMo Theatre in Albuquerque. Hard as she tried, she just couldn't get away from reminders of Karl. She hadn't had a lot of time to fret about him—or who he was with—and that was probably a good thing.

She had asked Melody about him the night before, but Melody said she didn't hear from him much anymore. "I know he's been busy moving," she added.

"Is she moving with him?"

"Angela? Oh I doubt it. She's got a good job in Washington."

The intimate environment of the house concert had been a lot of fun, Caitlin thought as she walked toward the theater's dressing rooms. Tonight, the band would be performing in a historic landmark before an audience of six hundred—about the same size as in Santa Barbara. Only now, Caitlin would be onstage for the entire show. Several costume changes were planned—and none of her outfits were pink.

Melody would be in the audience, Caitlin knew, but what about Paul? Would he be there?

He hadn't come to the concert the night before, Caitlin had realized when she went to bed. Everyone was always so wired after a show. They'd all stayed up late, laughing and eating and talking about how everything went. Caitlin joined the others for a quick snack and a cup of tea and then went to bed. She'd had a long, full day.

After tonight, the group would have three days to relax before they headed to Colorado. There would still be time to see Paul, Caitlin thought, if she really wanted to. But she wasn't sure she wanted to. Maybe someday, but not yet. Their parting was still too recent.

The band was called back to the stage for an encore, and then the crew got busy packing up the instruments and equipment to load onto the bus. Caitlin grabbed a bottle of spring water and walked out to the lobby of the theater to see if anyone she knew was hanging around. The deejay from the radio station came up to greet her.

"Did you enjoy the show?" Caitlin asked him.

"I did," he said. "It's different. Hard to categorize, which makes marketing a little more challenging. Not really folk or rock or pop. But elements of all of them."

"And some country," Caitlin said. "At least, for 'Road Angel,' which I wrote."

"Yeah, that was catchy. Not really the kind of thing I listen to, but you might find an audience for it."

"The way I look at it," Caitlin said, "a lot of groups have a few songs where they try to say something meaningful, whether it's about politics or spirituality or to raise awareness about issues like the environment or child abuse—think Suzanne Vega's 'Luka.' Our music is infused with positive messages—we aim to share love and peace, and hope and inspiration. But sometimes we just want to have fun and share our joy. I think people can relate to joy."

"Can I quote you on that?" the deejay asked.

The question surprised Caitlin, but she was surprised by many things these days. Life was becoming a wonderful journey, with new revelations and blessings appearing on a regular basis.

She thought for a moment and said, "Yeah, I guess," not sure if the man was even serious. "What's your name again?"

"Al," he told her.

"Okay, Al. Well, thanks for coming out tonight."

Caitlin shook his hand and then walked to her dressing room to change out of her costume.

∞ 72 ∞

*S*unday was a lazy day. Everyone slept late and then lounged around the house, catching up on personal calls, writing letters, or journaling.

A signup sheet for using the computer in Lu's home office was posted by the desk. Caitlin hadn't checked her email in a while and found she had new messages when she signed in. Several actors she'd worked with at the Playhouse had said they wanted to stay in touch, and two wrote to let her know what they were doing. Caitlin replied, telling them both that she'd left the Playhouse and was now on tour with a band.

"I've recorded a couple of songs," she wrote, "and plan to focus on music for a while."

On Monday, the weather was perfect for outdoor activities. Luisa said she had things she needed to do around the house, so, other than leading taiji, she didn't arrange any group activities.

"A bunch of us would like to go for a hike," Sky told her, but Lu didn't want them taking the bus into the forest. She suggested they find something to do that everyone could participate in.

"Maybe drive into Santa Fe and park somewhere central. People can branch out from there. There's plenty to do around the Plaza."

"We can take the bus?" Sky asked.

"I don't see why not," Lu said, glancing at June.

June agreed. "We can use Melody's car if we need to go shopping."

"Oh, I don't think we'll need to," Lu told her. "We can stock up in Boulder."

"Okay," Lu told Sky. "It's settled. Today's the day, though, if you're going into town. We leave Wednesday, so tomorrow will be spent loading up the bus and getting ready. There will be free time, too, but not for the whole day."

Caitlin was the only one who stayed behind with Luisa and June. After the rest of the group left, she walked over to the casita.

"Have you got time today or tomorrow for a massage?" she asked Melody.

"Today's my day off," Melody said, "and I promised to help Lu put up some curtains."

"In my bedroom, I hope!" Caitlin said. Sleeping late had been a challenge with bright light streaming in.

"No, sorry, I think these go downstairs," Melody said. "I could fit you in tomorrow."

"Okay," Caitlin said as she followed Melody to her treatment room to check her calendar. "I can probably work around your schedule. I don't seem to have too many responsibilities. Well, aside from the music!"

"That's no small thing," Melody said. "I haven't seen you since the concert Saturday, but I wanted to mention how great you were. Both nights. Your last song brought tears to my eyes."

"Oh, 'Shining Star'? Yeah, I wrote that for my mother. She came to the concert in Santa Barbara, did I tell you that?"

"No, we haven't been in contact much since you left here. How many of your songs were you able to record in L.A.?"

"Just two. One that I wrote while I was on the road, and one that I wrote after I got there."

"Did the band play either of them at the concert in Albuquerque?"

"'Road Angel.' I wrote it for them, and they included it on their album."

"Oh, I loved that one! But I hope you get to finish your album before long," Melody said. "Have you decided what you want to do after the tour? That's pretty exciting about the Fourth of July!"

"National television! I don't think I really believe it yet."

"This is your moment."

"I know. I hope I don't blow it. And no, I don't have a clue what I'll do after. I'm focusing on everything that's happening between now and then."

"The future has a way of taking care of itself."

Caitlin touched the cool, smooth surface of the gong she had given Melody and said, "I called Kimo, you know. Just before the band left L.A."

"Yeah?"

"She was there with him."

"Angela, you mean."

"Mmm. It was noon and he was still in bed. I'd been starting to have ideas about us being together. After all those memories surfaced during the ceremony I did out at Pecos. I told you about that, didn't I?"

"A bit."

"But I guess he's moved on."

"How long has it been since you last saw him?"

"Oh, gosh." Caitlin thought about when she left Virginia for the lake house and said, "You were there when I drove away. That was right after Hallowe'en, wasn't it?"

"1997."

"So that's about two and a half years ago."

"Sounds right."

"Anyway," Caitlin said. "What time tomorrow?"

"Let's say two," Melody said. "That will give me a chance to eat lunch first."

"Okay, I'll see you then. If not sooner."

Caitlin ruffled Lucky's fur and then walked back to the house to see what June was cooking up.

The house was quiet with just three of them there for dinner. Luisa and June had made a salad, pasta, and steamed broccoli. Lu put on classical music and opened a bottle of wine. Barefoot and dressed in a long flowing skirt and a sleeveless top, she seemed softer—sensual, even.

"Do you think you'd ever get married again?" Caitlin asked both women.

"Oh, I don't know," Lu said. "I wouldn't rule it out, but it's not something I'm looking for right now."

"Ditto!" said June.

The two women seemed to work well together, Caitlin thought. *They've got their own partnership, and it probably works better than most marriages.*

Caitlin lifted her glass and said, "To friendship."

"To friendship!" Lu and June repeated as they all clinked glasses.

∽

Caitlin had never gotten a massage from Melody before, but they had seen each other naked at the spa, shortly before Caitlin moved into Paul's house. As Melody's skilled hands loosened her tight muscles, Caitlin lay on the table pondering all the amazing changes that had happened in her life since she left the lake house.

Toward the end of the session, Melody sprinkled a blend of essential oils along Caitlin's spine and gently spread the oils over her skin. Then, she toned various sounds into her chakras.

Caitlin remembered her vision, after she'd left Pecos, of a time when she and Melody were priestesses. Caitlin seemed to be the high priestess. She thought about Melody's confession that she had been jealous of her at one time. Had Melody viewed her as a rival in more than one lifetime? Was she done with that pattern yet? *Time will tell,* Caitlin thought as she dressed.

She left a check on the kitchen table to cover the massage and Lucky's needs. The group would leave early in the morning, and she wasn't sure if she would have another chance to say goodbye.

"I'm coming back for you," she told Lucky. "So don't get too comfortable here."

Before opening the front door, she yelled, "Thanks, Mel. For everything."

"Just a sec," Melody shouted from the treatment room, where she was getting things ready for her next client. She poked her head out and said, "Remember to drink plenty of water!"

Caitlin acknowledged the advice with a wave.

Returning to the area had been satisfying, Caitlin thought as she leaned back against her seat the following morning. But seeing Melody and Lucky again reminded her of Karl.

Melody didn't suggest calling him this time. Maybe she thinks I waited too long to tell him how I feel.

Caitlin hadn't completely given up on the idea of a relationship with Karl, but she had no reason to think it would ever happen. That thought made her sad, so she kept her mind busy and avoided thinking about him.

This could be a long day. Too much time to think.

She liked sitting in the middle of the bus, by the window, and she was glad she had brought her own pillow. Though people took naps at various times, and the monotonous highway made sleeping attractive, the band's schedule thus far hadn't required driving all night, and Caitlin hadn't spent any time in her sleeping compartment. With twelve beds for thirteen people (one person always stayed awake to help the driver keep alert), someone would have to sleep on the table that converted into a bed if all the bunks were in use.

Someone who can sleep through anything! Caitlin thought.

People kept themselves occupied in various ways during the long hours of travel. June could frequently be seen knitting, and Lu was often working on her laptop. When André got restless, he drummed on anything within reach until someone asked him to please stop. Pete and Matt sometimes worked on a new song; Sky practiced juggling. Others played board games or card games or listened to music through headphones.

Caitlin had brought along both earplugs and headphones for times when she wanted to escape into her own private world. The bus was quiet at the moment, but with so many young, energetic performers on board, the sound could get a bit loud at times. Nonetheless, she preferred the group's liveliness to the loneliness she had endured at the lake house.

Solitude has its place, she thought.

But this phase of her life was so much more enjoyable!

To everything, there is a season.

She had to trust that love would again be in season sometime in her future. Somehow, somewhere—with someone.

∾ 73 ∾

*F*or Caitlin, it was love at first sight. The Colorado Rockies took her breath away, and she couldn't take her eyes off the mountain range that lay to the west of Interstate 25. This was her first trip to Colorado, and she was certain it wouldn't be her last.

In Boulder, Lu again sent Caitlin and Pete to a radio station for an interview. The station manager had agreed to give away tickets to the upcoming concert, Lu reminded them when she dropped the pair off. She handed Caitlin a large envelope and said, "Here's a packet for him. I'll be back in an hour or so."

"Aren't you coming with us?"

"You two can handle it," Lu said before driving away in the car she had rented for the day. "I need to check out the concert venue."

Caitlin pursed her lips and avoided looking at Pete as they walked toward the entrance.

Once they were on the air, Pete responded quickly to the deejay's questions and ignored questions and comments that were addressed to Caitlin. By dominating the conversation, he came off as rude and self-centered—which benefited Caitlin. Women called in to the station requesting to hear *her* song and complaining that Pete wasn't letting her get a word in. So it was still "Shining Star" that got played instead of "Road Angel."

Caitlin had written both songs—and sung both songs on the recordings. She was proud of both, and she was happy that either of them got played on the radio, even if the only time that happened was while she was sitting in the booth with the deejay. She'd had enough of Pete's attitude, but she wasn't sure how to address it.

That night, she turned on a radio in the bedroom of the cabin in the foothills near Loveland where the group was staying and then went to the bathroom to brush her teeth. She paused when she heard "Shining Star," wondering if someone was playing it downstairs.

When she realized it was playing on the radio, she spit out the tooth-paste in her mouth and said, "Oh my god!" before letting out a whoop.

She wanted to share her excitement with someone, but Cara wasn't in the room. She put a robe over her nightgown and dashed into the living room.

"It's on the radio!" Looking around for a stereo system, she said, "'Shining Star' is on the radio!"

Seth knew where the stereo was and turned it on. By the time they found the right station, the song was ending.

"By request, that was 'Shining Star' by Caitlin Rose. Caitlin was here in the studio earlier today, talking to Smokin' Joe Reynolds. Her band, the Road Angels, will be in concert tomorrow night for one show only. There's still a few seats available, so come on out and hear 'Shining Star' live and in person! Congratulations to all our listeners who won tickets to the show. And remember: you heard it here first!"

"All right!" Matt said when a commercial came on. "A plug for the show."

Caitlin felt embarrassed by her outburst. The song was hers, not the group's; naturally, they wouldn't be as excited as she was about hearing it on the radio. Maybe Pete wasn't the only one who resented the attention she was getting. Surely some of them realized that the band would be drawn into the spotlight along with her.

She didn't normally enter communal areas wearing bedroom attire and suddenly felt self-conscious. She hadn't even taken time to put on slippers! But hearing her song on the radio was a thrill beyond compare.

She slinked back to her bedroom, hoping she could calm down enough to get to sleep.

Breathe, she reminded herself as she turned out the light. *Just breathe.*

The stir created by the radio interview brought people out to the show, which sold out. But Pete's resentment only grew.

As she walked to the stage on Friday evening, Caitlin realized that she and Pete didn't sing any songs together. One or the other of them sang lead. They didn't have any duets. They didn't have to cozy up to each other onstage. Most of the time, they ignored one other.

The acrimony, however, was apparent to others in the band—and prompted a lecture from Luisa on Saturday.

After a morning hike, everyone returned to the cabin for lunch. The kitchen team prepared a simple meal of soup, salad, and sandwiches, and after cleanup Lu raised the matter of "group harmony," stressing the importance of cooperation, teamwork, and good will. She gave Pete and Caitlin an assignment to be completed by evening: learn the Beatles song "We Can Work It Out."

"We're going to play this first at our next performance," she said.

"Instead of 'Road Angel'?" Caitlin asked.

"Yes. And at every show after that, if necessary."

Caitlin understood Lu's message: resolve your differences, and quickly. And though, in her mind, Pete was the one with the problem, Caitlin knew that her distaste for him was growing, and she didn't want to feel like she was avoiding anyone in such a close-knit group. Maybe they *could* work this out.

The two of them agreed to meet in the loft before dinner.

"Got any ideas about how to approach this?" Caitlin asked Pete when he arrived.

He shrugged. "Seems pretty straightforward. I know the lyrics, and I can play the tune on the guitar. Do you want to play keyboard?"

"Yeah, I could do that," Caitlin said, sitting at the keyboard. "I don't think it's too complicated."

She tried out a few chords and then got an inspiration. "Hey!" she said suddenly. "What do you think about this . . .?"

"We're ready!" Caitlin shouted down from the loft. She turned to look at Pete, who was dressed in shorts and a t-shirt and wearing socks and sneakers.

"I brought a cap, too," he told her.

Caitlin turned it backwards on his head.

"Oh, and this—" she said, pulling one of his socks up and the other down.

The idea was to pretend they were children. Caitlin had put her hair in pigtails and buttoned her sweater incorrectly. She also brought props—items she had found in the cabin that were available for guests and their families to use: crayons and drawing paper, marbles, a stuffed tiger, and lots of throw pillows that she had collected from chairs and couches.

The scene was set. Caitlin was sitting on the floor, drawing with the crayons, when the rest of the group arrived. Pete was building a house of playing cards a few feet away, his back to Caitlin.

They had recorded their instruments earlier, and when everyone was seated and quiet, Pete turned on the music so he and Caitlin could sing along to it. Then he snapped a rubber band at the back of her head.

"Ow!" she said, turning to stare at him. "Whatdya do that for?"

Pete sang the first two lines of "We Can Work It Out."

Caitlin got up and kicked his house of cards. Then she sang the next lines of the song. Together they sang about working it out— but they each had their arms folded and were turned away from each other.

Next, Pete walked over to see what Caitlin had been drawing. He ripped her paper as he sang the beginning of the next verse.

Caitlin picked up his bag of marbles as she sang her next lines. She held the bag upside down; the marbles scattered. Again, they sang about working it out and not having time to fuss and fight—as they played tug of war with the tiger.

As Pete again asked Caitlin to try to see things his way, he pulled her hair. She countered with the next lines—and a punch to his arm. They sang about working things out—as their hands gripped each other's necks.

For the final verse, they again alternated their lines—and threw pillows at each other, ending with the promise to "work it out."

Their audience was in stitches as they both bowed—and then shook hands.

"Early night tonight, everyone," Lu said before the group dispersed. "We leave very early in the morning. We'll be on the road all day, and then you've got a show in the evening."

"Where?" Sky asked.

"Overland Park," June said. "Near Kansas City."

Lu and June had booked the country club that Martha and Ray had recommended for an early evening performance on Sunday.

"We won't be eating breakfast here, so let's get everything put away now," Lu said.

Lu helped Caitlin carry a few pillows downstairs.

"I usually like to arrive in town the day before a concert so everyone has a chance to rest before performing," she said. "But the country club is a small venue, and you've all got some experience behind you now."

"Oh, sure. It will be fine," Caitlin said. "We can sleep on the bus."

She hadn't actually tried sleeping in a bunk yet, but she had a feeling she might want to in the morning.

∾ 74 ∾

*C*aitlin closed the curtain beside her bunk and stretched out on the thin mattress, hoping to sleep a little longer. She wanted to be well rested for the band's performance that evening.

She wasn't sure what her mother was thinking when she invited them all to stay with her and Ray, but so be it. It was a nice gesture, even if Caitlin had mixed feelings about the idea. The group would stay in Overland Park for two nights before stopping at the lake house for a night on the way to Tennessee.

Maybe I didn't think through what I'd be getting myself into, either, Caitlin thought.

She had imagined that many of the men would want to camp out. But what if it rained? That possibility hadn't occurred to her before now. The lake house was way too small to comfortably accommodate everyone.

And there's only one bathroom.

Showers would have to be spaced out if they hoped to avoid running out of hot water. The more seasoned members of the group were accustomed to having to occasionally skip showers for a day—or more. But where would they be staying after the lake house? The whole group could have to camp out for all Caitlin knew.

The band wouldn't be performing in Nashville, though a few people had talked about looking for a place to play to garner attention.

"What, like a shopping mall?" Caitlin had asked at dinner the night before.

"Or a park maybe," Sky had said.

"Or a street corner," Allison said.

"Like a doo-wop group?" Caitlin asked.

Everyone found that image amusing.

"Outside the Grand Ole Opry, maybe?" Jordan said.

"Why not?" Caitlin said. "I think 'Road Angel' might do all right on the country charts."

Matt was itching to play at the iconic Bluebird Cafe; he'd been talking about it for days. "I think you have to audition first," he'd said.

No one brought up the big event, their upcoming performance in Washington. They hadn't been given many details about it yet, though they understood that they needed to be in town before Independence Day for rehearsals.

Caitlin remembered that the dress rehearsal the night before the show was open to the public. She hadn't ever attended that when she lived in the D.C. area, but now she kind of wished she had.

For such a huge event, the amount of organizational details must be staggering, she thought as she lay in her bunk. Just coordinating among the National Symphony Orchestra, the D.C. police and mayor's office, staff at the Capitol, and military liaisons would be difficult enough, not to mention all the celebrities and performers involved. But the team that put on the event had been doing it for years; they probably had a system in place to ensure that everything ran smoothly.

Not your responsibility—or your problem! Caitlin reminded herself before falling back to sleep.

When she finally crawled out of her bunk later in the morning, Caitlin asked June if she had missed breakfast.

June replied without looking up from her game of solitaire. "It's self-serve today. There's boiled eggs, toast, cereal, and the usual condiments and fruits."

Nuts, bananas, oranges, and apples were always readily available if anyone wanted a snack between meals. People were free to buy chips or cookies or protein bars if they wished, but they weren't provided. Still, Caitlin had noticed, few people chose to eat such foods in front of Lu. Everyone sought her approval, and they were well aware of her views on many subjects. They all tried to be on their best behavior when she was around, but that didn't mean that people were able to hide their flaws and imperfections. With as much time as they all spent together, under sometimes-stressful circumstances, people's shadow sides were bound to emerge sooner or later.

Pete had already brought attention to himself—and to Caitlin— with his petty outbursts. Caitlin hoped any other differences or quarrels that arose in the group could be resolved amicably. She knew that members left the group for various reasons—including being asked to leave when things *couldn't* be worked out.

June seemed to want to focus on her card game, so Caitlin sat at a different table after filling a bowl with yogurt and topping it with granola and slices of banana. Sitting alone, she realized she felt a bit melancholy.

Maybe I'm just tired, she thought as she looked out the window.

Or maybe she felt uneasy about returning to Kansas as part of a group that she would have viewed with suspicion at one time. Her old life, and the people in it, were conventional. Her new life was anything but.

Was she worried about how her mother, stepfather, and their friends and neighbors would view the Road Angels, or how Lu and the band would view *her* after learning more about her past?

Maybe both.

She hadn't talked much about herself or her past—she wasn't sure if Lu even knew about the Crash, though everyone knew she had once had a career as an attorney. She didn't have anything to hide—she was proud of her accomplishments. Her past didn't define her, and she was wary of labels. People tended to make assumptions about lawyers as well as actors and musicians.

Undoubtedly, Martha had photos of Caitlin and Bobby around the house—in photo albums or on the wall, maybe. Martha liked photo collages, Caitlin recalled.

Mother and daughter had made progress in accepting each

other—or at least in keeping their disapproval to themselves—but they also hadn't seen much of each other in the last couple of years. Caitlin wanted to avoid creating any scenes in front of the group if she and Martha fell back into old patterns.

As for the group, Caitlin wasn't especially close to anyone. She admired Luisa, and she appreciated June's efforts on behalf of the band. She got on well with almost everyone else. She agreed with the others that Pete was very talented—more so than she was, when it came to songwriting ability and skill with a guitar. Matt was also talented as a singer and guitar player. But the guys could get a little rambunctious at times, and energies would be running high after the band's performance on Sunday. At a minimum, everyone would be feeling chatty—and sweaty. They would want to unwind for a while before going to bed, and they would all want to take showers. The hot water heater might not be able to keep up, Caitlin thought as she rinsed her bowl in the sink. Some people might end up taking cold showers. *Either that or wait until three o'clock in the morning!*

Because her mother and stepfather were the hosts, Caitlin felt responsible for how things went during the band's stay. June would be flying back to L.A. right after the show, and Lu planned to take her to the airport and then stay at a nearby hotel for the night. Would people behave differently without Lu and June around?

Knowing Luisa's background as a therapist, Caitlin sometimes wondered if Lu's reasons for starting the group had as much to do with psychology as with music. Was she secretly trying out methods of behavior modification or experimenting with ways to influence interpersonal dynamics?

Not that that would be a bad thing—Caitlin trusted that Lu's motives were pure. She seemed to genuinely want to help people improve their lives—and their characters—by teaching them about wellness and personal growth. She didn't just tell her students to read a book and meditate or pray. She provided tips for reprogramming negative thought patterns and encouragement for making lifestyle changes. She practiced the mind-body techniques she taught, gave her students an experience of conflict resolution, and demonstrated a visionary leadership style.

But Caitlin did sometimes wonder what went on in Lu's head. What did she really think of the different people in the group?

She's probably not as opinionated as I am, Caitlin thought. *Maybe she really does value and accept each of us the way we are.*

Lu gave a lot to the group. What motivated her to continue with this endeavor year after year? Was selfless service part of her spiritual path? Undoubtedly, she had touched a lot of people's lives.

Caitlin wondered what Lu had been like when she'd worked as an agent—or when she'd been married to Paul. Had she catered to him before a life-changing experience set her on a new path, or had she simply grown tired of her life in Santa Fe? Had she always been interested in spirituality, or had she once been driven to succeed and make a name for herself?

Whatever the reasons for her choices, Lu was an inspiration and a role model. And whatever the outcome of this tour, Caitlin was glad she had agreed to be part of it.

∾ 75 ∾

*W*ith the discord between Caitlin and Pete resolved—or, at least, quiescent—Luisa announced that the set list would remain unchanged for the show at the country club in Overland Park.

"Just our songs," she said.

Caitlin glanced at Pete, knowing he would be happy that Lu was satisfied they had worked things out between them. Pete winked, and Caitlin smiled.

The turnout for the evening was respectable, and the audience— very different from the New Age crowd in Sedona or the band's loyal fans in California—was polite and congenial. They responded especially well to "Shining Star," which Caitlin introduced. She noted that her mother was a member of the club "and I'm sure many of you know her." (Martha, of course, was beaming.)

Lu took June to the airport before the show was over. Caitlin entertained her mother's friends while the bus was being loaded. Many of them remembered that Martha had come to Virginia to help out after the Crash. One of Martha's friends from church told Caitlin she had prayed for her then and was glad to see she was doing so well. Caitlin appreciated all the prayers and cards she had received, but reminders of the past were painful, and she was eager for the evening to end.

Her cousin Joni was also there. Joni was the daughter of Martha's brother, Jimmy. She was a couple of years younger than Caitlin, just as Jimmy was a couple of years younger than Martha. Jimmy's son, Dean, had died of leukemia at age ten, and Jimmy had never fully recovered from the loss. Caitlin suspected that Joni felt protective of her father and reluctant to do anything that might cause him further pain. She had stayed in Olathe, where Jimmy owned an auto repair shop, and worked in a store that sold women's clothing. She and Caitlin had never shared common interests. Still, Caitlin appreciated Joni's effort to come out and see her.

"How are your parents?" Caitlin asked. She couldn't remember the last time she had seen Jimmy and Carol but guessed they had probably come to the party Martha threw for her when she graduated from law school.

"Oh, they're fine," Joni said.

Well, what else would she say? Caitlin thought later. *It's hard to catch up on twelve years in five minutes.*

The small talk that often passed for conversation didn't interest her much, especially now that she had experienced the genuine sharing that occurred in Lu's group. She doubted she would ever again be content to brush problems aside and pretend everything was "fine."

Her exploration of the farther reaches of human nature was a large part of why she wasn't interested in looking up old friends while she was in town. They wouldn't understand the first thing about shamanic ceremonies or energy fields or telepathic communications, and those who were staunch Christians would think the devil had gotten hold of her.

But pride was also a factor. Her friends from college and law school had gone on to have successful careers as stockbrokers and accountants and doctors and lawyers. They were living in comfortable homes in affluent neighborhoods. They were living the kind of life that Caitlin had always expected she would have. And while she wouldn't trade hers, she knew that, in their eyes, she would be seen as an oddity. They might even feel sorry for her. Attempting to explain her choices to them would be too exhausting.

And for what? To chat about old times?

Ray interrupted Caitlin's conversation with Joni to ask if she wanted to ride to the house in his car. "Thanks, but I feel like I should stay with the group," Caitlin told him.

Martha overheard and asked, "Can I come with you? I'm so curious what it's like, traveling in that bus."

"It's nothing special, Mom, but I expect that would be okay. Lu and June won't be there, so we should have room. It's pretty cramped, with fifteen of us."

"Well that way I can tell the driver how to get to the house," Martha said as they boarded the bus. "You've never been there."

Caitlin ignored the remark, which she assumed was intended to emphasize her failure to visit before now.

She showed her mother the sleeping area and the kitchenette and then sat at one of the tables. "We've got coffee and tea and fruit," Caitlin said as the bus pulled out of the parking lot.

Rick had driven much of the way from Colorado, but Troy often drove in town. He had delivered pizzas when he attended a junior college and said he liked driving all kinds of vehicles.

"I started driving farm equipment at a young age," Troy had said one morning at Lu's house in Tesuque. He and Rick and Caitlin had lingered at the breakfast table while they waited for taiji practice to begin.

Troy was quite a bit younger than Rick, but he seemed mature for his age and the two of them often hung out together. Both of them seemed highly introverted to Caitlin. She'd asked Troy what had drawn him to the group.

"My parents were followers of Rudolf Steiner's teachings, so I went to a Waldorf school and the whole bit."

"I'm not very familiar with Steiner," Caitlin said.

"He was the founder of Anthroposophy," Troy said.

"Try saying that ten times fast," said Rick.

"So you were already steeped in esoteric philosophical traditions," Caitlin said. "Is that what you're saying?"

"Yeah, I guess."

"And you like computers."

Troy shrugged. "I like guitars. I was good at math, and my parents wanted me to have some practical skills. They know firsthand how hard it is, being on the fringe."

"What do they do?" Caitlin asked.

"They have a biodynamic farm in Upstate New York."

"Is that like organic?"

"It's beyond organic. It has a spiritual component to it and even uses some astrology."

"Huh," Caitlin said. "Such interesting people in this group!" Thinking that Troy looked a bit scrawny she asked, "So were you raised vegetarian?"

"No, not really," he said. "We didn't eat pork, though. Some chicken. Lots of eggs and dairy products. Pretty normal stuff I guess."

"And you have a degree in computer science," Caitlin said. Troy hardly looked old enough to have completed college.

"Associate's degree," he said. "I think I'm done with school."

"I'm a lifelong learner myself," Caitlin said. "But that doesn't necessarily require being in a classroom."

Martha walked to the front of the bus to give Troy suggestions on where to park as he neared her house. Before getting off the bus, she told Caitlin, "I'll get some refreshments ready."

Caitlin brought her pillow and her overnight bag inside. Large suitcases were hard to access and were mostly used to store extra towels and a change of clothing for times when the group hadn't had a chance to do laundry for a while. Thus far, the band had been staying at accommodations with adequate facilities, and hygiene hadn't been an issue. Even perfume was prohibited on the bus. Strong odors of any kind quickly became obnoxious in the shared space.

Martha gave Caitlin her pick of the two guest bedrooms. Both rooms were furnished with a queen-size bed. Caitlin chose the room at the end of the hall and offered to share with Cara. Crystal, Marya, Allison, and Jordan drew lots for who would sleep in the other room. Marya drew the shortest lot and decided to sleep on the pullout sofa in the living room—with Pete.

"Lu and June aren't here, so what the heck!" Caitlin heard her tell Crystal.

The rest of the men camped out wherever they could find space and a bit of privacy. Sleeping bags and bedrolls were laid out in the living room, the family room, and the dining room.

Martha piled sheets, pillows, and blankets on a chair in the living room in case anyone needed them. "Towels are in the bathrooms," she said.

The two guest bathrooms both had showers, and Ray offered use of his and Martha's bathroom anytime the door to their bedroom was open.

Jordan and Allison decided to share the queen bed in their room; Crystal would sleep on an air mattress on the floor.

Caitlin didn't offer to share her bed, and Cara found a spot on the floor for her air mattress.

Curious to see the rest of the house, Caitlin wandered out to the living room after unpacking a few things. Marya was on her way to shower when Caitlin passed her in the hall.

The show had started and ended earlier than usual, and as Caitlin had expected, the atmosphere was boisterous.

Martha was in the living room, asking if anyone wanted a bottle of beer, when Caitlin arrived.

Pete and Matt looked at each other and grinned. "Sure, I'll take one," Pete said casually. Matt followed with, "Me too."

Caitlin remembered the bottle of wine Luisa had opened in Tesuque when only three of them were at the house and figured alcohol wasn't completely off limits. She sat in a recliner and said, "I haven't heard Lu say anything about alcohol."

André said, "I think it's one of those things that's discouraged but not prohibited. Like junk food."

Pete had been a member of the band almost as long as Cherry and considered himself an expert on all things Road Angels. "It's rare," he said, "but Lu does serve it on special occasions. Usually wine and beer. No hard liquor."

"No daiquiris or margaritas, even?" asked Crystal, who had come out of her room to join the others. She sat on a cushion by a window that looked out onto the backyard and deck. The outside lights were on, Caitlin noticed.

"I don't think she would object if you ordered a mixed drink in a restaurant," said Seth as he unrolled his sleeping bag in a corner of the room. "Just so you don't, like, get drunk."

"Yeah, I think that's the main thing," said Matt. "We're not a rock band with groupies and casual sex. We don't have wild parties with drugs and booze."

Marya snorted. "No! We're in bed by nine most nights!"

"Not all of us," said André.

"Yeah, our idea of a wild night is staying up until midnight and maybe telling crude jokes when the girls aren't around," said Sky, who had just finished showering in the master bathroom.

Caitlin knew that André, Seth, and Sky often stayed up late, jamming in the rehearsal studio.

"So that's what you guys are up to when you disappear together," she said. "Anything else we should know about? Have you got a stash of porn hidden away someplace?"

She winked at Sky, who just laughed. Caitlin doubted they would be having this kind of conversation if Luisa were present. The situation was awkward enough with Martha hovering about.

Martha handed cold bottles of beer to Matt and Pete and then set several more bottles on the coffee table.

Caitlin could tell that that her mother was very interested in the conversation. She was undoubtedly curious about what went on in the group—and probably relieved to hear they didn't regularly engage in wild parties. In many people's minds, rock bands were associated with drug use, groupies, and trashed hotel rooms.

Martha returned to the kitchen to get more beers after Sky, André, and Troy grabbed the ones she had just brought.

Caitlin followed her mother into the kitchen and asked, "Did you get any wine?"

"I didn't buy extra, but I think we've got a bottle or two in the cabinet. The white's not chilled, though."

"Okay, I'll see if anyone wants red."

I know I wouldn't mind a drink about now! she thought.

She found a bottle of merlot and asked Ray for a corkscrew. He had been showing Rick his album collection.

"Vinyl is superior for sound quality," he was saying as he and Rick entered the kitchen together. "In my opinion."

"Ray mostly listens to classical music," Martha said. "But I think he enjoyed your concerts," she told Caitlin. "Didn't you, dear?" she asked her husband.

"Oh, yeah, sure," Ray said. "Great fun."

He opened a drawer and found a corkscrew, then took the wine bottle from Caitlin to remove the cork.

"We'll have a game of chess tomorrow, if you've got some free time," he told Rick.

"I'd like that," Rick said. "It's been a while since I played."

Rick explained to Caitlin and Martha that he had spotted a chess set in the den, where he and Troy would be sleeping.

Ray offered Rick a wine glass, which he accepted after a moment of hesitation. Caitlin figured she was probably the only one who noticed. Ray filled Rick's glass and then handed the bottle to Caitlin. She filled a glass for herself and took a sip before setting the glass on the counter.

"There's plenty of beer but only one bottle of red wine, if anyone would prefer that," she told the group in the living room.

"Ooh, I would!" said Marya, who had finished her shower.

"And me!" Jordan said eagerly.

Caitlin quickly grew drowsy as she lounged in a recliner and listened to the group's chatter. After her mother and stepfather retired for the night, she said goodnight to everyone and padded down the hall.

Cara was already asleep when Caitlin turned off the lamp by her bed. Cara was often quiet in a group setting, Caitlin had noticed. She seemed to prefer one-on-one conversations.

She'll be a good asset for the group, Caitlin thought. *Balance out some of the more forceful personalities.*

Cara had a good ear for music and might help with lessons for the band members who were less proficient with their instruments.

Caitlin crawled under the covers and breathed a heavy sigh.

It's a good thing we don't all want to be center stage. Then there would really *be tensions.*

∾ 76 ∾

*T*he next morning, Caitlin carried empty beer and wine bottles to the recycling bins in the garage. The alcohol had helped ease her fears about how everyone would get along while the band was staying with Martha and Ray.

Just one more day to get through.

She closed the door to the garage and noticed a van in the driveway when she glanced out the window. Luisa had arranged to have meals catered so that Martha would have less work to do.

"Caterer's here," Caitlin announced. While she watched, a car pulled up beside the van. "Oh, and Luisa's here, too," Caitlin told her mother. "Your neighbors aren't going to like all this traffic."

Martha joined Caitlin at the window. "Bosh," she said. "It's only a couple of days. I warned the ones who are real close by. And I promised them a copy of your album when it's done."

Caitlin groaned and followed her mother to the kitchen. "I've only got two songs recorded! At this rate, it could be years before I finish a whole album."

"Oh, well," Martha said as she put on her apron. "They will have forgotten about it by then. In any case, it's not your problem. So don't worry about it."

Martha opened the front door and then chatted with Luisa while the caterers brought in their wares. Caitlin heard mention of a shopping trip to pick up groceries for the lake house and said, "I was thinking about making pancakes while we're there, so you might want to pick up a mix and anything else you can think of. Maple syrup, maybe."

Neither Lu nor Martha responded, so Caitlin didn't know if either of them would follow up on her request. She shrugged and took a seat at the dining room table.

The caterers served a delicious brunch and then carted away the dirty dishes. Caitlin appreciated her mother's efforts to help everyone feel at home. Sometimes Martha tried too hard, but perhaps that was to be expected. Caitlin had shut her out for a time, and though their rift had been resolved, they were still figuring out how to *be* with each other—as adults, as family. Caitlin expected Martha to accept her new direction, and she had to be willing to accept that Ray played a big role in her mother's life now. So far, they seemed to be adapting, and Caitlin was determined to be on her best behavior during her stay.

In the afternoon, Matt and André tossed a football in the backyard, where Crystal, Jordan, and Allison were sunbathing. Pete and Marya went for a walk in the neighborhood. Rick played a couple of games of chess with Ray, and Cara found a shady spot outside to read a book.

Caitlin washed her hair after everyone else had showered. She didn't know when she would have another opportunity and warned everyone that there was only one bathroom at the lake house—so they should all shower while they had the chance. "It's an old water heater down there," she said.

"Where do you go after the lake house?" Martha asked Caitlin that evening.

"I'm not really sure. I usually ask June that kind of thing, and she's gone back to L.A."

"Well, Luisa would know," Martha said.

"Yes, of course," Caitlin said, "but I don't like to bother her with endless questions. I'm just along for the ride. Lu makes announcements to the whole group when she's ready to tell us something."

"Where will everyone sleep? That house is awfully small."

"I'm hoping the guys will want to camp outside."

Unless it rains! Caitlin thought.

In the morning, Caitlin asked her mother if she could take one of the vases filled with fresh flowers that the caterers had brought to decorate the dining room table.

"Take them all if you'd like."

"Nope. Just need one," Caitlin said as she removed a bouquet of flowers and wrapped the stems in a wet paper towel. "Actually, I don't need the vase. Just the flowers."

"Planning to visit your father's grave?"

Caitlin nodded. "Yeah. If there's time. And it doesn't rain."

"The forecast looks good," Martha said. She handed Caitlin a plastic bag and a rubber band to wrap around the stems of the flowers. "It's a nice group," she said. "Your band."

"Not really my band, but yeah," Caitlin said. "Good people. Thanks for letting us all stay here. You'll be doing laundry for days."

"Yes, but I'll be talking about the concert for weeks!" Martha said giddily. "And I have to let everyone know about the Fourth of July. So exciting!"

"I'm trying not to think too hard about it myself," Caitlin said. "Hopefully by then I'll feel a little more confident about performing."

"What are you talking about?" Martha said as she put a few dishes in the dishwasher. "You were on the stage all that time in Santa Fe."

"Playing in a band is different," Caitlin said. "Singing on national television is *very* different!"

"You'll do fine," Martha said. "This was probably your destiny all along. I'm just sorry I didn't encourage it sooner. You always wanted to be a performer. But, well . . . you know your father's views about all that."

"Yeah," Caitlin said wistfully. "But I think even he would have been impressed about the Fourth."

"Oh, I don't doubt it," Martha said, closing the dishwasher door. She turned to face Caitlin. "Now. You're all packed and ready to go?"

"I am," Caitlin said. "I think Rick is driving again today. I just hope it doesn't rain."

"It's not going to rain!" Martha said confidently. She hugged Caitlin and said. "Oh, I'm so proud of you, I could just burst!"

Caitlin felt her eyes tearing up as she pulled away from her mother's embrace.

"It's been quite a journey," she said. "Give my thanks to Ray."

"I will. He was sorry he couldn't be here to say goodbye, but he had an early appointment."

"You've both been good sports about keeping everyone entertained," Caitlin said. "It's a diverse group, so that's no easy task."

"I'll walk out with you," Martha said. "I want to say goodbye to Luisa. Those caterers made a huge difference."

Caitlin sat in her usual seat on the bus and waved goodbye. Now that the visit was over, she was glad she'd had an opportunity to perform in the area. She knew how much it meant to her mother, and she had enjoyed seeing Martha and Ray's home and meeting their friends. Rather than being a hindrance, the group's presence had helped ease the tensions that sometimes surfaced between Caitlin and Martha when they had only each other to focus on.

After conferring with Ray, Rick had decided to take interstate highways as far as Springfield, Missouri and then U.S. highways from there.

The bus should arrive at the lake house in about five hours, Caitlin thought as she checked the time on her watch. She leaned back in her seat and closed her eyes, thinking, *I better rest while I can.*

∞ 77 ∞

A light rain was falling when Rick stopped at a gas station in Springfield. While he filled the tank with fuel, a few people visited the restrooms or bought snacks. Seth got behind the wheel after everyone was back on the bus. About thirty minutes later, the skies cleared.

"Welcome to Shannon County!" Caitlin announced when the bus passed a highway marker on U.S. Route 60.

"I think my father chose this area partly because of the name of the county," she told Cara, who was sitting next to her.

"Oh, was he Irish?"

"Very Irish!"

Before long, the bus crossed the low-water bridge that led to the lake house. Seth parked in the gravel driveway, and everyone got off the bus.

Caitlin unlocked the front door and opened the windows to air the place out. Allison needed a bathroom, so Caitlin showed her where it was. Then, she walked around outside to see how everything looked. Her mother had hired a landscaping service to get the property cleaned up when she was down at Easter, she'd said, but the grass again needed mowing.

Caitlin walked over to where the bus was parked. Rick, Matt, Seth, and Troy were unloading air mattresses, sleeping bags, blankets and supplies.

"Anyone have a hankering to mow some grass?" Caitlin asked.

"I wouldn't mind," Troy said. "If you have a rider mower."

"I do! Let me show you where it is."

Caitlin led Troy to the barn. "We might even have some gasoline," she told him on the way. "Camping will be ever so much more pleasant if we can clear away some of the growth. You don't need to mow the whole property, just the area close to the house would be great."

"How much land do you have here?" Troy asked.

"I think it's twenty acres," Caitlin said.

After making sure the mower started and Troy knew what he was doing, she walked back to the house to figure out sleeping arrangements.

She showed Luisa to her father's bedroom and told Cara to take the top bunk in the bedroom she and Bobby used to share. She would sleep in the bottom bunk. Undoubtedly, she would be up late and up early making sure everyone had whatever they needed.

Crystal and Marya decided they would sleep on air mattresses in the study; Jordan and Allison were game to try sleeping outside in a tent. Caitlin pulled her family's old tent out of the hall closet.

"I'm afraid it might be a little musty," she told the pair. "It hasn't been used in a long time."

"That's okay," said Jordan. "I'll douse it with perfume and we'll hardly notice!"

"It sleeps four, as I recall," Caitlin said. "You know how to put it up?"

"Haven't got a clue," said Jordan.

"We're city girls," Allison said.

"This will be our first time camping."

"We thought it would be an adventure."

"Come on," Caitlin said, leading the girls outside. "Let's find a good level spot for you."

The trio walked across the freshly mowed grass.

"Watch out for snakes," Caitlin said. "Especially in the tall grass." She waved to the acreage in the distance, beyond where Troy was now mowing.

"Oh!" Jordan said.

"By the lake might be nice," Allison said. "Is that a lake or a pond?"

"We always called it a lake," Caitlin said. "There's a canoe in the barn if anyone wants to take it out." She stopped about fifty yards from the house and asked, "How about here?"

Jordan looked around and said, "Um, how about over there?" She pointed to an area that was much closer to the house.

Caitlin laughed and said, "Ah, okay. A *backyard* adventure."

"Baby steps," said Allison.

Caitlin chose a spot about a hundred feet from the house and then showed the young women how to set up the tent. She knew that Jordan was a recent college grad from Dallas and asked about her plans for the future.

"Jordan's going to join her father's company," Allison said.

Caitlin couldn't tell if she detected a note of envy or disdain in Allison's tone but guessed she had her own ideas about what Jordan should do with her life.

"And what does Jordan think about that?" Caitlin asked, glancing at Jordan.

"Oh, I'm fine with it. That's always been the plan. I don't have any brothers, so I'm supposed to take over someday. My degree is in business. But I wanted some time off first."

"Her father told her she could have a year," Allison said, "and she went to all these cool places in Europe. But then she met Cherry at a festival in California and she wanted more time so she could hang out with the group for a while."

Caitlin was curious now. "And?" she asked the women. Jordan let Allison finish the story.

"And her father cut her off!" Allison said.

Caitlin looked at Jordan and said, "Really?"

Jordan shrugged. "He said I was on my own if I wanted to be a penniless musician; he wouldn't support me. I told him I didn't need his money. Expenses are all paid by the band!"

"'I'll see you at Christmas,' she told him!" Allison said, clearly amused.

"So you'll stay with the band until then?" Caitlin asked.

"Probably more like Thanksgiving," Jordan said. "I'll start work in January, and I want some time to visit with my friends while they're in town for the holidays. My family always has a big to-do then."

"That was brave of you, following your heart and not caving in to pressure from your dad," Caitlin said.

"Oh, I just knew this was something I had to do," Jordan said. "Even if he cut me off completely. Though I didn't really think he would."

"No way," Allison told Caitlin before she went to find an air mattress to use in the tent.

Caitlin walked back to the house as Troy was returning the mower to the barn. She entered the kitchen through the back door and was approached by Matt.

"I was thinking a campfire might be nice," he said. "Have you got a fire pit?"

"I don't know," Caitlin said. "I don't think so."

"It wouldn't be hard to make one," Matt said. "I'm sure some of the other guys would help. We'd just need some bricks to line it. Or concrete blocks, if you have anything like that."

"Oh, okay," Caitlin said, thinking for a moment.

Lu entered the room and said, "A fire is a great idea! The summer solstice is tonight."

Marya joined the others who had gathered in the small kitchen and asked, "What time is the solstice?"

"I'm not sure exactly," Lu said. "June would know."

Caitlin thought Lu seemed a little stressed and scattered without June around to carry some of the load. She turned to Matt and said, "Why don't you go poke around in the barn and see if you can find any bricks out there? I can show you where it is."

"I know where it is. I saw it when we drove in."

Matt departed, and Caitlin told Lu about the general store nearby. "It's about five miles from here. If we need more ice for the coolers. Or marshmallows to roast!"

"I brought marshmallows," Lu said. "I also brought sparkling wine. And your mother told me about the beer, by the way."

"Oh!" Caitlin said, surprised and yet not surprised. Her mother was known to be a chatterbox. She meant no harm, but Caitlin had wished on more than one occasion that she would Just Keep Quiet.

"You've all worked hard. It's time for a little party."

Pete walked into the kitchen and said, "I heard that!"

"Have you guys found a place for your tents?" Caitlin asked him.

"Yeah, I think so. We were just waiting for Troy to finish mowing."

"He's done now," Caitlin said. "I think Matt's going to dig a fire pit if you want to check on his progress. There should be a spade and other tools somewhere—either in the barn or in the shed."

"Is the shed locked?" Pete asked on his way out.

"I don't think so," Caitlin said. "What's for dinner?" she asked Cara, who was putting food into the refrigerator.

"I think we decided on veggie burgers and baked potatoes and a tossed salad, didn't we?" Cara asked Lu.

"That sounds right," Lu said. "I'm going to shower while I have the chance. Why don't you go ahead and get started on dinner prep."

"I think there are some folding chairs around here somewhere," Caitlin told Cara. "I'll look for those. Let me know if you need anything. Who else is helping with dinner?"

"I think it's still Seth and Jordan and me," Cara said. "And Crystal and Sky on cleanup."

And me, no doubt, Caitlin thought.

She found a card table and chairs in the shed along with the umbrella for the round patio table; with help from Marya and Rick, she carried them to the deck behind the house and then retrieved a plastic tablecloth from the house to cover the card table.

The patio table would seat six, she thought as she stood outside on the deck; another four could sit at the card table. The redwood deck chairs could also be used if people wanted to eat outside, and a picnic table by the lake would be another option if anyone wanted to be a little more separate from the group.

Caitlin told the dinner team to set the food on the dining room table as there wasn't much counter space in the kitchen. The chairs that were part of the dining set would provide indoor seating as needed, but Caitlin guessed that most people would want to be outside as much as possible.

By the time she was ready to sit and eat, she was exhausted.

"Caitlin, we saved a seat for you," Lu said. She was sitting at the round table with Matt, Pete, Crystal, and Marya.

"Thanks," Caitlin said, sitting between Pete and Matt. "Are we having wine?"

"At the bonfire," Lu said.

"Did you find bricks?" Caitlin asked Matt.

"A few," Matt said. "We dug a pit, and we had enough bricks to line it, but if you really want it to look nice, you'll have to get more to finish it off. It'll work fine for tonight, though."

"I can't wait to see it," Caitlin said.

"Wait until it's dark!" Pete advised.

"I'll probably have to, with all there is to do yet this evening," Caitlin said.

"You know, we could stay another day," Lu said. "If everyone wants to. But that would mean skipping Nashville. We can't do both. We have to get to North Carolina by Friday, and we'll want to stop somewhere between here and there."

"Isn't Allison from Tennessee?" Pete asked, looking around to see where Allison was sitting.

"Memphis," said Crystal. "Are we going through there?"

"No," Lu said, taking a bite of her veggie burger. "We'll already be past Memphis by the time we get back on Interstate 40."

"I thought Allison might have a suggestion about a place to stay in Tennessee," Pete said.

"Why don't you ask her?" Lu suggested.

"Okay," Pete said before leaving the table.

"I didn't mean right this minute!" Lu said after he'd left.

"What's going on in Asheville?" Crystal asked.

"There's an outdoor festival on Saturday afternoon, and then we're playing at a metaphysical church on Sunday. Two services."

"Is that the church you told me about?" Crystal asked Marya, who nodded.

When Pete returned, he said the only place Allison knew about was an hour west of Nashville. She and her parents had stayed in one of the cottages during a family reunion, though most of the rooms were in the main lodge as she recalled. "She said it was nice," Pete said.

"Thanks, Pete," Lu said, finishing her meal. "I can call them in the morning and see if they have availability."

"We could take a vote," Matt suggested. "About staying here another night."

Caitlin suspected Matt would vote for a full day in Nashville, but she was okay with whatever the group decided.

"I was just thinking there's no need to rush and feel stressed," Lu said. "We've got some flexibility built into the schedule."

Lu seemed inclined to stay put for another night, Caitlin thought, and her preference was likely to be the deciding factor.

Sure, Caitlin thought. *She's got the comfortable bed!*

∾ 78 ∾

*A*fter dinner, the group gathered in the living room for a quick check-in. They had used disposable plates and utensils to save water, which made cleanup easy.

The first item on Lu's agenda was deciding whether to leave in the morning or stay at the lake house an extra day.

"We've got enough food," she said, "though meals won't be anything fancy. We'll find some good restaurants when we get to Asheville, I imagine."

After briefly discussing their options, the group took a vote. Pete and Matt were in favor of going on to Nashville. Rick and Caitlin abstained, and everyone else voted to stay another night, as it was apparent that Luisa favored that choice.

"But we'll at least drive through the city, right?" Matt asked. "We can't be right there and not have a look!"

"We'll see," Lu said, moving on to the next item on her agenda.

"With our fire tonight we join with groups all over the planet that are celebrating the point where, here in the northern hemisphere, we receive the maximum amount of sunlight. We mark the beginning of summer by acknowledging the solstice—Sol being Latin for that great ball of fire, our sun, which seems to stand still during this time."

Pete and Matt asked to be excused so they could get the fire started. Lu nodded before continuing.

"In ancient Rome, the sacred fire in the Temple of Vesta was tended by the Vestal Virgins. The ashes were removed once a year and taken to the Tiber River during the June festival of Vestalia, which was a time of purification. During the festival, women brought offerings to the temple, and the Vestal Virgins prepared a special cake using grain, salt, and water—all of which had been ritually prepared. The water was taken from a sacred spring, and the vessel it was carried in was not allowed to touch the ground outside the temple."

As Lu continued talking about the Vestalia festival, Caitlin's mind drifted back to her experience with Kimo at the Shannon Pot four years earlier, at solstice time. She remembered waking in the morning and finding a plate of wafers by the campfire. Kimo swore he hadn't brought them, and Caitlin knew she hadn't, either.

No Vestal Virgins had prepared those cakes; they were in Ireland. However, Caitlin had read in Athena's book about some of the rites of ancient Goddess worshippers, and she knew that many ancient traditions bore similarities. In the Hebrew Bible, the prophet Jeremiah detested the offerings made to the "Queen of Heaven"—which included cakes made by the women. Surely the wafers had been left for her and Kimo by the mysterious group they had encountered. Most mysterious of all was the man with the shaman's drum. The voice Caitlin had heard in her head, both on the flight to Dublin and during the ceremony at the Shannon Pot, seemed to belong to him.

One more thing to ask Karl about, she thought before returning her attention to the group.

"Everyone set for a place to sleep?" Lu was asking. "Anyone planning to sleep in the bus?"

Rick raised his hand.

"Okay, last item on the agenda," Lu said. "I brought sparkling wine, as well as sparkling apple juice for anyone who prefers a nonalcoholic treat—or who is underage. Is everyone old enough to drink alcohol?"

June would know everyone's age, Caitlin was thinking when Lu asked her about the legal drinking age in Missouri.

"I think it's still twenty-one," Caitlin said.

Several people pointed to Allison and teased her about being the only one who was underage.

"Oh, you can't be serious!" Allison protested. "My birthday is next week!" She leaned toward Jordan and quietly said, "And it's not like I've never had a drink before."

"Caitlin?" Lu said. "What do you think? You're the lawyer—and it's your property."

"I'll take responsibility for her," Caitlin said.

"Great," said Lu. "I'll need volunteers to carry a cooler down to the bonfire."

Cara and Marya brought marshmallows, graham crackers, and chocolate bars to make s'mores. Crystal passed around a package of napkins. Rick poured wine into plastic cups, and Troy—barely twenty-one himself—handed them out.

When everyone had been served, Jordan raised her cup to Allison and said, "Happy twenty-first birthday, a little early."

Others chimed in, "Happy birthday to Allison!"

Lu offered the next toast. "To Caitlin. Thank you for inviting us."

"Thank you to Caitlin!" the group said in unison.

Caitlin reciprocated with, "Thank *you* for inviting me to be part of the tour! To Lu!"

"To Lu!" everyone shouted.

Caitlin also singled out others who had been helpful, especially Troy, for mowing, and Matt, for suggesting the fire pit.

"And the guys who built the fire," Marya said.

"And Rick and all our drivers," Crystal said.

When the toasts died down, Cara held up her flute and said she wanted to demonstrate her progress. She had been practicing the flute solo from Chicago's "Colour My World" for weeks and played it perfectly.

"So if we go back to playing at weddings that will fit right in," said Pete, who had been first in line for a wine refill.

"Why would we do that?" asked André.

"Well, who knows where we'll be after our shining star moves on to greener pastures," Pete said.

Caitlin was watching the marshmallow at the end of her stick turn a golden brown when the comment registered. She looked over at Pete, who was sitting directly across from her, and said, "Oh—You mean me?"

She'd hoped he had gotten over his resentment. *Maybe it just went underground.*

Lu intervened before tensions could escalate.

"Pete, you're out of line. I invited Caitlin on this tour and she's been a tremendous asset. It's true I didn't ask your opinion, and I didn't put it to a group vote. Maybe that was a mistake. I'm still learning things, too. If I've offended anyone, I apologize. Some decisions need to be made quickly."

Pete shrugged. "It's your group. You can do what you want."

"It's *our* group," Lu said, looking around the circle at each person, "and you're all integral parts of it—not just the lead singers."

She turned to Pete and said, "What's really bothering you, Pete? You clearly resent the attention Caitlin is getting, but what's underneath that? Can't you be happy for her? What would help you feel more accepting of her role here? Or of yours?"

"I wonder—" Caitlin said.

"Caitlin?" Lu asked.

"Well, I know Pete writes songs, too. I wonder if what he's really wanting is to record an album of his own songs. Like I hope to, someday."

Everyone looked at Pete.

"Pete?" Lu asked. "Do you think that might be at the root of your . . . feelings?"

Nice work, Lu, Caitlin thought. *Don't label it envy or anything else.*

"Well, sure I'd like a chance to record my own album," Pete said, scratching at the ground with a stick. "What musician wouldn't?"

"Let's hear what you've got," Lu said.

Everyone else murmured their encouragement.

"Go for it, man," said Matt.

"Play something for us," said Marya.

"What—now?"

"Sure, why not?" Lu said. "Go get your guitar. We'll wait. We don't have anywhere we need to be."

Pete sheepishly left the campfire and returned with an acoustic guitar.

"Well, this is the most recent one," he said before playing a song about a woman with green eyes who he was, apparently, in love with—only she didn't know he existed, or, if she did, she didn't share his interest.

Everyone applauded enthusiastically when Pete had finished, and he smiled for the first time that evening.

"Feel better now?" Lu asked.

"Yeah," Pete said, grinning. "Guess I just needed a little lovin'."

"Well, I can't snap my fingers and get you a record deal," Lu said, "but I'll help in any way I can."

"Me too," said Caitlin. "Call me if you ever need a backup singer."

Pete looked genuinely touched. "Thanks," he said sincerely, looking directly at Caitlin from across the campfire. "I'm sorry I've been behaving badly. It won't happen again."

Let's hope not, thought Caitlin.

"Hug! Hug! Hug!" the group chanted.

Caitlin and Pete obliged, meeting halfway and sharing a warm embrace.

"Apology accepted," Caitlin said.

Caitlin had just gotten into bed when she remembered the flowers that were lying on a table inside the bus. She walked out to the bus and rapped on the door, which was closed to keep out flies and mosquitoes and any critters that might wander in.

"Rick?"

Rick opened the door. "Yeah?"

"Sorry to disturb you. I forgot something."

"No problem," he said. "Come on in."

Caitlin found the flowers and asked Rick if he had everything he needed before walking back to the house.

"I'm all set," he said.

"Okay, have a good night."

Caitlin put the flowers in a vase and filled it with water before turning out the light in the kitchen. Through the open back door, she could hear Jordan and Allison giggling in their tent.

She smiled, remembering the first time her parents had allowed her to bring friends down from Topeka, soon after her graduation from high school. Jenny had gotten a red Mustang as a reward for graduating in the top ten and she was eager to take it for a spin. She drove Caitlin and two others—whose names Caitlin could no longer recall.

I'd forgotten all about that weekend, she thought.

She left the outside lights on in case anyone needed to come inside during the night.

Just don't let the screen door bang! she thought as she lay down in the lower bunk.

She'd had a few close friends in high school and an extensive social network during her undergraduate years at KU. She had kept in touch with some people for a while, but working at OSP, she'd been too busy. She had lost track of most of her law school classmates, too. After the Crash she'd had little energy or desire to reconnect, and the last couple of years had been a whirlwind of activity.

A class reunion might be fun sometime, she thought, but she was more interested in looking ahead than behind.

Better get some sleep. Morning will come all too quickly.

∾ 79 ∾

Cara set out the usual breakfast selections of coffee, tea, fruits, yogurt, granola, nut butters, and toast. She boiled a dozen eggs on the stove while Caitlin mixed batter for pancakes.

Marya was in the shower when Luisa emerged from her bedroom.

Late, for her, Caitlin thought as she poured some of the batter onto a hot griddle. She smiled, remembering the time Lucky got into a bowl of flour when she wasn't looking. He was so tiny then!

"I just realized—there's no reception here!" Lu said, looking at her phone with a puzzled expression.

"Nope," Caitlin said. "There's no landline, either. Well—there is, but it's not connected at the moment."

Allison and Jordan entered the kitchen, complaining about mosquitoes.

"I had one buzzing in my ear all night!" Jordan said.

"I'm covered with itchy red welts!" Allison said.

"We're out in the boonies here," Caitlin said. "The wilds of Missouri!"

"We want to sleep in the house tonight!" whined Jordan.

"Pull up a floor!" said Caitlin.

"How's everyone feeling this morning?" Lu asked when everyone was present. "Rick, how was it, having the bus all to yourself?"

"Kinda weird, actually. But okay."

Pete was grumpy, as he often was when he first got up, but it was Crystal who'd had too much to drink the night before. "I've got a massive headache," she said.

"Okay, you can be excused from kitchen duty this morning," Lu said. "Drink some herb tea and then join us on the lawn for taiji after breakfast."

Caitlin slid the last of the pancakes onto a plate and added butter and maple syrup. She carried her plate and her mug outside and sat by Cara, who was enjoying a cup of coffee on the deck.

Cara looked out at the lake and said, "It sure is peaceful here."

"Yeah," Caitlin said before tasting her pancakes. "I spent the winter here a couple of years ago. Just me and my cat."

"Oh, the one Melody is taking care of?"

Caitlin nodded. "He was just a kitten then." She sipped her tea and said, "I wrote a bunch of songs while I was here. One of them is kind of dark and despairing. I was going through a lot at the time. Well, you'd understand. Grief and all."

Cara drank her coffee and quietly said, "Yeah."

It suddenly occurred to Caitlin that Cara's seeming aloofness might be a phase she was going through. If she was still grieving her mother's passing—or recovering from the stress of being a caregiver—she probably *wouldn't* feel very sociable.

"Anyway, I always imagined an arrangement with piano and strings. If we have a chance sometime, maybe we could play around with it. You still have a cello, don't you?"

Cara nodded. "I didn't bring it to California with me, though." After a pause, she asked, "What's the name of the song?"

"'Phoenix Heart.' It's one that I'd like to record eventually."

"I'd love to hear more of your work," said Cara.

Caitlin doubted that she and Cara would ever get together after the tour ended, but who could say where any of them would be in five years? *I hope it doesn't take me that long to finish my album,* she thought.

Crystal came outside to collect trash. "Taiji in ten," she told Caitlin and Cara.

"Okay," said Cara.

"Thanks," said Caitlin.

"I better go get ready," Cara told Caitlin.

Caitlin rushed to finish eating her breakfast. "I'll be right there."

The cleanup crew was nearly finished in the kitchen when Caitlin went back inside. Her father had never installed a dishwasher, so everything had to be washed by hand. She drank the last of her tea and then washed her favorite mug in the sink.

The group was meeting by the lake for taiji. By now, everyone knew the whole routine. Luisa no longer gave instructions, though she still positioned herself in front of everyone so people could easily follow along.

Maybe the group's good vibrations would help transform the lingering memories of the sorrowful past that she had come to associate with the property, Caitlin thought as she walked outside.

Maybe it's time to visit Dad's grave.

In the afternoon, Caitlin helped Jordan and Allison take down the tent. On her way back to the house, she saw Rick and Troy and told them about the chess set in the study. Troy said he'd like to learn how to play; Rick said he'd be happy to teach him.

Pete and Marya walked off hand in hand to find a quiet spot to be alone. Crystal, Jordan, and Allison put on their swimsuits and took their towels—and suntan lotion—to the lake. André, Sky, and Seth went to the bus to jam, and Matt and Cara paddled around the lake in the canoe.

Luisa didn't seem to know what to do with herself without a

telephone or Internet service—or June. She sat outside in the shade for a while, writing in a notebook. After she started sneezing, she disappeared into her room.

While everyone was occupied, Caitlin took the flowers from the vase and walked to her father's grave.

She laid the bouquet on the ground and kneeled down. Quietly, she said, "I'm in a good place now, Daddy. I hope you are, too." Her eyes teared up when she added, "I miss you."

She heard a stir and looked up to see an owl on the branch of a nearby tree. Hadn't she seen an owl the last time she was here?

Weird, she thought, and headed back toward the house.

On the way, she spotted the mat from the front door that she had moved after Lucky left a dead squirrel on it.

She shook her head and smiled. She hadn't expected to be back here so soon—and she certainly hadn't planned on returning to Washington this summer.

Coming full circle, she thought. *Or maybe it's a spiral.*

∾ 80 ∾

*A*fter Lu vacated the master bedroom, Caitlin stripped the sheets from the bed. *Mom will have to take care of these next time she's down*, she thought.

She walked through the house, checking to make sure everything had been put away, turned off, locked up. She closed all the blinds and was about to start folding a blanket when Pete walked in.

"Need some help?" he asked.

"Uh, sure."

Pete held two corners and Caitlin held the other two. They folded the blanket in half and then quarters, then Caitlin folded it again before taking it to the hall closet. "Thanks," she told Pete. "I'm almost done."

"I'm not here to check up on you. I just wanted to say— I didn't ever not like you. It wasn't about that. The opposite, if anything."

"Oh. Okay."

Caitlin resumed checking off the items on her list. *Trash: emptied. Stove: off.*

"I'll be right out," she told Pete.

"Sure," he said before leaving.

Caitlin locked the front door and returned the key to its hiding place beneath the flower pot. She was glad she had invited the group to come. And, she was very ready to go.

Lu called the lodge in Tennessee as soon as she had cell phone reception. Because the group only needed one night, and it was a Thursday, she was able to arrange accommodations.

When the bus arrived at the property, she checked in and then announced that the men would share two of the four cottages and the women would share the other two. "I've got a room in the lodge," she said.

Crystal joined Cara and Caitlin in the largest cottage, which had two small bedrooms. Caitlin took the queen bed; Cara and Crystal shared the room with twin beds.

"The Three Cs," Caitlin said as they brought their overnight bags inside.

Lu came by to check on everyone and said, "We're not likely to find organic food anywhere around here. Probably not even vegetarian fare."

"Maybe at an Italian restaurant," Crystal said. "You know, pasta and veggies—that sort of thing. Salad."

"Pizza, worst case scenario," Cara added.

"Good idea," Lu said. "I'll ask our host for suggestions. Maybe he's got a menu for a local place."

Ten minutes later, Lu returned with a menu. "They'll deliver," she said. "If they can handle such a large order on short notice."

Caitlin glanced at the clock on the wall of the tiny kitchen. "It's only five o'clock. They should be able to handle it."

"You three figure out what you want and then pass the menu on to the guys next door, along with your orders. Let's get this done quickly so we're not eating at midnight. We'll all eat together in the dining room in the lodge."

Caitlin decided on lasagna with a side of broccoli and a small salad.

"I'm guessing this is going to come with some bread, but make sure that's the case," she told Crystal, who had agreed to take everyone's orders and deliver the tally to Lu.

Before heading to the shower, Caitlin added, "And ask Lu if there was any wine left over."

Crystal groaned. "Okay, I'll ask. But I don't think I'm ready for any more wine just yet!"

Lu brought the last bottle of sparkling wine to the dinner table and poured a small amount into everyone's glass for one last toast.

"Here's to the final performances of the tour, in Asheville and Washington!"

"To Asheville and Washington!" Caitlin repeated along with the others.

Matt asked again if they could drive through Nashville the following day. "I'd like to at least *see* the Bluebird," he said.

"All right," Lu said with a sigh. "If we get an early enough start— and you do the driving."

"How early?" Matt asked.

"Early enough that we don't get caught in rush hour traffic."

Matt thought for a moment and then grinned and said, "Deal!"

"I think the Bluebird has an open mic night," Allison said. "You don't have to audition for that."

"Have you been there?" Matt asked her.

"No, but I used to wait tables in Memphis and I'd hear the musicians talk. They were pretty friendly. That's what made me want to be part of a band, so I took singing lessons and learned to read music. I never could quite get the hang of the guitar, though."

"Did you go to college at all?" Marya asked Allison.

She shook her head and said, "No, I didn't like school much."

"Yeah, me neither," said Marya.

These were the two women Caitlin would be singing "America the Beautiful" with on the Fourth of July.

So when are we going to start rehearsing? she wondered.

She wanted to avoid a repeat of her first concert experience with the band, in Santa Barbara, which started on a sour note because they hadn't had time to rehearse.

We need to start practicing—and soon.

∾ 81 ∾

*C*aitlin watched from the window beside her seat on the bus as Rick took a photo of Matt in front of the Bluebird Cafe, which wasn't open yet. Allison had also gotten off the bus; she looked over some of the flyers that were posted by the door.

The unassuming café was nestled amongst retail shops in a shopping center that was located on a busy road. Caitlin turned to those sitting behind her and asked, "What's all the fuss about?"

"A lot of famous musicians got their start at the Bluebird," Seth said from two rows back.

"Oh yeah, the Bluebird is legendary in these parts," said Marya. "There's a tv show on cable that broadcasts some of the performances, but it's only available in the South. One of my friends in Asheville was telling me about it."

"How long were you in Asheville?" Caitlin asked Marya, who was sitting across the aisle from Seth.

"About a year."

"And how long have you been with the group?"

"About a year!"

"So you've been on tours before."

Marya nodded. "Uh-huh."

"Have you played any outdoor festivals, like we'll be at on Saturday?"

"No, but I know the group has." Turning to Seth, Marya said, "You've been around longer than me. Did you play any outdoor festivals before I joined the band?"

"Just the equinox festival near Santa Fe. I think that was two years ago."

"Fall or spring?" Marya asked.

"Spring. It snowed!"

"I remember that day!" Caitlin said. "That was when I auditioned for the Playhouse! I'd just gotten to town, like, the day before. Melody invited me to come to the festival with her and her friends!"

"Yeah, we were there. Though I don't think I ever met Melody, until this trip."

"Huh!" was all Caitlin said. Was she somehow connected to the members of the group—on a soul level, perhaps? Everything seemed to be fitting together, like pieces in a puzzle.

Allison returned to her seat on the bus, and Rick got behind the wheel. Matt sat by Luisa, who was sitting two rows in front of Caitlin. "There's an open mic night every Monday," he told Lu. "Maybe we could stop on the way back?"

Caitlin could tell that Lu was getting exasperated by Matt. *She probably can't wait for June to get back!*

June usually insulated Lu from everyone's questions and requests; anything she couldn't directly handle she brought to Lu's attention, but in manageable doses. Lu wasn't accustomed to a steady stream of interruptions.

"We can try," Lu calmly told Matt. "But I'm not making any promises."

After lunch, Lu called a restaurant in Asheville that Marya had recommended.

"What did they say?" Marya asked when Lu's call ended.

"They can accommodate us. As long as we get there before 5:30."

"All right!" Marya said, to no one in particular. "I love that place!"

"What time do they open?" Sky asked Lu.

"Five."

The bus arrived in downtown Asheville just before 5:00 p.m. Troy, who had been driving since Knoxville, dropped everyone off and went to find parking while the group was seated in the restaurant's private dining room.

Caitlin ordered a trout dinner with sides of rice and mixed vegetables. "And chocolate mousse for dessert," she told the server.

Lu announced that the group would be staying at a developing ecovillage in the hills about thirty miles from town.

"A what?" Caitlin asked.

"An ecovillage is an intentional community that's designed to be sustainable," Lu said. "Living off the grid, that sort of thing."

"So this place is kind of rustic," Caitlin said.

"I've been there," said Marya, "though I've never stayed overnight. I went to a workshop on permaculture. They're going to be building for a very long time."

"Permaculture?" Caitlin asked.

Was she the only one who was unfamiliar with these new trends? She looked at Cara, who shrugged her shoulders as if to say, "Beats me."

"It originally referred to agriculture," Marya said, "but it's a philosophy that can be applied to any ecosystem, really. The focus is on renewable resources and minimizing waste. So they collect rainwater and use composting toilets."

Sky seemed excited about visiting the ecovillage, but Caitlin wasn't sure what to expect, and she was tired of shared accommodations. Everyone's nerves were getting frayed from nights in different places and long days on the bus.

It was after dark when the bus arrived at the ecovillage, so the group headed straight to their cabin. All the beds were twin size. Lu got her own room, and Caitlin shared a room on the upper level with Cara. She didn't pay a lot of attention to where anyone else was sleeping, but she heard Rick say he would rather stay on the bus than sleep on the couch. Troy decided to join him.

During the night, rain pelted the skylight in her room, and Caitlin didn't sleep well. No one was in the mood for a tour of the property in the morning, and the rain continued all day on Saturday. The solstice festival wasn't canceled, but it wasn't well attended. The Road Angels were just one band in the day's lineup, so they didn't perform a full set. "Shining Star" wasn't part of the set list, but "Road Angel" was.

Reminded how humid summers on the East Coast could be, Caitlin hoped the weather in D.C. would be more favorable on Independence Day.

The group ate pizza at an Italian restaurant that offered gluten-free options and then returned to the ecovillage. Matt brought in some board games from the bus; he and Pete and Sky and André were deciding what to play when Caitlin went to her room. She wasn't surprised to find that Cara was already there. Frustrated by the lack of privacy, she wrote in her journal and went to bed early.

By Sunday, the rain had let up. The Church of Life members were enthusiastic participants at the church's two services, and the band lingered afterward to enjoy refreshments and sign autographs before returning to the ecovillage for another night.

Lu stood at the front of the bus and announced that the band's CD had sold well, making up for Saturday's lackluster sales. "I was thinking we might stay another night or two and get acquainted with some of the residents at the ecovillage," she said.

"Cool," said Sky. "Maybe we could organize a drum circle if anyone's into that."

"We really need to start rehearsing for the Fourth soon," Caitlin said. "I'll be playing piano for 'Shining Star,' right?"

Lu nodded.

"I'll need a piano to practice on," Caitlin said, "and Allison and Marya and I need to start rehearsing 'America the Beautiful.'"

Until now, she had gone along with the group's agenda without complaint, but the time had come to insist that her priorities outweighed other interests. Her future could very well be determined by one night. Her chance might not come again.

Lu walked down the aisle and sat next to her. "That's fair," she said.

"Did I tell you I was invited to testify at a congressional hearing in the middle of July?" Caitlin asked.

"No, I think I'd remember that."

"It concerns vaccine safety and a case I'd worked on when I was at the Department of Justice. Anyway, I'm feeling like I need to get to Washington and really focus, now that the rest of the tour is done. I don't know where you were planning on staying in the D.C. area, but I'm probably going to want my own room—at least for a day or two before the Fourth. I'll be happy to pay for it."

"Not to worry," Lu said. "I'll take care of it."

But Caitlin was worried, and she tossed and turned that night. The thought of going back to D.C. brought up all the pain of the past—the breakup with Jayson, the conflicts with Neil, the Crash, the end of her law career. She had left there feeling weak and wounded. Lost. She'd had some great experiences in the last couple of years, but the tour was coming to a close and soon she would be on her own again. Where was she going to go after the Fourth? She couldn't put off thinking about it forever.

Doesn't mean I need to think about it right now! she told herself. *One step at a time.*

She put soft foam earplugs in her ears to block the sound of the air conditioner, but she still couldn't sleep. Her mind refused to be still.

Knowing that Sam had been the driver of the GMC that crashed into her car, she felt like a fool for falling for him in Hawai'i. She also felt sad about Karl and wondered if she would even see him while she was in Washington. Would their meeting be awkward?

Best to wait until after the Fourth to see him, she decided. Or maybe after the hearing. If their reunion didn't go well, she might be upset and unable to think clearly.

Come on, you're a professional now, she thought. *Get it together!*

Professional? What did that even mean? Surely it didn't mean she would never have moments of insecurity and self-doubt.

The group had been performing in small venues, not huge arenas, and Caitlin was fine in that kind of setting. But was she polished enough for The Big Time? Was she ready? She felt powerless to stop the surge of panic that threatened to overwhelm her.

She sat up in bed and took a deep breath. Would it help to talk to someone? Should she wake Cara—or Luisa?

She had handled lots of high-pressure situations in the past, she reminded herself.

Yeah, but the whole country wasn't watching!

This was the opportunity she had wanted, wasn't it? Did she want to back out now?

Hell no!

The group would be there with her, and she was grateful for that. They would surround themselves—and her—with a force field of peace and love. Wasn't that what they had all been learning how to do with the various practices Lu had been teaching them?

Caitlin lay back down, assuring herself: *I can do this.*

She smiled, remembering how she had joked with Paul when he asked her if she was ready for the opening night of *Millennium Blues*. "I will be," she'd said, after giving him a momentary scare when she first uttered a simple "No."

And I will be ready on the Fourth. I have to be.

As her panic subsided, she realized that she had, at times, felt a bit judgmental about things people had shared in the group that seemed silly or petty to her.

So your brother wouldn't let you use his skateboard when you were kids—this matters now why? Get over it already! she would think.

Lu didn't minimize anyone's pain, but she urged everyone to keep moving through the darkness until they emerged into the light. A few people in the group had had to deal with serious problems—abusive relationships, parental desertion, betrayals of trust. Marya had been the victim of a crime; André had been a member of a street gang.

Caitlin hadn't felt the need to take up the group's time by revisiting events from her past. She did, however, want help quelling her fears about the future.

In the morning, she asked Lu if she could be in the center of a healing circle.

"I'm feeling a little freaked out about going back to Washington. I went through a lot when I lived there. And worked there. As a lawyer. I'm also kind of nervous about performing on national television."

The healing circle was a practice Lu had used a couple of times during the tour when someone was struggling. The person who was the focus of the group's attention stood in the center of the circle. With palms extended, the others directed healing energies toward the person. Lu called it a Love Bomb. Adopting a ceremonial air, she stood outside of the circle and spoke affirming words.

She ended the ceremony for Caitlin by saying, "You are the phoenix, rising from the ashes of destruction and despair, transformed. Vibrant, strong, empowered!"

As Caitlin basked in the positive energy sent her way, the others joined hands and raised their arms as they said, in unison, "And so it is!"

∾ 82 ∾

"*A*re we even getting paid for the Fourth?" Caitlin asked Lu as the bus neared the Virginia state line.

"Yes, but it's at scale, which isn't a lot. We have to cover travel expenses and lodging."

"Well, hopefully it will pay off with future bookings. And CD sales!"

"I'm not worried," Lu said. "It's a wonderful opportunity, and I'm really looking forward to it. I know it might be a little stressful, but hopefully it will also be fun."

"If I really want to be a performer, I've gotta get over my fears sometime," Caitlin said.

"Do you?"

"Do I want to be a performer? Oh, yeah. I always have. Though I'm not sure I'm cut out for arena concerts, and I'm not looking to get signed by a record company. I want to retain ownership of my songs."

"You want to stay independent."

"Yes. I don't want to feel pressured to finish an album or cater to some executive's idea of what will sell."

"You want to stay true to yourself," Lu said. "And your music."

"Exactly."

"The house where we'll be staying this week has a piano, by the way."

"Great."

"And a pool."

"The gang will love that!"

Lu had called in a favor and found a house in Potomac, Maryland where the group could stay until Sunday; after that, they would be at a hotel in Washington for three nights, including the Fourth of July.

"What happens after the Fourth?" Caitlin asked.

"We'll head back to L.A. Maybe take a break in August."

"Is June coming back soon?"

"She's flying in tomorrow," Lu said. "She'll get a car at the airport. So we'll have a way to get around without taking the bus everywhere."

"We're getting low on groceries," Cara said. She was sitting in front of Luisa and turned around to join the conversation.

"Yes, I'm well aware of that," Lu said. "We'll just have to make do for now."

"There's a food co-op in Montgomery County," Caitlin said. "If we don't get in too late, we could stop by there on the way to Potomac."

"Excellent idea," said Lu.

"I don't remember the exact address, but a friend of mine would know. If I can borrow your phone at the next rest stop, I'll see if I can reach him."

The reception along their route was too spotty to try calling from the bus, and even though she didn't plan to talk to Karl about anything intimate, Caitlin wanted privacy for the call. Melody would also know how to get to the co-op, but with a legitimate reason for calling, Caitlin wanted to remind Karl that she would soon be in the area.

The next rest stop was in Bristol, and Caitlin learned that the city on the Virginia-Tennessee state line was considered the birthplace of country music.

She felt a pang of longing when a young couple with a child passed by. She hadn't ever wanted to be a full-time stay-at-home wife and mother, but she hadn't ever experienced the kind of support provided by the group before, either. Her time with Luisa and the Road Angels had changed her. And though she hadn't met many of the residents of the ecovillage, the idea of intentional community had struck a chord. Whereas members of Lu's group all lived together in one house, other groups of people were creating communities where people lived in separate households yet shared a similar kind of lifestyle. They weren't necessarily related by blood or marriage, like tribes and extended families that settled in close proximity to their relations. These were people who created a community together because they wanted to be part of something larger than themselves and saw the benefits of sharing resources with people who shared their values.

The choice of marriage or career didn't have to be either/or, Caitlin realized. Maybe she could have both if she was part of a supportive network. She was ready to get off the road for a while, that much was clear. She had fulfilled some of her ambitions, and she was ready to think about settling down.

And just because the timing was off with Karl didn't mean it always would be. Together or not, they were connected. *That kind of soul connection lasts.*

Luisa handed Caitlin her flip phone after she was done with her calls. Caitlin entered the number for Karl's landline and then paced back and forth until he answered.

"You're home!" she said. "It's Caitlin."

"I wasn't sure when I might hear from you again after you hung up on me last time," Karl said.

"Sorry about that. Everyone was waiting for me. Which they kind of are now, too. We're at a rest stop, so I don't have much time."

"Do you want me to call you back?" Karl asked.

"No, this isn't my phone, but we wanted to pick up some things at the co-op later and I couldn't remember exactly how to get there. Can you give me directions?"

"Sure," Karl said. "I was just there over the weekend."

Caitlin wrote down the directions and nodded to Lu when she saw that everyone was getting back on the bus.

"So you're almost here," Karl said. "Where will you be staying?"

"We'll be at a hotel in D.C. right before the Fourth, but for this week Lu found us a house in Potomac that has a piano."

"Sweet."

"Yeah, I always liked that area."

"Somehow that doesn't surprise me."

"Well, listen, I've gotta go, but I hope we'll have a chance to get together sometime."

"Let me give you my cell phone number," Karl said. "I'll still have that after this landline goes away."

Caitlin wrote the number down as Matt honked the horn.

"I heard that," Karl said. "You better get going."

"Yeah, I'm eager to get there," Caitlin said.

Her heart sank when Karl said, "Just so you know," afraid he was going to announce that he was engaged or some other news she didn't want to hear. "I leave tomorrow for Pennsylvania," he said. "I'll be there till Sunday, but good luck with everything."

Relieved, Caitlin said, "Okay, thanks," and then hurried back to the bus. She handed the phone—and the directions to the co-op—to Lu and then wrote Karl's phone number in her journal, where she kept the photo of him that she had been carrying around since she left Virginia.

She was glad they had talked—and glad to have his cell phone number—but their conversation was also unsettling. For so long, he had wanted to get closer. Now, she was the one craving intimacy.

Wanting to tune out the world—or at least the thirteen other people on the bus—she put on her headphones and looked through her CDs. June had given each of them a copy of the band's CD while they were in Sedona, but Caitlin hadn't listened to it yet. She'd heard the band's songs so many times during rehearsals and shows, they sometimes stuck in her head for days after a performance. She decided on Mozart music and closed her eyes, visualizing a positive reception from the live audience that would gather on the West Lawn of the Capitol on the Fourth of July.

And from Karl.

The bus arrived at the co-op half an hour before closing. While Lu filled a cart with the usual items—fresh fruits and vegetables, granola and rolled oats, yogurt, rice, beans, pasta, soy milk, almond milk, nuts and nut butters—the rest of the group dispersed to find their favorite cookies, candy bars, chips, and flavored drinks.

Caitlin found the scene comical. The orderly, carefully managed functioning of the group that she had witnessed in Los Angeles had deteriorated into something resembling chaos as the Road Angels, tired, perhaps, of constantly trying to be on their best behavior—and restless from being cooped up on the bus all day—let self-restraint lapse, however briefly. With performances on Saturday and Sunday, the group had skipped taiji as well as their evening check-in. Caitlin had a feeling they would be skipping check-in tonight as well. Even Luisa's halo seemed a bit tarnished, she thought, though she didn't see any junk food in Lu's cart.

She walked to the candy aisle and chose an organic dark chocolate bar with dried cherries. *Better get two.*

On the way to the checkout lanes, she noticed a selection of freshly baked breads and pastries and remembered liking the co-op's spinach-feta croissant. She took the last one, as well as an oatmeal cookie.

Back on the bus, she unwrapped one of the candy bars and bit off a piece. She put the rest away for another time, thankful she had tamed her chocolate addiction and could now enjoy a small amount without needing to devour the whole package.

As she carried her things to the room she would, again, share with Cara, Caitlin felt withdrawn and sullen. After enjoying a brief period of solitude while she showered, she got ready for bed.

Just a few more days, she thought, sinking down into the plush pillowtop mattress. *Then I'll have my own room!*

She loved performing but questioned whether she was suited for national tours, much less international travel. She wanted fans, of course, and she had liked all the venues where the band had performed.

Surely with a little effort—and luck—I can find the right balance.

Would she have been better off staying in Santa Fe and continuing to star in musical theater productions at the Playhouse?

Quit doubting yourself, she thought as she got out her earplugs.

She had no regrets about joining the Road Angels on tour, but she wouldn't be getting back on the bus after the tour was over. She planned to fly to L.A. to get her car and then drive to New Mexico to pick up Lucky.

I just need to get through the next few weeks. Then, after the hearing, I can think about what to do with the rest of my life!

〰 83 〰

*T*he kitchen team had breakfast ready when Caitlin joined the group in the dining room on Tuesday morning. Crystal served French toast as a special treat, and Cara poached eggs for the first time. André found a citrus juicer in the pantry and made fresh orange juice.

After everyone was served, Lu tapped on her glass with a spoon and said, "I talked to June last night."

"She's still coming in today, isn't she?" asked Rick.

"Yes, but she told me there's been a change in the program for the Fourth."

"Oh," said Marya. "That doesn't sound good."

"A well-known entertainer wants to sing 'America the Beautiful.'"

A chorus of groans and disappointed murmurs erupted in the group.

"Who is it?" asked Seth.

"She didn't say," said Lu. "It's a man, I take it."

"So where does that leave us?" Matt asked.

"Caitlin will go on before him with 'Shining Star.'"

"That's it?" Pete said. "The rest of us are out?"

Lu shrugged. "Looks that way."

Caitlin wished she could hide under the table. Her big moment would be overshadowed by guilt if her opportunity came at the expense of the band's chance to appear on national television. She thought for a moment and said, "Unless—"

All eyes were on her.

"When I was writing 'Shining Star,' I had a longer ending in mind. Kind of a choir effect for a coda."

"Go on," said Lu.

"Well, it's probably easiest if we just try it out. After lunch, maybe? I'll need to find my notes."

∞

Caitlin practiced the alternate version of "Shining Star" while the lunch team cleaned up, and then everyone gathered around the piano.

Caitlin sang the song from the beginning. Toward the end, she said, "This is the final chorus."

> Even though you've gone away
> I love you from afar
> You're still the light that guides me home
> You are my shining star

She stopped playing and said, "Then, here, you all could sing:"

> Love is the bond we share
> I feel it everywhere
> You know I'll always care
> Your light will guide me there

"And one more verse:"

> We'll meet among the stars
> My home is where you are
> The distance is not that far
> When you're a shining star

"And then I'd repeat the final chorus, and maybe you could do some oohs and aahs or something. Shall we try it?"

"All of us?" asked Crystal.

"Why not? You don't need to sing loudly. At least you'll be onstage!"

With Rick and Lu as their audience and Caitlin as their leader, the band rehearsed the song several times and then waited for Lu's response.

"It could work," Lu said. "As long as the production team agrees."

"Why wouldn't they?" Pete said. "They won't know the difference if they've never heard the recorded version."

"I wouldn't be so sure that they haven't," June said from the back of the room.

She set her handbag on a chair so her arms were free to hug everyone who came over to welcome her. After the commotion had died down, she explained her remark.

"I didn't get a chance to tell Lu this last night, but 'Shining Star' has been climbing up the Adult Contemporary chart. It's currently in the top ten and shows no signs of slowing down."

Everyone congratulated Caitlin, who was stunned.

"How?" she asked.

"Rick included it in the promo package we sent out to radio stations, and they've gotten a lot of requests from listeners. Which doesn't surprise me because I've been getting a lot of inquiries about *you*! That's part of why I couldn't get back sooner. The phone has been ringing off the hook. You, my friend, have got yourself a hit record!"

"Does that mean it's available for sale?" Caitlin asked, wondering what else might have transpired without her knowledge.

"No," June said emphatically as she took a seat. Caitlin followed her lead, sensing a longer conversation was coming, and everyone else did the same.

"A lot of pieces need to be put into place first, and for obvious reasons, that should be done quickly. I've got the paperwork ready for registering the song with the Copyright Office; that really should have been done already. In fact, being so close by, someone might even take it to the Library of Congress in person."

"I'll go," said Rick.

"Next, you'll need a manager who can advise you about distribution and rights and your different options," June said.

"Can't either of you do that?" Caitlin asked, looking from June to Luisa.

"We've got our hands full," June said, "and you're moving into a different league. But we can recommend a few people who might take you on."

"Okay," Caitlin said. "I'd like the song to be available somewhere, even if I don't have a full album ready to go."

"Absolutely," said Lu. "After the Fourth, people will be looking for it."

"Yeah," said Pete. "And you never know if your first hit might be your last."

"Pete!" said June.

"What? I'm just sayin'." Pete shrugged. "There's a lot of one-hit wonders out there."

June rolled her eyes.

Caitlin ignored Pete and focused on her next steps. "Are these managers all in L.A.?" she asked June. "With the time difference, I might even reach someone today."

"I can make a few calls to introduce you and check on availability," June said. "I just need a little time to get acclimated."

"I can do it," said Lu. "You should have some lunch and get settled. I'll show you our room."

Luisa helped June carry her things upstairs, and Matt announced that he was going to check out the pool if anyone wanted to join him. About half the group thought that was a great idea and left the room to get ready.

"You should have a website, too," Rick told Caitlin. "The Internet is expanding rapidly, and that's where you can post news about your work and any appearances you've got scheduled."

"That's a good idea," said Caitlin.

"You know I built the band's website. I've been thinking about doing that as a sideline. Maybe focus on bands and musicians."

"Creating websites?"

"Yeah. It was a pretty steep learning curve for the first one, but I think I could put together another one pretty quickly, if you want me to give it a go."

"Sure! I can pay you for your time."

"Not necessary. I'll need some sample projects for my portfolio. There may be a few fees involved, though, with domain names and hosting."

"I don't know what you're talking about, but just let me know how much I owe you."

"Super. I'll get started on it right away. I'm guessing you'd want your name as the name of the website?"

"I guess. Just use your best judgment."

"Okay. It won't be anything fancy, now. But at least you'll have an online presence."

"I thought you did a good job on the band's site," Caitlin said. "And I guess I have you to thank for all of this."

It had never occurred to her to ask why the radio stations she and Pete had visited in Albuquerque and Boulder had a copy of her song, which wasn't on the Road Angels' debut album.

"I thought it deserved a shot," Rick said. "I'm glad it worked out. It's a good song."

Caitlin walked back to the piano to get her notes. She closed the keyboard cover and then walked slowly to her room.

She would have to make some quick decisions about marketing for "Shining Star." She could change course later, if necessary, as she learned more about the music business. Her focus thus far had been on figuring out how to find venues for live engagements and getting her music recorded. She hadn't given much thought to what she might need to do once she had a fan base.

She took a deep breath and shook her head in disbelief. "Shining Star" was a hit! On the radio!

Imagine that.

"Rainbow Bridge" had been well received when the band played it at New Thought church services. With such an eclectic style, Caitlin wasn't sure how to choose material to fill an entire album.

That's why I need a manager.

Luisa pulled Caitlin aside before dinner and handed her a sheet of paper with the phone number for Ron Ventura, the only one of the managers she had contacted who was willing to take Caitlin on as a client.

"Okay," Caitlin said. "I don't know one from another, and I like it when my choice is clear. If you think this guy is okay, I'm willing to give him a shot. I can make adjustments later if I'm not happy."

"I don't need to tell you this, but be sure to read any contracts carefully before you sign anything. Managers' fees are pretty well set. You won't have a lot of room to negotiate, but you'll have some."

"Yeah, I know entertainment law is its own specialty," Caitlin said. "I need advice from an expert."

"This guy isn't a lawyer, but he can advise you about things like distribution and publicity and promotion. We decided to go with CD Cat for distributing the band's CDs, but that was for a full album. I'm not sure if they handle single songs. Ron should know. Or Rick might. He's the one who set up the account with CD Cat."

"I guess without a record deal, I don't have much hope of getting my music into record stores."

"The way I understand it, record stores are on their way out," Lu said. "I think you're wise to stay independent. Knowing what I do about you and your music, I don't think a big record label would be a good fit for you in the long run. Some of them may express interest if things go well on the Fourth, but with the new technologies that are emerging, I think greater opportunities for artists to connect with their fans are going to make it possible to eliminate a lot of the middlemen. The Aquarian Age will bring more power to the people. Or at least more demand for equal playing fields, across all spheres."

"So it's a good time to be an artist," Caitlin said.

"There are bound to be some bumps in the road. Just stay adaptable—and alert."

"I'll try to avoid the potholes!" Caitlin joked as they walked together to the dining room.

Caitlin sat next to Rick at dinner and asked him about CD Cat. "This is all completely new to me," she said. "What is it and how does it work?"

"It's an online retailer that started a couple of years ago. Basically, artists send copies of their CDs to the company and the company fills orders and sends out a check every week if there have been any sales. They charge a fee for each sale, and there's a setup fee for each CD, but it's reasonable."

"Do you know if they handle singles?"

"I think so, but I'd have to check," Rick said. "Do you want me to call them?

"Maybe. First, let me see what I can find out from this manager that Lu put me in touch with."

After dinner, Caitlin called Ron Ventura from the landline at the house.

"I've only got two songs recorded," she told him. "Would I make a CD for two songs or just for 'Shining Star'? Who actually makes the CDs? I'd need to get copies to send to CD Cat—or wherever—as well as artwork. How fast can all that be done?"

"Realistically, you're not going to have CDs available for sale by next Tuesday," Ron said. "The best you can hope for, if you go the CD route, is to have an account set up so people can place orders. You'll need advertising so people know where to find you and your music. You could go with a digital download file, which would be readily available, but there are greater risks for piracy, and yes, you do have to consider who your fans are and how familiar they are with newer technologies. A lot of people still like to have a physical product that they can hold in their hand."

"My mother doesn't use the Internet," Caitlin said. "I haven't even been using it for all that long."

"Right now, less than four percent of music sales are made online—and CD sales have been declining. But in five years, the majority of sales are going to be made via the Internet. And in ten years, most of the files will be digital."

"How do you get paid? What would our agreement look like?"

"I take a percentage of sales and any other deals I set up for you. I typically start with a one-year contract so neither of us is locked in for long if we're not a good fit."

"Do you mind if I take a night to think about it? This has all been sprung on me out of nowhere and I need to consider the bigger picture in my decision."

"I think that's wise," Ron said. "It's been a pleasure talking to you. Let me know what you decide."

"Thanks," Caitlin said. "I appreciate your interest."

After check-in that evening, Caitlin rehearsed "Shining Star" with the band. Then, Rick wanted to talk about some of his ideas for her website.

"We could do a video of you singing 'Rainbow Bridge' and put that on the site," he suggested. "Maybe add some photos of you onstage next week."

"Are you going to take them?"

"Sure, if they'll let me. I'm guessing the journalists with press passes will get the best spots for taking pictures, but we'll get photos somehow."

Caitlin thanked him and then went outside to sit on the back deck.

She thought about her conversations with Luisa, Rick, and Ron Ventura. She knew that Rick enjoyed working in the studio—and on the computer—more than running sound at live events. He was a fan of the band's music and wanted to stay involved with the music scene in some fashion, but he didn't especially enjoy touring and was looking for a career path that would give him more autonomy.

"I'm not really a group person," he'd told her once. "In case you haven't noticed."

He was good with details, Caitlin thought, and willing to learn new things. Maybe he could be her manager. He had already given her some good ideas, and she trusted him. She would be happy to be his first client if that was something he wanted to pursue. Lu might have work for him in the future as well. If he wanted to focus on websites, that was okay; she would sign with Ron Ventura. Either choice would have advantages and disadvantages. Ventura would have contacts and experience that Rick lacked, but she already had a relationship with Rick and knew they would work well together.

The choice would be his to make, she decided—so she better present the idea to him right away in case he wanted time to think things over before making a commitment.

He was in the dining room working on the computer when she went back inside. "I can show you the CD Cat website," he said.

"That's such a strange name!" Caitlin said, pulling up a chair beside him.

"I think it's short for catalog," he said. "But I don't know."

"Oh, look at the cat on the record label!" Caitlin said when she saw the company's logo. "Say, that gives me an idea for my album. I've got a song called 'Pause.' I could call the album 'Pause' and use a picture of my cat's eyes and maybe have a streak of paw prints running across the cover. What do you think?"

"Sounds clever," Rick said.

"Well, I haven't recorded the song yet, so that's all down the road. Which is what I wanted to talk to you about."

∾ 84 ∾

*W*earing high heels, a sleeveless red sequin top, and black satin pants, Caitlin walked to the piano. The band followed, single file. Organizers expected over a million people to attend the millennium event, which would be seen on television by viewers all over the country.

The show's rehearsal on Monday had gone well, though a lot of time had been spent waiting around. Rick took photographs of Caitlin while she was onstage.

He didn't hesitate to accept Caitlin's offer and said he would help her in whatever way he could. With the situation evolving rapidly, they decided to address immediate concerns and consider their options over the coming weeks. They trusted each other enough to proceed without a signed contract, and with the tour over, Rick didn't have a lot of work he needed to do for the band. He could devote his full attention to Caitlin.

With Rick on her team and the band on the stage with her, she felt confident. Seated at the piano, she took a deep breath and played the beginning of "Shining Star." The memory of her audition at the Playhouse, when she started out off key and asked to begin again, flashed through her mind. But thoughts of that awkward moment couldn't shake her composure. She was prepared to show the world what she could do. Her only weakness was her lack of experience in front of the camera. She would just have to do her part and play and sing and leave it to the professionals to figure out how to capture the performance. If she started looking around—at the audience, the band, or the crew—she would lose focus. And then she would be in trouble.

"Here is your foolish child, running reckless like the wind," she sang.

The song flowed effortlessly from one verse to the next and soon the Road Angels were singing their part along with her. The group had worked out harmonies for the last line of the song, with the band singing "You are my shining star" along with Caitlin for a climactic ending worthy of a Broadway musical.

Caitlin was beaming when she stood up. The group gathered around her before they all left the stage. This was what mattered: sharing her music. Whatever the critics would say, however the audience would respond, this was her moment and nothing could ruin it. If everyone loved the song, that would be a bonus. An influx of orders for her CD would be fantastic. But hearing her music come alive—accompanied by the National Symphony Orchestra, no less!—and supported by a group of people she had come to love was, in itself, rewarding.

Only one thing was missing. Or, rather, one person.

∾ 85 ∾

*L*uisa stepped inside the band's tent near the stage and handed Caitlin a dozen red roses.

"Beautiful," Caitlin said, inhaling the fragrant aroma. "That was sweet of you."

"They are beautiful. But they're not from me."

Lu stood aside and Melody and Karl entered the tent.

"You guys were here for the show?" Caitlin asked, hugging each of them.

"You were awesome," said Melody. "All of you," she added when she saw other familiar faces.

"Unbelievable," said Karl. He gave Caitlin a warm embrace.

Realizing Melody wasn't in New Mexico with Lucky, Caitlin asked, "Hey— What did you do with my cat?"

"He's at my place," Karl said. "Waiting for you to come home."

Overcome with emotion, Caitlin broke down in tears. All the stress and excitement, heartbreak and ecstasy, worry and relief came pouring out of her. Karl held her close, and everyone else left to give them some privacy.

Caitlin pulled away to find a box of tissues. "I really need to get cleaned up," she said. "I was already sweaty and now I'm a mess!"

"Will this help?" Karl handed her a bottle of water.

Caitlin laughed. "A bit! Give me a few minutes to get changed and splash some water on my face."

Karl waited outside while Caitlin changed into the casual clothes she had brought with her—a cotton skirt and top and sandals that were easy on her feet.

"Let's go find a good spot to watch the fireworks," Karl suggested. He was wearing a white button-up short-sleeved shirt and khaki shorts.

"A walk will do me good," Caitlin said. "It takes a while to come down off the high after a concert."

"I can imagine," Karl said. "And we need some time alone. To talk."

"Yes," Caitlin said.

But neither of them said much as they walked the length of the National Mall.

Karl's skin was tanned and his hair, Caitlin noticed, was neatly trimmed. Not too short, not too long. *Just right.*

"It's a beautiful night," she said.

"Yeah, you got lucky with the weather."

After another awkward silence, Karl said, "Your mom must be over the moon."

Caitlin laughed. "Oh, yeah. She probably called all the local newspapers to make sure everyone knew that her daughter would be on television!"

Karl chuckled.

"My father was a journalist, you know."

"I'd forgotten that."

More silence and then Karl asked, "What are your plans now?"

"I don't really have any, other than staying around for a couple of weeks until I testify."

"You're testifying? Where? About what?"

"I'd written to a congressman who's chair of a committee that's investigating vaccines—thimerosal, in part, but also other issues about vaccine safety. I got a letter inviting me to testify, so I figured while I'm in the area . . ."

"What about your music career? Are you going to stay with the band or go out on your own?"

"I'm not going to join the band, and they'll probably take a break in August anyway. I want to finish my album, but not right away. I need to write a few more songs first. I've got a manager now, though. That's a start."

The fireworks were just starting to pop when Caitlin and Karl reached the Lincoln Memorial. They walked up the stairs and sat on an elevated ledge not far from one of the two marble tripods that decorated the entrance to the monument.

"Oh, I got you something," Karl said, removing a mobile flip phone from his shirt pocket. "You'll need a phone to handle all the offers that will be pouring in."

Caitlin smiled and took the phone. She flipped it open and said, "Yeah, I guess it's time I stopped borrowing other people's phones!"

Karl leaned toward her and pointed to a button below the screen. "Here's where you find the contact list. I've added my number, so you've got no excuses for not keeping in touch," he said.

Then he smiled that smile, the one Caitlin had missed. The one that complemented the sparkle in his eyes.

She put the phone in her purse and said, "You'll have to let me know your schedule. So I'm not calling at an inconvenient time."

"Oh, you mean Angela? We're not together."

Caitlin looked at him, waiting for him to say more.

"I told her I needed to be with someone who shares my vision and is willing to commit to an alternative lifestyle."

"And she wasn't?"

"I knew she wasn't ready to leave her life here. I also knew she wasn't the one *I* wanted to commit to, long-term. But I figured I'd let her think she chose to end it. No hard feelings that way."

"Hmm," was all Caitlin said.

She watched as bright, colorful patterns appeared in the sky near the Washington Monument and then said, "I've come around to your way of thinking about a number of things in the last couple of years."

Karl turned toward her and said, "Yeah?"

Caitlin wanted to reach out and touch him, but she needed to know what he was thinking—and feeling. She had so much to tell him, and this might be their only opportunity to talk in person. Searching his eyes, she said, "We made love, didn't we?"

"At the Shannon Pot," he said, and then looked away. "Yes."

"I remember," Caitlin said. "I remember all of it. That must have been hard for you, when I didn't."

Karl shook his head and let out a deep sigh as he looked down at the ground. "I knew I'd never be able to convince you that we belonged together. And I didn't really want to try." Turning to face her, he said, "You had to find out for yourself. But yeah, having come so close only to lose you again— It was hell."

Caitlin put her hand on his and asked, "What did you see? During the ceremony."

Karl pulled his hand away and ran his fingers over his hair before clasping his hands together. "That was . . . hard."

"You were very withdrawn in the morning. I didn't know if it was because of me or—"

"No, no. It had nothing to do with you. Well, not nothing, but I was shown images from other lifetimes."

"Me too!"

"We were together in Egypt."

"The temple! I know! And I was with Melody in ancient Greece!"

Karl smiled weakly before turning serious again. "After the army destroyed the temple and separated us, I . . . I took my own life."

"I guess you weren't sentenced to eternal damnation," Caitlin joked.

"Eternal, no. But I've had to learn how to stay strong through the dark periods. And to not lose faith."

"Or give up too easily."

"Or give in to addictions and other attempts to escape the pain. I had to find my way back to a path of love and service. Life-affirming rather than self-destructive. You know?"

Caitlin nodded and said, "Yeah. I do."

She collected her thoughts and then asked, "But who was he, exactly? The shaman. I heard his voice in my head before I even landed in Ireland."

"Really?"

"Yeah, I was half asleep and I didn't know if I was imagining things or hearing things or what. I've slowly been piecing together different parts of the puzzle, but so much of it remains a mystery."

Karl smiled at her. "Keeps life interesting, doesn't it?" Looking away, he said, "My sense is—and I don't know this for a fact, but my sense is that you and I are part of the same soul group and he's like a guide who tracks our progress."

"But he was real, right? Like, a flesh-and-blood person?"

"Oh, yeah, I think so. There was a group there, at the Shannon Pot, and they were in the midst of a ceremony and he was the leader. I don't think it was an accident that we found them. And I don't think he necessarily lives in Ireland."

"So you think he, what, telepathically planted the idea that we should both come to Ireland?"

"Maybe," Karl said. "I think he probably has followers that study with him—you know, like in an ashram or temple setting. I've had dreams where I seem to be there, in a class or something. Maybe they travel to different regions for important ceremonies."

"Wow. If that's true . . ." Caitlin was at a loss for words. "Life gets more interesting by the minute!"

Karl turned to her and said, "So, now that you know my deepest, darkest secrets—what do you think?"

"About what?" Caitlin said. "About you?"

Karl got down on one knee, pulled out a ring, and said, "Yeah. What do you think?"

"Oh my gosh!" Caitlin said. She covered her mouth with her hands and then quickly removed them. "Are you asking me to marry you?"

The ring wasn't a diamond, and Karl hadn't actually asked her to marry him, so she wasn't sure.

"Looks that way," Karl said. "And this pavement is kind of uncomfortable on bare skin."

Caitlin took the ring and put it on her finger. It fit perfectly. She took Karl's hands in hers as they both rose to their feet and kissed passionately. The grand finale of the fireworks display exploded in the sky to the cheers and applause of onlookers.

Caitlin and Karl laughed, though they knew the applause wasn't for them. They stood watching the last streams of light and then sat and talked for another hour while the crowds dispersed.

Karl told Caitlin about his plans to build first a clinic and then an intentional community with gardens and shared facilities on his property in Pennsylvania.

"Can we have an orchard?" Caitlin asked.

"You want an orchard? We'll have an orchard."

She told him about the ecovillage near Asheville where the band had stayed.

"I know about that place," Karl said. "They're doing some ground-breaking work there. Pardon the pun."

"I can't say I saw much of it. It rained while we were there, and I was tired of being on the road."

"Maybe we can visit a few of these places and get ideas about how to go about forming a community of our own."

Caitlin thought for a moment and then said, "I'll have to go back to L.A. to pick up my car. Why don't you come with me? We can drive back together and maybe stop at a few places along the way. I've got some stuff in storage in Santa Fe that I need to get."

"There's a cohousing community in Santa Fe," Karl said.

"A what?"

Karl explained a little about the Danish model that had been adopted by communities in the U.S. and elsewhere.

"Is it like a commune?" Caitlin asked.

"Everyone owns their own home, but it is a cooperative venture, with parts of the property owned in common. The residents make decisions together and usually share some meals as well as skills and resources."

"So how is that different from an ecovillage?"

"They both attract people who want to live in community and be involved with their neighbors. There are a lot of decisions that have to be made—everything from the initial building design to the kinds of food served at community meals. But ecovillages go a step further in terms of a focus on environmentally friendly measures—organic food, sustainability. Cohousing often has a multigenerational emphasis, with families and seniors and singles all looking to support each other in various ways. But really, it's a model that has a lot of flexibility. It's all about intention. It's important to be clear from the start about agreements to avoid running into problems later."

"Having a shared vision," Caitlin said.

"Yes. The better defined the vision is, the easier it is to attract the kind of people who want to help create it."

"Sounds like you've done your homework," Caitlin said. She agreed that visiting existing communities would be a good way to see these principles in action and talk to residents about community life.

"I've got a lot of ideas," Karl said. "But I'm open to suggestions."

They held hands as they walked toward the Metro station at Foggy Bottom.

"I'm tired," Caitlin said. "Can't we take a cab?"

"Sure—if we can find one."

Karl sounded skeptical, but Caitlin remembered Melody's Parking Angel and said, "Let's try! The roads should all be open by now."

"True."

They walked to Constitution Avenue and hailed a cab with no difficulty. Once inside, Caitlin asked Karl if he wanted to come back to the hotel with her.

"Nah," he said. "I left my car at the Clarendon Metro. And you should get some sleep."

The driver dropped him at the Foggy Bottom station and then took Caitlin to the hotel where the Road Angels were staying.

She smiled dreamily as she replayed the evening's events in her mind. She was exhausted but also elated. This was the best night of her life, and she wanted to savor every minute of it.

Karl's words weren't very romantic, but the setting was. She wouldn't have guessed he would ever get down on one knee and present her with a ring. She hadn't even known if he believed in the institution of marriage. She wouldn't have been surprised to learn that he favored polyamory or some other unconventional arrangement. She was pleased to discover that at least some of his ideas were normal. Relating to him day to day would be too much of a stretch if they didn't have *some* things in common.

Maybe he was more conventional than he liked to let on, Caitlin thought. Or maybe he, too, had changed in the last couple of years.

There was still so much they didn't know about each other. Were they crazy to think about getting married when they hadn't even dated?

When you know, you know, she concluded.

Melody had always said their union was written in the stars. *Maybe she was right.*

∾ 86 ∾

"**D**id I wake you?" Caitlin asked when Karl finally answered the phone after seven rings.

"In a matter of speaking," Karl said. "Oh, you mean this morning? No, I was already up. I'm getting ready to go for a run. My bike's in Pennsylvania."

"I'm going down to breakfast and I want to give everyone my new number—but I don't know what it is!"

"Hang on. I'll look in my phone."

"You mean you haven't memorized it?" Caitlin teased.

"No one memorizes phone numbers anymore," Karl said. "I don't even know *my* new number."

Caitlin wrote down the number and said, "Thanks. What's the plan?"

"Melody's on her way over there. She took my car. She'll bring you back here whenever you're ready."

"Okay. It may be a while. I need to meet with Rick after breakfast."

"See you when you get here."

Caitlin took her time getting ready. As she showered, she thought about her engagement to Jayson. She had dreamed of an elegant wedding attended by prominent lawyers and politicians as well as friends and family. She would have wanted a designer gown then and lots of bridesmaids. She would have wanted to be the center of attention.

Now, she would be satisfied with a simple ceremony. She didn't need to impress anyone, and she was more interested in starting her new life with Karl than in putting on a show. She'd save the glitz and glamour for the stage and keep her private life private. Simplicity was more Karl's style anyway. Though, she did still want a tasteful affair and a beautiful, memorable experience. An event that would be fun and enjoyable for everyone—and low stress for her.

Simple elegance. No need to sacrifice quality.

They would have plenty of time to plan a wedding and reception, she thought as she dressed.

For now, Karl is busy with his career and plans, and I'm busy with mine.

"There she is!" Luisa said when Caitlin arrived at the restaurant.

Lu, Melody, June, and Rick were sharing a booth; the rest of the group sat at tables nearby.

"Looks like everyone has already eaten," Caitlin said. She waved to Cara before squeezing into the booth next to Melody.

"Yes, but we're not in any rush," June said. She poured cream into her coffee and stirred it with a spoon.

Melody gave Caitlin a big hug. "Congratulations! I'm so happy for you!"

Caitlin looked around and said, "Ah, I guess you've told everyone."

"I did, but only because I have a proposal of my own, and I wanted to run it by the group first."

"Okay, let's hear it."

"I'd like to plan your wedding," Melody said. "It will be my gift. And I knew your friends in the band would all want to be there."

"So we took a vote," said Lu, "and it was unanimous. If you get married in the next three weeks, we'll play at your wedding. Or reception. Or both!"

Caitlin took the menu the waiter handed her and said, "Three weeks!"

"We know you have that hearing coming up," Melody said. "So we were thinking maybe the following Saturday."

"Does Karl know about this?"

Melody grinned and nodded. "Uh-huh. He's cool with it."

"What are you all going to do in the meantime?" Caitlin asked Lu and June.

"It's all arranged," June said. "The band is going to Upstate New York and I'm going back to L.A. But I'll come to the wedding, if you decide to have it."

"What's in New York?" Caitlin asked.

"Troy's parents have agreed to an outdoor concert on their farm," Rick said.

"Pete and Matt have some new material they want to try out," June said. "And Marya is keen to sing lead on a few songs."

"Huh," said Caitlin. The show would go on without her. *As it should,* she thought.

She opened her menu and said, "Can I have a minute to think about what I want to eat? Or has someone already ordered for me."

Hearing the edge in her voice, she realized she felt stressed. She stared at the menu, thinking: *Now I've got* three *things to worry about in the next few weeks: the hearing, getting my music launched, and planning my wedding! Nothing like being put on the spot. Sure, it will be a help if Melody handles all the arrangements. But our tastes are so different . . . and I'll still have to find a dress and figure out who to invite and . . . I don't really appreciate all this going on behind my back. Oh, I know they mean well, but it is my wedding!*

She closed the menu and said, "Oh, what the hell."

I would *like the band to be there,* she thought, *and they're already here. You can be sure they wouldn't all come back at a later time. Who else would I even invite, besides my mother? I haven't really kept up with anyone since the Crash. The important thing is to formalize our union and get on with our new life together. I'm not attached to the particulars, and I expect Karl would go along with whatever Melody and I decide.*

"Okay," she said, and then took a drink of water. "But I don't want any gifts. Put that on the invitations."

"No gifts," Melody said as she wrote on a pad of paper that Caitlin hadn't noticed before.

"Well—state it a little more tactfully," Caitlin said, thinking, *Yup, this is exactly what I'd expect from Melody.*

Melody looked up, as if waiting for Caitlin to dictate the wording—so she did.

"Your presence in our lives is the greatest gift you can give," Caitlin said. "We would be honored to have you join us for this special occasion as we declare our love and pledge our lives to each other. Something like that."

"How many invitations do you think you'll need?" Melody asked.

"I'm not expecting many guests, but I can't speak for Karl. Find out if there's a minimum order, and give me a choice of styles, please."

"No friends from your old job?" Melody asked.

"No, and Pennsylvania is kind of far anyway."

"Pennsylvania?"

"You were planning on doing this at Karl's house, weren't you?"

Melody put down her pen and said, "Oh." After a pause, she nodded and said, "I hadn't really thought about that, but we could. It might be a little more complicated, but I've been wanting to see his property. I guess I could go up there and make the arrangements. It's kind of a rural area, as I understand it. There won't be as many choices. For caterers or places for people to stay."

"I'm fine with simple," Caitlin said. "And that's not as far for the band to travel from New York."

"True," Melody said.

"And then everyone will know where to find me from here on out."

Turning her attention to Rick, Caitlin said, "Can we meet after breakfast? When do you all head out?"

"We're staying another night," Rick said. "Everyone wanted to do a bit of sightseeing. So, sure."

"Okay. I won't keep you for long."

"As long as it takes." Rick stood up and said, "I'll be in my room. It's number 515. Just come on up when you're ready."

June also got out of the booth. "I'll let the others know what's going on."

"I've got some calls to make," Lu said. "And you two have a lot to talk about!"

Caitlin and Melody got out of the booth so Lu could leave and then they sat across from each other.

"When exactly is the hearing?" Melody asked.

"The eighteenth."

"We're looking at the twenty-second, then," Melody said, glancing at her day planner. She looked up and said, "Twenty-two is a master number, you know."

"Okay," said Caitlin. "Is that a good thing?"

"It's powerful."

Melody had started a list of arrangements that would need to be made: flowers, cake, decorations, food. "What about bridesmaids?" she asked.

Caitlin thought for a second and said, "No. No bridesmaids."

She would have to have a maid of honor, though, and Melody would probably be offended if she chose someone else, considering all the trouble she was going to.

"Just a maid of honor."

"Do you know who you'll ask?"

"Not anyone from the band, I guess," she said, thinking out loud. "I've got a cousin in Kansas—I just saw her when we went through there. But we're not exactly close. I guess I'll have to invite her and my aunt and uncle to the wedding. I doubt they'll come, though. Same with my relatives in Massachusetts. And I should send an invite to my brother. He lives in Sydney. There's no way he'll come. He might not even get the invitation in time!"

"Can't you call him?"

"Ah, well, that's complicated, and life's complicated enough at the moment. But I'll send him an invite."

"Maid of honor?"

"Oh, right. Would you like the honor? I mean, you're already doing all the work. I can't think of anyone more appropriate. Especially considering how long you've wanted Karl and me to get together."

Caitlin noticed a troubled look on Melody's face.

"Would that be too weird, considering your history with him?" Caitlin asked.

"No . . . It's not that," Melody said. She seemed almost embarrassed as she leaned forward and whispered, "I don't have anything to wear."

Caitlin knew that she would be responsible for most of the expenses. Karl wasn't earning much yet, and he'd just built a new house. Melody wouldn't want to spend money on a dress she probably would never wear again.

"I'll get your dress when I get mine," Caitlin said. "Just give me your measurements."

Melody seemed relieved when she said okay, but she grew excited when Caitlin asked, "What color do you want?"

"Oh, I get to pick?" She thought for a moment and said, "Mmm . . . purple!"

"Purple it is," Caitlin said.

"Great! We'll have purple accents for the invitations and decorations. And the flowers!"

Caitlin's breakfast arrived. She stuck a fork into the omelet she had ordered and thought, *I guess we're really doing this. For better or for worse.*

∽ 87 ∽

I hope Melody confers with me about any important decisions, Caitlin thought as she walked down the corridor to Rick's room. She knocked on the door, eager to think about something other than wedding plans.

Rick opened the door and invited Caitlin to join him at the table, where Lu's laptop was open.

"Melody's waiting for me, so I can't stay too long," Caitlin said. "But we should at least get started on putting some plans into place."

"I've been learning about the different charts the music industry uses. 'Shining Star' is number one on both the Adult Contemporary chart and the Adult Top 40," Rick said.

"I've never even heard of Adult Top 40."

"It's fairly new."

Opening various computer files, Rick showed Caitlin the progress he had made on her website.

"I'm still working on some of the other pages, but the home page is set up, and it gives information about how to order 'Shining Star' from CD Cat."

"So they do accept singles?"

"Yep, everything's in process."

"What about 'Rainbow Bridge'? Are we releasing that now, too?"

"I was thinking we might save that for your album. We should go through all of your songs sometime and decide which ones fit together. I don't think we want to mix totally different sounds that would appeal to different listeners. You might give that some thought."

"I have," Caitlin said. "'Rainbow Bridge' is already recorded, as you know. A few of the other songs I've written could work for an album—'Phoenix Heart,' which I'd like Cara to play cello on, and 'Gone for Good,' which I wrote about my father, and 'Pause,' which I already mentioned. I don't think 'Veil of Illusion' would fit. It's kind of a negative view of marriage!"

Rick laughed. "Oh!"

"I won't be wearing a veil when I walk down the aisle," Caitlin said. "I won't be promising to obey, either!"

"Congratulations, by the way," Rick said.

"Thanks. When things settle down, I'll have more time to write."

Caitlin thought for a moment and then said, "I sang 'Wonderin' Fool' when I auditioned at the Playhouse. That one might work as a single, actually. I don't think it would fit with the others. It's got a different feel."

"Okay, we might think about recording that next. Get another single out quickly."

"You know, I'll have to go back to L.A. to get my car," Caitlin said, thinking aloud. "Maybe we could record it then, if David is free. I have no idea how much his fees are, or whether we have the budget for that."

"One song shouldn't be too bad," Rick said. "And I heard from the morning shows. They're interested in having you on."

"Would I have to go to New York City? Because I really don't have the time for that right now."

"One of them is here for the week, actually. They're on location at different spots around D.C."

"Let's go with that one."

Caitlin stood up and said, "You've got my number, so let me know where I need to be and when. I'll be staying in Arlington until the hearing."

"Will do."

Melody drove Caitlin to Karl's house and helped carry her things inside. "It's pretty sparse, just so you know," Melody said.

Karl greeted Caitlin with a kiss. "There's my fiancée," he said. "Thanks for bringing her," he told Melody before she left to spend the afternoon with friends.

"Not a fiancée for long, it seems," Caitlin said, closing the front door. "She really takes an idea and runs with it, doesn't she?"

Karl laughed. "Oh, yeah, if Melody has her mind made up, it's easier to just go along with her. You don't want to butt heads with a ram, believe me!"

"I know, I lived with her, too." Caitlin sighed and said, "Well, if you're okay with leaving all the plans to her, then I guess I am, too."

"The wedding is just one day," Karl said. "We've got the rest of our lives to make a mess of things ourselves!"

"You mean I get to blame her for everything that goes wrong on my wedding day?" Caitlin joked. She put her arms around Karl's neck and said, "You know, July twenty-second is only four days before my birthday. Don't think you're going to get off easy every year. I still want my special day and our special day!"

"Sweetheart, I'm gonna make every day special!" Karl said.

He picked her up and carried her to his bedroom, where a queen-size mattress and box spring had replaced the twin bed Caitlin remembered from her stay nearly three years earlier.

Their first—and only—time making love was in Ireland, at the Shannon Pot on the summer solstice, four years earlier. They'd known each other for nine years now. In that time, their friendship had matured; their love had blossomed. Caitlin was ready now to commit to Karl—heart, mind, and body.

Lucky woke Caitlin from a nap. Karl was still sleeping, so she picked up the cat and walked through the house to see what furnishings remained. She would be living there for two weeks, and part of that time she would be there alone.

"Except for you," she told Lucky. "You know, you've come full circle, too. I was staying here when Kimo introduced us. And just like Starcatcher, you've been off having adventures! Pretty soon you'll have a proper home—probably for the rest of your life."

Caitlin's eyes teared up at the realization that in a matter of weeks she would be a married woman and starting a new life. Unexpected as it all was, moving to Pennsylvania with Karl felt right.

Melody had been staying in her old room upstairs, where a sleeping bag was cushioned by a foam pad on the floor. Downstairs, a couple of folding chairs were set up in the living room, but the lamps had been removed, as all the rooms had ceiling fixtures. A few dishes, pots and pans, and cooking essentials had been left in the kitchen.

Caitlin filled Lucky's bowl with fresh water and went back to bed. Karl stirred.

"I'm hungry!" Caitlin said. "Can we order in?"

"Chinese?"

"Sure!"

"There's a menu in a drawer in the kitchen. Order whatever you want. I'm gonna take a shower."

Caitlin phoned in an order from the landline and then put plates and utensils on the small desk in Karl's office. While she waited for the food to arrive, she hung some clothes in the closet in the bedroom, which also had shelves she could use for shoes and jeans. She didn't see a dresser anywhere, so she organized the undergarments in her suitcase and then closed it to keep out her curious pet.

After dinner, Karl helped Caitlin set up the voicemail on her phone and then he showed her photos of his house and property. "I could take you up there, but there's not a lot to see yet."

"It'll be a surprise," Caitlin said. "You know, most of my stuff is still in storage here. I'll call this week and see when it can get moved."

"Uh . . . How much do you have?"

"I got rid of some things when I sold the townhouse, but I kept most of the furniture. How big is your house?"

"About 2,000 square feet. Three bedrooms."

"So one of those could be the nursery. The other is your study?"

"Right now it is," Karl said. "Once the clinic is built, I'll be spending most of my days there."

They carried their plates and the empty food containers to the kitchen.

"How many patients do you have?" Caitlin asked.

"In Pennsylvania? None."

"But you still have a few here?"

"A few. As long as I have at least three I'll keep coming back every month. My friend Barry said I could crash at his place. He travels a lot."

"For work?"

Karl nodded. "He works for the Agency for International Development."

"Humanitarian aid," Caitlin said. Her neighbor in Alexandria worked for AID and Caitlin had learned about some of the agency's programs from him.

"Did you invite Barry to the wedding?" she asked.

"I haven't invited anyone yet. Have you?"

"No! I was going to call my mother today, but I got distracted," Caitlin said with a grin. "I'll do that tomorrow, after you and Melody leave."

Karl turned out the light in the kitchen but left the outside lights on.

"Is she coming back tonight?" Caitlin asked.

"Far as I know," Karl said. "She's got a key."

He followed Caitlin to the bedroom and started to undress. "You'll need a car to get around," he said. "I can take you somewhere in the morning if you want to rent one."

"Okay." Caitlin thought for a moment and said, "You should call your parents right away. Give them some time to plan. How often do you usually talk to them?"

"My father's not well," Karl said. "I don't think he can travel, and I don't think my mother would come without him. They're older, you know."

"Right."

"But I was thinking we might visit them when we go to California to get your car."

"Okay! And I may try to record one song while I'm there. That would be cool, to have you in the studio with me."

Caitlin brushed her teeth and then asked, "What about your friends from all the groups you were involved with here? Any of them you want to invite?"

Karl was already in bed. "No, if we were getting married here, then yeah, they'd all want to come. But I'm not close to many of them. They're acquaintances more than friends. I don't know how many of them I'll stay in touch with when I'm no longer living here. I've been busy with other things the last couple of years."

Caitlin lay down beside him and said, "I get it. I'm not planning to invite anyone I used to work with at OSP or at Legal Aid. So I guess it will be a very small wedding."

"Are you okay with that?"

"Yeah, we don't need fancy," Caitlin said. "We just need our friends around us. And like you said, the wedding is just one day. The marriage will last a lifetime. I hope!"

"I hope so, too." Karl kissed her and said, "Let's get some sleep."

∾ 88 ∾

*C*aitlin snuggled up next to Karl in the morning and said, "I'm not changing my name, you know."

"Did I say you could have my name?"

"I like my name."

"I like it, too," Karl said. He kissed her before going to shower.

"I'll start breakfast," Caitlin said. "Good morning, cat!" she said when Lucky jumped onto the bed. "I'll bet you're hungry."

She fed Lucky and then looked around the kitchen. *No blender.* Melody would have to do without her morning smoothie.

Caitlin sautéed potato, onions, red pepper, and asparagus and then topped scrambled eggs with feta cheese, but she only found two dinner plates on a shelf in the cupboard. She would give those to Karl and Melody. She chose a smaller salad plate for herself.

Melody came bounding down the stairs and cheerfully said, "Good morning!" She had brought her own blender, a slender immersion mixer that didn't require a pitcher.

"I was thinking we could sit outside on the steps," Caitlin said. "The weather is so pleasant this morning."

"Okay," Melody said. "Did you see the strawberries I bought?"

"Yeah, but I wasn't sure if you were saving them for anything special."

"There's enough for all of us. I'll cut some up."

Melody put her ingredients into a large glass, stuck the blender into the mix, and turned it on.

"Will your boyfriend be coming out to see you at all while you're in Pennsylvania?" Caitlin asked as she and Melody took their plates outside to sit on the front steps. Karl arrived soon after.

"No, he's on tour in the Northwest this summer," Melody said. "I might join him after the wedding. Though I'm also thinking about riding back to Tesuque with the Road Angels."

"On the bus?" Caitlin asked.

"Yeah! I thought it might be kind of fun. Lu plans to stop in New Mexico for a few days on the way back to L.A."

"Have they got any concerts lined up? I hope the show on the Fourth brought them some attention, too."

"Oh, yeah, they've been getting lots of calls, but most of their events are scheduled pretty far out. I think Lu wants to do another couple of shows in New Mexico. Maybe Albuquerque again, and also in Santa Fe."

"I'm glad to hear it," Caitlin said. She already missed the group. *Even Pete,* she thought with a smile.

"I need to talk to them about the music for the ceremony," she said. "And you need to talk to me about any important decisions," she told Melody. "Agreed?"

"Agreed."

Karl took Caitlin to rent a car and then she followed him back to the house.

"You're sure you'll be okay here by yourself?" he asked as they walked toward the back door.

"You have no idea how much I've been longing for some time to myself!" Caitlin said. "I've got that appearance on the morning show tomorrow and then the hearing to prepare for. I'll have plenty to keep me busy."

They walked inside and were greeted by Lucky but saw no sign of Melody.

"Okay, I'll see you Sunday," Karl said, pausing for a kiss. "I've got clients scheduled on Monday, Tuesday, and Wednesday."

"I'll call the movers and make arrangements for getting my stuff."

"After the wedding would probably be best."

"I doubt they could do it before then, but yeah—that would be a real mess with boxes everywhere."

"I'll do what I can to get the house in order. I only just moved in, remember."

"Did you buy a new bed for your house?" Caitlin asked.

"I did. And it's *our* house now."

"Has Angela slept in it?"

"She has."

"Hmm."

"Is that a problem?"

"I'll have to think about it."

They had both had other relationships, other lovers, but Caitlin liked the idea of starting their new life together in a new place that had no associations with the past.

I should probably be more worried about having sex with him so soon after he's been with her than about where they've been sleeping, Caitlin thought. She was enjoying the sex, so she'd best get over any concerns she had about someone who was no longer a threat.

"Have you talked to her?"

"I haven't, but we parted on friendly terms."

Caitlin watched as Karl packed a cooler with a few items from the fridge. "Meaning, you might," she said.

"I expect I might hear from her at some point."

"So she doesn't know you're getting married."

"No. That would upset her, I think."

Caitlin thought about the wounded look on Paul's face when she turned down his offer of marriage. She hadn't seen any point in mentioning Paul's proposal to Karl. Paul wasn't a threat to their relationship, and she didn't want Karl to obsess about it, so she wouldn't obsess about Angela, either, she decided. She wouldn't ask a lot of probing questions about how they met and whether she was pretty and what Karl had liked about her. She might not know everything *about* Karl, but she knew *him*—and she trusted him.

"Are we going to have a guest room?" she asked.

Karl closed the lid on the cooler and said, "I thought we might have a guest *cottage*."

"Ooh, I like that idea!"

"That way, clients could stay overnight. But, in the meantime, the future nursery can be the guest room."

"So you agree? No birth control? We don't have a lot of time to mess around."

"Oh, I hope we'll have lots of time to mess around," Karl said, squeezing Caitlin's rear.

"You know what I mean," she said with a grin.

"Yeah, I do, but let's agree we won't make assumptions. We'll say what we mean, so everything is clear."

"I agree we shouldn't make assumptions," Caitlin said, "but I don't want to have to spell everything out, either. Language isn't the only way to communicate."

Karl kissed her and said, "Fair enough. I'll go find Melody. We need to get going."

"Call me when you get there."

Caitlin called Karl's mobile phone soon after he left to ask if Internet service was set up at the house. "I was thinking I might buy a laptop," she said, "while I've got some time to figure out how to use it."

"Good idea," Karl said. "I've been pretty happy with mine. Why don't you shop around and then tell me what you're thinking of getting."

"My manager, Rick, and Troy—one of the guys in the band—both know quite a bit about computers. I thought I might ask them for a recommendation. Keep it simple."

Karl was quiet for a moment and then said, "Do what you think is best."

"I'll let you know what I find out."

Was he upset that she didn't want his advice? Caitlin wondered when she hung up the phone. *So much to learn about each other.*

She entered the number for Ray and Martha's house into her phone and saved it to her contacts list before placing the call.

"Thought I'd let you know my new phone number," Caitlin said when her mother answered.

"I didn't recognize it when it showed up on the caller ID. Where is that area code?"

"Pennsylvania. Get out your suitcases—this time you're coming east!"

Karl called that evening after he and Melody had eaten dinner. "Melody says the invitations will arrive there in the next couple of days," he told Caitlin. "So you'll have to get stamps and send them out. I'll make up a list of names and addresses."

"Have you thought about a best man?"

"Yeah, I'm going to call Barry and see if he's available. He's been a good friend for quite a few years."

"Did I ever meet him?"

"I don't think so. He never came to any of the dinners I used to have at the house."

"How did you meet him?"

"Basketball."

"Okay, I hope that works out. Can you put Melody on? I want to ask her who will officiate. And since we're getting married in Pennsylvania, one of you will have to look into the requirements. Legally speaking."

"Yeah, sure. I'll get her."

"Do you remember Charlotte?" Melody asked Caitlin. "She was at the new moon ceremony we had in Arlington before you left."

"I remember the ceremony but I'm not sure I remember who she was. Why?"

"She's now an ordained minister in the Church of Religious Science."

"I don't know that church. It's not that weird one, is it? The one all those celebrities joined?"

"Oh, no. This organization was started by Ernest Holmes and later it became a church, though the centers are not about worship—more about teaching and practice. Holmes taught a lot about the power of mind and spirituality as a science. You cool with that or do you want a real minister from, like, a Christian church?"

"Did you already talk to her about the wedding? What did she say?"

"She was open to the idea but needed to check her calendar, since she'd have to be gone overnight."

"Sounds fine. Just keep me posted."

Too much to think about, Caitlin thought as she switched off the light and closed her eyes. She knew she'd better get some sleep or she would have dark circles under her eyes in the morning, when she would, again, be appearing on national television.

Maybe I need a publicist or an agent or someone who can help me prepare for these things. Rick's expertise only goes so far.

∾ 89 ∾

The network sent a limousine to take Caitlin to the National Zoo. The team from the morning show had been visiting different attractions around the area all week, and today the focus was on the Smithsonian Institution.

"I hadn't realized the zoo is part of the Smithsonian," Caitlin told the hosts of the show when she arrived at the zoo.

She never watched the morning shows, and Karl didn't have a television, so she hadn't been able to familiarize herself with the format. She didn't know much about the two-hour show, except that her segment would be the last.

"You probably won't be on the air for long," Rick had told her. "They'll ask you a few basic questions as chitchat and then you'll perform your song. That's pretty much it."

Rick had put together a cover for Caitlin's CD using one of the photos he had taken at the rehearsal for the Fourth of July concert. The image was flashed on the screen, along with the URL for CD Cat's website, when the host announced that a "special performance" was coming up after a commercial break. Caitlin stood by and watched on a monitor.

She had decided to wear a casual gold top and a chic hat to keep the sun out of her eyes. Her black pants were the same pair she had worn for the concert on the Fourth, back from the dry cleaners. She would probably be seated at a grand piano the entire time, so she didn't figure anyone would be critiquing her fashion choice.

Curious onlookers were gathered around the piano. Some people sat on the ground so they wouldn't interfere with the cameras.

Once they were on the air, the host introduced the show's "musical guest."

"You're joining us live from the National Zoo in Washington, D.C., and we're here with Caitlin Rose outside the Panda House, which has been empty since the death of the giant panda Hsing-Hsing last November," the man said to the camera. Turning his attention to Caitlin, he said, "And you'll be performing your hit song, 'Shining Star' today, is that right?"

"Yes, that's right."

"Did you know that Hsing-Hsing means 'Shining Star'?"

Caitlin grinned and said, "No, I didn't!"

"Seems fitting that you're here at this particular moment in time."

"Very fitting indeed! Thank you for having me."

"Any plans for an album?"

"It's in the works."

"All right, then, here with 'Shining Star' is Caitlin Rose."

Another commercial break followed Caitlin's song, and then the weather anchor joined the host for his closing remarks before the cameras stopped rolling.

Caitlin shook hands with the members of the team; one even asked for her autograph, as did several of the bystanders. The crew packed up and Caitlin returned to Arlington in the limo.

She had asked her mother to record the show and bring the videotape when she came for the wedding. As Pete would no doubt be quick to point out, her fame could be short-lived.

She heated up leftovers for lunch and then drove to an electronics store to buy a computer. She had occasionally used a laptop when traveling for OSP, and she was familiar with word processing and a few other functions, but she had no real preferences about computer brands or models; she just needed to be able to save her lyrics and maybe record her music while she was working on it.

She would also need a printer, she realized when she was browsing in the store. If she made any changes to her testimony before submitting it, she would have to print it out again.

She bought a small tape recorder, a laptop, and a printer and headed back to Karl's house. If she couldn't figure something out, she would ask Karl or Rick or Troy or—someone.

∞

By the time Karl returned on Sunday, Caitlin had set up the printer and learned about the different search engines that were popular for navigating the Internet. Rick was nearly done with her website, and he wanted her feedback whenever he added new text or images, so they were in frequent communication by phone and by email.

He had started compiling a list of email addresses, he wrote in an email. "That way, you can send announcements directly to your fans and you won't have to rely solely on advertising to get attention."

As long as Rick would manage the list and draft the announcements, Caitlin had no objection.

She gladly put the computer aside on Sunday evening so she could spend time with Karl. "Is Melody finding her way around okay?" Caitlin asked him as they walked through the neighborhood after dinner.

"She'll be fine for a few days," Karl said. "She's used to being on her own. I took her to rent a car, so she has a way to get around. She has already lined up a tent and tables and chairs for the reception. And a platform. For the band. And for dancing."

"We should decide what song we want for our first dance and maybe practice every evening between now and the wedding."

"The music is your department," Karl said, "but I'll dance with you anytime, anywhere. With or without music."

He demonstrated his point by twirling her around on the sidewalk. Caitlin giggled and kissed him. She was looking forward to seeing what Melody had cooked up for their wedding. Not having to manage all the details—and stress—of planning and arrangements made for a nice change. She could just show up and enjoy herself.

I could get used to this! she thought.

On Monday morning, Caitlin read her testimony to Karl after they finished eating breakfast. Unfamiliar with the committee's procedures or the details of the hearing, he had no suggestions and thought her speech sounded fine.

They returned the rental car and then Karl dropped Caitlin at the

Clarendon Metro station before driving to the chiropractor's office where he still saw patients on a part-time basis.

Caitlin took the Orange Line to the Capitol South station. As she walked toward the Rayburn House Office Building, she recalled going with her mother to the nearby U.S. Botanic Garden during her recovery to paint roses. Those paintings were in storage, along with most of her other possessions.

Getting them back will feel like Christmas! Caitlin thought as she walked down Independence Avenue. Her things would arrive later in the summer, after she and Karl returned to Pennsylvania from their cross-country honeymoon trip.

She delivered a copy of her testimony to the staff of the Committee on Government Reform and then wandered around the building to see where the hearing would be held the following week.

When she first moved to Washington, the possibilities had seemed endless. She was young and enthusiastic and eager to work within the legal system to create a better, stronger, fairer country. Engaged to another lawyer, a career in music was the farthest thing from her mind.

Had it not been for Sam's interference, she could have had a long career at OSP. Her work there had been fulfilling, but demanding. Even then, she knew she would need to make some changes if she hoped to have a family and a more balanced life. Her job had been all-consuming. She wouldn't let that happen again. She did want a family, and she wanted to build a life with Karl. She might want to go out on tour again someday, but she had no idea when that might be, so she didn't see any point in discussing it. There were too many unknowns. No doubt they would encounter many unexpected opportunities as well as challenges over the course of their marriage. By establishing a strong connection, rooted in love and trust, they would navigate the course together.

That was the plan, anyway. Despite the best intentions, plans could go awry.

∾ 90 ∾

*T*he afternoon was hot and humid when Karl dropped Caitlin at the Clarendon Metro station the following Tuesday. She smiled as she watched him drive away in his convertible, remembering the tiny car they had rented in Ireland.

He had arranged to donate his old furniture to a local nonprofit and needed to be at the house when the truck arrived. He planned to pick Caitlin up after the hearing and whisk her away to Pennsylvania.

They had driven up to Gettysburg after learning that Pennsylvania required a three-day waiting period before a marriage license would be issued. (The license was good for sixty days and would be recognized anywhere in the state.) After they completed the necessary forms, they visited the Gettysburg Address Memorial in the National Cemetery and then ate lunch at a historic tavern before returning to Arlington.

Caitlin had spoken to Charlotte, the minister who would officiate at the wedding, about the ceremony. Charlotte gave her a few suggestions to share with Karl so the two of them could be thinking about their vows before they all met in person on Friday.

But right now it's time to focus on the hearing, Caitlin thought as her train left the station. *I can think about vows and wedding details later!*

She hadn't brought any conservative clothing on the tour, so she'd needed a new outfit to wear to the hearing. She had settled on a bright blue short-sleeved silk top, navy slacks, and a classic navy blazer that she could use later to dress up a pair of blue jeans. *Add a fun scarf, some bangles, and a quirky hat and voila! A whole new look.*

For the wedding, she'd found a lovely sleeveless gown made of ivory silk that showed off her slender figure—and didn't need any alterations.

Melody had called to ask her what she would be wearing for the ceremony. "It's probably going to be me giving Karl advice on what to wear and I don't want you two to be wildly mismatched."

"That would not be good," Caitlin agreed.

"So, a tux, then?"

"Probably the best choice," Caitlin told her.

And I'm thinking about the wedding again! she realized as she prepared to get off the train.

There had been a lot to think about in a short time, and her life was about to change—dramatically. But she felt at home with Karl. Sure, there would be differences to be worked out, adjustments to be made—by both of them. They would learn to consider someone else in their decisions and choices, to work together toward common goals—and to allow each other freedom to pursue dreams and interests they didn't share.

Caitlin exited the station and walked to the Rayburn House Office Building, ready to share her thoughts with the committee.

The whole subject of vaccines was controversial, she knew, and the last hearing this committee held on vaccine safety had been televised on C–Span. She didn't notice any television crews as she walked to the hearing room, but undoubtedly reporters would be looking for a story, and she was prepared to talk to any journalists who approached her. Being the celebrity of the moment, she could use the spotlight to help raise awareness about the health risks associated with exposure to mercury—something she believed was beyond dispute, whether the exposure occurred because of amalgam dental fillings or tainted fish or from some other source.

As mercury was the focus of this hearing, Caitlin assumed that Congressman Burton wanted to hear about the thimerosal case she had worked on at OSP. But she knew that the committee was examining different issues concerning vaccines. She was a lawyer—not a doctor or scientist. She planned to confine her remarks to the subject she knew best: the law.

She entered the hearing room and sat in the back of the room. The staff had told her that she would be on the second panel of witnesses.

The room was quickly filling up with parents, witnesses, and reporters. Seated on a raised dais were the twelve members of the Committee on Government Reform who were present—enough for a quorum. A few staffers sat behind the committee members.

Representative Burton, the chairman of the committee, called the hearing to order and stated the purpose: to hear the reasons why mercury was being put into vaccines that were given to infants and children.

Caitlin knew that the American Academy of Pediatrics and the U.S. Public Health Service had issued a joint statement the year before recommending the removal of thimerosal from vaccines. *The committee probably wants to find out if that recommendation is being followed,* she thought.

Congressman Burton noted that the committee had been investigating vaccine safety for the last year with the aim of strengthening the vaccine program. From his opening remarks, Caitlin learned that thimerosal was present in over 50 licensed vaccines. But the parents who had contacted the committee were also concerned about the other potentially hazardous substances, such as aluminum and formaldehyde, that were commonly added to vaccines as part of the manufacturing process.

Caitlin's name was read along with the names of the other witnesses who would be testifying that afternoon. Following opening statements by several of the committee members, the chairman swore in the seven witnesses on the first panel, including a doctor who had treated many autistic children. Several parents of autistic children would also testify. One of them was an attorney, another was a doctor. Some of the witnesses had prepared slides that were projected onto a screen on the wall.

Listening to the researchers and health care professionals who spoke about the different forms of mercury—as well as the similarity between many of the symptoms of mercury toxicity and autism—Caitlin recalled the research she had done four years earlier, before the subject of thimerosal in vaccines had received widespread attention.

She had expected that controversy would erupt once parents became aware of the potential hazards presented by the thimerosal that was added to some of the vaccines that were routinely recommended for young children. With ever-increasing numbers of vaccines being given, some children received as many as nine different vaccines on a single visit. Until recently, no one had bothered to add up how much mercury exposure that amounted to—or considered the risks to babies whose brains were still developing—despite the knowledge

FULL CIRCLE 393

that mercury is toxic to humans and is especially damaging to the brain. Now, people wanted answers and demanded action.

To most of the witnesses on the panel, the hazards of using mercury as a preservative were obvious, given its documented danger when consumed in fish or present in emissions. They didn't think removing thimerosal from future vaccines was enough. They wanted a recall of the existing supply of vaccines that contained it. To date, the FDA had not issued any recalls.

Committee members addressed questions to a few of the witnesses, and then the second panel was called forward. Name cards were placed on the long table, which was covered with a white cloth. Caitlin sat at the end. She would be the last to speak.

Representatives from four federal agencies joined her at the table: Environmental Protection Agency, Food and Drug Administration, National Institutes of Health, and the Centers for Disease Control and Prevention. Burton asked them all to stand and raise their right hands.

"Do you solemnly swear to tell the whole truth and nothing but the truth so help you God?"

After agreeing, they all sat back down.

The official from the EPA said her agency had no authority to regulate mercury in vaccines but she could speak about mercury in land, air, and water. The FDA's representative said that although no evidence of harm had been found, vaccine manufacturers had been urged to reduce or eliminate the use of thimerosal in vaccines. As a result, many more vaccines were now available that did not contain thimerosal.

Congressman Burton announced a recess before the next witness's testimony, so Caitlin went to find a rest room.

The testimony of the witnesses on the first panel had been informative, and she felt a deep appreciation for people in all walks of life who took chances, lent a hand, and did the right thing for selfless reasons, even if speaking out or taking action cost them jobs, friendships, or clients. People like Karl, who had chosen a profession helping people. He was passionate about wellness and was continually learning and striving to do more. Perhaps his utopian experiment in community living would fail, but at least he was doing something he believed in and creating a positive environment for himself and others. Someone had to stand up to people like Neil, who were only out for their own gain.

Caitlin went back to her seat and reviewed her notes as people returned to the hearing room, many of them chatting amongst themselves. Some of the witnesses seemed to know each other. She was an outsider here.

Or maybe I'm a bridge, she thought.

She knew how to talk to lawyers and judges—and bureaucrats—and she also understood the concerns of citizens who believed the government wasn't doing enough to regulate the corporations that polluted rivers and aquifers and destroyed lives, farms, habitats. In the worst cases, government agencies—and employees—concealed damaging information and allowed exploitation of resources. Waste, fraud, and inadequate oversight sometimes led to disastrous consequences. Then, investigations were launched in an effort to hold someone accountable. But if lessons weren't learned, a similar scenario would play out another day in another arena.

When the hearing resumed, the CDC's spokesperson stated that vaccines don't need to contain thimerosal and some vaccines never have. He expected all routinely recommended childhood vaccines to be thimerosal-free by the following year. A doctor from NIH said it was clear that vaccines were safe for the vast majority of children.

Caitlin was introduced next. She pulled the microphone closer and read from her prepared testimony after acknowledging the committee members.

> I'm Caitlin Rose and I served as an attorney for the Office of Special Projects, or OSP, an agency within the U.S. Department of Justice, from 1992 until 1996. Claims concerning vaccine injuries that fall within the jurisdiction of the U.S. Court of Claims as part of the Vaccine Injury Compensation Program are normally handled by the Civil Division of the Justice Department. Though I did work briefly for the Civil Division

before accepting a position at OSP, I did not handle vaccine injury compensation claims. I did, however, speak to some of the attorneys who handle these claims after I was assigned responsibility for a class action suit brought in federal district court against vaccine manufacturers on behalf of children who allegedly had been injured by the mercury-based preservative thimerosal. The United States was not a party to the case, but the Justice Department often files an amicus brief in cases that have the potential to affect federal interests in order to help the court understand the position of the U.S. government.

From my review of the case, in 1996, I believed the plaintiffs had stated a cause of action that deserved to be adjudicated in a court of law without the interference of the Justice Department. However, the decision was not mine alone to make. Before any actions were taken, I was involved in a serious motor vehicle collision that effectively ended my legal career. I later learned that my successor at OSP filed a brief recommending dismissal of the lawsuit, and the defendants' motion to dismiss was thereafter granted.

Mister Chairman, as you know, adverse effects are a known risk for vaccines. We all hope that our loved ones will not become statistics, and if they are injured, we hope they will be able to find the care they need. We expect that they will be treated fairly throughout the process. But expecting families to prove that a vaccine caused their injuries in order for their claims to be successful is, in many cases, expecting them to fail.

My understanding is that the compensation program established by the National Childhood Vaccine Injury Act of 1986 was intended to be a nonadversarial proceeding that would provide swift resolution for injured parties without the need for lengthy litigation—and yet, in too many instances, that is exactly what is occurring in what is commonly known as Vaccine Court.

Now more than ever, when taxpayers are funding research and companies are marketing more and more vaccines, the necessity for independent oversight at all stages—research, funding, approval, and distribution—is essential. Information about the manufacturing process is necessary for informed consent to the administration of vaccines to be meaningful, and timely reporting of adverse events is necessary for monitoring to be useful. Are adverse events truly rare or are they more common than has previously been believed? We all have an interest in knowing the facts. And when plaintiffs and petitioners are successful at securing a settlement after harm has occurred, that information, too, should be available to the public. Manufacturers claim their practices are proprietary and need to be shielded from disclosure, just as policy makers worry about declining rates of vaccination, or rising rates of litigation, and seek to keep the facts shrouded in secrecy. Everyone worries about liability. The result is a scarcity of information, which makes ascertaining the truth difficult, if not impossible.

As part of your investigation into matters concerning vaccine safety, I urge this committee to examine how the Vaccine Injury Compensation Program is functioning in practice, and, in particular, the roles played by the Department of Health and Human Services, which conducts the medical review of petitions, and by the Department of Justice, which represents HHS in court. I believe many petitioners would say that, in their experience, the process has become highly adversarial. However, representatives from these agencies can provide the necessary information for this committee to determine whether changes are needed to ensure that petitioners' claims are being handled in a fair and timely manner.

Caitlin decided not to say anything that would point to wrongdoing by Neil Morton—not because she was worried about him coming after her again, but because she didn't have any solid evidence, only suspicions. If he didn't change his ways, his shadowy dealings would be discovered eventually. She wasn't interested in retaliation. She sought to expose the flaws and inadequacies in government policies and industry practices. She hoped the committee's investigation would bring attention to the mercury and other potentially harmful substances that were added to vaccines as preservatives and adjuvants.

As with her appearances on the morning show and on the Fourth of July, her time in the spotlight was brief. The committee was running out of time in questioning the second panel of witnesses, so no questions were addressed to her. A transcript of the hearing would be available to anyone who was interested in reading it, including the committee members who had not been present at the hearing.

Caitlin had put her views on record; that was her main objective in testifying.

I hope more information is available by the time we have to decide about vaccinating our children, she thought as she walked down the hall. *And I hope Karl and I can agree about which vaccines are worth the risks.*

Money, time, sex, chores, rules, discipline—marriage and family life would require many choices and would highlight the differences between them. They would both have to be patient, understanding, and willing to compromise to avoid conflict.

Like every other couple, we'll just have to do the best we can.

She turned on her phone and searched for Karl's number. Before she could press the call button, she heard her name.

"Cait!"

She turned to see Neil Morton. *Looking polished, as always,* she thought.

Neil walked toward her and said, "I enjoyed your performance."

"It wasn't a performance. It was the truth."

"Oh, the hearing. Yeah, well, one version of the truth, maybe. No, I meant on the Fourth."

"You were there?"

"No, my wife doesn't like crowds. We watched from home."

Caitlin stared at him, incredulous. "Your—"

Neil showed her the gold ring on his finger. "Last month."

"A June wedding. How sweet." Caitlin held up her hand to show Neil the opal ring Karl had bought for her while he was in Australia. "You beat me by a month."

"Ah. Congratulations. Can I expect an invitation?"

"It's going to be a small wedding."

Neil leaned forward as if to confide a secret. "Believe it or not, I want you to be happy." Standing straight, he said, "That's why I called the producer and—"

"Hang on," Caitlin said as she tried to comprehend what Neil was saying. "Are you telling me *you* arranged the invitation for the Fourth?"

Neil puffed up his chest but before he could answer, a statuesque beauty wearing an official name tag walked over and stood beside him. Neil put his arm around her and introduced her as "Julia." He told her he would join her in a minute. She smiled and went back inside the hearing room.

"Well, I guess I should thank you, then," Caitlin said. "I certainly never expected such a gesture."

"My attempt at a peace offering."

That was probably the closest thing she would ever hear to an apology, Caitlin knew. Neil wasn't one to ever admit wrongdoing or error in judgment.

He straightened his tie and said, "We're all a mix, you know. Shadow and light."

"Hmm," Caitlin said before turning to leave.

"You did good work," Neil added.

Caitlin stopped and turned, waiting for him to say more. Was he talking about the hearing?

"As a lawyer, I mean. But you'll have a bigger audience now. For your bleeding-heart agenda."

"Thanks," she said, and muttered "I think" as she continued on her way.

She appreciated the acknowledgment. She *had* done good work when she was a lawyer. She had worked hard and made sacrifices. She could no longer function in the same capacity as she once had, but she would continue to speak out about matters that needed attention, especially matters that no one seemed to want to address.

She paused and turned to ask Neil about something that had been bothering her ever since he had unexpectedly shown up in Santa Fe. He was just about to go back inside the hearing room when she called out to him.

"Say—"

He turned toward her and they both moved a few steps closer.

"How did you find me, anyway? In New Mexico."

"I was summoned," Neil said. "By our friend Sam Burns."

Caitlin felt the blood draining from her face. "How did *he* know I was in Santa Fe?"

"Because he was in Santa Fe."

Caitlin tried not to let on how distressing this news was to her. "Why?"

Neil shrugged. "I don't know. I didn't see him. But I guess he liked your show."

Caitlin shook her head and turned toward the exit. She would have to digest this new information, wrap her mind around the fact that Neil and Sam were connected in some way. If she was going to be a public figure, she'd better get used to the idea of losing some of her privacy.

She took a deep breath and stepped outside, eager to begin the next phase of her life. A swarm of photographers and reporters gathered around her.

"What's your interest in this issue?" one of them asked. Several microphones were thrust toward her.

"My interest is that of a concerned citizen and, hopefully, a future parent," she said. "In our zeal to eradicate disease, we must not lose sight of safety considerations and the need for continued research and adequate testing, as well as reporting of adverse events. We need information about potential dangers and we need transparency from government agencies. As consumers, we must be granted the freedom to make choices about our health care."

Other questions were shouted at her, but Caitlin tuned them out when she saw Karl's convertible parked on the street. He was standing beside the car and holding a bouquet of red roses.

Caitlin smiled and told the reporters, "Now if you'll excuse me, I've got a dream to catch!"

∾ 91 ∾

*K*arl held the door open for Caitlin.

"Where's Lucky?" she asked him.

"The carrier wouldn't fit, so I left him with Barry. He'll bring him when he comes up on Friday."

"Oh, okay," Caitlin said, settling into her seat. She sniffed the fragrant bouquet Karl had given her. "These are lovely," she said.

He was waiting for the traffic to clear. Once they were on their way, Caitlin asked, "Are you planning to keep this car? I'm just wondering how practical it's going to be if we're living in a rural area."

"It's not *that* rural. The driveway is gravel, though. And it's long." Karl sighed and said, "I don't know, I hadn't really thought about it. But you're probably right. Could be time for a change."

Caitlin was hungry, so Karl suggested Lebanese food. "I've never been to the Washington restaurant, but we went to the one in Arlington once."

"I remember," Caitlin said, reaching for his hand.

"We might as well enjoy a nice meal. Traffic will be lighter later on."

"Fine by me."

While they waited to order, Caitlin told Karl about the chelation method one of the witnesses had described for removing mercury and heavy metals from the body. "Is that something you're familiar with?" she asked.

"I've heard of it, but I haven't ever used it—yet," Karl said. "I want to be able to treat a variety of conditions. And keep my own family healthy," he added with a wink. "Eventually, I want to invest in ozone therapy and infrared saunas and emerging technologies that not only diagnose issues but also help resolve them. I've seen demonstrations of computerized programs that measure a whole range of responses to different possible stressors—viral, bacterial, emotional, whatever. Some of them have the capability to imprint a homeopathic remedy with the frequencies that can help bring the person back into balance, or clear the source of the problem."

"Sounds promising," Caitlin said as she looked over the menu.

"Yeah, first things first," Karl said. "That's all down the road."

She had sent a wedding invitation to Jasmine Wells, Caitlin told him. "I'm hoping you might be able to help her son, Marvin. You remember me talking about him? He's the autistic boy I bought a piano for. I wonder if he ever learned to play it. I was giving him lessons, but we hadn't gotten very far when . . ."

Caitlin didn't finish the sentence. Talking about the Crash still upset her.

"I can try to fit it in," Karl said, "though it will be a hectic time. Maybe I could meet with them in the morning if they stay overnight in the area."

"Jasmine barely gets by," Caitlin said. "She was waiting tables when I knew her. And you know how expensive special needs can get." She thought for a moment and said, "We'd probably have to put them up somewhere."

"See? This is exactly why I want to build more housing on the property!" Karl said.

"I'm not arguing!" Caitlin said. "But I do wonder how you plan to pay for it all."

"The community should pay for itself. People who want to build will buy parcels. The residents will all have to agree on communal building projects, like a common house, that we would use communal funds for."

"A common house?"

"It's where everyone gathers for meetings and meals and yoga classes or whatever. You'll see when we visit a few communities. Sometimes the common house has guest rooms—for interested visitors as well as for family and friends of residents who don't have space for guests in their homes."

"I imagine we'll have community gardens, too," Caitlin said.

"Oh, yeah. We'll grow a lot of our own food, and we'll use solar and other renewable resources as much as possible. I'd like the clinic to be certified as a green building. My hope is that everything we create will serve as a model that other people can replicate."

They placed their orders and then Karl told Caitlin about his plans for the clinic.

"The idea is to involve other professionals so we have a truly integrative practice—a holistic M.D., nutritional counseling and testing, massage therapy, vibrational medicine. I'd like to create a center where we have qualified staff that can evaluate different kinds of therapies and not accept every claim that gets made. Treatments and outcomes need to be studied so that some of these unconventional approaches gain acceptance if they're shown to have validity. I've met practitioners who are experimenting with new technologies for treating imbalances in the meridians and the energy field that can be detected before disease even manifests. The possibilities are really exciting."

"Yeah, but how will you find professionals who are willing to move to Pennsylvania and commit to a new venture?"

"I have to have something tangible to offer them first. I'd like to form an organization and hold annual conferences where we could all share our ideas and experiences. Support each other—because this is all happening outside of mainstream medicine, and you know there will be allegations that it's all nonsense—or worse."

Their waiter brought their appetizers. Caitlin spread hummus on a slice of pita bread and took a bite.

"So the first step is building a clinic? Have you come up with a design, or how far along are you in that process?"

"I hired an architect to design both the house and the clinic. I may have to join a practice in a nearby town for a while to save up some money and get my name out there."

"Hopefully I'll have some income from my music. I'll need to put some of it back into my music career, but some of it can go toward household expenses—and a college fund. Kids are expensive!"

"Have you got their names picked out, too?" Karl grinned and licked baba ghanoush off his fingers. "I've talked to some folks who work with rammed earth and straw bale construction and other natural building materials," he said before eating a dolma. "They're sometimes looking for places to hold workshops, and they build a small structure as part of the program. I was thinking maybe they could build us a cottage and we can see how that goes. How the building looks—and holds up. It probably won't be anything fancy, and we might have to finish whatever they start ourselves, but it would bring people together and it could be fun!"

Caitlin's brain was tired. The hearing had required intense focus. She knew nothing about natural building materials or techniques, and now wasn't the time to try to absorb new information. She had enough to think about with wedding plans.

We need to write our vows soon! she thought.

The waiter brought their entrées to the table. After he left, Karl took Caitlin's hand in his and said, "So—before we go announcing our plans to the world: does this sound like a lifestyle you want to embrace? It's not for everyone, so I'd certainly understand if you say no."

Caitlin smiled and said, "I know it won't be easy, and I may have days where I wonder what I've gotten myself into, but: yes." She laughed and added, "My mother always said I was impulsive!"

After tasting her order of lamb stew, she said, "I never would have imagined four years ago—or even two years ago—that I'd consider such a thing, but saying a lot has changed would be stating the obvious."

It was as if, in the back of her mind—or maybe somewhere deep in her heart—she had always known that she and Karl would end up together. It wasn't so much a question of what she *wanted*; something about their union seemed inevitable. But they had both needed to be ready—and they'd each needed to have whatever experiences would help prepare them for the journey ahead. They would be forging new paths with no guidebook to show them the way. A lot would happen through trial and error.

And guidance, Caitlin thought with a smile.

She could see now that marrying Jayson simply hadn't been her destiny, she thought when she and Karl were back in the car. And a career in law had never been her dream. She had learned a lot, and some of her training might prove useful in the future.

"I may need to draft a contract for Rick's management services," she told Karl. "I'll start researching all that after we get back from our honeymoon."

I'm getting married in four days! she thought with a smile. Talking about their plans felt a bit surreal.

Perhaps it was no accident she'd visited the Ananda Center and the ecovillage in North Carolina—just as her trip to Ireland seemed to have been preordained. And if children were a part of her future, she knew she would have to make sacrifices and put the needs of her family—and the community, if Karl's plans took off the way he envisioned—ahead of her own for a time. The challenge would lie in finding balance and learning to surrender what she thought she needed or wanted without completely losing sight of her identity and desires. Being in relationship and also staying true to herself.

Maybe someday she would have her own recording studio, just as Karl planned to have his own clinic. Or maybe she would find other musicians in the area to perform with on occasion.

One way or another, music would always be an important part of her life.

∼ 92 ∼

*A*fter they crossed the Pennsylvania state line, Caitlin asked Karl, "What's the best place for people coming to the wedding to fly into—Philadelphia?"

"It's about an hour's drive."

I guess that's a yes, she thought.

Lawyers were trained in the proper way to interview witnesses—and they were taught to instruct their clients about the proper way to answer questions addressed to them during a deposition, hearing, or trial.

"If you're asked a question that calls for a yes or no answer," Caitlin used to tell witnesses, "don't launch into an explanation that gives more information than is necessary. Wait until you're asked another question."

She had learned to choose her words carefully long before she ever met Melody or Luisa—or Karl—but she hadn't always applied the same care to her thoughts and language outside of work. Now, she found herself getting irritated when people went off on tangents or didn't directly answer questions that were put to them. She often had to remind herself that she hadn't always been so careful herself. Sometimes she could be patient, but when she was tired she was easily irritated.

Hopefully she would be patient with her children, she thought, though undoubtedly she would fail to meet her own standards, which were high, at times. She expected a lot from Karl, too, but she didn't expect him to be perfect.

"So your clinic won't be too far for people driving from Philadelphia or even New York City, and you can continue to build a practice in the D.C. area in the meantime."

"That's the plan," Karl said.

He didn't seem to be in a talkative mood, and there wasn't much scenery to look at in the dark, so Caitlin closed her eyes and rested until Karl exited the highway.

"That's the inn where people will be staying," he said as they drove through a quaint town. "This county is one of the three original counties established by William Penn."

About twenty minutes later, Karl turned onto a dirt road. Melody had turned all the outside lights on, so the house was easy to spot, even from a distance.

"How did you pick this place?" Caitlin asked.

"It was already an organic farm and I knew the owner. I came to a couple of gatherings here," Karl said. He turned to Caitlin and said, "I invited you to one of them."

"Hmm," Caitlin said. She still didn't recall everything about her life in Virginia, but perhaps that was normal. *No one remembers everything,* she sometimes reminded herself.

"Is it still being farmed?" she asked as Karl parked the car next to a detached garage.

"Uh-huh. That brings in a little income."

Caitlin's mind flashed back to her trip to California with Sam several years before. As they approached his house near Joshua Tree, she asked him a few questions about his life there. He accused her of interrogating him.

Her body tensed at the recollection. Here she was, again, in a remote area with a man she hardly knew. Until two weeks before, she hadn't seen Karl in over two and a half years. Sure, they'd stayed in contact—and she'd known him better, and longer, than she had ever known Sam. But they were different people now. Maybe this whole idea of "soul mates" was utter nonsense. Maybe she was living in some fantasy world that bore no relation to reality.

She sat frozen in place when Karl got out of the car, afraid to move or even to breathe. Was she repeating an old pattern?

Karl walked around to the passenger side and opened Caitlin's door. To her surprise, he extended his hand and helped her out.

"Watch out for the gravel with those heels," he said. "What the heck—I'll just carry you over the threshold now!"

"Ohh!" Caitlin said as he swooped her up in his arms. *Life with Karl will never be boring!* Of that much, she could be sure.

He carried her into the house through the front door and said, "Welcome home, princess!" as he set her down.

Melody came out of the kitchen and hugged them both, and then she and Karl unloaded the car while Caitlin looked around.

The house was one level and equipped with the usual amenities—washer and dryer, dishwasher, central heat and air. Two of the bedrooms were close together; the third was down the hall.

"I love the hardwood floors," Caitlin told Karl on one of his trips from the car. "The kitchen cabinets are nice, too. Do we have well water?"

"I've had it tested," Karl said. He put her suitcases by the bedroom door and went back outside to get more things.

That didn't answer my question, Caitlin thought. *Is this how every conversation is going to go?*

She was pleased to see that the house was sparsely furnished. There would be room for her furniture.

Melody brought Caitlin's gown bag to the living room and said, "I think I can guess what's in here!"

"Let me show you your dress!" Caitlin said as she unzipped the bag.

"Very nice," Melody said. "I can't wait to try it on. And to see you in yours!"

"I better go hang it up," Caitlin said. "Maybe in your closet, so Karl doesn't see it?"

"Sure."

Caitlin followed Melody to the room at the end of the hall. *Good, Karl and I will have some privacy if we're feeling amorous!* she thought.

She looked around the guest room, thinking, *I could paint in here if the light is good.*

"I love this color," Melody said, admiring her gown before hanging it in the closet.

"I'm glad you like it," Caitlin said. "The place looks nice."

"I've been crazy busy getting everything ready," Melody said.

"Well, I really appreciate it," Caitlin said.

"How'd the hearing go?"

Caitlin shrugged and said, "About like I expected, I guess. I read my prepared statement and that was that."

Karl brought the last items from the car and closed the front door. He took Caitlin by the hand and said, "Let me show you what I brought you from New Zealand."

He led her into the spacious bedroom they would be sharing and handed her an unwrapped shoebox that had been sitting atop his dresser. Caitlin opened the lid and saw a pair of sheepskin slippers.

"Try them on," Karl said. "I got some for my mom, too. She loves hers."

Caitlin sunk her tired feet into the plush layer of soft wool and grinned. "Oh, these are wonderful!"

She walked into the en suite bathroom and said, "I'm thinking of taking a bath. Are those jets I see in the tub?"

"Yep."

"Nice!"

Karl smiled and said, "I'd join you, but I've got some things to take care of yet tonight, so—enjoy your bath. Towels are in here." He opened the door of the linen closet before leaving.

Caitlin wrapped herself in a large towel after soaking in the tub. She brushed her teeth, unpacked one of her suitcases, and then climbed into bed to wait for Karl. Her fears were unfounded, she realized. She was home at last.

Relaxed and content, she fell sound asleep.

∾ 93 ∾

*B*arry stopped by on Friday to meet Caitlin, drop off Lucky, and get a quick tour of Karl's property. He introduced his girlfriend, Tatiana. She stayed in the house with Caitlin while Karl showed Barry the site where he hoped to build a clinic.

"Do you also work for AID?" Caitlin asked Tatiana.

"Yes, that's how we met. We are going on three years now."

"No plans to get married?"

"No, not really. We are happy as we are."

"This was all pretty sudden for us."

"So I heard! This will be quite a change for you, living out here."

"My life has been full of changes. This is just the latest surprise!"

Tatiana nodded. "Attorney turned performer. Or maybe all trial attorneys have a little performer in them, yes?"

Tatiana clearly knew more about Caitlin than Caitlin knew about her. She spoke with a slight accent that Caitlin was trying to place when Karl and Barry walked in.

The two couples walked outside when they heard a horn honking repeatedly. The sound grew louder as the Road Angels' tour bus neared the house.

Barry and Tatiana decided it was a good time to be on their way. "Karl says there's a nice restaurant at the inn, so we can have dinner there," Barry told Tatiana.

They would be staying at the same inn as Martha and Ray, Luisa and June, and Charlotte Odom, the minister who would be officiating at the wedding. Melody had gone into town to pick up Charlotte and bring her back to the house so they could all discuss the ceremony.

"See you tomorrow, buddy," Karl told Barry before he and Tatiana drove off.

"Thanks for bringing Lucky!" Caitlin shouted after them.

She was excited to see her friends in the band and hugged each person. She introduced Karl, who shook hands with everyone—except Luisa, who gave him a warm hug.

Caitlin showed them all around and said, "Come back in a few years and we'll have a guest cottage. But for now, all I can offer is a few extra tents and sleeping bags."

"And mosquito repellent," Karl added.

"*We're* staying in the bus!" said Allison, who was standing next to Jordan.

"We'll tough it out," said Matt, tossing a sleeping bag to Pete.

"Oh, hey, Pete," Caitlin said, pulling him aside. "I wondered if you might sing something at the wedding."

"Me?"

"Yeah, I was thinking about 'Longer' by Dan Fogelberg. Did the band ever play that at weddings? I thought maybe Cara would play her flute. She sounded pretty good when she played 'Colour My World' by the campfire. That could be a good song for our first dance."

Pete said, "Yes, I know 'Longer.' And I'd be honored. Though I think Matt has a better voice for 'Colour My World.'"

"Okay. I'll talk to him, too."

Caitlin had told her mother that Friday would be a busy time with final preparations and the band's arrival, hoping that Martha and Ray would wait until Saturday before coming to the house, but she wasn't surprised to see them drive up.

"Is this it? You know, we just had to come and find it. I couldn't take a chance on getting lost tomorrow. How are you, dear?" Martha said before kissing Caitlin's cheek.

"Hi, Mom. I'm fine," Caitlin said, hugging her. "Ray, let me introduce my . . ." Caitlin looked at Karl and said, "You know, I really don't like 'husband' and 'wife.' We have to find another way of referring to each other."

"Uh . . . partner?"

"Spouse, maybe. Anyway—Ray, this is Karl."

"Are you changing your name, dear? I never got a chance to ask."

"Nope. Our kids will be hyphenated."

"Sounds painful," said Ray.

They all laughed and then Caitlin said, "I can give you a quick tour of the house, but then I really need to get all these people settled."

"Oh, we remember," said Ray with a wave to Rick.

"Rick's my manager now," said Caitlin.

"Is that right?" said Ray. "Nice fellow."

Caitlin's phone rang, so she let Karl show Martha and Ray the house while she answered it. Not many people had her number yet— and most of them were right there.

"That was Jasmine," Caitlin told Karl when she finished with the call. "She's married now!"

To Martha, Caitlin said, "Do you remember— Oh, that was when I wasn't talking to you."

Mother and daughter walked outside to where Ray had parked his car while he and Karl stood talking on the front porch.

"I'm sorry about the way I behaved then," Caitlin said. "I never should have cut you out of my life like that."

Martha touched Caitlin's cheek and said, "Your father's death was a big shock for you. You were just trying to find a way to cope."

Caitlin's eyes teared up. "Yeah, but you're my mother, and I love you, too."

"We're fine now. All's well that ends well?"

Caitlin smiled but she still felt emotional. "I miss him." Looking around, she said, "I wish he could be here for this."

"He is," Martha said. "In spirit."

Ray laid a hand on Martha's shoulder and said, "We should let these kids take care of their guests." He extended a hand to Karl and said, "Karl, a pleasure. She's quite a gal, our Caitlin. But I'm sure you already know that."

"From the first time I laid eyes on her," Karl said, gripping Ray's hand.

Karl put his arm around Caitlin while she watched the car drive away. "You were saying that Jasmine is married. Is she coming to the wedding?"

"Yes! She was waiting to see if her husband could get off work. They'll drive up tomorrow and find a motel. I told her you'd offered to see Marvin Sunday morning. I guess he must be around eleven now. Jasmine said he's doing a little better, but she would appreciate any suggestions you might have to offer."

"I can't do much in one visit, but we can get acquainted and then follow up later, in Arlington," Karl said as he and Caitlin walked toward the bus.

"Do you want a tour of the bus?" she asked him. "This is probably the last time I'll see the inside of a tour bus for a while," she said as she prepared to board the bus.

Walking down the aisle, she thought of her phone conversation with Karl just before the bus left Los Angeles—and all the hours between then and now when she'd feared their chance had passed them by. Now, here they were—about to be married.

She turned and gave him a big hug. "I'm so happy," she said. "Don't ever let me go."

Karl stroked her hair and kissed the top of her head. "Not a chance," he said.

The atmosphere was always festive when the Road Angels were around, Caitlin thought as she ate the last of her dinner. *They bring community with them.*

The tent and tables, set up for Saturday's wedding, were being put to use already—as was the porta-potty. Melody was waiting until morning to put up decorations and spread tablecloths, she'd told Caitlin. "Don't worry about a thing," she added.

Caitlin looked over at Karl, who was engaged in an animated discussion with Sky. *Probably talking about ecovillages,* she thought. She was glad Karl would have a chance to get to know some of the members of the group.

"I'm hoping we might have some time to talk on Sunday morning," Caitlin told Rick, who was sitting to her right. "Before the group gets on the road."

Rick nodded and said, "Luisa and June will be at the inn, so I'm sure we won't take off too early."

The restaurant at the inn would be catering the reception, and Rick would serve as the wedding photographer and videographer.

He'll probably want to put photos on my website, Caitlin thought. She would talk to Karl first and make sure he was okay with making their wedding photos public. *Good thing he understands the need to attract attention,* she thought. *His projects won't ever get off the ground if no one knows about them.*

Cara was sitting to Caitlin's left. Caitlin talked to her about her idea for two songs. Cara seemed excited about the chance to play her flute.

"I'm definitely ready for 'Colour My World,'" she said. "I'll go practice 'Longer' right now. On the bus!"

After Cara left, Matt asked Caitlin if she wanted to see the set list for the reception.

"Nah. I trust you guys to come up with a good mix. Besides, there won't be very many guests besides the band! So, enjoy yourselves."

Everyone pitched in for cleanup and then Luisa, Charlotte, and June left for the inn in Melody's rental car.

Karl and Melody could be in charge of the group's needs, Caitlin thought; they knew the house and property better than her. She kissed Karl and hugged Melody and then went to bed.

She wasn't following most wedding traditions, like "something borrowed, something blue," but she did insist on sleeping apart the night before the ceremony. Karl would be sleeping in the room next door to hers.

The future nursery, Caitlin thought with a smile.

∾ 94 ∾

*C*aitlin glanced at the clock on the nightstand. She could use some help with the row of buttons at the back of her gown, and the time for her to make her entrance was fast approaching.

She hadn't seen Karl yet today—she had stayed in the bedroom to make sure of it. Melody had brought her breakfast and then returned later to take away the tray.

Caitlin had taken her time getting ready. After a soak in the tub, she fixed her hair and applied her makeup. She'd bought a pearl necklace and matching earrings while she was shopping for the gowns and shoes. She put those on and then moved the opal ring Karl had given her from her left hand to her right. They had chosen matching gold bands with delicate scrollwork. Caitlin opened the top drawer of the dresser and removed the small box that held Karl's ring. She looked inside and then set the box on top of the dresser.

Melody knocked lightly on the door and then entered the room, wearing the purple charmeuse-and-chiffon gown Caitlin had bought for her. Sleeveless with a low back and a side slit, the dress was perfect for Melody's toned figure, Caitlin thought.

"You look fab," she said. She couldn't wait to see Melody's expression when she discovered the surprise Caitlin had arranged for her.

Melody looked down at her attire and said, "It fits," as if that was the most positive thing she could say about Caitlin's selection.

Melody helped with the buttons on Caitlin's gown and then handed her a bouquet of purple-and-white calla lilies and white roses before picking up her own bouquet of purple irises and white roses.

"Ready?" Melody asked, her hand on the doorknob.

"Ready!" Caitlin said. "Don't forget the ring."

"Right!"

As soon as Melody opened the door, Jordan began playing organ music on the keyboard that had been set up in the back of the living room.

Folding chairs had been arranged on two sides of the room to create an aisle that Melody and Caitlin could walk down. Barry and Karl stood waiting with the minister in front of a table covered with white linen and decorated with flowers, candles, and amethyst crystals.

While Melody walked slowly down the aisle, Caitlin greeted her mother, who stood behind the last row of chairs. Martha smiled and nodded approvingly as she looked her daughter over.

Caitlin thought she was too old to be given away, but she wanted a gesture that marked the rite of passage. With her embrace, Martha gave her blessing to Caitlin's union with Karl and sent her forward into her new life. Then Ray escorted Martha to their seats in the front row.

Caitlin began her walk down the aisle. As she neared the altar, she glanced from Melody to Billy, who was sitting in the second row, behind Martha and Ray. Melody followed Caitlin's gaze, and Caitlin caught the look of surprised delight on her face before turning to look into Karl's welcoming eyes. Together, they stood in front of the minister, who spoke after the music stopped.

"Friends and family, welcome. We are gathered here to celebrate the union of Karl and Caitlin and to bear witness as they pledge their love, and their lives, to one another. Before we begin, let's take a moment to acknowledge those loved ones who are not present."

To Caitlin's surprise, her thoughts traveled to Ireland, where she had researched the Rose family tree. She remembered the connection she'd felt to her great-grandmother, Katie Moran, and wondered what Katie, with all her healing talents, would think of the new healing methods Karl was pursuing. Caitlin liked to think that her father and Katie and Grandmother Clayton would be pleased with the direction her life was taking. She was looking forward to meeting Karl's parents, and she planned to bring them photos and maybe a video of the wedding, since they hadn't been able to attend.

Charlotte spoke about marriage being a life-affirming and life-altering choice. Each partner agrees to be accountable to the other. They both commit to nurturing and maintaining the health and vitality of the relationship. "Selfishness has no place in marriage," Caitlin heard Charlotte say. She was glad that Rick was video-taping the ceremony. She was focusing on her vows and not closely following the minister's remarks. She would be able to replay the whole ceremony later on.

She and Karl had agreed to keep their remarks short. They both wanted their vows to be attainable—embellishments about their timeless love being written in the stars and soaring hearts and other flights of fancy they would save for anniversaries and poems and private moments. Declarations publicly stated should, they agreed, be the promises they intended to keep and the goals they were willing to commit to working toward.

They'd written a statement together that they would each recite, and they had agreed they would each start with some personal thoughts. But first, they invited any guests who wished to participate to choose an index card from a basket on the altar and read what was written there. After their meeting with Charlotte, they had written short quotes from poems and literature and even pop songs. Some were humorous, some wise. All reflected sentiments Caitlin and Karl both shared about love and commitment. Barry, Cara, June, and Jasmine all chose to come to the front and read something.

When it was time for her to speak, Caitlin looked into Karl's eyes and said:

> Karl. Your easygoing yet steadfast nature calms me. Your playful spirit brings me joy. With you by my side, I know I can face whatever trials and challenges lie ahead. To you, I give my heart. From this day forward, we're a team. I will share with you life's blessings and sorrows, and take as much interest in your hopes and dreams, your worries and concerns, as in my own. I will strive to be patient and kind, generous and supportive, forgiving and appreciative. Together, we will forge an unbreakable bond that will endure throughout our lives, and the fruits of our union will inspire and uplift everyone around us as we co-create a center filled with love, beauty, and harmony.

Caitlin paused to catch her breath and then she recited their joint statement:

> I vow to practice compassion and loving kindness. I recognize that only healthy individuals can create a healthy marriage, and I accept responsibility for taking care of my physical, emotional, psychological, and spiritual needs and well being.
>
> I will approach our life together with a cooperative and optimistic spirit. I accept that we are different, and I trust that we can work together to find solutions to any problems that arise. I will respect your individuality and independence, even as we become more and more interdependent. From this day forward, our lives are joined. For better and for worse, I will love you forever.

As she had expected would happen, Caitlin choked up when she spoke the last line. Their declarations carried more weight, she realized, when spoken aloud in a ceremony witnessed by others. *The power of ritual,* she thought as Karl began to speak.

Caitlin looked up at him expectantly. She was eager to hear what special words he had chosen to preface their joint statement.

He smiled at her and said:

> Caitlin. My life changed the day I met you. It's taken us a while to find our way to this altar, but I would wait a thousand years to be united with you. I cherish you as much as life itself. You inspire me to be the best man I can be. Your gentle touch soothes my spirit, your knowing glance gives me assurance. When I am with you, I am home. With you in my life, I can achieve greater things than I could ever hope to accomplish on my own. I will aspire to always be worthy of your love and respect, and I promise to be faithful and loyal, in thought and in deed. I will strive to be honest, fair, and receptive, and to listen with an open mind and open heart.

Caitlin's heart felt full as she listened to the words Karl spoke. She wiped away a tear as he, too, recited their joint statement.

They had a few moments to relax while Pete sang "Longer," and then the minister asked them each to respond to the questions she posed.

"Do you, Caitlin Rose, freely and wholeheartedly consent and agree to marry Karl Owen?"

"I do," said Caitlin.

"Will you care for him in sickness and in health, through good times and bad, and remain faithful and true as long as your marriage shall endure?"

"I will."

"Do you, Karl Owen, freely and wholeheartedly consent and agree to marry Caitlin Rose?"

"I do," said Karl.

"Will you care for her in sickness and in health, through good times and bad, and remain faithful and true as long as your marriage shall endure?"

"I will."

When they exchanged rings, they each said, "Wear this ring as a symbol of my devotion and endless love."

Charlotte then declared, "By the power vested in me by the Commonwealth of Pennsylvania, I now pronounce you married!"

The guests cheered and applauded as Caitlin and Karl kissed, but the ceremony wasn't quite over yet. Charlotte said, "Please join me in a blessing for Karl and Caitlin." She bowed her head and raised her hands. Everyone else in the room did the same.

"May you be surrounded by love and light as you embark on a lifelong journey as partners and companions. May you be blessed with good health and good fortune, and, by living in accordance with your highest principles and aspirations, may you fulfill your dreams and attain your purpose, both individually and as a couple. May your lives be filled with an abundance of beauty, love, friendship, and joy."

The recessional music started after Charlotte said, "I present to you the bride and groom!"

Caitlin felt a mixture of exuberance and relief as she and Karl walked hand in hand down the aisle and then outside, where they would greet their guests and pose for photographs.

"My beautiful bride," Karl said, admiring her. After a thoughtful pause, he asked, "Is 'bride' okay?"

Caitlin laughed and said, "Bride is great! But thanks for asking."

She planned to enjoy every moment of this newlywed phase, beginning with the reception. Martha, Melody, and others were ready and willing to handle the details and ensure that everything went smoothly, and Caitlin was happy to let them. Soon enough, she would be inundated with chores and responsibilities as she and Karl got down to the work required to start a new life.

∾ 95 ∾

*C*aitlin had told Melody she didn't want rice—or anything else—thrown at her after the ceremony.

"Just good wishes," she said. "I'm always open to those!"

While the guests mingled and enjoyed the appetizers and refreshments being served, Caitlin posed for photographs. Lots of photographs. With Karl; with Melody; with Martha and Ray; with Karl and Martha and Ray; with Melody and Barry and Karl; with Luisa and June; surrounded by the Road Angels.

"And I want to get some just of you," Rick said. "You look absolutely radiant!"

When Caitlin was finished with the photographs, Melody approached her and said, "I can't believe you brought Billy here!"

"Well, I need a cat sitter, you know, while we drive back from California. I figured I had to make it worth your while to stay here a little longer. He's only got a week before he has to be in Seattle, so you'll be here on your own part of the time—if you're okay with that. Karl's car will be here, and if something comes up that you need to leave before we get back, you can board Lucky somewhere."

"How are you getting to the airport tomorrow?" Melody asked.

"Ray will take us. He and my mother want to see some of the historic sites in Philadelphia while they're here."

"Maybe we'll do a little sightseeing, too," Melody said when Billy joined her and put his arm around her.

"Oh, yeah," Billy said, "I want to run up the steps of the museum, Rocky style."

Billy and Melody went to get drinks when Martha approached.

"It was a lovely wedding, dear," Martha told Caitlin. "Bobby sends his love. He would have come, you know, if you'd given him a little more notice."

"I should call him."

"Yes, you should. I've been getting calls from relatives I haven't heard from in years. Everyone was so excited when they saw you on television! I even heard from your father's sisters."

"Aunt Mary?"

"Yes," Martha said, nodding. "And Maureen. You know, if you wanted to do a concert in Boston, you'd have a lot of eager fans."

"That's an idea," Caitlin said. "Maybe this fall."

"Oh, it looks like dinner is about to be served. I should find my seat," said Martha.

Caitlin joined Karl at the head table. Melody had hand-written each menu and name card and placed a red rose at each place setting. Candles lit the tables, and a string of lights surrounded the tent.

Melody tapped her glass of champagne with a spoon and then stood to make a toast. "To my dear friends Caitlin and Karl. I am so blessed to know you both and to be a part of your special day. May your life together be a never-ending song of love."

Glasses clinked all around, and Caitlin and Karl smiled at each other and kissed. He no longer attended AA meetings, but he continued to avoid alcohol, so a non-alcoholic sparkling wine had been included among the beverage choices.

Barry stood next. "I don't claim to be the best man here," he said, "but I'm honored to stand up for this man and his lovely bride on this joyous occasion. For it is, indeed, love that makes the impossible possible. Never doubt the power of love to heal, to unite, and to make life worth living." He raised his glass and said, "Salud!"

"Here, here," someone shouted.

Everyone was quiet while Charlotte said a short blessing before the meal and then lively chatter and bursts of laughter filled the air.

Caitlin tasted the main entrée, salmon in puff pastry topped with a light cream sauce, and asked Karl how his vegetarian version was. She had approved the menu, which included sides of asparagus, green beans topped with sliced almonds, and a salad. For the tiered dessert, she had suggested a carrot cake with cream cheese frosting.

Rick took photos as Caitlin and Karl cut the cake, and Cara joined the band when it was time for the first dance.

"That's our cue," Caitlin told Karl. He took her hand and led her to the dance floor.

After Matt sang "Colour My World," the band played "At Last," which Allison sang. Caitlin and Karl continued dancing, and Melody and Billy joined them on the dance floor, followed by Martha and Ray and Pete and Marya, who weren't needed for that song and were able to enjoy a break from performing.

Most of the musicians in the band knew covers from their days playing at weddings and conferences, so Caitlin trusted them to entertain the guests in her absence.

"I'm going to change clothes," she told Karl. "You might want to do the same."

He gave her a puzzled look.

"I think Melody laid out some clothes for you," she said. "I'll meet you by the garage in ten."

When Caitlin went inside, she saw that the folding chairs had been removed and the rest of the furniture had been put back the way it was before the ceremony. The altar, however, remained. Marvin was on his hands and knees in the living room, looking under the couch, and Jasmine was at the kitchen sink rinsing a glass.

"Thank you for coming, Jasmine," Caitlin told her. "I'm sorry I haven't had a chance to talk."

Karl had invited his architect as well as the man who had sold him the property, but Caitlin hadn't met them yet.

"That lady—Luisa—she gave me a CD of the band's music," Jasmine said.

"Oh, good. I hope you like it," Caitlin said. Lucky rubbed against her legs. "No cat hair on this dress, please!" Caitlin said as she lifted her gown.

"I di'n know you was a celebrity now. That's awful nice of you to think of us."

"I've often thought of you and Marvin and wondered how everything is going."

"We doin' all right. Ya know, we still got that old piano."

"Does Marvin play it?"

"Well, I wouldn't quite call it playing. But he does take an interest in it."

Caitlin chuckled and said, "Well, good."

They looked outside to where Henry was standing. He was drinking a beer and talking to Ray.

"I'm so glad you have someone to lean on," Caitlin said.

Jasmine nodded and said, "He's been very patient with us."

"You've been through a lot. I hope things continue to go well for you. I've got to get changed now. I have something to show Karl before it gets dark."

"Thank you, an' I wish you all the happiness this world can offer."

"Oh, look," Caitlin said, pointing. "Maybe what he needs is a cat!"

Marvin was petting Lucky—and smiling. It was the first time Caitlin had ever seen Marvin smile. Lucky, however, looked desperate to be rescued.

"Oh, you'll survive!" Caitlin told him.

Before closing the door to the bedroom, Caitlin asked Jasmine, "You'll come back tomorrow, then, to meet with Karl?"

"Right after breakfast, uh-huh," Jasmine said.

Caitlin kicked off her shoes, removed her jewelry, and unbuttoned her gown. *That went well,* she thought.

She changed into cotton pants and a long-sleeved top and went outside to wait for Karl. When she saw Melody, she beckoned to her.

"Did you get a chance to go to the nursery?"

"Yes, it's all ready," Melody said.

"Thanks," Caitlin said with a grin. "Everything was lovely. The food was terrific. I can't thank you enough."

"I'm so glad you're happy!" Melody said.

"You'll get the bedroom ready?" Caitlin asked.

Melody nodded and said, "I will."

When Karl arrived, Caitlin took him by the hand and said, "Come with me."

He had given her a tour of the property two days before. He pointed out the area he envisioned for houses, a playground, and a common house. Continuing to walk to the field beyond the future community, they'd arrived at a spot that they agreed could be a good place for an orchard. Caitlin led him back there now.

A potted tree was sitting on the ground beneath an elm tree; beside it was a shovel.

"What's all this?" Karl asked with a laugh.

"An apple tree!" Caitlin said. "I'm ready to put down roots. Literally!" She put on a pair of gardening gloves and handed another pair to Karl. "I thought this would be our own *private* ceremony. Just the two of us."

"Let me guess—I'm supposed to do the grunt work," Karl said, picking up the shovel.

"We-l-l," Caitlin said flirtatiously. "I can help fill the hole up with dirt!"

"All right, Miz Rose," Karl said as he broke the ground with the shovel. "May this tree thrive here all the days of our lives."

"Thank you, Mister Owen. May it bear sweet fruit that nurtures and sustains us." Looking around, she added, "And from these humble beginnings, may our gardens flourish as we grow and expand our network of kindred spirits."

When they had finished planting the tree, Karl said, "Let's seal it with a kiss" before kissing Caitlin.

When he released her from his embrace, she looked up and saw a bird take flight from a branch of the nearby tree.

"Here in spirit," she murmured.

"Huh?"

"I was just thinking of something my mother said earlier," Caitlin said as she took Karl's hand and walked back to the house with him. "Let's go pack!"

"California, here we come!"

"I hope your mom likes me."

"Does your mom like me?"

"I don't know!" Caitlin said. "She will. I guess we should plan to stop and see her and Ray on the way back. Oh, and I want to show you the lake house, too."

Karl put his arm around her and said, "I always knew life with you would be an adventure."

"Just so it's not a rollercoaster," Caitlin said. "I've had enough highs and lows."

"A magic carpet ride?"

Caitlin laughed and said, "Maybe my next song will be about wedded bliss."

"I'll give you something to sing about!" Karl said, spinning her around.

"Let the honeymoon begin!"

They entered their new home and left their shoes by the door. Karl opened the door to the bedroom. The room was aglow with candlelight. A heart made of rose petals adorned the bed.

Lucky sped past them and jumped up on the bed, making himself comfortable in the center of the heart.

Caitlin smiled and shook her head as she carried him to the hallway. Before closing the bedroom door, she said, "You know I love you, furball, but don't push your luck!"

End of Volume Two

Acknowledgments

A heartfelt "Thank you!" to everyone who has supported me throughout this writing journey, whether through comments on drafts, road trips for research, or encouragement and friendship.

Special thanks to Robert A. Ford, who freely shares his theatre expertise (with me and with others) and to Annette Olsen, who is always ready to accompany me on piano or guitar (or join me for breakfast).

Finally, I appreciate the work done on the cover and interior by Michelle at MW Design.

About the Author

Jilaine Tarisa is a retired attorney with a background in psychology (Master of Arts). She lives in the United States and enjoys travel, photography, theatre, and music.

Learn more at jilainetarisa.com.